Gayle Siebert
www.gaylesiebert.com

Author's photo by www.ckellyphoto.com

Other books by Gayle Siebert:

Secrets Series:

The Pillerton Secret

The Dark River Secret

Lisa Rogney Series:

Wembly

Call Me Lisa

Silver Buckles

The Bear Mountain Secret

By Gayle Siebert

ONE

THE PHOENIX

HE'S ALWAYS BEEN lucky. Some people might not agree. He didn't think so himself when he was growing up and the old man used his fists on him. That stopped once he was big enough to put the bastard on his ass and things were okay after that. It would have been worse if he'd gone to live with his father because then it wouldn't have been the little girl who was thrown in the river with a caved-in head, it would have been him.

He stands on the berm surveying the construction site around him. Everything's nearing completion; the trucks filling the parking area are for electricians, gasfitters, HVAC and security system techs. The tile setters are packing up their tools. The big truck just rolling in is delivering the overhead garage doors.

The explosion and fire destroyed the old building, but like a phoenix, the new improved version is rising from the ashes. Aside from the prow-front two-storey great room and log construction, it's vastly different than the original. Bigger and better.

The location is remote; it's rainy, cold and snowy half the year but in summer, a cool respite from the heat, and fresh, clean air year round. Right in the middle of the world's largest grizzly bear population. Book a wildlife tour and you're pretty much guaranteed to see at least one, or in fall when the chum salmon are running, dozens. Hiking trails will become ski-doo runs in winter. Separate tracks for skiing and snowshoeing. There'll be a covered skating rink, and in due course, a string of horses for trail rides. Something for everyone, for every season. Who wouldn't want to vacation here? There would be plenty of tourists even without the club members. Perfect cover for the real purpose of the facility.

The project manager appears at the side door to greet the driver of the newly-arrived truck, looks up at him and waves. He raises his good hand in acknowledgement.

Yes, he's always been lucky.

His luck began when he was born a boy and his father's wife wanted a girl.

TWO

BEST PIE

THE COWBELL OVER the door jangles and a small, dark-haired girl in cowboy boots, purple tulle princess dress, and a shiny red cape printed with Supergirls sails into the diner. "HI AUNTIE FRANNY!" she calls out.

"Hey, Lisey," Franny, behind the cash register, responds. "You drive here all by yourself today?"

"NO SILLY! THEY'RE COMING." She points out the window to a man in a cowboy hat with a smaller girl on his hip, just passing the sign on the boulevard that declares Dot's Diner has the "Best Pies North of Kamloops!"

"Okay, let's get a table for you, then." Franny picks up a menu, and leads the girl through to a booth by the window. Lisey climbs up on the bench and Franny slides a colouring placemat and a bin of crayons in front of her.

In a moment the man comes through the door, sees Franny and Lisey, and comes to deposit the child he's carrying on the empty bench before sliding in beside her. "She got away on me again, Franny. Don't tell Astrid."

"You'll have to be a lot quicker to keep ahead of that one, Denver," Franny says with a chuckle.

"Well, it's dangerous." He turns to Lisey with a frown and says, "Elise, you know you're not supposed to run through the parking lot like that. You're supposed to hold my hand..."

"I KNOW. I SORRY." But she doesn't look up; she's got the black crayon in her small fist and is obliterating the kitten's face.

Denver sighs and says, "What can you do?"

"Short of a leash, not much," Franny agrees. "Just the three of you today, or will Astrid be joining you?"

"Nope," Denver says, "just us. Wilson's getting his cataracts done today, obviously can't drive, so Astrid took him. She wanted to do some shopping in Prince George anyway. I had some things to deal with at the mill, so the girls had to spend a few hours in the office. I promised to treat them if they were good, and the ladies said they were. I thought Dairy Queen, but Elise wanted to come here."

"I WANT PIE!" Lisey declares, the booming voice incongruous coming from her slim little body.

"Well," Franny says, "Pie it is! If Daddy says it's okay."

"Gettin' close to supper time and Astrid and Wilson won't be home until late, so I think a grilled cheese sandwich or something first," Denver says.

"I WANT PIE!"

"Okay, Lisey, you can have pie after you eat some supper."

The small blonde girl pops her head out from behind her dad and says, "pie!"

"Tell you what, Lisey," Franny says, "I'll make you your special grilled cheese sandwich, okay? You know, with the smiley face on it. How about that?"

Lisey looks up at Franny through narrowed eyes and asks, "WIFF KITTY EARS?"

"Sure, with kitty ears."

"KA-CHUP WISTERS?"

"Ketchup whiskers."

"PICKLE EYES?"

"Pickle eyes."

"NOT BIG PICKLE EYES!"

"Nope, just the right size pickle eyes."

"OKAY."

"What do you say, Lisey?" Denver prompts.

"OKAY *PLEASE!*"

"That's very polite, Lisey. I guess everyone in the place heard you," Denver says with a shake of his head.

Franny grins, then turns to the other little girl and asks, "What about you, Kylie? You want a grilled cheese sandwich like Lisey's?" But Kylie has already burrowed back behind her father's arm.

"NO! KYLIE WANTS CHIKAND FIGGERS."

Denver sees the amused looks from the grand-parent-types at the next table. He smiles and says to them, "four years old with a drill sergeant's voice."

"FOUR AND A HALF!"

"Maybe she'll be a stage actor," the white-haired woman chuckles. "No trouble hearing *her* at the back of the theatre!"

"Or a contract negotiator. A little bit's cute, but lately we negotiate everything, right down to the clothes she's going to wear, all day, every day. Which explains what she has on, if you're wondering." He sighs and turns his attention back to Franny. "Wilson's no better at it than I am. We both feel like we came out on top if we can get her to wear panties."

Lisey gives him a dark look before refocusing her attention on colouring, now adding heavy red streaks.

"Well, panties are over-rated anyway," Franny says.

"I like how you think. Astrid doesn't agree, though."

Franny chuckles and gives his shoulder a fist bump. "You know what you want, Den, or should I bring you a coffee or a beer while you decide?"

"Yeah, a glass of beer would be good, milk for the girls, and I'll have a look at the menu."

"I WANT A CHOCKLIT MILKSHAKE WIFF WIFF CREAM ON TOP. KYLIE WANTS A STRAWBERRY ONE WIFF WIFF CREAM ON TOP."

"Okay, milkshakes, then," Denver agrees. "How come you're working the floor today, Franny?"

"Just getting ready for the dinner rush. We're short-staffed anyway and one of the girls called in sick. You wouldn't think it would be so hard to get servers. Course all the ones that quit for the summer will be wanting jobs again once their kids are back in school, right about when we slow down and don't need them."

"The joys of being the owner, eh?"

"Yup. Never a day off, just like your business. I wouldn't have it otherwise. Besides, it's a good thing we're busy now; once winter sets in and the tourists are back at home, we'll be tight again. Still workin' that loan off. Good thing Bill's on steady, even though it's the short early shift for fire season."

"Yeah. Looks like we'll have to shut down logging completely pretty quick, though. Just waitin' to get word."

"You can't help that."

"No. Makes it hard for the guys, though. But they'll all be back at work before too long, if we get some rain soon. You might be busy all winter, too, what with that lodge opening up. They got trails for cross-country skiing and snowshoeing, snowmobiling and so on, apparently they think they'll have as many customers in the winter as in summer."

"Well, if that's true, maybe some of them will stop here for lunch on their way through."

"I imagine they'll want to come to town, too, and come in here for some of that pie, if nothing else."

"I hope you're right." Franny puts her pad and pencil into her apron pocket and scurries off.

Three men wearing ball caps with Dark River Forest Products embroidered on the crowns come through the door. Franny calls out, "You guys sit wherever you want and I'll be right with you!"

They head for a booth at the back, but hold up beside Denver. "Hey, Boss," one says, "no Missus Boss today?'

"She had to go to Prince George," Denver tells them, "but don't worry. She'll be back Monday to make sure no one's slacking off."

THREE

THE BISCUIT TIN

FRIEDA FLAMAN STUMPS her way along the narrow walkway through her corn patch to the shed at the lane, a small bag of garbage on the seat of her walker. She doesn't need the walker, really, but the concrete is so broken and frost-heaved after five decades of Saskatchewan winters it's treacherous going anytime, and especially if she's carrying something.

The whole sidewalk needs to be torn out and replaced, but on her pension there's not much money left by the end of the month. Certainly none to put aside for a new path to the back lane she only uses to take the garbage to the bin. Her grandson Trevor has no problem with the broken sidewalk and he usually takes it out for her when he stops by on his way to the new high school two blocks over, but she forgot to get him to do it this morning, and the garbage truck should be coming by in a few minutes.

When she rounds the corner of the shed, she sees garbage strewn across the lane. The garbage can is on its side, and laying there with the rumpled Kleenexes, Oh Henry! wrappers and Styrofoam meat trays is the lid, flattened.

She heaves a sigh, pulls the bag off the seat of her walker, and sits. Why would someone drive over the lid? Hardly any cars use the lane and it's not like the lid is invisible. Now because of other people's carelessness she has a mess to deal with and she'll need a new garbage can besides. *Damn that mutt of Clarkson's,* she thinks.

Of course she'd never say *damn* out loud, but it feels kind of good using foul language in what her daughter calls her inside voice. It's nothing compared to the F-word everyone uses now. That young man with the green hair and tattoos and earrings sprouting from his lips and eyebrows used it when he yelled at her for parking in the handicap zone outside the Co-op last week, just because she'd forgotten to put her tag up on the dash. Kids have no respect these days.

I'll have to go speak to Clarksons about keeping their damn dog in their own damn yard again, too, for all the good it did last time. Isn't it just like those people in the new part of town! They seem to think just because they've moved out of the big city they can let their dogs roam. Well, they'll find out! Next time I see him on the loose, I'm going to call the Town Office! And look at that, he's been digging a hole!

She gets garden gloves and a rake from inside the shed, scrapes the garbage into the can, then sets the can upright again. That done, she decides to organize the odds and ends of wood that have accumulated around the bin over the years and deal with the hole the dog dug under the roots of the forsythia that winter killed. Maybe the dirt is loose enough now she can pull it out. Maybe the damn dog did something good after all.

The rake is useless at pulling the dirt away from the roots, so she bends over and uses her hands. The scent of the soil is primal and enjoyable and she hums as she works. When she's cleared much of the dirt away from the roots, she grabs the dead shrub and pulls. It's stubborn. She leans her weight against it. Finally, it gives; off balance, she stumbles back a couple of steps, only to be grabbed from behind. She lets out a shrill "AAKK!" and her heart thumps alarmingly.

"Mom! What are you doing back here?"

"Chrissy! Can't you give a body some warning? You scared the daylights out of me! One of these days you're going to give me a heart attack and I'll fall over dead right before your eyes."

"If that happens can I have that pearl pin you always wear on your coat?" Chrissy chuckles. "Don't be silly, Mom, you're strong like bull."

"And schmart like tractor, isn't that how it goes?" Frieda clucks her tongue and tosses the dead shrub toward the woodpile. "You should've shown up sooner so you could clean up the mess that darn dog of Clarkson's made."

"That's the thanks I get for saving you from landing on your ass? I would've pulled that out for you, if you told me about it."

"I told Doug about it."

"You don't really expect him to do stuff like that, do you? I can't get him to do any work in the yard at home; he sure isn't going to come over here—"

"And look at the lid for my garbage can! Someone ran over it. It'll never stay on the can now. Don't suppose you can buy just a lid?"

"I don't think so. Have the garbage guys take the can along with the garbage today and I'll pick up a new one for you next time I'm at the Co-op. Maybe a plastic one with wheels so you can leave it by the stoop and just have Trev wheel it out on garbage day. Then you won't have this problem. You can pay me back in corn, which is what I've come to get."

"If I do that, what's to stop that darn mutt coming right into the yard and dumping the garbage all over my patio? And don't those plastic things break in the winter?"

"We can put a bungy on it if we need to, and then the worst he could do would be to roll it around. And they're pretty durable. I've had mine for years. Anyway, looks like the garbage is cleaned up, so what are you doing still poking away here?"

"Well, that darn mutt dug a hole but I guess it's not all bad. I wouldn't have been able to pull out that dead shrub otherwise."

"Was he trying to burrow under the shed? Maybe he was after a rat. What's this?" Christine brushes past her mother, pokes in the loose dirt for a moment, and comes up with flat tin box. "Why'd you throw this away, Mom?"

She takes it from Chrissy to examine all sides before handing it back, declaring, "That's not mine. I've never seen it before."

"Oh? Maybe it's Dad's stash."

"It's too small for a bottle."

"I meant weed. You know, marijuana."

"Oh. Ha ha! He didn't smoke marijuana."

"You sure about that?"

"Course I'm sure! He was dead five years before they legalized it."

"You think that stopped him? Why do you think he came all the way out to the shed to smoke?" Chrissy shakes the tin and rubs some of the dirt off with her sleeve. "It looks old. Quite pretty, eh? And there's something inside." She works at the lid but it's rusted and refuses to budge.

"Be careful," Frieda says. A shiver courses through her despite the heat of the south Saskatchewan summer. "Maybe you shouldn't open it."

"Why not?"

"It could be anything. Maybe something awful. I got a bad feeling, a terrible feeling all of a sudden. Like a goose walked over my grave."

"What's with you and dying and graves today? Don't be so maudlin! It could be something good, too, like jewelry or money! Or maybe even weed." The lid gives and Chrissy pulls it off to reveal a package of letters tied in a ribbon. "Rats! Nothing but a bunch of letters."

Frieda takes the little bundle, slides the ribbon off, and sorts through them. "Looks like they're all from the same person, although who? There's no return address." She passes the bundle back to Christine. "They're addressed to Louise Klein. She lived in the big house kitty corner. Remember?"

"Yeah, who could forget! She died a few years ago, right?"

"Yes, just before the place blew up. That was some explosion! Remember I had to get new windows? Good thing the insurance paid for it. There were bits and pieces of that old house strewn all over town."

"That must be how this tin got here! I wonder why Dad didn't find it back then."

"The forsythia was alive then. He must not have seen it."

"That Klein woman! The kids all thought she was a witch and were afraid of her. One Halloween I caught Trev and his friends with a carton of eggs, on their way out to egg her house." She puts the letters back in the tin, closes it up, and they start back to the house.

"Trevor? Really? Not Trevor!"

"Even kids like Trevor get up to nonsense once in a while, Mom. And as pranks go, that one's pretty harmless. I doubt she'd notice, and it sure wouldn't've made that place look any worse."

"No. And I can see why they'd do it. Pretty exciting, sneaking up to that scary-looking old place in the dark on Halloween! I think she almost deserved it. I don't imagine she gave out treats."

"Never did when I was a kid."

"I know you'll think it's silly," Frieda says, "But her eyes! They were sort of *penetrating*, so dark you couldn't see any pupils, and she seemed to look right through you. All the years she lived so near, I don't think she ever spoke more than a few dozen words to me, and one dozen was when I went over to see if she needed anything after her husband disappeared. That's got to be forty years ago, but I still remember those eyes! All that time living so close, and I never got to know her. She was really involved with that church group, the Children of Noah, you know?"

"Yeah. It's still around, but you can't join without going through some sort of interview."

"How do you know that? Did you try to join?"

"You're kidding, right? It's just what I heard. To get in, you gotta know the secret handshake or something. Seems ridiculous because most churches are happy to have new members."

"Well Louise Klein was right in tight with them, the big wigs always coming and going, all hours of the day and night."

They reach the comparative cool of the shaded patio. Frieda pushes the walker aside and sinks into the cushioned chair next to the table.

Christine puts the tin box on the table and takes a chair across from her mother. She says, "Just as well you weren't friends, Mom, being as she 'disappeared' her husband and kept his body!"

"Well, no one knew about that, of course, might never have been found out if her daughter hadn't been kidnapped and they were searching everywhere for her. That was after Louise died, though. I saw that girl working out in the yard when she came back for the funeral. She remembered me and said hello. We had a nice little chat. I always felt sorry for her. Sure don't blame her for running away. Just lucky she wasn't in the house when it exploded."

"That's right, she had a daughter. Kathy?"

"Yes."

"She was ahead of me in school so I never really knew her. Still don't, other than I think she works at the insurance office."

"She does, and she married Rick Schoenfeld. Hermina's son."

"Poor girl!"

"Why poor girl?"

"You must know what he's like! Wonder how he got so good looking. He must take after his father."

"You don't remember his father?"

"Hmmm. Not really."

"Well, in his youth, he was really handsome. Knew it, too. Fooled around, 'playing the field' they called it, until finally one of them got pregnant. And didn't she put him through! He was always having to buy her things. She had a mink coat, full length, not just a muskrat jacket like the rest of us. And jewelry! So she would let him back in the house, is what everyone said. His house, the Schoenfeld family farm! And her in her expensive coat, flashing all that jewelry, dressed up like that for the ladies aid meetings. But maybe she had good reason to be mad. The talk was that he never quit his tomcatting. Don't look at me like that! And if you ever tell anyone I said that—"

"I won't. I guess Rick takes after his father in more ways than just his looks, then," Christine says, "and if you ever tell anyone I said that!"

"At least his wife is good looking. Was a hairdresser. Now she works at that investment office. First wife, that is. Kathy is pretty, too."

"Yeah. I hope for her sake he's smartened up. She deserves better, growing up with a mother like that. And it looks like her mother had more secrets than just a body stashed in the house. Wonder why she kept these. Definitely not a woman's handwriting. A boyfriend? Wonder if it was before or after she killed her husband. Maybe it's the reason she killed him! This is *too* juicy! Let's have a glass of wine, and read them!"

"Well, it's kind of early but I guess I'm ready for a glass of wine," Frieda says.

"I know I am."

"You always are."

"Says the woman who buys her wine in boxes."

Christine goes into the house and comes out with the gala keg and two glasses. She sets them on the table next to the biscuit tin, fills the glasses, then gets the letters out of the tin. She brings the bundle up to her nose and sniffs. "Musty! Hope they're not ruined." She shuffles through, sorting them by the dates on the postmarks. "Which one should we read first? I think I'll start with the oldest and read them in order. Postmarks aren't the greatest—ever heard of Dark River, B.C.? Looks like they're decades old."

"You know, Chrissy," Frieda says after a sip of wine, "I don't feel right about this. I don't think we should read them. They're personal. They rightfully belong to her daughter."

Christine sits back and with a sigh, returns the letters to the tin. "I guess you're right. I'll take them to work with me and give them to Rick the next time he comes in."

The garbage truck comes rumbling down the lane. Christine trots out to ask the driver to take the can and its flattened lid, too.

FOUR

THE LETTERS

LETTERS. STILL IN envelopes, addressed to her mother, ripped open along the flap. Actual letters such as people wrote before there was e-mail, almost as old as she is. The handwriting is messy; more printing than writing, definitely masculine.

"I'm afraid to read these," Kathy says; she tucks them back inside the rusting Lebkuchen Schmidt box, closes the lid, and looks up at Rick.

"Oh?" he says, eyebrows lifting. "Why? I thought you'd be glad to get them. There must be a reason your mother kept them all these years."

"She kept everything, remember?"

"Yeah, but jumbled up in cardboard boxes, not in a tidy bundle like this. And tied in a ribbon? These must be special. I bet they'll tell you a lot about her."

"That's what I'm afraid of." She sets the box down on the kitchen table between them, takes a sip of her coffee, shrugs her shoulders and sighs. "I think I know enough about her. Looks like these are from before she murdered my father."

"Maybe it'll explain why she did it. Or maybe, they're *from* your father and will tell you more about him."

"I don't care why she did it, if you're thinking she might've had a good reason and I'll forgive her!"

"No, Runty, I don't think—"

"And I doubt these are from my father. I don't remember ever seeing anything he wrote and although I don't know much about him, I do know he was educated. His handwriting would be more, well, tidy and ordered, actual writing, not printing like he never got past grade four."

"Maybe he, and we're just assuming it's a *he*, only printed the address and the letters are in writing."

"Well, my father wouldn't have spelled Pillerton with only one L, either. And no return address on the envelopes? Besides, he was living here, with my mother. Why would he write to her?"

Rick shrugs. "You're right, I guess. Who else—" His phone sounds a text alert. He picks it up off the table, reads the message, sends a quick response, and slides it into his shirt pocket as he gets to his feet. "Thought I'd putz around here for the rest of the day but now I have to go out again."

"What's wrong?"

"Ryan's at the lentil field. Same old problem with the cutter bar on the swather. I'm gonna hafta run into Regina and pick up that part after all. Hope we don't have to bring the damn thing back to the shop to switch it out." He bends to kiss her, then rubs her shoulder. "See you tonight, Runty."

"Never a Saturday off."

"Not at this time of year. A farmer's life."

"Don't forget, we're going to Sarah's for supper."

"Her first family supper in her own home, how could I forget?"

"You want to drop in on your mother when you come back, and see if she wants to come here for a bit before we leave? You could give her a lift."

"Why can't she just walk over? And why would you want her to come here? Is there something you haven't cleaned well enough she could take care of for you?"

"I just thought it might be nice for her. She hasn't been spending much time in the yard. And you know she hasn't walked over here since she broke her hip. Maybe I can think of something for her to do. You know, so she feels useful."

"I didn't know you liked her that much. She hasn't exactly welcomed you into the family with open arms."

"She's mellowing. I feel sorry for her."

"Don't let her poor old woman act suck you in. She's as healthy as a horse."

"I think she's lonely, over there all by herself."

"If she hadn't made such a stink about Ryan and Sarah sleeping together they'd probably still be living there, so she's only got herself to blame."

"Doesn't make it any easier for her."

"You're sweet, Runty." He plants a kiss on her head, checks to be sure his wallet is in his hip pocket, and gets a drink of water from the fridge. When he turns back, he asks, "what did you say you were going to town for, anyway? I could pick something up while I'm out."

"I need to shop. I told Sarah I'd bring a salad."

"Seriously? With a garden the size of ours you have to buy lettuce?"

"No, not lettuce silly! I need avocadoes. She asked me for a Southwestern salad."

"Oh my gawd, don't tell me we're out of avocadoes!" He barks a laugh.

"I have to swing by the office to sign some cheques, anyway."

"Talk about farmers never having Saturdays off! Why can't Godzilla do it, she lives right in town. And when is she going to start paying you for all the extra hours?"

"Management doesn't get paid overtime, you know that. We knew it would be worse than ever once we bought into agency. Doesn't matter. We need a few other things, too. I might as well shop for the week."

"Okay then, pick up a six pack while you're at it." He grimaces and continues with a groan, "I sure hope there's going to be something besides rabbit food."

"Maybe I should get a dozen beer and some chips so you can fill up on that. And rabbit food? You know it's not like that!" She clicks her tongue and frowns at him. He wiggles his eyebrows and grins.

"I don't know what Jeanie's bringing," Kathy continues, "likely dessert, since that's her speciality. Your mother can usually be counted on for potato salad. I could get her to make it while she's here. Sarah's making vegan molé chimichangas, not too spicy, she said. You can eat those, it won't kill you."

"Never would've believed a daughter of mine would come back from university a brainwashed vegan, and us raising cattle!"

"You mean enlightened, an *enlightened* vegan. And I wouldn't call those two old cows in the pasture with the horses, raising cattle."

"I should've shipped them with the rest before you got so attached. You see the looks Mutti gives me every time she brings the subject up?"

"She doesn't like the horses, either, even after Jeanie and I started riding, and you'd never ship them. Better not tell Mutti we're looking for younger replacements! Anyway, I'm sure Sarah will make a few chicken molé chimichangas since Ryan is a carnivore too, but if not, she's making hot dogs for the kids. You can have a couple of those, while the *grownups* eat the good food."

"Only if I can sit at the kids' table."

"I'm sure that would be fine. You'd fit right in." Despite herself, Kathy chuckles at the mental picture of this broad-shouldered six-foot-three man on a tiny chair with his knees up around his ears, hulking over a low table surrounded by Jeanie's kids. "But don't worry. I'll put some chicken on your salad. Even though it means I have to handle your meat."

"I love it when you talk dirty! And people wonder what I see in such a bossy little runt." He heads toward the door, picks his ballcap off the row of hooks and settles it on his head.

"More likely they wonder why a sensible woman like me ever hooked up with the likes of you."

"They just credit your good taste," he says as he turns to face her, favouring her with the wide grin that crinkles his eyes and still gives her a pleasant rush. "See you later, Runty." The door closes behind him.

Kathy gets to her feet and goes to the window in the living room with her coffee and the tin box. As she watches Rick's truck disappear through the gap in the grove, she feels the familiar tug of hollowness at his leaving even for a short time, and marvels again at how she was lucky enough to have a second chance at happiness with her high school sweetheart. And how "Runty" has become an endearment, as pleasant as a kiss.

She sinks into her favourite chair. With the box beside her on the lamp table, she finishes her coffee. *I should water the garden before it gets any hotter,* she thinks. *I'll do that before I go to town.* Then she picks up the box and examines it as gingerly as if it might be booby-trapped. Before the fire and the years of rain, snow and mud, it must have been pretty; despite the rust, the embossed figures still show red and blue and metallic gold paint.

How could a simple tin box survive the fire and explosion that destroyed her family home and wind up in the Flaman's yard, intact? Is it a blessing or a curse that Mrs. Flaman found it half a decade later and realized where it came from? Then gave it to her daughter who works at the Gas-N-Go, who gave it to Rick when he was there this morning?

She goes to the kitchen and makes another cup of coffee, then comes back to her chair and polishes the top of the tin with her shirt tail. It's something she would have been drawn to as a little girl. Odd she can't remember ever seeing it, not when she was little, and not even when she moved back after her mother's death.

Remember, she thinks, *you didn't make much progress sorting through all the stuff accumulated by three generations of your predecessors in that house before it all went BOOM! It could've been anywhere, and you might never have found it.* Rick or her friend Penny might have found the box, saw it contained only letters, and passed it over like so many of the other boxes full of old papers. They were looking for a will, not letters, after all.

She heaves a sigh and wonders again what their lives might be like if the fire and explosion hadn't happened. If she'd left the beautiful but faulty 1920's Art Deco lamp in the attic instead of letting Penny move it into the spare bedroom where she was staying. Hundreds of gold American Double Eagles, all gone. All but one. She strokes the coin on the chain around her neck, her only connection to her family, a reminder a decision that seems insignificant at the time can change the course of a person's life. Like opening the door to let in the man who nearly killed her.

She touches the scar where her earlobe used to be, not realizing she's doing so. She is always conscious, though, of her mutilated index finger. The sight of it still gives her a jolt of rage and she feels no guilt at being glad the monster who did it was murdered.

At last, she mutters, "Might as well get it over with." She finishes her coffee, takes a deep breath, opens the lid and pulls out the letters. Arranging them in chronological order according to the postmarks, she selects the oldest one and begins reading.

Hunny bun,

Yore pregnant? I thought you were on the pill. Why do you think its mine? I aint saying it aint just dont know how you can be sure. You no are plans we aint ready for this and so I think the best thing would be to get rid of it. I no this is a tough time for you. Its awful for me to being so far away from you. I want you to come live with me you no that but camp is no place for kids. You say you will leave are little girl with him. Thats a good plan. She thinks he's her Daddy and he's got a good job, steady job and so on. Married you even tho you was preggers and he's got a House too but not for much longer ha ha!. You wait til you have the house then you sell ~~THE~~ it leave the kid with him and come live with me. Thats are plan remember? Get rid of this one to and be more careful until its a good time for us to start are own family. I gotta go you no I love you and I am always yore Teddy Bear xoxox

Hunny Bun

Why did you wait so long now its to late to get rid of it? dont worry I will do right by you I told you that but You should stay there until the babies born. Its safer for you to have it there so yore close to a Hospital. Dont tell him you want a divorce until after when you and the baby are safe. Its good in a way as its more ~~ammuni~~ ~~amunishin~~ better for getting the house you have 2 kids who need it get the car too. Any way think about it its just a few months. Mean time Im getting a place for us like I told you and I will get one with a room for the baby to if you want to bring this one with you and when Im done this job and I have a place I will come get you. Its only a few more months until we are together forever. You know I always loved you remember all those days out in the hills? are speshul place? You were only thirteen but ~~the~~ ~~hottest~~ ~~little~~ ~~p~~ some hot number I think about it all the time of coarse now I got lots more resent memories. Ha ha!

Xoxox lots of hugs and kisses! yore big teddy bear. Xoxox

Hunny bun,

You no I can't phone you except when I aint in camp. Theres only one phone and its in the Office they don't let us grunts to use it. Why aint you slept with him all this time you just need to do it now RIte AWAY so when the babies born he will think it is his just early. I wont be mad you slept with him. I never thought you wernt sleeping with him its just some thing you have to do. If you think I dont hate the idea of him being with you like that you can forget it but I wont be mad. Sorry this is so short had to hurry to get it on the truck to be mailed. I will phone you when Im out of camp in a couple weeks.

You no I love you and will always be yore big Teddy Bear

xoxox

Hunny bun,

You never slept with him? Not never? How the hell does he put up with that? I no FIRST HAND how good you are at other things but JESUS! Really? You call that saving yer self for me but really? What kind of man puts up with that? But anyway, Just cuz I said I wouldnt be mad about you sleeping with him dont mean I been cheating on you. How do you get that?How could I cheat on you anyway Im living with a bunch of men and I aint no fudge packer as you well no ha ha! Yore right, we could live in yore house easy but how many times did we talk about it unless you get rid of _him_ it aint yore house and I got nuthin there and a good paying job here. Thats why Im out here in the bush in the first place and why Im getting a place for us here. Im only out of camp one week in six so I dont have that much time to look thats the only reason I havent found a place yet plus there aint a lot of places to rent in Dark River. Hey you remember Barney Jeffries from school? I run into him out here. Hes got a girl in Pilerton to (like me! I bet she aint as pretty as you tho) If you cant get rid of it thats OK, we will have are own place and a place for the baby to like I said. I cant wait til we get are own place and I can love you any time I want. Its been offel windy here all week. We got blown out 2 days. Lots of time to work on that coarse I told you I was taking but other than that nuthing to do but sit around. Played poker last nite and lost all my money. Even had to bum smokes. Got an advance on my pay so I can win it back tonite.

Love BIG TEDDY Xoxox

My sweet little Hunny Bun

Please honey PLEASE dont be mad I didnt tell you Im married. Yore married to after all. I didnt tell you cuz she dont mean nuthing to me. She aint like you, nuthing like you. Yore so beautiful and shes years older than me the guy's call her my mother, face like a mud wall besides. Ask Barneys girlfriend who went running to you to blab. I told Barney he better strayten her out about that and make sure she goes and tell's you the hole story. Why would I hook up with you if I was happy with her? I was so glad you saw me again when I was back home I could not believe I could be so lucky you would love me like you did when we were kids and after, you no, the first baby, after I been away for so long I was sure not going to tell you about her then! I would of if I could of found a good job there so I could stay there. You no I tried but I aint cut out to be no plow boy or to grunt bags at the feed store for minumum wage no future in that so I had to come back here so I thought it was just better not to say nuthing. I will get a divorce for sure as soon as the REALLY BIG DEAL that is going to make me rich is done. Yore the best thing that ever happened to me. I never went looking for a girl why would I when I have you? She was the cook here in camp but dont worry shes gone now and I never see her. Her father own's the company. I only married her to get cozy with her old man. Hes already gave me a nice piece of land as a bribe to marry her thats how old and ugly she is. Ha ha So if you think Im having a good time with her you can forget it. I only done it to make that _REALLY BIG_ deal I told you Im cooking up with the old man fly. I only love you. Right now the land I got out of him is nuthing but trees but its rite across the road from the mill wich Im gonna get outta him next and you won't believe the house I'm going to build on it! For me and you and are baby if you bring it. We'll be together for sure just give me a little more time. When you get rid of _him_ we can sell that old house and all those lots in Pilerton like we talked about. They got to be worth a bundle it will give us a real good start. With that and with what Im getting in this deal Im talking about I will be _RICH!_ I will buy you anything you want just snap yore fingers. Start thinking about what kind of fancy new car you want! And I will buy you the _BIGEST DIMUND_ ring you ever seen.

I want to tell the world yore mine Hunny Bun and I will soon but right now if my wifes father found out about us he would make a lot of trouble for me _FOR US_ and Id end up with nothing and I want the best for you. So we just need to keep are secret a little while longer and think about us all three of us being together in are little love nest. Yore beautiful how could I love anyone else with you in my life? Every nite I go to sleep and dream about you. Please say yore not mad and you no I love only you.

You no Im always going to be yore own Teddy Bear and wont never love no one else.

Xoxox

Dear Louise,

Im sorry I was short with you on the phone. The other guys were hanging around the phone booth making faces and smart ass comments waiting to make calls to. Ya of corse Im glad hes gone didn't I say that? But I told you not to tell him you wanted a divorce until after the baby was born. I have a question. You never ansered me. Did he sine off the property before he left? If he didnt you wont be able to sell it without him sineing. So if you didnt get it sined over make sure you get yore lawyer and get in touch with him and get that done *PDQ !!!*.

I cant come live with you, you no that, it would Rock the Boat for yore divorce and that really Big Deal I told you I'm working on and besides we still need moolah or how are we going to live?

I just got yore letter and had to rite back in such a hurry   to catch the mail truck because you no it just turns around and goes rite back.

Love Hank.

Louise

No you wont be able to sell the property if he hasnt sined it over I told you that. I looked into it but you go ahead and ask yore lawyer if you dont believe me. I dont no why yore lawyer never done it in the first place maybe you need to get a better lawyer but it aint to late *GET IN TOUCH WITH HIM AND GET HIM TO SINE IT OVER TO YOU NOW* get your lawyer to do it if you don't want to. If you dont get that done you can forget it.

Hank

Louise

Ya yore right my last letter sounded mad cuz I was mad, real mad, and now its worse. You always was as dum as a *post but I never* new you could be this _dam STUPID._ Now you cant sell that place not for years *maybe not never.* I wont tell no one what you done but if you think Im going to wait around you can forget it. Dont blame me you done this yore self you _STUPID_ _BICH._ I dont believe you that you never slept with him or that baby is mine *anyway but dont worry* I will fix every thing. Some one will come see *you when the baby is born* you just give it to them. Make sure _NO ONE_ finds out yore pregnant or there will be questions like what happened to that baby and I cant help you then. If you tell any one that kid is mine or if you make trouble with my wife I will have no choice but to tell them what you got in that old furnace.

At the family dinner later, they talk about how amazing it is that the tin biscuit box was found intact, the letters inside only slightly water-damaged.

"Oh, letters to your mom?" Jeanie asks. "Are they all from the same person? Who?"

"Well," Kathy begins, "it looks like they're all written by the same person, but there's no name or return address. I haven't had a chance to read them yet. I'll find out who they're from when I do." Heat rises up to her face. She feels the weight of Rick's stare and looks his way. He's frowning. Grateful he doesn't call her on the lie, she gives him a tremulous smile before asking Jeannie, "How is Faith feeling about starting kindergarten?"

"She's super excited! Mostly because I won't let her wear her new sparkly shoes until then."

IN BED LATER, Rick draws her into his arms, strokes her hair and says, "Okay, Runty, why don't you tell me why you lied to my family about the letters."

Kathy takes a deep breath, snuggles up against his big, comforting male body, and explains why she has to go away for a while.

"I WISH YOU'D WAIT until I can go with you," Rick says as he navigates through traffic into the Regina airport, watching for the sign for the hourly parking. "I know you think you only have a slim chance of finding him, but I'm worried about what might happen if you do."

"Nothing bad will happen, dear. I have my lucky charm!" She lifts the gold chain with its heavy gold coin pendant to prove it before tucking it back out of sight under her T-shirt.

"How is that thing lucky?"

"Oh, it's not, really. I just like to look at it once in a while, thinking about how close I came to being a millionaire."

"Are you really sorry? Would you have married me if you were a millionaire?"

"Of course I would have! I feel like I am a millionaire, with you for a husband."

"Aww, what a perfectly sucky thing to say." He takes her hand and brings it to his mouth to kiss her knuckles before releasing it again. "But thanks."

"Anyway, I look at it and remember how we fell in love in that old house."

"Yeah."

"But we never found those letters. Sometimes I wish they were never found. But they have been, and I know my father wasn't who I thought he was, and I have to go and find my real, or at least my *biological* father."

"I know. But will you really be able to approach strangers? Men especially? Will you really be able to go to his house, all on your own? You never know what kind of person he is."

"The worst thing, assuming I even find the guy, might be he hasn't got a clue what I'm talking about." Kathy pats Rick's thigh. "You don't have to park; you can just drop me off."

"Not a chance. I'm still hoping to talk you out of going." He follows the arrows into the parking area and slows to look for an empty spot. "You can't predict what he's like now. What reason do you have to think he's any better than he was back then? He sounds like a bad bastard! Sex with a thirteen year old?"

"Maybe he was thirteen too? Mom was sixteen when I was born."

"Yeah, and then he abandoned you both? Running off is one thing, lots of assholes do that. But stringing her along just to get the property? And he knew your mother killed your, *er*, the man you thought was your father and didn't report her! You know someone murdered someone, you even know where the body is, and you don't report it? A bad bastard in anyone's books. If he'd turned her in, think how different your life would've been."

"Yeah, it may have been worse. I might have had to go and live with him! And what happens to kids with no other relatives when their only parent goes to jail for life? You hear horror stories about foster homes."

Rick shrugs. "I guess that's true."

She reaches for his hand; he takes it off the steering wheel and tucks her hand in his on his thigh. "I agree he was a bastard," she continues, "but think about it. How much of a threat can he be? He must be seventy, for Pete's sake."

"Maybe not that old, maybe in his sixties, and unless he's sick he'll still be stronger than you, Runty. Besides, that pendant won't stop a bullet."

"Oh, now you're getting carried away. Bullet? This is Canada!" She pulls her hand out of his, gathers up her purse, digging through it to check that she has everything, and scrolls through her phone for her boarding pass.

"Well, he's a redneck. He likely has a gun. I have one, after all. Even that old single-shot Cooey of mine can kill a person."

"Well, I bet that if he's even still alive, he's probably drinking beer, tinkering on his rusted-out pickup behind a one-bedroom bungalow with old chesterfields for patio furniture, thinking he's doing great if he has steak on Welfare Wednesday and can still walk to the Seven 11 on the corner to buy cigarettes without getting an angina."

She reaches across the seat and strokes his thigh. "Anyway, it's not much to go on, a guy named Hank, last name unknown, not even a previous address, who worked in some kind of camp somewhere around Dark River four decades ago? He's likely not even still there. But if he is, I want to meet him at least once. And if I have a brother or sister, I have to try and find them. Who knows? I might have a bunch of half-sisters or half-brothers too! A family! You can't understand, since you've always had your sister and aunts and all those cousins. Your whole big family. I've never had anyone."

"My family is your family now, Runty."

"I know. But it's not the same, at least not now that I know I might have blood relatives."

"Yeah, I know. We've been over this a dozen times."

"I've done all the on-line searching I can. Looked for adoption records. Posted it on Facebook, got lots of shares, came up with nothing. I have nowhere else to start looking. Assuming I find him, and assuming he's willing to talk to me, he might not know where the baby ended up or what his or her name is now. It's probably a fool's errand."

"Well, I think so, but it looks like you're determined. How long do you think you'll be away?"

"I have no idea. Depends on what I find or if I find out anything at all. Could be a few days maybe? I've booked a week off work. Godzilla nearly had a coronary but it's my vacation time; she shouldn't begrudge me that, even though it's short notice. I wish you were going with me, but I know you can't get away at this time of year."

Rick aims the SUV into an empty slot, puts it in park and turns the engine off. "I'll go pay for parking," he says, face grim. He slides out of his seat and heads off to the ticket spitter.

Kathy gets out, pulls her duffle bag out of the back seat, sets the strap of her purse across her body and adjusts her sunglasses. When Rick returns with the ticket, he comes around to her side and puts it on the dash. He takes the duffle bag and holding hands, they walk to the vaulted glass canopy that looms over the building's entrance. From the sidewalk there's a view through to the tarmac thanks to banks of windows on both sides of the building. A DeHavilland Dash 8 with WestJet logo is there, door open, staircase in place.

"Looks like that's your plane," Rick says, putting the duffle bag down and drawing her into a hug. "Can I at least tell everyone you've gone to visit relatives?"

Kathy heaves a sigh and shrugs, "Well, I suppose so. I just worry about the questions, you know, about my family. Or should I say, lack of family? When I come back and haven't found anyone."

"And I worry people will think we've had a fight and you've left me."

"Why would anyone think that?"

"You know people like to believe the worst. There has to be another reason for you being away other than you've gone on vacation without me."

"It's not a vacation, but you're right. We wouldn't want that. It was scandalous enough when the most popular boy in school married the least popular girl, even if it took you twenty years to get around to it."

"I was an idiot, you should've been my first wife, I admit it." He kisses her before releasing her. "We better get you checked in."

"I'll just go right through. You don't have to come with me."

"I want to."

"No, let's not prolong it." She stops just outside the doors. Her eyes fill. She sniffs. "Please?"

"You don't have to go, Runty," he says softly. He pulls her back into his arms. "If you want to spend money on a holiday, let's make it Mexico, in February. We can still cancel your ticket and go back home."

"No. No, I *do* have to go. I'm being a baby. It's just that it's the first time we've been apart."

"I know." After a bit, they stand apart; Rick picks up the duffle bag and hands it to her. "One week, Runty. No longer, okay?"

"Okay."

"Promise?"

"Promise. I'm only taking this one carry-on. When I run out of clean underwear, I'll come home. Cross my heart and hope to die."

As he stands arms akimbo, watching her walk purposefully through the automatic doors, down the concourse and away, not turning to look back, he mutters, "Stubborn!" Still, he wonders why her parting words make him uneasy.

FIVE

THE RECRUITER

HE ENTERS THE room, stands for a moment looking around while his eyes adjust to the low light, then goes to the bar and slides onto a stool. The bartender brings a J & B on the rocks; he picks it up and swivels his stool to look past the couples gyrating on the small dance floor to the noise blasting from the jukebox. In a booth on the other side there's group of three heavily made-up young girls. They appear awkward. Nervous. Maybe worried about being carded. But they have tall drinks in front of them. They're giggling; two get up to go to the ladies' room, tugging the hems of their short skirts, a little unsteady on three-inch heels. The drinks on the table are apparently not their first.

He drains his drink and summons the bartender. "Hit me again," he says.

The bartender nods, and when he returns with the fresh drink, says, "I see you spotted the talent I called you about."

"Hard to miss."

"What do you think? Too young to be lookin' for what they're lookin' for don't you think? They look nineteen to you?"

"Sixteen. Maybe not even."

"That's what I thought, too. Good for that finder's fee we discussed?"

"For sure. Give 'em another round. And a couple shooters each. Let 'em know they're from me. Clear out the corner booth. After I move there, give them my card and ask them if they'd care to join me."

The bartender spends a moment reading the card just handed to him and says, "if the boss comes in and sees them—finds out I didn't card them—I'm out of a job."

"Don't worry. I'll get you something. You won't be unemployed for long."

The bartender shrugs and nods, then moves off, busying himself behind the bar. When all three girls are back at the table, he heads out with the drinks, dropping them off in front of them.

The man at the bar watches as the bartender says something to them, turns and points at him. When the girls look his way, he smiles and acknowledges them with a nod and a lift of his glass.

He turns his back to them, checks his look in the mirror behind the bar and wonders if it's time to start wearing his hair shorter. Military style, maybe. But then he reminds himself hair the length it is, just slightly over his shirt collar, makes him appear non-threatening. And with the glasses? Downright nerdy even. And definitely younger than his years. Thankfully his hair is still thick and receding only slightly, with just enough grey at the temples to make him look old enough to be the self-made millionaire and uber-successful talent agent he claims to be. He congratulates himself on still appealing to teenage girls. He clink-clink-clinks his diamond pinky ring on his glass, checks his Rolex Oyster, and sorts through email and his Facebook feed on his phone while he waits.

Soon, the girls have consumed their shooters and are well into their newest drinks. He puts his phone in his pocket, slides off his stool and strolls to his usual booth in the corner.

SIX

A PROMISE

ASTRID IS AT the table in the lunchroom eating a sandwich and chatting with Mary Ann and Janine from the accounting department, when Denver comes in. He greets them with, "Hey!" but doesn't slow as he hurries into the back hallway leading to the washrooms.

"Jeez, Den," Astrid says when he returns and goes to the coffee machine, "the biffy at the field office out of commission again?"

"Dunno, haven't made it there yet. Had a lot of coffee at lunch. Should've hit the can before I left Dot's but it didn't seem important until about ten minutes ago." He puts a fresh pod in the Keurig, fills his cup, then takes a chair at the table.

"And the first thing he does is get more coffee." Astrid says.

"Oh *ja*, of course, comes with being of Norwegian extraction." He takes the empty chair next to Astrid, has a sip from his mug, and asks, "What's up with you ladies today?"

"We were just talking about the traffic," Mary Ann says, "how there's a lot more truck traffic than there used to be. It's beating the crap outta the highway. You must've noticed the grooves in the pavement. Rattles your teeth bouncing over them to make the turn into the yard here!" Mary Ann shakes her head, then gets up and takes her mug to the sink.

"The grooves are bad enough, but what about the potholes!" Janine contributes. "I see more roadworks in our future. We'll really have something to complain about then."

"Never saw so many trucks," Mary Ann continues. "Weird, too. The laundry trucks I can understand, probably because of that resort up on Bear Mountain opening again, but so many from that shredding company? Who needs so much shredding done now that everything's paperless?"

"I hadn't noticed we're paperless, Mary Ann," Astrid says, "and we've still got decades of old files taking up space. Why don't you call them and get a price on doing our shredding, since they're going right past our door anyway? We need that back room cleared out and we'd burn out our little shredders if we tackled all those years of records."

"I'll see if I can catch the company's name next time I see one of the trucks," Mary Ann agrees. "Out of curiosity, I Googled shredding services but didn't come up with anything close."

"Huh. Maybe a new start-up? Still, in this day and age, you'd think they'd get a website up first thing."

"You'd think so," Denver agrees, "but why pay someone to shred documents? Just get one of the guys to haul that crap all out to the yard and burn it. Not until the rainy season, of course."

Astrid shrugs and says, "I guess that's a better idea."

Janine drains her coffee and says, "Well, back to work." She gets up, goes to the sink and rinses her mug, then follows Mary Ann out the door.

When the door closes behind them, Astrid turns to Denver and says, "you had lunch at Dot's?"

"Yeah. I ran into Evan Briggs at the bank and he insisted, so we went to Dot's. You know they have a sandwich named after me?"

"Yeah, I know. And as I tell you every time you mention it, Denver sandwiches were a thing long before you were born. But maybe there's other people you haven't told yet that will believe you. You're such a hero in Dark River they probably think more than a miserable egg sandwich ought to be named after you. A park maybe. Street, at least."

Denver grins at that, but there's no humor on Astrid's face. She feels the clenching of her insides, the jolt of angst that still prompts an adrenalin rush when she thinks about what Denver did that made him a hero. "But you went for lunch with *Evan Briggs*? Of all the people in Dark River, you had lunch with *him*?"

"I don't expect you to be friendly to him," Denver says, his grin evaporating. He leans forward in his chair, takes off his hat and gives his head an all-over scratching before continuing: "He's a likeable guy and lucky for us, he likes us too. He's a great connection. Don't forget—because of him we got that great order. Remember? We were the only locals that got anything out of that project, except of course for the motels and restaurants and so on, the spin-off—"

"I know!" Astrid snaps, then sighs. "Sorry. Just, it was great for us, but why us? And why didn't he hire locals for any of the work there? Something seems off."

"That general contractor they used must've been the low bidder."

"I guess. But a contractor from Saskatchewan? For a huge log building? When we've got Timber Kings right in Dark River? It still doesn't make sense."

Denver's brow creases as he studies his wife. "Yeah. But it's a legit company."

"As far as we know!"

"Yeah, as far as we know. You checked them out, didn't you?"

"I did. But I still don't get it. Hauling equipment all that way? Setting up bunkhouses for the labourers instead of just hiring local subs? How can they possibly be the low bidder with costs like that?"

"Babe, we don't know the ins and outs. Not our place to question who the shareholders hire."

"But what if it's because they're connected somehow? What if it starts up again?"

"Oh, that's what you're worried about. The way Briggs explained it, the old lodge was owned by, like, money managers, bonds and stuff. I don't understand it all, but it'd be like our RRSP fund. We have no say in how the companies in the fund are run. How could the shareholders know—"

"Don't say it like it's a crazy idea! You said Hank Junior had some deal he wanted you in on, something about selling your ranch. I know he and Hank Senior went to Edmonton and met someone to talk about selling this property. They said it was some billionaire, through an agent or something, in Saskatchewan—"

"There's a few companies in Saskatchewan, babe."

"But what if there's something I couldn't find out online? Company ownerships can be convoluted. There could be a connection to the old lodge—"

"I've heard those rumours, too, but I don't believe it. You think there's like, some rape-murder club franchise and they all stick together?"

"Don't act like it's impossible! You know what that woman is saying about Heather's House! Everyone acts like she's crazy. I suppose you think *I'm* crazy, too!" This last comes out louder and more like a sob than she would have liked; the bolus of fear and dread in her stomach is growing; even knowing she's safe, even after all the counselling, memories flash through her brain, vivid and terrible.

Denver slides his chair closer and pulls her into a hug. "Aww, Astrid, I'm sorry, I don't think you're crazy. I wish there was something I could do to help you get over this." He cups her chin and leans in to give her a kiss. "Don't worry, babe, you're safe! Those murders were a long time ago and all the bad people were killed in the explosion. There's no reason to believe Briggs has any connection to them, but I'll handle the business with him. You won't have to be anywhere near him. I won't let anyone hurt you. I promise. Okay?"

After a moment, she relaxes and says, "okay."

"Maybe you want to book another session with Doctor Malone?" he suggests. "Not that I think you're crazy, but she seems to help you."

Astrid takes a breath, shrugs, and says, "sure."

"I love you," he says. He kisses her gently and gives her a squeeze before getting to his feet. "I have to swing by Heather's House. They had a little scuffle there this morning. Had to call the cops."

"Oh my god! One of the husbands showed up?"

"No, one of the clients flipped out. The one that's been saying things—"

"Why didn't anyone call me?"

"I didn't realize they hadn't. Maybe they thought I'd pass the message along? Anyhow, it was over before they called me. Just wanted us to know I guess. But I thought I'd check in anyway, find out what I can. And I have to get to the field office, too, so I'd better hustle." He goes to the door, pulls it open, and is halfway out before turning around and saying, "Oh, before I forget, Briggs says they're doing more landscaping at the Lodge and want some full dimension yellow cedar for boardwalks and so on. Can you see where we can get logs? Dunno how much they'll need yet, so you don't need to commit to anything, just see what the supply is like."

Astrid takes a deep breath, leans back in her chair and says, "I think we sawed some last year and might still have some in the yard. I'll see what else I can get, once we know how much they need."

"Okay. See you at home."

"There's a dinner meeting at Heather's House."

"Oh yeah. Do I have to go to that?"

"You're on the Board, aren't you?"

"Well," he says with a sigh, "I guess I'll see you at the meeting, then."

Astrid watches his retreating back and as the door closes behind him, she bites her lower lip and thinks, *he won't let anyone hurt me? No one can always be there.* Some promises are impossible to keep.

SEVEN

WELCOME TO DARK RIVER

FROM THE PASSENGER loading stairs, the Dark River airport terminal building looks no bigger than a double car garage. *At least it shouldn't take long to get through it,* Kathy thinks as she follows the few dozen passengers deplaning.

Since she had only a carry-on she doesn't have to wait for baggage, and goes in search of the washroom. As she passes the kiosk with the green sign declaring it to be Economy Car Rentals, she says to the young woman behind the counter, "I have to rent a car. But I really need a bathroom break first! Can I leave my suitcase here?"

"Umm..." the girl frowns; Kathy doesn't wait for her to continue, and strides off toward the washroom signs only to find the door to the women's is locked. Someone beat her to it, and she's taking her time.

Kathy breathes a sign of relief when at last the woman comes out. She pushes into the small room and thinks, *well whatever you were doing in here that took so long, it wasn't cleaning the place up!* The garbage bin is overflowing, the soap dispenser is drooling pink ooze onto the counter, and there are odd bits of soggy toilet paper in puddles on the floor. She's careful where she steps and sets her purse in a dry spot on the counter.

Done in the washroom, she heads back to the car rental kiosk. The young woman manning the desk reluctantly puts down her phone. She doesn't offer so much as a smile as she explains the choice of three vehicles. Kathy gets the keys to the Kia Sorrento, then although the girl has gone back to studying her phone, she asks, "by the way, do you know anyone by the name of Hank?"

The frown on the girl's face deepens; she doesn't look up but clicks her tongue with a *tsk* and says, "nope," before lifting a backpack onto the counter and stashing her phone in it. She gets to her feet, turns her back to Kathy and pulls down the first of the enclosure blinds.

Teenagers, Kathy thinks. *Pissed off because I delayed her leaving by five minutes. I sure hope everyone in town isn't so unfriendly.*

She stands uncertainly looking around, wondering if there's anyone else she can ask. The baggage handler is nowhere to be seen and all the other passengers have left. The gate is closed across the gift shop entrance. The Air Canada, West Jet and Interior Air check-in desks are in darkness. No more flights for quite a while, then. The tourist information kiosk, the size of the old outhouse on the farm, has a sign reading "Closed".

With a sigh, she heads out to the parking lot. The Sorrento is in the first row, and in less than fifteen minutes since she got off the plane, she's on the road following the signs to Dark River.

At the edge of town there's a sign reading: "Welcome to Dark River! Population 5,000". She crosses a bridge and takes the offramp onto what looks to be the main street; not much further along, there's a large illuminated sign reading Riverview Motel above a modern-looking building with enough cars in the lot to suggest it's lucky she wasn't any later getting here. She turns in, parks in front of the office and goes inside to the front desk.

The smartly-dressed desk clerk looks up over her glasses, gets to her feet as Kathy approaches and says, "good afternoon. How may I help you?"

"I'd like a room, please."

"You're in luck! We have one left."

"Only one?"

"Yes. Sorry, but this is our busy season."

"On the second floor, I hope?"

"No. Sorry," the desk clerk says.

It's expensive. "Oh, umm, I, er, that's a bit pricey."

"It's one of our deluxe rooms, and we're on summer rates, sorry."

"Okay, well, it's more than I wanted to spend, and I'd really rather not be on the ground floor. I guess I'll try another motel. Is there something else near here?"

"Well, there's Dodd's Auto Court, on the other side of the river, back toward Prince George. About a half-hour's drive I guess." She selects a pamphlet from the rack on the counter, opens it to a street map and circles the star marking Dodd's Auto Court. "But they don't have a second floor."

"Oh." Kathy catches her lower lip in her teeth. She could drive on, but she'd be getting further away from her search area, may not have better luck, and what if she ends up having to sleep in the car? She tells the desk clerk she'll take the room, negotiates a better price for a stay of a week, and provides her credit card information.

"By the way," Kathy says once the paperwork's done, "I know it's a long shot, but I'm looking for a guy named Hank, who worked in some kind of camp near here about forty years ago. You wouldn't by any chance know anyone like that?"

"Hmmm. That's not much to go on. I think a lot of guys worked in camp then. Still do, for that matter. I don't know anyone named Hank, though, but then, I've only been here a few months."

"Oh, you're a newcomer! I thought people mostly moved away from these small towns. What brought you here?"

The clerk takes her glasses off and holds them by the stems; she shrugs and says, "you're right, most people are heading the other way. I was at a crossroads in my life, you know, lousy job, divorce. My car crapped out and even my cat ran off. One night my luck changed. I met a man who offered me a job up here, this job. He even got me a cut rate on the rent of a duplex one of his buddies owns. Sounded good, so here I am. What about you? Are you looking for a job? He might be able to set you up with something, too."

"Me? No, I'm just here short-term, trying to find Hank."

"If you don't find him, will you need a job?"

"Oh, no! It's not like that."

At the narrow-eyed look the clerk gives her, Kathy feels as though she should elaborate, but resists the urge.

In a moment, the clerk continues, "Forgive me for saying, but you don't have much to go on."

"I know." Kathy sighs, then brightens. "Say—the man who got you this job—maybe he'd know more?"

"Might, I suppose. I can't give out his phone number, but next time I'm talking to him, I'll ask."

"That would be great. Maybe give him my phone number?"

"Sure. And you could ask around the Fisherman's."

"Fisherman's?"

"The Fisherman's Pub. It's a favourite watering hole for rednecks. Oh! I hope you don't mind I said redneck! It's not an insult. I actually like rednecks!"

"I like them, too, I guess. Married one." They share a chuckle. Then Kathy says, "So. This pub ...?"

"Oh, yeah, the pub's been there over a hundred years. A little rough, but it has its charm."

"And it's called The Fisherman's? Are there fishermen around here? We're a long way from the ocean."

"Guys come here for fly fishing. The Dark River is quite famous for it. There's these fish that come up from the ocean, cutthroat trout they're called. Good fighters, keep fighting for a long time, at least that's what they all tell me."

"Seems kind of mean," Kathy says.

"Oh, mean? They don't hurt them, you know. They use hooks that don't have barbs on them and then they let them go.

Kathy swallows the urge to tell her that of course it hurts them. How would anyone like being dragged around by a hook in their mouth, barbless or otherwise? Every living creature feels pain! But she's not on a PETA consciousness-raising mission. She's looking for someone, and The Fisherman's would have been there when Hank was writing those letters. It might be the kind of place he would have headed for as soon as he got out of camp, eager to start spending his wages.

"How do I find it?" she asks.

The desk clerk studies the map again, then circles another spot. "It's out on the Old Rupert Road down by the bridge. Just continue north on the highway. There's a sign where you have to turn off."

"I'll check it out." Kathy reads the clerk's name badge and says, "Thanks, um, Kiersten!" She takes the map, buoyed by the feeling they've made a connection. How nice to find someone so small-town friendly and helpful! It's encouraging after her experience with the car rental clerk.

Key card in hand, she heads back outside to park the Sorrento in the assigned spot right outside the door to the room that will be home for a week. It's the last room at the end. Far enough off the road there won't be traffic noise.

The room is clean and tastefully decorated. There's a separate sitting area with a flat screen TV, a table by the window, and a patio door leading out the back to a walkway that adjoins the pool deck. Being one of the deluxe rooms, it has a private patio enclosed by a fancy block wall on the back and wrought-iron railings on the side and front. It's inviting, with shady as well as sunny areas, ceramic pots with shrubs and trailing flowers, and a bistro set. At her approach, small birds fly out of holes in the wall. The forest is only meters away, tall trees surrounded by dense underbrush. Branches overhang the patio, dropping needles and cones on everything.

At the other end of the long building there's what must be the restaurant, two-storey tall windows on its prow front blazing with reflected sunlight. Inside a fenced area with deck chairs and umbrellas, there's a pool. Across a stretch of lawn, a river gurgles lazily along. A man on a mower is making his way along the pool fence before he disappears around the back. The afternoon sun gives the patio, the entire area, a warm glow.

She brushes needles off a chair and sinks into it; leaning back against the wall, she enjoys the scent of newly-mown grass, the late afternoon sunlight warm on her face. The patio is nice. If only Rick was with her! Would it be sensible to cancel this expensive room and get the next flight back to Pillerton? She really is on a fool's errand. Five thousand people live in Dark River, almost twice as many as Pillerton. How many Hanks could there be now, let alone over the past four decades? Not that many, really, maybe only thousands!

She wonders what Rick is doing. She gets out her phone and sends him a text to let him know she's arrived and where she's staying. Once sent, she quickly sends another: "Miss you already. Love you." He's probably at Big Al's Pub, so it doesn't hurt to remind him he has a wife, just in case Dolores Murray is hovering around.

It's not Rick's fault women are attracted to him. He still has that movie-star grin and a cocky bounce in his step, but he's not the cock-of-the-walk he was back in high school. Gone is the player who took her home from the dance early so he could go to the afterparty with someone else. The someone else who's the mother of his only child. But maybe there's still enough of the old Rick that women pick up on. Or is she just being foolish? Worrying about nothing?

Rick! She is missing him. She gives herself a mental kick. *You didn't come here to lay around feeling homesick! Get going! Get out to that pub and start doing what you came here to do! Maybe one night is all you'll need.*

She decides to freshen up, then take a leisurely drive to familiarize herself with the town before searching out The Fisherman's. It's bound to have pub grub and may even be an okay place for dinner. If there are no vegan options, there will likely be salad and if all else fails, at least French fries. She won't ask whether they use lard or vegetable oil in their deep fryer.

EIGHT

SILVERFACE

HE'S WASHING HIS hands after a satisfying dump when his office phone rings. He debates hurrying to answer it, but instead dries his hands and wipes water spots off the taps with the towel before poking it back into the ring.

He leaves the bathroom, heads into his office and sits at the desk. Illuminated by only the monitors and a desk lamp, the room is dark, but the phone is in the pond of light on the desk top. No cell service here, it's a land line and very few people have the number. Fewer still would call so late. He plays the voice message, then picks up the handset and returns the call.

"What's up?" he asks. As he listens to the answer, his forehead creases in a frown. Finally he says, "You're right to call. You don't need to do anything, but for chrissake keep your mouth shut."

He clicks the hang-up button and drops the handset on the desk. Leaning back, he scans the monitors without really seeing them, rocking and swiveling for a moment, wondering what kind of fool would come looking for someone with so little to go on. And for what reason? A good-looking young woman, all on her own. She should count herself lucky the man she seeks is dead.

He sits up straighter and makes a sound like a low, animal growl. He's just made the connection: there is that one loose end in the will. The old man said it was unlikely to ever come up, so unlikely that he would probably never have to deal with it. What was the point of including it in his will, then? A little fucking late to start feeling responsible! But the old bastard was stubborn and couldn't be talked out of it. In fact, it was the only time they argued. Once was more than enough. After that, he pushed it out of his mind and went on believing the five million dollars would be his on the five-year anniversary of his father's death. That was way off in the future, after all. Or it should have been. That anniversary is just a few months away, and this woman chooses now to come crawling out of the woodwork?

He scratches the nub that's the last remnant of his ear and runs a palm over the shiny scar tissue where hair no longer grows. The hair on the unscarred part of his scalp is stubbly. Overdue for a shave. Annie is coming tomorrow to deliver his weekly grocery order and do the cleaning. She always stays long enough for a fuck and to cook meals for him to eat through the week. He'll get her to shave his head. He can do it himself, of course, but she does a better job. And he enjoys the touch of the woman.

He gets to his feet, straightens his robe and tugs the belt tight, then turns off the desk lamp as he leaves the office. If not for his uneven steps, the slight dragging of one foot, he would be silent as he moves barefoot along the dark hallway to the kitchen. He flicks on one bank of undercabinet lights and gets a bowl. He fills it with Vector, pours milk over it, and sprinkles it with sugar before going to the living room, where he stands at the middle of the wall-to-wall, ceiling-to-floor windows, looking out as he eats.

Bright moonlight silvers the clearing in the forest surrounding his house and puts the tall firs and dense underbrush into stark relief. It's always still and peaceful at this time of night. He slides the patio door open, steps out onto the deck and draws a deep lungful of the pungent forest scent. Crickets chirp beneath the hot tub and further off, an owl hoots. It's primal.

Annie complains that it's dark and depressing under the huge old Douglas firs. She says the house is too close to the forest, it should have been in the middle of the clearing, more trees need to be taken out at the back to let more light in. She says he wouldn't be so depressed if his house wasn't so dark.

He never acknowledges her comments. She doesn't live here and no matter how often she hints at it, she never will. He can't deny he enjoys her impressive tits, though. That they're implants doesn't bother him, but her thinking he's depressed or has other mental issues she keeps wanting him to talk about pisses him off. She doesn't know him, not at all. It's not her fault. He has only ever had one true friend and she wasn't even a girlfriend, just a friend. A sweet girl friend he grew up with. Since then, he's never let anyone get close to him and he sees no reason to change now.

He could live in the spacious master suite at the Lodge, but he prefers this house, as small as it is. Taking the trail through the forest on his Kubota Sidekick, he can be at the Lodge in under half an hour. It takes twice as long by road, but he seldom goes that route.

As much as it's annoying at times that there's no cell phone coverage, he loves the womb-like sanctuary and feels enfolded in the ancient forest. He can be himself. No one here to gawk or turn away. And he can always drive the Sidekick to the top of the hump if he needs to make a call on his cell. He wouldn't give up the view, limited though it seems to Annie. He never tires of it.

But tonight he's looking out across the small cleared area at the tall trees, silvered by light from the full moon, without really seeing them.

Why would *she* show up now? No one was supposed to know about the money. But then, she wasn't supposed to find out that the transfer of the title to her mother's house was illegal, and she did. Now she's here. Maybe her snoopy lesbian lawyer friend who got the title transfer to the house overturned will show up next. This isn't good.

Movement at the edge of the clearing draws his attention. It's the bear, a huge male grizzly. Like the trees, the fur on his hump is silvered by moonlight and the large white spot on his face gleams.

Bears are supposed to sleep at night, but more and more, this one is as likely to show up at night as during the day. Since he killed Brutus, he seems to think he can wander the property at will, day or night, unchallenged.

He glances back at the fur tacked above the fireplace, the head with its snarling teeth so unlike the dog's usual expression of interest and curiosity, and shakes his head.

Brutus was a good dog. He'll always have that place of honour in the cabin.

The Rottweiler got in a few licks of his own, ripping the bear's face open and leaving an eyeball dangling. The eyeball was gone the next time he came around but it took weeks for the flap of skin to necrotize enough to fall away. The raw meat under it was angry-looking. It must have been excruciatingly painful, probably accounting for the lengthy roaring sessions that could be heard for weeks.

Unlike his own ruined scalp, the bear's fur is growing back. White, yes, but at least it's growing back. The wound healed but the roaring sessions have continued as if he's found something else to rage about. Maybe he has. Maybe it's the fact of this cabin, an intrusion into his traditional range. Maybe he's mentally ill, if a bear can be mentally ill, from the pain of the wound or maybe he got a brain infection through the empty eye socket. Or maybe he's just angry at being scarred for life. He, of all people, understands that.

At first, thinking only of justice for Brutus, he wanted to shoot the bear, rationalizing it would be a kindness. He set up his C-14 Timberwolf MRSWS on the deck, trained the sights on the bear, and followed his movements for better than ten minutes. Several times he had a clear shot with the red laser dot right in the middle of the bear's massive forehead, a perfect kill shot. But he couldn't pull the trigger.

He has a grudging respect for the mutilated beast and feels a kinship with the animal. They were both drawn to Bear Mountain, after all. The thought came to him that the bear found him because it's his spirit animal, in the flesh.

In the manner of some indigenous people, he renamed himself, his inspiration for the name he chose coming from the Viking Berserkers. He can't wear a bear skin as they did, so he settled for a tattoo on his scarred shoulder. Lumpy whorls beneath one eye make it three-dimensional. Life-like. He thought of naming himself "Bear", but discarded that idea in favour of "Bearon". No one will ever see it written; on email and so on, he's just "B." And on legal documents—well, only his lawyer and a couple of others know his real name. Just those few people with a need to know, and they're sworn to secrecy. Spoken, it's common enough. And when people shorten it to "Bear", it's perfect.

Once he accepted the fact of the bear, he came to appreciate having it patrolling the woods around his retreat. He started putting food at the edge of the clearing. Then came the morning he came into the kitchen to find the bear on the deck outside the patio doors, looking in. For terrifying minutes Bearon thought he was going to smash the glass and come inside. In that moment, he realized that spirit animal or not, there had to be boundaries. Since the bear didn't respect the cleared area as being Bearon's territory, he had a two-meter high, barbed-wire-topped chain link fence built around the perimeter.

The fence is electrified, making it doubly secure. Now when an invited guest comes, he presses the button by the front door or clicks the command on the computer, and the driveway gate opens. Everyone else takes their chances at the enterphone.

He watches the bear approach the man gate at the back where the tray of kibble, raw meat and a watermelon waits. He seems wary of the fence. He's smart.

I should give him a name, too, he thinks. In the moonlight, his "grizzly" hump almost looks white. The spot on his face glows. *Silverface?*

"Silverface," he says.

The bear looks up, suddenly as still as if frozen, seemingly fixing his one eye on him. Bearon feels a jolt of panic and takes a quick involuntary step backwards into the house. His bad leg catches on the doorsill, setting off sharp needles of pain in his hip. He nearly falls, catching the jamb with his damaged hand to save himself, and barely avoids dropping the bowl. Milk and cereal slop out. He slides the door shut with a loud thump. The bear watches for a moment before returning his attention to the food. He doesn't look up at the house again.

He looked me right in the eye! That was a threat! He blames me for my dog mutilating him!

He has a fleeting thought he should get another dog, or maybe two, to patrol inside the fence. Then he gives himself a mental shake. *You're being paranoid. There's no way the bear can get past the fence. He might have heard me but he couldn't have seen me well enough to make eye contact. Not at this distance. No. He and I are bonded. He feels a kinship with me as I do with him. You over-reacted. He just responded to the name.*

Silverface it is.

NINE

RETIREMENT PARTY

"WE HARDLY EVER go out for supper. If we have to pay a sitter, why can't we at least go someplace nice? I don't know why you guys like that place, anyway."

"Because, babe, it's homey, the beer's cheap, and it's only ten minutes away," Denver says. He was late getting home so he's just coming out of the shower now, sandy hair slicked back, whiskers freshly scraped off. He hasn't done up the snaps on his shirt front and Astrid never tires of admiring his body, even though his tan stops in a Vee at his neck. He still has that six-pack. How does he stay so lean and fit now that he spends more time in his truck or behind a desk than on a horse or throwing bales? Unlike herself, he doesn't even spend time on the treadmill or Bowflex.

"Yeah, homey if you live in a cave," she says. "All those dark beams, low ceiling, and frickin' giant moose antlers for decoration? And the smell! Decades of spilled beer, cigarette smoke, and I'll bet the sewer backs up every time the river rises. It's a wonder the place doesn't get shut down."

"There's a couple pitchers of Queen Elizabeth when she got crowned, too," Wilson points out.

Denver chuckles and says, "Seventy-year-old pictures and the sweet smell of more'n a hundred years of spilled beer and backed-up sewer! What's not to like? I'll take you somewhere nice next time. How about the Riverview for our anniversary? It would be fitting, returning to where we had our first date."

"Sure."

"Come on, babe, where's your enthusiasm? We can go any where you want, any time you want. Wilson is always happy to stay with the girls, you know."

"Yeah, I know. I guess I'm just tired," she tells him.

"You seem to be tired a lot, babe," Denver says.

"It's been a busy week. Lots going on at the office, and on top of it, that woman's accusations. And there won't be an end to it unless she admits she isn't telling the truth."

"MAKE HER TELL THE TROOF, MOMMY!"

Astrid and Denver turn to look at the small girl with the big voice, sitting with her sister on the rug in the living room. They're building Lincoln Log corrals for Breyer horses.

"Little pictures have big ears," Astrid whispers. She turns her back on the girls and herds Denver further into the kitchen. "Anyway, I bet she thinks Heather's House has lots of money and she might as well have some of it. After all Heather's House did for her, she makes up a lie to blackmail us? Voices coming from inside the linen service van?"

"She's delusional. Drugs messed up her head."

"I wonder if it's a good idea to have the linen service, anyway. The driver's a man. You know the policy about men inside the fence. If we could get a woman barn manager we could replace Jake, too. We wouldn't have to fire him, maybe give him something over at the yard. A woman helping the girls with the horses would be a better fit. And the linen guy. Maybe we should stipulate the driver has to be a woman? You know, I wouldn't have agreed to the linen service if they hadn't offered it as a donation. It's so generous of them and such a benefit for us I hate to make waves."

"Well, there must be a woman that can do the job. Meantime, how about they tell us when they're going to be coming around and we push the laundry cart out to the gate for them?"

"That's a good idea," Astrid says. "But aside from that, maybe we have an obligation to follow up with the women when they leave."

"That's what some of the board members are saying and Doctor Malone is pushing it. It would add to the work load. We'd need a few more staff, for sure. And you know how often they just bug out without a word to anyone."

"Maybe we should look into it when that happens, though? Maybe they're still too vulnerable to just be let loose like that. What if that woman is right?"

"It's pretty far-fetched, but suppose she is. We have nothing to do with it."

"But what about the police? Did you ask Jacques? What did he say?"

"She flipped out when she was at the Detachment, just like she did at Heather's. She's at Nechako Manor now.

Apparently, she's been in and out of there a few times over the years, always hearing voices, complaining she's being followed. Jacques called to update me this afternoon. Told me this in confidence, so it stays here."

"Of course. Okay then. Maybe it will come to nothing."

"Yup, I imagine it'll die a natural death. No use worrying about it, babe. And this little retirement party will be just what we need to get all our minds off it. You're all fixed up and you look so pretty, you don't want to waste it! Give the guys a chance to see you without your ball cap, although now that I think about it, it's not really fair to them, knowin' all they can do is look and I'm the lucky guy who gets to take you home." He grins, then takes a more serious tone. "I know the place is kinda rough but the guys are comfortable there and it's customary for the boss to present the watch."

"I'll stay home," Wilson offers, "I don't mind."

"I think we can afford to pay a sitter," Denver assures him, "that's not the point."

"Don't be silly, Wilson," Astrid says, "You deserve a night out more than anyone and you like those guys, don't you? When you all get your heads together over in your corner solving all the world's problems it's as if no one else exists. You can argue all night about whether Guy Lafleur had a better wrist shot than Bobby Orr, or if GM is better than Ford. You wouldn't want to miss that!"

"Don't forget Dora Mae," Denver says. He's finished closing his shirt and loosens his fly to tuck it into his jeans, then zips up and fastens his big silver belt buckle. "She's been askin' all week if you were comin'. You got an admirer there, Wil! When're you gonna give that poor lonely widow woman more'n a smile?"

Wilson shrugs and turns away.

Astrid notices Wilson's ears turning red. She says, "Well, we sure don't want to disappoint Dora Mae!"

"We won't stay late," Denver promises as he heads to the door. "I'll go pick up Jessie now. Can you two be ready to go as soon as I get back?"

Astrid nods and Wilson says, "Ay-yuh."

As Denver goes out the door, Astrid watches with amusement as Wilson follows him out to the porch. He keeps his almost non-existent backside to her but he's gone to the cupboard where the shoeshine box is kept, and is bent over, giving his boots a buffing. He's not shining his boots and wearing his bolo tie with the silver and turquoise slider for the guys.

Denver returns with the sitter in under fifteen minutes. The girls are fond of Jessie so after the excited greetings, they take her hands and tow her into the living room to show her their horse ranch, so engrossed in telling her all about it they barely look up to say good-bye.

THEY ARRIVE AT the fisherman's and enter the low-ceilinged, dark room to find half has been sectioned off for the noisy Dark River Sawmill crowd. It's hot and stuffy with the heat of so many bodies coupled with the warm August night; even with the double doors giving onto the patio next to the river being wide open, there isn't enough of a breeze to move the air.

Wilson joins his group of friends at their usual table in the corner under the moose antlers while Denver and Astrid work their way through the crowd, engaging in the usual small talk with everyone they pass. The press of bodies is oppressive. At last they're outside, where there's shade from the huge old firs and the breeze from the river, slight though it is, stirs the bushes surrounding the patio. Astrid draws a deep breath of the cooling evening air and sighs.

Caterers in white chef's coats are busy setting the long food table. Rows of tables and chairs have been arranged around the flagstones. Women from the office are at the table closest to the river. Mary Ann looks up and beckons.

"I'll join the girls," Astrid tells Denver. "You go ahead and circulate."

A server is working her way through the crowd; Astrid orders a liter each of house white and red and a jug of draft for the group to supplement the bottles of wine Dark River Sawmills contributed to the party. The mood is light, the mosquitoes aren't too bad thanks to the perimeter of citronella torches, and the meal of Caesar salad, mashed potatoes, herbed carrots and roast beef with horse radish and gravy is very good.

Mary Ann and her boyfriend come to sit with them to eat. Dora Mae somehow managed to get next to Wilson in the queue at the buffet and they join them, too. Despite Wilson being his usual reserved self, Dora Mae is cheerful and laughs easily; conversation is lively and enjoyable, and the hour passes quickly.

After everyone has been through the dessert table, it's time for the speeches. Astrid goes to stand at the head of the table where Barney and his wife sit, and turns to face the crowd. Once the chatter hushes, she says, "You all the know the reason for this party is to see Barney off onto the next phase of his life. I'd say we're doing it in style! The meal was great, and we have the staff party fund to thank for putting it on. Let's give the catering staff a hand for doing such a good job." After the enthusiastic applause, she continues: "Yeah, sounds like you enjoyed the food. Show them some love by dropping a little something in the tip jar."

She turns to Barney as she addresses the crowd: "As you know, Barney works in the yard, and since I don't spend much time out there, I don't see him often. Still, I feel like I know him better than any of the other guys, and I have since my first day on the job. I know him intimately, you might say. I might know more of you guys intimately, too, but I haven't stumbled into the men's washroom by mistake since." Everyone laughs.

"It wasn't yer fault!" Barney says loudly enough to be heard in the back. "Them A-holes thought it would be funny to pull a joke on the new boss lady by switching the signs around!"

"Yeah, and I'd still like to know whose idea *that* was!" Astrid responds. "But seriously, it's been a great experience working with all of you, and Barney, you are a big part of it. I know you and Irene are looking forward to becoming snowbirds and you're getting your nice new motorhome ready to go.

"This company, by any of its names, was a huge part of your life. For anyone to work for the same company for forty-five years in any business, but in this business especially, is remarkable. There is no way to adequately repay you, but there's a little cheque in the envelope, and I know I speak for all of us when I say we hope when you look to see what time it is, you'll think of us. It goes without saying, I hope there will be no swearing when you do."

Astrid allows the chuckles to dwindle before continuing. "Seriously, though, you will be missed." She hands him the box with the watch. Everyone claps as she returns to her seat.

"You did good," Denver whispers, taking her hand. She gives his hand a squeeze.

Barney stands up and gives his acceptance speech, tearing up at one point, and promises to keep in touch. After various of his co-workers finish telling their own Barney stories, the party begins to break down into groups. Wilson returns to the table under the moose antlers, leaving Dora Mae with Barney and Irene.

"I see why he's been a bachelor all his life," Astrid remarks. "Anyway, I know it's early, but I'm ready to leave when you are."

"I'm ready now. Canucks are playing tonight. If we go now and you take Jessie home, I can still catch part of the last period."

"Thought you were recording it."

"I am. But I'd rather watch it in real time, at least the end. Unless they're losing badly. If they are, I'll just delete the recording and save myself gettin' pissed off watchin' tomorrow."

"Ahh. But isn't it still pre-season? Does the game even count? You could just check the app on your phone."

"There's that," Denver agrees, "but three hours is long enough for the bosses to hang around putting a damper on the party."

Together they go to see if Wilson wants to stay. "I don't mind coming back later to get you," Denver tells him.

Wilson jumps up and comes away from the group with such speed that as they walk out, Astrid says, "sorry to tear you away."

"I'm more'n ready to go. Can only stand so much stupidity," he snorts. "Goddamn George Mahoney, never done nuthin' for ranchers and goddamn Carson thinks he's the greatest!"

"Oh. Politics. One of those nights."

"Wisht we'da stuck to trucks or hockey! If you hadn't come along I mighta had to punch that stupid Carson's lights out."

"You wouldn't!" Astrid exclaims. "He's got six inches and a hundred pounds on you!"

"You worried about Wilson?" Denver asks. "It's Carson you should worry about."

As they're outside heading toward the truck, someone calls from the side of the building, "Give me a minute, Denver?"

Denver turns and sees a man in the pond of light from the kitchen door beckoning him. "Sure, Brent," he responds, then hands the keys to Astrid and says, "go ahead. I'll catch up." He goes to stand beside Brent. "What's up?"

"I hope you don't think I was rude. I just thought your good wife might not want to hear this, you know, because it might remind her of, well, of what happened."

"Okay ...?"

"Well, there's a woman been asking about Hank. Said he was working at a logging camp thirty-five or forty years ago. I said I didn't know anyone by that name, and that's the truth, the two of them both bein' dead now, but I overheard one of the other guys telling her he knew a Hank, but he got killed in an explosion. He was talking about Hank Junior. He wasn't one of that group Junior ran with, too much younger, but a lot of them young guys looked up to that shithead for some reason. Girls got sucked in, too. He had some kinda, er, charm."

"Yeah. Charisma. I never felt it but my brother and my ex-wife did, I guess."

"Oh, that's right, your ex was there when it went up—"

"How'd you know that?"

"Small town, Denver, ain't you used to that by now? Anyhow, I guess charisma's a handy quality to have if yer gonna be a serial killer. If you knew him you remember he threw Senior's money around like he was a big fuckin' cheese and that impresses a lot of dumbasses. Anyway, she said something like, no, he'd be too young."

"She's lookin' for someone and all she's got to go on is a first name?"

"Yeah, just a first name and that he worked in camp. Which camp? She had no idea there was more than one, and a-course didn't know the name of it. And such a long time ago."

Denver shrugs. "You know how it is. Since they unsealed the adoption records, there's lots of people looking for their birth parents. Could be why she's looking for him now."

"Could be, but wouldn't she know his last name?"

"Yeah, she would at that."

"She didn't say he was her father, now that you mention it, but something like she's looking for her sister or brother and he's the only one who can help her find him or her, something like that. Could be Hank Senior, I think. Sure as hell couldn't be Junior. 'Sides bein' too young he never did a day's work far as I know but I seem to remember the old man talking about workin' out at the old Bear Mountain camp, like he was proud of it, as if just about all the fallers around here didn't work in camp one time or another. He sure liked to brag himself up, always goin' on about how he was a self-made man, started off in camp and worked up to owning the whole works. Never bothered to mention everything he had he got by marryin' the boss's daughter. Sure had a lot of people around here kissin' his ass, too, even guys my age callin' him *Mister* Hazen, like he was special. That little group of his was special, all right. Glad you took 'em all out."

"Well, I didn't, actually—"

"You're the one who got the gals out, though."

"Well—"

"Anyhow, I didn't tell her Junior's father went by Hank, too. I thought she might be out to make trouble for you. Maybe she read about the explosion, how it wiped out the Hazen Sawmills family, and dreamed up a story, thinkin' to claim she's related so she could tap into your good wife's inheritance or something."

"After all this time?"

"Ain't been all that long. What, three years?"

"Nearly five."

"That long, eh?" Brent shrugs. "Well, someone else might tell her, but at least it won't be me. She asked me to ask around and to let her know if anyone came up with anything."

"You get her name?"

"Kathy. And she's staying at the Riverview, Room 110. Just thought you should know."

"Yeah, thanks," Denver says. They shake hands, then Brent turns and goes back in the kitchen door.

Denver is about to turn away when movement in the bushes next to the walkway attracts his attention. Someone is there, spying? He takes a few steps closer to investigate. A man in dark pants and hoodie comes stumbling out, zipping his fly, head down and mumbling. Denver shakes his head, then turns and continues to the truck, where Wilson and Astrid are waiting inside.

"What did Brent want?" Astrid wants to know when he gets in.

"Nothing, really." He takes a sharp breath, glad it's dark and Astrid can't see he's embarrassed at the lie. He starts the engine, backs out of the parking stall and aims the truck up the driveway to the road, avoiding looking at Astrid. He feels the weight of her stare and is relieved when she faces forward again.

As they approach the one-lane bridge, they pass a man in dark clothes walking on the narrow gravel shoulder. "Jeez, didn't see him until the last second!" Denver exclaims.

"You see how he's lurching along? I thought he was going to stumble out right in front of the truck." Astrid says. "He shouldn't be walking out here in such dark clothes."

"Probably didn't plan to walk," Denver says. "I think he's the guy that was in the bushes takin' a piss when I was talking to Brent. Pretty shitfaced, I think."

"Least he ain't stupid enough to drive in that condition," Wilson observes.

Once across the bridge, they pass a row of vehicles parked there. "Overflow from the pub," Denver says. "Didn't think it was that busy. And why park halfway into the bushes like that? And I think it was a Range Rover. You see it, Wilson?"

"Yup," Wilson responds, "guess the owner don't care about scratchin' the paint."

"Expensive vehicle like that and you don't care about the paint? Wonder whose it is."

"Seems kinds outta place, don't it?"

"Yeah, it does. Wonder who around here has the money to shell out $200K for a vehicle."

"People have different priorities and you don't know how deep in debt they are, either," Astrid points out. "Same with Barney and Irene. I wouldn't have thought they would have the bucks to buy that expensive new motor home, especially at this point in their lives. I sure hope they didn't take on a lot of debt for it."

"I heard they mighta sold their house," Wilson says.

"Oh, I hope not!"

Denver turns on the stereo, relieved Astrid isn't pressing him about his conversation with Brent. He hates lying to her, but she doesn't need a reminder of her ordeal.

His thoughts turn to that Range Rover as he wonders whose it is.

TEN

TABLE TALK

THE ROOM IS not much bigger than the table. According to its history, it was built where it stands, filling the only part of the room where there's a full-height ceiling. Made of thick slabs of clear fir trimmed with native maple, it has been worn shiny by the elbows that have rested on it and bellies that have rubbed up against it over the past hundred-plus years.

From his seat at the head, Bearon looks at the possessors of the bellies in front of him and has a fleeting thought they should make use of the workout room at the Lodge, but knows they won't. The hot tub, sure; the pool, maybe, but the rest? Never. The lawyer is a weedy little runt and will never change but the other three are becoming more rotund by the day, happy to keep buying bigger clothes. The upside is, they'll probably die off before they get much older, but he'll be stuck with the lawyer forever.

He snaps his thoughts back to the present, pulls the balaclava away from his mouth, and says, "Okay, let's get started."

The big man at the far end noisily demolishing the super-size plate of nachos in front of him breaks away from his food and says, "we ain't gonna wait til Reardon gets here?"

"No, Preach, nothing we have to discuss today concerns him."

"Good. I don't trust him."

"Why not?"

"He's too...I dunno," Preach looks up and they make eye contact for a heartbeat before he looks away. "Too slick, I guess."

"You mean he looks fit and prosperous? That's why he's good at his job."

"I could drive a Porsche if I wanted one, too."

Bearon dismisses the comment with a wave of his hand; he turns to the barrel-chested fifty-something man at his elbow and says, "So, Brent, when I was leaving here last night I heard you telling Danielson about that woman."

"Yeah? So?"

"So? We decided he—*they*—didn't need to know. That it would be better if she didn't connect with Danielsons and that she didn't find out about Hazens, so she would go back to where she came from."

"I know that's what you wanted, Bearon," Brent says as he pushes his empty mug toward Evan, who's pouring beer from the pitcher, and watches as his mug is refilled.

"Yet you pulled him aside to tell him," Bearon growls.

"Yeah, it's what you wanted, but you never consulted any of us," Brent responds after a long draft of his fresh beer. "Say it is Hank Hazen Senior she's looking for, why do you give a shit? She finds out he's dead, goes home, end of problem."

You don't know shit, Bearon thinks.

"Fuck, Bearon, if I didn't tell him, someone else would. I heard she's been asking all over town," Brent continues, giving him a sideways glance. "You don't think she'll go into Dot's and ask there? If she gets a hold of Franny, she'll tell Danielson's wife, no doubt about that. He might as well hear it from me. He's a pretty big player around here, if you ain't noticed. Someone we're better off having on our side."

"You forget he blew up the old Lodge?"

"Propane leak, I heard."

"That's what I heard, too," the lawyer says, giving his heavy five o'clock shadow a scratch. "And about that woman, Kathy, I think she said her name was—"

"You talked to her too?" Bearon asks.

"Not me, but some of my gals did. She came into the office. They gave her the link to the Community News, you know there's a bunch of info in their archives, maybe even that old phone book of town residents. Remember that?"

"Oh yeah," Preacher says, "used to be able to pick up a copy at the Community Center. Haven't seen that for a while."

"Me neither. Anyhow, I heard them tell her about Hank at the bowling alley, and off she went." He takes a draft of his beer, and continues: "We all know you blame Danielson for blowing up the old lodge, but it's in the past. Forget about it. If you can't forget about it, at least admit it turned out good for you, and let's get on with whatever it was you called us out for. I need to get going."

With a sharp intake of breath, Bearon struggles not to respond. It turned out good for him? None of these guys knows shit. But that's the way it has to be.

After a moment, he says, "yeah, Kevin, you worried your wife will make you sleep in the guest room again if you're ten minutes late? Oh, now I remember. She's got your balls because it's *her* family money."

"*Jesus*, Bear!" Evan hisses.

Bearon gives Evan a sharp look. For a moment, the only sounds in the room are Preacher's lip-smacking and the murmur of conversation from the pub below. Then Bearon exhales and says, "This deal is going to make us so rich Kevin's wife's money will look like chump change. Keep that in mind." He drums the fingers of his good hand on the table and thinks for a second about what to say that would put Kevin in his place. But the moment has passed.

He continues: "anyhow, let's move on so we can get outta here. I don't want to be here any longer than I have to, neither. You'll all be happy to know this is our last meeting in this room. Next time we meet, it'll be in the board room at the Lodge."

"Didn't know the boardroom was finished," Brent says.

"Yeah, or at least it will be before our next meeting. But the big news is, we have a ceremony to organize."

"Ceremony? Have the Illustrious Leaders told you when they're coming?" Preacher asks.

"Yeah, this week-end."

"What? I can't be ready by then! And besides, we don't have an Acolyte. We'll have to tell them to postpone it."

"I know it's short notice but they've been anxious to see the Lodge so they jumped on the chance when something else fell through and their weekend opened up. They're bringing their Acolyte, and she's a hottie! Wait'll you get a load of her! But more important, this is our first full communion. I thought they sent you the sermon, Preacher, so what's the problem?" Bearon asks.

"Yeah, they emailed it to me. Some nonsense from the Book of Esther, King Ashermuckky sent for his wife when his heart was merry with wine and when she told him to pound sand, he tossed her out and took up with Esther. That's all I remember. I haven't figured out how to say his name, forget memorizing the whole passage! No way I can learn it by this week-end! I'll hafta read it."

"Jesus! You're gonna have to up your game. Bad enough we don't have many members for this first Ceremony, and you're gonna read your sermon?"

"No one told me I was going to have to give it so soon. It's not enough time."

"No one really listens anyway, at least not at a Ceremony, so if he reads it, no big deal," Evan intercedes. "As for numbers, I told them how it is, not all of the Pastor's old congregation has stayed with us, so it's a work in progress. As long as you can show the Pillerton guys you're growing, you'll be okay. Think about Pillerton! For years—decades really—they only had a couple dozen. Three Elders for that tiny congregation! They had a solid bank account thanks to their real estate and mortgages or it wouldn't have worked. Dark River doesn't have that, of course."

"No, not yet we don't, but meanwhile we got product that doesn't take decades to make a guy rich," Bearon points out.

"Of course," Evan agrees. "I didn't mean to dis what you got going on here, and I think they'll be pleased with progress to date, but you gotta do something to attract new members. Preach, get the Pillerton guys to send you all their sermons and start blasting out some hellfire and brimstone! Maybe we should think about advertising, too. Your picture on a bus stop bench or something. But the services are important for attracting ordinary members and for the cover story. If you can't up your game, Dark River Chapter will have to recruit someone else or maybe parachute someone from the parent company in, and Preacher goes back to being good old Wally who owns the motels."

"What d'you think I been doing, Evan, sermonizing every fuckin' Sunday to that bunch of old biddies in the meeting room at Riverview? The dregs left over from the old congregation? Not my fault no one takes us serious. We wanna make something more of this, we need a better venue."

"I don't imagine you object to all of them pouring into your restaurant for Sunday brunch, though," Bearon says.

"Wally's right," Kevin contributes. "All we need is a bag full of money."

"Don't have to spend a bundle, Kevin. We could get a big old house, the kind that would be designated heritage status if they have such a thing in Dogpatch," Evan says, "something that really only needs a little tiddling up. We used an old house in Pillerton for years."

"One of my clients who passed away a couple weeks ago lived down at the end of River Street," Kevin tells them. "I haven't been in the house but I drove by. Looks a little run down but it's a big Victorian two-storey. Big lot. Nice, private riverfront property. One of the nicer old houses in *Dogpatch*." He gives Evan a hard look.

"Other than the Al Capone Tunnels being protected, I don't remember any property being designated heritage in Pillerton," Bearon says. "I don't know that it's all that much better than Dark River."

"No disrespect intended," Evan says with a shrug, then turns to Kevin. "Who inherited it?"

"Her son. He lives in Victoria."

"So, would he move here? Keep it as a rental?"

"He doesn't want it. Asked me about realtors."

"We should take a look at it," Bearon says. "If it'll work, make him an offer before a realtor gets involved."

"Lousy time to be laying out cash, though," Brent says.

"Gotta spend money to make money, right Evan?" Preacher opines. "You'd give us a mortgage on it, wouldn't you, Evan?"

"I, uhh, well, sure, I could run it by the Big Guys if that's what you want, but you won't need a mortgage," Evan responds. "There's a shipment going out in a couple days, remember? We're gonna have bucks to wash, so this comes along at a good time."

"Get someone on the son in Victoria," Bearon says. "Check him out. See if we can do something with him. Is there a way we can get to him? Loan him some money with the house as collateral? Some weakness he might have? Gambling? Coke? Pussy? You get on that would you, Kevin?"

"I'll get on it," Kevin agrees.

Bearon tips his beer for a good long draft, then wipes his lip with his hand, leans forward and says, "We're gonna be the Big Guys now, boys. We're gonna make what the old man cooked up look like Monopoly. The Children of Noah angle was only a means of providing the girls for his gentlemen's club. We're going to be bigger than he ever dreamed."

"Ahh! The girls," Preacher sighs. "They're not girls, though. They're a bunch of fat old broads. Not sure I can get it up for them."

"I'd of thought being married to Georgia or whatever her name is, you'd of figured out a way," Bearon says. "Take your Viagra and pull the hoods up over their faces. You'll do fine."

"Yeah, that'd be a lot like fuckin' Georgia."

"There's some nice pussy in the congregation too. At least one new member. She's thirty something but she's still at least a seven. You all seen her, works for you, Preacher," Brent says, with a lift of his chin in Preacher's direction.

"Yeah, at the Riverview. Reardon's fuckin' her."

"I'm nervous, though," Brent tells them. "Can we really fly under the radar? The gentlemen's club is one thing. Even the drugs. It's the other…"

"Getting cold feet?" Bearon asks with a scowl.

"I'm just sayin. We have to be careful."

"We *are* careful. We're upstanding businessmen. Pillars of the community. The Lodge is going to be a big boost to the local economy. Dark River loves us."

"I wouldn't be so sure about that," Kevin says. "Clients of mine talk. Lots of 'em are pissed none of the construction jobs went to locals, that you didn't hire any trades from around here. People are asking why not. And then there's the fact you have to be a member to even get in the gate."

"Yeah, I've heard there's some bitchin' about that," Bearon says. "I've been thinking, maybe we open to the public one week-end a month or something. Just so all the nosey bastards can come and take a look. Have a nice dinner. Nothing to see here, folks, kinda thing. If we charged enough, they wouldn't wanna come back a second time."

"Maybe they will, though," Evan says. "Not a bad thing. Another revenue stream never hurts."

"We got another problem," Preacher says. "That crazy broad runnin' around tellin' everyone Heather's House is kidnapping women. Stokin' fears about another serial killer. I hear whispers about the new Lodge bein' just like the old Lodge."

"*What?*" Bearon hisses.

"Yeah. Fuckin' cop actually looked into it, snoopin' around the hotels because we have the linen service. You know, not for linens, we do our own, but for the entrance mats and so on. He followed the truck along its whole delivery route, watchin' and askin' everyone at every stop. Just lucky the driver twigged to it, cut his route short and only delivered legit stuff. And of course, didn't pick up the cargo."

"Don't tell me they're still at the Dogwood house?"

"Hell no!" Brent chimes in. "The driver came and killed some time here. At closing time, he went and picked 'em up. Made sure he wasn't followed."

"That fuckin Frenchie cop! Ain't he got nuthin' better to do? Dunno why they didn't send him somewhere. He's been here longer than anyone else. Instead they move our guy out and promote him!" Bearon scowls. "I wonder what made him suspicious about the truck, though."

"Because that's the truck that picks up Heather's House's laundry. They bundle them away with the sheets, according to the crazy woman. The cop told the driver she claimed to have heard voices coming from inside. Yellin' for help. He asked the girls working at the desk if we ever noticed anything like that. Asked to talk to the housekeeping staff and even wanted to see inside the truck."

"Jesus! He look inside?"

"Yeah. Driver had to let him have a look. Opened the back door for him. He didn't climb in. No live cargo anyway so it was a small risk."

Bearon pinches the bridge of his nose, exhales loudly. "He didn't notice the box being shorter inside than out?"

"No."

"Jesus H. fuckin' Christ!"

"Maybe we should switch trucks. Use the shredding truck instead," Preacher suggests.

"For chrissakes, Preach, how would that work? It's for long hauls. Nobody needs shredding every week!"

"I guess," Preacher shrugs and drains his beer.

"We better beef up the soundproofing on the linen van. I'll tell Clint to get it done." Bearon leans back in his chair, eyes closed for a moment, wishing he could take the balaclava off because he's got an itch and it's impossible to scratch it. All he can do is put it out of his mind. He says, "for a while at least, no more girls from Heather's."

"Jake won't like that," Brent points out. "It'll cut into his earnings big time."

"It's the new reality. If he doesn't like it, he can quit. You really think he'll walk? He's still got a captive customer base for the other stuff there without hardly lifting a finger."

"Not a good idea to take 'em from around here anyway," Kevin says. "This town is too small."

"They're low hanging fruit, like hitchhikers and runaways. At loose ends when they leave Heather's," Bearon opines. "But you're right. This town is too small. We all agree, then? No more from Heather's. Or anywhere around here?"

Everyone voices agreement. Bearon continues, "people will quit bitchin' about not being able to have dinner or go to the Grotto without a membership if we let 'em in once in a while. Or that they didn't get work when it was being built now that we're hiring permanent employees."

"Speaking of employees, who've we got at the mill now that Barney's gone?" Kevin asks.

"No one, but I got feelers out," Brent tells them. "Got the word out with the mill guys that come in here. Not much interest so far. It ain't as attractive as before the fuckin' government legalized pot."

"People could always get their weed lots of places. We'll be cheaper than the legal stuff. Better hours too. And the government stores won't have the rest of the stuff we supply," Preacher reminds them.

"Yeah. Might take some time but there's bound to be someone workin' at the mill that would like a little sideline. And a new motor home."

"Maybe we don't need someone at the mill. Just get a freelancer," Bearon suggests, "someone who can intercept the fallers when they come to town from camp with their pay burnin' a hole in their pockets. Better to have someone here, Brent. Ask yourself, where do guys go as soon as they're out of camp? The Fisherman's and Dot's. Not the mill. Don't need the expense of another motorhome."

"I don't want this place connected to it."

"If he was a freelancer, no connection to this place. He gets busted, you know nuthin' about nuthin'."

"Makes sense, Brent," Kevin opines.

"I guess," Brent says with a shrug. "As for Barney, he put in a lot of years for us. Worked for the old boss long before you came to town." Brent takes a swig of his beer to wash down a mouthful of tortilla chips before continuing, "plus, that motorhome ain't brand new. I got a good deal. And as it turned out, with the little twat you're so worried about showin' up now, it's good timing, him headin' south. He's the only guy still around who would remember Hank from camp."

"He wouldn't of been stupid enough to yap," Preacher says.

"Who knows? Might of thought there was no reason not to tell her." Brent says. "Who wouldn't wanna spend some time with a pretty little thing like her? Impressin' her with all he knows about the Hanks."

"Pretty, huh?" Kevin says.

"Yeah, she'd be about the right size for you," Brent tells him, "but since you don't like 'em once they got hair on their pussy I doubt she'd even give you a chubby."

"Speaking of chubbies, I was wondering, are you sure the gals, you know, the True Believers, will really fuck everyone at the Ceremony?" Preacher chimes in. He's finishing his nachos and talks around the last mouthful, spewing crumbs as he peels melted cheese off the plate and licks his fingers. Kevin pushes his barely-touched plate over to him. He accepts it with a grunt and a nod.

"I'm sure," Evan replies.

"How do you know for sure, though?"

"How d'ya think? I've been to Ceremonies."

Bearon says, "I been to Ceremonies in Pillerton, too. I get a chubby thinking about *that*! The Illustrious Leaders, you, Preacher, and you, Brent—or should I say, Elder Martin? Elder Hayward?—put on the red robe and they'll be falling over each other to fuck you."

"What about me?" Kevin asks.

"You're Inner Circle, so of course, you too. It's their ticket to salvation."

"You think any of them are shaved?" Kevin asks.

"I guess we'll find out," Bearon replies.

Brent continues. "But the others, guys who are just here for a holiday. Why would they fuck them?"

"They fuck whoever we want them to or they don't fuck us. Believe me, the last thing they want is to be cut off.

They'd lose their communion rights. But that's off in the future. For right now, we fly in call girls, like before."

He sits back, moves his plate closer and works a chip loaded with melted cheese and jalapeno out of the jumble. He puts it in his mouth and chews thoughtfully. "Don't worry, you'll get all the pussy you want and once our membership list starts growing, we'll be well on our way to becoming millionaires, besides."

"Thought you already were." Preacher has polished off Kevin's nachos, takes a long draft of beer and slams the empty mug down. He looks at Brent and asks, "are we going to get more of this?"

"Sure," Brent says; he gets to his feet and sidles around behind the chairs to the stairwell, stopping at the top, he looks back and asks, "anyone else?"

"Nothing for me. I gotta get going," Kevin says.

"That's enough beer for me, Brent," Evan says. "How about bringing up a bottle of Courvoisier?"

"For a small town guy, you sure got big city tastes, Briggs," Brent responds. "That stuff ain't cheap! It'll go on your account."

"Not big city taste. Big money taste! Put it on my account, then. And bring glasses for everyone. Unlike the rest of you assholes, I'm not cheap. Maybe if you'd drink something other than Lucky for a change, you would acquire a little class."

"I like Lucky," Preacher declares. "Besides, I want class, I drink Dos Equis!"

"You got the beard, but it'll take more than that to give you class, or make you interesting," Kevin says, and everyone chuckles.

As Brent thumps his way down the stairs to put in the drink order, Preacher calls after him, "More nachos! Or better yet, chicken wings! Or some of them dry ribs!"

"Don't you have your own restaurant?" Brent calls back. "Next meeting, you supply the food!"

Bearon shakes his head, studying his plate as the bantering goes on around him. Sure, he's a millionaire on paper, but in reality, he's broke. Building his cabin, small as it is, nearly bankrupted him. Maybe he overspent on the Lodge. No matter. His barren bank account is a temporary inconvenience, to be solved when he gets the money from the will. He has no plans to share it with anyone, and he certainly doesn't want it frozen while that woman's claim works its way through the courts. Especially since the ruling would be in her favour. In truth, her showing up now is more than a minor inconvenience and he hasn't yet worked out what to do about it.

"The money train can't start soon enough to suit me," Preacher says, "as long as it's under the table so Georgia can't get her greedy fucking mitts on it."

"It'll be so under the table even the rats can't find it," Bearon tells him. "For now, we got a Ceremony to plan."

ELEVEN

DOT'S

KATHY DRAWS A sharp breath and stirs in her chair. The hair on the back of her neck bristles with the feeling of being watched.

She puts her book down on the bistro table and stands to have a look around. The only other people nearby are a young couple walking hand in hand toward the restaurant, and further off, a few people lounging under umbrellas or sunning themselves around the pool. A boy cannon balls off the diving board, prompting squeals from girls in the splash zone.

She steps close to the block wall to look through one of the holes and sees nothing but forest. *Of course there's no one there, silly. Why would anyone be skulking in the bushes watching you read?*

She shouldn't be spending time reading as if she's on vacation but she needed a break to recharge her batteries, boost her enthusiasm, restore her energy or do *something* to get herself back on task. It seems as though she's been on the run ever since she got to Dark River and her quest is looking more and more hopeless.

There have been leads. The owner of the bowling alley turned out to be a Pakistani who immigrated less than thirty years ago. He said he picked a Canadian name when he got here because nobody could pronounce his Urdu name. A mechanic at Northern Transmission (too young). An elderly man in the Elm Street Senior's Residence (he was an accountant for fifty years, did books for logging companies but no, he never worked in the bush and never heard of Pillerton although he went to Prince Albert once).

She found an old list of Dark River residents and their phone numbers in the archives of the community newsletter, and has made dozens of phone calls to any listings with the initial H for their given name. Most numbers were out of service or now belong to others.

Many people have told her about two guys, father and son, both named Hank. It was shocking, big shots who turned out to be serial killers. Both died in an explosion. She'd heard of them of course; unless you lived under a rock, you heard about them, but she hadn't made the connection. At the time the news broke, a remote town in northern British Columbia called Dark River meant nothing to her. Still, she could kick herself for not realizing Hank is a common form of Henry like Bill for William, and included it in her online searches.

Since hearing so much about those two Hanks, she's found an abundance of information online: five year old newspaper reports from around the globe, often with photos. She breathed a sigh of relief when she concluded the father didn't look like her, but the son! As much as she wants to, she can't convince herself there's no resemblance. It's bad enough everyone knows her mother killed the man she thought was her father, and now she might be related to serial killers? Henry Junior would be too young to be her father, but he could be her sibling, and Henry Senior would have been the right age.

The cliché *be careful what you wish for* comes to mind. If those two are blood relatives, she would have been better off never knowing. Maybe she should go home while she can still tell herself Hank Hazen Senior didn't write those letters. But she knows it would always niggle at her and the only solution is to find someone who can tell her more about the Hazens in hopes it will prove they're not who she's looking for. Anyway, she's paid for the room to the end of the week and there are a few more places she needs to check out.

Approaching strangers is so far outside her comfort zone she's surprised she has even been able to do it. It's empowering to know she can, but at the same time, mentally and physically exhausting. So, about two o'clock she got a sandwich and a coffee to go at the motel restaurant and came out on the patio with a paperback she picked up in the gift shop, planning to read for half an hour. A respite from her search and a mental break from stewing about the Hazens. Now she's well into the book and starting to get hungry. A check of her phone confirms it's nearing supper time.

She debates following the young couple to the restaurant to try the vegan cauliflower curry on the "Daily Specials" menu posted in the lobby, or heading back out to other places she hasn't been yet. She decides on the latter, thinking of a place she's driven past several times. It looks like it should apologise for existing, yet the sandwich board on the boulevard boasts that it has "The Best Pies North of Kamloops!" She hasn't eaten there, and maybe she should have. It looks old enough to have been there fifty years and might be a place loggers or miners would frequent. If nothing else, she can always have a slice of pie. Or just ask around and then come back to the motel for that vegan curry. And maybe, just maybe, change her return flight home to tomorrow.

She picks up the sandwich wrapper, empty coffee cup and paperback and goes inside, flicking the lock lever on the patio door behind her. In the bathroom, she tends to the call of nature, then washes her hands and face and spritzes a cloud of perfume to walk into. Gloss on her lips and a sparkly barrette to hold her hair behind one ear, and she's ready. She heads out the front and climbs into the Sorrento.

Once on the main drag, she slows as she approaches an intersection with a Chevron service station on the corner, and makes a right turn. Half a block further along is the diner she had in mind. An awning over the front windows with "DOT'S DINER" in tall red letters supports three hanging baskets; those and tall ceramic pots with shrubs in them flanking the door are the only cultivated plants. A narrow paved lot fronts the road with vehicles angle parked both up against the building and facing the no-post barrier that separates the lot from the street. A sign on the corner of the building indicates more parking around the back, so she steers the Sorrento there.

The back lot isn't paved and is so rutted and potholed she's glad she rented the SUV instead of the sedan. There are a few eighteen wheelers here, along with big pickups, some towing trailers. A large cube van for a linen service is parked at the far end next to the bushes. It reminds her of the lot behind Al's Place in Pillerton. Always at least a few farm vehicles there. She experiences a tug of homesickness.

She finds a spot not far from the dumpster by the rear door, puts the SUV in park, pulls out her phone and calls Rick, only to hear his voicemail greeting: "It's your dime! Shoot!" as if you could call anyone for a dime even if you could find a payphone. But he seems to think it's funny. Is it a line from a movie? she asked him once. No, it reminds him of his father. It's how he always answered the phone in the days before cellphones when there were payphones everywhere. She says, "I'm at this place called Dot's Diner for supper. Hope someone's feeding you! I'll call again later. Love you!"

There's no worry about Rick not eating. If he goes near his mother, she'll stuff him like a *Galushki*. The mental image of Rick a giant cabbage roll with just head, arms and legs sticking out gives her a chuckle; she's smiling as she leaves the vehicle and walks the short distance around the front to the entrance.

A cowbell jangles overhead as she pushes the door open and steps inside. She's surprised at the décor. It's bigger than it looks from outside. A long counter flanked by bar stools separates the more formal booths and tables from the work area and pass-through and the colour scheme suggests a recent renovation. It's pleasant. She thinks it must be a good place to eat after all, judging by how busy it is. There's the noisy confusion of people in ball caps and cowboy hats and bareheaded, bearded and clean-shaven, in jeans and shorts and sweat pants, all chattering away as they eat. Mouth-watering food smells. The clatter of cutlery and crockery overlays it all and there are half a dozen TV screens silently running hockey highlights, baseball games and Global TV News.

A couple of turquoise-and-white-shirted women and a young man are busy behind the counter. One is putting the makings of a fresh pot of coffee in the Bunn. The man picks up orders off the pass-through and heads out into the dining area with them. The heavily made-up woman with an inch of dark roots in her blonde hair looks up and makes eye contact with Kathy. As if Kathy is a block away, she calls out, "If you don't wanna sit at the counter, hon, stay put 'n' I'll be with you in a sec!" The buttons on her shirt struggle to remain closed across her breasts and she's left the top several open, showing impressive cleavage. Her smile is warm, and Kathy smiles back. After a moment, the woman takes the full carafe off the coffee machine and comes out from behind the lunch counter. "Right this way, hon," she says, and leads Kathy to a two-person booth against a short dividing wall.

"Busy place," Kathy remarks as she puts her purse on the bench and slides in beside it.

"Yeah, drives me nuts sometimes but hey! It's job security, ya know?" She drops a menu on the table. "My name's Annie. I'll be your server. Have a look at this, hon, 'n' I'll be right back." She scurries off, topping up coffee mugs as she goes.

The menu is a single laminated sheet. Offerings harken back to the diner's roots: liver and onions, roast turkey dinner, even a Denver sandwich. Kathy is surprised to find a Beyond Meat burger and a couple of other vegan options on the menu.

When Annie returns, she orders the mushroom tortellini in creamy cashew sauce with a side salad and treats herself to a glass of house white. It's only a short wait before Annie brings her meal, and before rushing off, calls, "give a shout if I can get you anything else, hon!"

The food and even the house white is decent and the tortellini is such a large order she's unable to finish it.

"I guess I should've had the senior's size," she apologises when Annie returns later and asks if she's still working on it.

"Would you like me to pack that up for you hon?"

"Yes, please," Kathy tells her. "You know, I was going to go to the restaurant at the motel for dinner but I'm glad I came here instead."

"Oh yeah? Which motel?"

"Riverview."

"Yeah, you were smart to come here! The food's half the price 'n' twice as good. Can I get you anything else? A slice of our world famous pie maybe?"

"Not allowed dessert when I haven't finished my supper," Kathy says. They share a chuckle, and Kathy continues, "thanks, but I'll come another time for that."

Annie picks up the plate and when she returns with the little box of leftovers and the bill, Kathy says, "I know you're busy, but quick question: I'm looking for someone by the name of Hank. He was working at a camp, a logging camp maybe? Somewhere around here about forty years ago. Would you have any idea who that could be?"

By now Kathy has come to expect raised eyebrows and clucks and even chuckles when she asks this question, and everyone always asks, what's his last name? Annie doesn't disappoint; she frowns and chews her lip, looks around for a second, then says, "Well, there's Hank Durkin over there." She calls out across the room, "Hey, Hank!"

A skinny forty-something man in a grey logger's sweater and a Canucks ball cap is seated at the counter. He spins his bar stool and looks over the heads of the other customers. "Yeah, Annie?" he answers.

He's too young. Kathy shakes her head and tells Annie, "No, that couldn't be him. He would've been a baby forty years ago. The Hank I'm looking for is sixty or even older."

"Nuthin' hon! My mistake!" Annie calls out, then turns back to Kathy and says, "Well, anyways, that's it, that's the only Hank I can think of. But you know, the boss has lived in Dark River *forever* and would know if anyone would."

"Could you ask him?"

"It's not a him, it's a her. I'll tell her you'd like to speak to her when she has a minute." She scurries off and Kathy watches her push through the swinging doors. Moments later, she comes back out alone. She picks up a coffee carafe and heads her way.

"She says she'll be out in a few minutes. Meantime, I'll top up your coffee for you."

"That's great, thank you Annie," Kathy says as she watches Annie pour. *Might be difficult falling asleep tonight,* she thinks, *but the coffee really is good.* She sips it as she scrolls through Facebook and checks her email.

Still no text from Rick. She sends him another text: "Are you still alive lol?" She's just hit send when a fifty-something woman with salt-and-pepper hair appears in front of her. She has a mug of coffee in her hand and slides into the booth across from Kathy.

"Hi," she says, "I'm Franny. Hope you don't mind if I sit. My feet are killing me."

"No. No of course not, Franny. I'm just glad you're taking the time to talk to me. I know you're busy. My name's Kathy."

"All good, Kathy. I was ready for a break," Franny says with a sigh. "Annie said you were asking after someone."

"Yes. I know it sounds crazy, but I'm looking for a guy named Hank who worked in camp somewhere around here about forty years ago."

"Well, that could be the guy I knew. He started off working in camp but ended up owning half of Dark River."

"Oh! A self-made millionaire?"

"He liked to brag he was but I don't think he would ever have been more than an average Joe if he hadn't married the boss's daughter."

"That sounds like him!"

"So, why do you want to know, Kathy?"

Kathy takes a sip of coffee and studies Franny's face for a moment. Deciding she can trust her, she says, "I'm looking for my biological father. And I may have a sibling I've never met. So where is this guy? How can I contact him, do you know?"

"You can't, unless you die and go to hell."

"Oh." Kathy's shoulders slump as the implications sink in. "But what about my sibling? I don't know if I'm looking for a brother or a sister ..."

"Too late on that, too."

Kathy sinks back against the upholstery and breathes out a deep sigh. "You're talking about the father-son serial killers."

"I am. And believe me, you don't want to be related to those two. But how could you be? I know Senior had a little girl, but she drowned when she was very small. I don't think they had another one...although you do look quite a bit like Bridey."

"Bridey?"

"Hank Senior's wife."

"No, Bridey wasn't my mother. I was born in Saskatchewan. Do you think Hank Senior would have cheated on his, er, on Bridey? Like on a trip to Saskatchewan maybe?"

"You know, I only knew the Hazens from the outside looking in sort of thing. Gossip, and what I might've overheard when he was in here with his cronies. The Hank Hazen I knew was always polite and pleasant. Good-looking, too. His son, Hank Junior, though! That's another story. Handsome, but cold, although maybe that's just what I realize now that I know... You know..." her words trail off; she takes a sip of coffee, then continues: "It was shocking to find out they were serial killers."

"I guess it would be." Kathy nods and takes a few deep breaths, her mind in turmoil. Both her father and the sibling she seeks, serial killers? And dead? She nibbles at a hangnail on her thumb, realizes what she's doing, and pulls her hand away from her mouth.

"Tell you what, Kathy," Franny says, "I didn't know them well, like I said, but my best friend worked for them, as a live-in housekeeper. She helped out because Bridey had MS. She—my friend—inherited the land and even the sawmill when Hank Senior died. She would be the best person to talk to. When I get to my phone and have a minute, I'll share her contact info with you. Just write down your phone number." She pulls a pad and pencil out of her apron and pushes it across the table to Kathy.

"Okay. Thanks." Kathy writes her name and number and passes the pad back.

"Well, back to work," Franny says as she gets to her feet. "Nice to meet you, Kathy. If you're staying in town a while, let's get together for a coffee. Maybe Astrid will join us."

"I'd like that."

"Okay! Talk to you soon!" Franny scoots off and Kathy watches as she goes behind the bar at the back and starts pouring drinks.

She takes her little box of leftovers and the bill to the cashier, pays, and leaves. By now most businesses are closed and although Dot's parking lot is still full, there are only a few cars on the streets. She decides to give up the search for tonight and go back to her room. She'll call Rick, then have a glass or two or maybe a whole bottle of wine and watch a movie.

She buys a bottle of Gewürztraminer from the Red Barn Cold Beer and Wine Store near the motel. As she pays, she asks the sole employee if he knows anyone named Hank.

The young man says he thinks there's a guy at the Mister Lube by that name. Yes, he's older, pretty old to be still working as a grease monkey, in his opinion.

"My mom says that'll be me if I don't go back to school," he tells her.

"Well, the world needs mechanics too," Kathy says; she completes the Apple Pay transaction and leaves, the sickening thought she might be related to serial killers tempered with cautious optimism. A grease monkey father beats a serial killer father in anyone's book.

Once back in her room, she sees the bed has been turned down and there's the little chocolate she's come to expect on the pillow. There's an apple on the desk. *I ought to get the deluxe room more often*, she thinks, *not that I ever go anywhere*. She shucks her shoes, picks up the remote and turns the TV on before twisting the cap off the wine and filling one of the coffee mugs.

With the wine on the night table and her laptop on the bed, she fluffs up pillows and climbs up, leaning back against the headboard. She calls Rick, but it goes to voicemail again. She tells herself he's more than likely at Big Al's and it's too noisy to hear the text alert. He's probably been spending a lot of time there since she left. She says, "Hi dear! Back at the motel now. Got a couple more places to go tomorrow. I'm going to watch a movie now but you can call me. Miss you! Love you!"

She notices that Franny has sent her contact information for an Astrid Ingebritson. It's not nine o'clock yet. Not too late to call.

"Hello?" a woman answers.

"Hello. Is that Astrid?"

"Yes. Are you Kathy?"

"I am."

"Franny said you'd be calling."

"Oh, good, umm…So you know why…"

"Yeah, unfortunately. I … well, let's put it this way. I really hope you're not related to the guy. Are you sure you want to know? If he's your father, you'd be better off not knowing. And as for me…I'd rather not stir up bad memories."

"I know a thing or two about bad memories myself," Kathy says, and takes a few breaths before continuing quietly. "I guess I'm hoping you can tell me something that proves it's not him."

"I see. Just a sec," Astrid says, and Kathy hears muffled voices as if Astrid has the mic covered. "Okay," she says when she returns to the call, "My husband thinks we should meet. He'll come with me."

"Oh…?"

"Would tomorrow morning about ten work for you? We can meet you at Dot's for coffee."

"Sure, that would be good. I'll see you there then. I'm short and have dark hair…"

"Franny's working tomorrow morning and she'll put us together, no worries."

"Thank you, Astrid. This means a lot to me."

"You may not thank me after we talk. See you tomorrow."

"See you tomorrow."

Kathy settles back against the pillows and tries to make sense of what Astrid said. The Hank she worked for was a murderer. Did he do something to her? Are those the memories she doesn't want to stir up? But then why would he leave her that property? How can memories about an inheritance be bad? She chews her thumbnail.

Her thoughts turn back to Rick. With a two-hour time difference, it seems rather late for a guy who always goes to bed early not to be at home, or answering his phone. She feels a surge of angst. *He's fine. He just didn't hear the phone. Maybe it's on the charger. Maybe he's in the shower. You can trust him.*

She chews her already ragged and sore thumbnail some more as she boots up her laptop, clicks on the Netflix icon, and scrolls through the movie menu. She selects *A Star is Born*, wondering if Bradley Cooper and Lady Gaga will have the same steamy magnetism Barbra Streisand and Kris Kristofferson did in the Seventies version.

But she can't focus on the movie. She keeps thinking of Rick, wondering why he hasn't called. After half an hour, she gives up on the movie and decides to take her wine outside, sit on the patio and enjoy the sound of the river along with the last of the sunset. She closes the laptop and sets it aside as she gets off the bed. With her phone in her pocket, she takes the mug and the bottle to the door.

It's not locked.

I locked it when I came in from the patio this afternoon. Didn't I? Yes, I'm sure I did.

She's puzzled, thinks about it for a few moments, then goes to the room phone and calls the front desk.

"Front Desk, this is Madeline. How may I help you?"

"Umm, hi, Madeline. I'm in room one ten. When housekeeping came in to do the turn down, would they have left the patio door unlocked?" she asks.

"I don't think so. They have no reason to use the patio door. Lorraine did the turndown tonight. I can ask her. Is there a problem?"

"Yes! Well, maybe. I locked the patio door before I went out, and it was unlocked when I came back just now."

"Are you sure?"

"Well, pretty sure. Is there a surveillance camera?"

"Just in the front. Is anything missing? Do you want me to send someone to come and check, you know, to make sure the lock is working properly?"

"Umm, no. I guess I only thought I locked it. But could you ask Lorraine if she had to open the patio door for some reason? I don't want her to be in trouble, and I wouldn't bother you but …"

"Not a bother, ma'am, I'll ask her and let you know."

"Okay, thanks."

She hangs up, and blows out a breath. Did she forget to lock it? It doesn't seem likely. But she just gave it a flick and maybe it didn't actually lock. What else could it be, if housekeeping doesn't use that door?

Her laptop is still here, of course. She checks her clothes in the drawers and closet. Everything seems as it was. Her suitcase, empty anyway, is where she left it. The papers on the desk are in the pile just as she left them. But her password notebook is closed. When has she ever closed it? It's usually open, folded back to the page listing the last password she needed to look up. But the laptop, the only item of value, still there in plain sight. Why not take that? No one would come in just to fool around with a little notebook full of scribbles! Unless…

She checks her online bank account. No new entries. No new entries for PayPal, either. Anyway, the passwords for those aren't in the notebook. As a precaution, probably completely unnecessary except to make her feel better, she changes the login password for the laptop. She makes it Rick's name and the year they married, so easy to remember she doesn't need to write it down.

The desk phone rings; she answers it, and hears Madeline's voice again. "I checked with Lorraine, ma'am. She confirmed she didn't open the patio door. She said she didn't notice anything out of the ordinary."

"Oh. Good."

"Is there anything else we can do for you?"

"No. Sorry I bothered you."

"Not a bother, ma'am. Let me know if you need anything."

"I will. Thanks." She hangs up the phone and thinks, *I'm letting my imagination run away with me. No one would come in just to look around and leave without the laptop, sitting right there in plain sight on the desk!*

But the door being unlocked coupled with the feeling someone was watching her earlier has her spooked. And adding to her unease, Rick. What's going on with him? Why hasn't he returned her calls?

She decides against going outside. After making double sure both doors are locked, she pulls the heavy draperies over the window and the patio door and gets into her nightgown. In bed, she pulls the covers up over her head as if burrowing into a hole and squeezes her eyes shut. But it's a long time before she's able to sleep, and it's not just because she drank coffee so late.

RICK PUSHES THROUGH the door into Big Al's, walks up to the bar and slides onto a stool. Marge is working the bar, spots him, and calls out, "your usual?"

"You bet," he answers. "I'll have a Big Al burger with fries, too."

While he waits for his pint, he swivels around to survey the room. Lots of strange faces in the place tonight. Big Al's has been busy since the murders made national headlines. It's gotten so he's almost a stranger in the old pub he's spent so much time in for the past nearly three decades.

He spots his old buddy Marty at a table with a couple of the new guys and thinks they might work for the paving company that just opened up north of town. He'd like some paving done around the shop, and is considering joining them when Dolores catches his eye. He smiles. Marge sets his pint in front of him and he's just taking his first good, long quaff as Dolores comes to sit next to him.

"Hey, handsome," she says, "sorry I had to leave in such a hurry last night. The ol' man came home unexpectedly, like I told you."

"Yeah. Shit happens."

"Well, he's back on the road today. Won't be home for a week this time." She leans one elbow on the bar and tips forward toward him. She's so close Rick can smell the perfume wafting up from her cleavage. As usual, it provokes a response. He takes in the scoop neckline of her T-shirt, his gaze settling on the tattoo that's mostly hidden in her bra.

"You dying to see the rest of it?" Dolores asks in a whisper.

THE VET'S TRUCK pulls out of the yard and onto the road. Rick watches from the tarmac at the barn door until the taillights disappear. He sighs, heads up to the house and the bedroom, where he puts his phone on the highboy. He goes into the ensuite, and starts the water in the shower while he strips.

He should have eaten his burger and come straight home. Hell, he should have gotten the burger to go. Instead, he missed the texts and calls, those from both Kathy and Ryan. When he saw Ryan's message that Dodi was in trouble, it was too late to call Kathy. She couldn't do anything anyway. Still. Maybe he should have sent off a quick text. He could have done that from Al's. Definitely too late now.

Ryan had already called out the vet and treatment was well underway by the time he got home. At that point, all anyone could do was watch and wait, hoping for a good outcome. Their hopes weren't realized.

He'll shower, then go to bed for an hour and get up again at first light. He has a grave to dig.

BEARON IS AT HIS DESK, studying the documents he's scrolling through on the center and largest monitor. Clint is certain he wasn't seen around the motel and left no evidence of ever being in her room. He opened the sliding patio door just by lifting and jiggling it until the lock let go. He went in, got the computer copying stuff onto the thumb drive, and photographed the papers on her desk.

That he was able to do anything with the computer is unexpected. He wouldn't have had time to try and guess passwords, but the silly girl had a little notebook with all her passwords written in it, even noting what each one was for, even the log-in for the computer itself.

There might be some interesting stuff on the memory stick, but he hasn't gotten to that yet. What piqued his interest are the photos of the documents on her desk. That fucking Klein woman kept letters the old man wrote to her forty-odd years ago and somehow, they were found.

The house burned down, didn't it? Why weren't they burned up? She must have given them to someone for safekeeping, her daughter maybe. But if so, why did the daughter wait so long to surface? Why didn't she just get in touch with the lawyers and claim her inheritance when that whole mess happened? It was national news, after all. Hell, it was international news. All those graves! And the trophies! Nineteen murders, and those are just the ones they found out about.

The only possible reason is that she didn't know about the inheritance then, and from the sounds of it, she doesn't know now. So what is she doing here? What does she hope to gain? If he never acknowledged her—if all she has to prove she's related is these letters—is that enough?

"Shit! Goddamn fuckin' shit!" He pounds the desk with his good fist. He flips to the series of photographs of the woman that Clint took while he was watching her. They're from a distance, but zoomed in, it's obvious she's aged well. How long has it been since he last saw her? Not ten years, but more than five. They were supposed to get rid of her. He left before that all came down but he thought they would have succeeded. Who was supposed to take her out? The bikers? It wasn't like them to screw up.

The will stipulates the lawyers were not to advertise. Anyone wanting a piece of the pie had to come looking for his or her biological father within five years of his death in order to get the money. Why? No reason other than the old man's narcissism and the fact he never passed up a chance to jerk anyone around. If no one stepped up, the five million plus interest would go back into the estate, and since Bearon is the only one still around to claim it, it's his. Or so he thought.

If this woman asks the right person, she'll find out about the Hazens. Someone has probably already told her about them. Maybe she'll just accept the fact they're dead and go back to Pillerton. Maybe she won't even think she could have a claim on the estate.

But it's only a question of time before she connects with Danielsons, thanks to fucking Hayward. Danielsons will surely tell her about the will. That they got the sawmill and the ranch from Hazen in his will. They wouldn't know if she is entitled to anything but they might suggest she contact the lawyers just in case. They know who the probate lawyers are and can put her in contact with them.

But still. She showed up asking for Hank without even knowing his last name. It just doesn't jive. There has to be more to the story. Is that lawyer friend of hers already digging into the will? No, she wouldn't have a place to start without the last name.

But he's not going to wait around until she finds out. He picks up the phone and punches in a number.

TWELVE

THEY MISSED

KATHY'S PHONE CHIMES. She pulls it out of her purse and sees Rick's picture. At last! She touches accept and is more than just glad to hear his voice.

"Good morning Runty."

"Rick! Why didn't you return my calls yesterday? I was worried something happened!"

"Well, uhh, something did happen."

Kathy feels a jolt like a punch to the stomach. "What? What's wrong?"

"Ahhh, ummm, Dodi colicked yesterday."

"Oh no! Is... Is she okay?"

"No. We, uhh, oh god, Kathy! We had to put her down."

Kathy sinks to one of the leather armchairs in the lobby and tears up. She glances around to see if anyone's watching. Not that she can stop the sobs if there is. She puts her free hand over her eyes.

"You okay, Runty? I'm so sorry, I didn't call you yesterday because I was hoping we could get her through it, and then we couldn't, and she was in so much pain ...

when she didn't get any better ... I didn't want to tell you last night. There was nothing you could do."

Kathy straightens, shakes her head, and swallows hard, still unable to speak. Rick continues, "She went quietly, Runty. She was old. She's had a good long life."

"I know," Kathy says at last. "Something had to happen sooner or later. I'm glad you were with her. I should have been there."

"You couldn't have done anything."

"No, I know. But you've had her since she was born. It must have been awful for you."

"Yeah. Such a sweet mare. I'm sure gonna miss her. Part of life, though." There's a catch in his voice and when he doesn't say anything for a minute, Kathy realizes he's struggling to hold back sobs. "But I won't say I don't wish you were here," he says at last. "How much longer do you think you'll need?"

"Well, I'm still planning to get on the flight I'm booked on, on Saturday. I have a few leads to check out today. This morning I'm going back to Dot's. They have world famous pies, don't you know."

"Better than Mutti's *Pflaumenkuchen.*"

"Well, that's the one cake she makes that I really like. In fact, I wish Italian prune plums were available all year round. But the *Streuselkuchen*—I'll never understand why you like that so much."

"And I don't know why you *don't* like it."

"It's okay the first day, I admit. After that it's a lot like eating your mattress."

"And yet, you eat tofu."

"Try it. You might like it."

"I doubt that."

After a brief lull in the conversation, Kathy asks, "how about Fancy? How's she coping, losing her friend?"

"I let her see, um, the body, of course. She's buried now and Fancy seems to be grieving, just hanging around where she saw her lying, then going back up to the barn to look in Dodi's stall."

"Poor Fancy. Poor you." Another lengthy silence. Then Kathy says, "You know, I think of you a hundred times a day, wishing you were here. The motel is nice. They come in every day and make the bed, clean up the bathroom, then at night they come back and do the turn down, which means they fold the sheets and blankets back, in case you wouldn't know how to get into bed otherwise!" She chuckles, but even to her own ear it sounds forced. "They leave a nice little chocolate on the pillow. And I wish I'd brought my swim suit! I told you about the pool that's not a hundred meters from my own private patio. It's been so hot, a swim before bed would be nice."

"I'm glad you're enjoying yourself."

"Not really enjoying myself, just making the best of it. It's not that much fun, no matter how nice this room is."

"I know. Are you at least gettin' somewhere?"

"Yes and no. I've had a few leads. A nice visit with an old man in the senior's residence that went on much too long. I couldn't get him to quit talking. I guess he's lonely. But everything seems to come back to these two guys, father and son, both named Hank, who were serial killers. You remember hearing about them a few years ago?"

"Oh, yeah. I guess I do. Didn't remember the names, though."

"Well, I Googled it. The news reports always call them Henry. No one around here called them that. Here they were known as Hank Senior and Junior. Just Junior. I might have found out online if I'd thought about searching for Henry and not Hank, or serial killers for that matter. What I was going to tell you before I got sidetracked is, the owner of Dot's put me in touch with someone who knew them."

"As if anyone would Google serial killers when they were trying to find relatives. You're not in danger, are you? I mean, those guys aren't still around?"

"No, they'd be in jail if they hadn't died in a fire."

"Oh, I guess I heard about that, too. How will you find out more about them then? Won't you have to ask their, er, relatives? That's not who you're meeting with, is it?"

"Not sure who she is or if she's a relative. Something about working as a live-in caregiver or housekeeper. Her name's Astrid, and she got an inheritance from the estate."

"She's probably related, then. But if they're dead, why don't you come home?"

"I did look at the airline schedules, but there's only two flights heading east out of here every week. I'd have to leave this afternoon and I'm not ready to give up. I want to talk to this Astrid, for starters. I'm fine with waiting until Saturday. If I left without finding out more, I'd always be wondering if I was related to them. I *really* hope it turns out I'm not."

"Well, be careful."

"I don't think there's a serial killer gene, if that's what you're thinking."

"I wouldn't be so sure. It was a father and son murder team after all."

"Nurture, not nature."

"I hope you're right, otherwise I need to be worried. You could have the double killer gene, one from each parent."

"Not funny."

"Sorry. But be careful. And keep me posted."

"I'm being very careful. Love you."

"You too. Bye."

She stashes her phone in her purse, digs out a Kleenex, wipes her eyes and blows her nose. Dodi. Poor sweet old horse. She'll be missed. Fancy's getting on, too. She'll be lonesome without her pasture mate. They've been looking for younger riding horses for a while, so this will speed up the search.

She gets up and goes into the gift shop. The medley of vanilla, cinnamon and lavender scents from the potpourri and fancy soaps in little organza bags is pleasant but she barely notices. She buys a pack of Dentyne, the reason she came into the lobby in the first place, and manages a smile for the cashier.

As she comes back out, she notices Kiersten is on duty behind the reception desk, holding up her favourite coffee mug with "I HAVE ONE NERVE LEFT AND YOU'RE ON IT!" in bold black and red letters, beckoning. She goes and says hello.

"Hey, Kathy," Kiersten says. "My break's coming up. Wanna grab a coffee?"

"Sorry, can't today. But thanks."

"Everything okay?"

"Well, no. I was on the phone with my husband just now. One of our horses had to be put down last night."

"Oh! I'm so sorry."

"She was old. She had a good long life." Kathy's throat constricts and she tears up again.

"Still, it's always hard."

"Yeah. I'll miss her." Kathy's voice breaks; she takes a Kleenex from the box on the counter and wipes her eyes again. "But on a happy note, I met someone who knows who I'm looking for."

"Oh, great! So you're off to meet him?" Kiersten asks.

"No, not him, a her. I was at Dot's Diner last night. The owner knows someone who worked for the man who's likely the one I'm looking for. It's my first solid lead! I'm really hoping she can tell me something. I'm meeting her at ten. Wish me luck!"

"Good luck!" The phone in front of her buzzes; Kiersten smiles and gives Kathy a nod, then answers it.

KIERSTEN IS TAKING her break under an umbrella next to the pool. The kids haven't come out yet, so she has the whole pool surround to herself. It's pleasant. She lifts her mug for a sip when her attention is drawn to movement on the patio outside 110. *That's odd*, she thinks, *Kathy's back already?*

She gets up and taking her coffee with her, leaves the pool enclosure. She heads down the sidewalk and through the open gate to Room 110's private patio area. The patio door is open, too, so she taps on the glass, then steps into the room and says, "Hey, Kathy! Back so soon?"

But instead of Kathy, a muscular young man with a shaved head and full sleeve tattoos comes out of the bedroom with a suitcase. With surprising speed, he drops it and lunges at Kiersten. She takes a quick step backward and bangs up against the doorframe. She drops the mug and it smashes on the concrete outside the door. Before she can turn and run, the man grabs her and pulls to him. He swings her around and slams her down on the floor before sliding the patio door shut.

"Stay down!" he hisses, and pulls the cords to close the drapes.

She yells, "Help!"

He drops to the floor on top of her, clamping his hand over her mouth. She bites down.

"Arghh!" he squawks as he jerks his hand away and slaps her, hard enough that she sees stars. "That was a slap! If you don't shut up, it'll be a punch next time. Okay?"

"Okay! Okay," she sobs.

"Okay. I'll let you up, but don't try nuthin'." He gets to his feet and stands over her as she sits up. Her eyes widen as he pulls a long knife out from under his pantleg.

"I won't tell anyone!" she shrieks. "I won't! I won't!"

"No, you fuckin' won't!" He scans the room and in two strides is at the patio door; he pushes the drapes away to expose the pull cords, and cuts them off. Bending over her, he jerks her hands behind her and wraps the cord around her wrists.

"I won't tell," Kiersten sobs. "Just let me go."

"Shut up!"

"I told you, I won't tell anyone! Believe me!"

"I said, shut the fuck up!" He pulls her to her feet and shoves her down on a chair. She lands awkwardly, wrenching her elbow.

He stands staring sightlessly at the wall above the TV, fists opening and closing. Finally, he pulls out his phone and after a moment, says into it, "Ahhh, a contingency happened. Got it solved though 'n' I'm headin' out."

He turns back to Kiersten and says, "Okay, lady, me 'n' you are goin' on a road trip."

He disappears into the bedroom area and comes back with pillows. He pulls the cases off and slices into one with his knife, then rips it apart and uses a strip for a gag. The case from the second pillow goes over her head. He pulls her to her feet and drags her to the patio door, parts the drapes and slides the door open. After a brief pause, he propels her out. She stumbles along and if not for him holding her arm, would fall. Bushes scratch at her legs as he pushes her along the rough terrain. Then she's shoved up against a car; the trunk lid opens, she's pushed inside, and the lid slams shut.

She struggles. Tries to scream but can only make muffled noises with no volume. Kicks and thrashes, but to no avail. In moments, she hears a door open and a soft thump as if something was thrown onto the back seat. The door slams shut, then another door opens and closes, the vehicle rocks as if he's settling into the driver's seat. Something beneath her rattles as the engine coughs to life; the vehicle lurches forward, changes direction, then stops briefly before turning left and speeding away.

KATHY STEERS THE Sorrento into the access to Dot's, slowing as she drives into the front parking area. It looks to be full. She may have to park at the back.

There are two men outside the entrance doors as if they have just come out. One carries a briefcase and has a shaved head; he's wearing a short-sleeved T-shirt and his arms are covered in tattoos. Just as she gets there, he trots down the steps and away. The other man looks right at her; he lifts his hand in a kind of wave, and smiles. *Do I know him?* she wonders. *No, of course not, but he must think he knows me.*

Ten A.M. is a busy time at Dot's, coffee time for lots of people apparently, but there's an empty parking spot at the end of the row just at the far corner of the building. As she goes to pull in, the bald guy steps down off the curb. His briefcase flops open and dumps its contents. He hunches down and begins scooping the papers off the asphalt, not so much as looking up as he sorts them into neat bunches before putting them away.

Great move, asshole, she thinks. He's making such a production of gathering the papers it's obvious he's going to be at his task for a while, so she continues around to the back lot.

She pulls into a spot behind the diner and has the door partly open when she sees the man who waved coming around the corner, striding purposefully toward her. When he breaks into a trot, she experiences a jolt of panic and pulls the door shut. He comes up to her window. She powers the window partway down.

"Good morning," he says with a wide smile.

"Good morning. Can I help you?"

"I don't think so, but I can help you."

"Oh?"

"I understand you're looking for Hank."

"Yes. How..."

"Annie mentioned it to me," he says, and gives her another brilliant smile. "I recognized you from her description." As he talks, he turns the cuffs of his dress shirt back, exposing tanned forearms lightly covered with blonde hair. "She didn't tell me you were so pretty."

He puts his hand up, curling his fingers over the top of her window. It's a common enough gesture, maybe just casual, but she's struck with the thought it's as if he wants to stop her from closing it. Or maybe it's just that he wants to make sure she notices his watch. It's a big one. The kind of watch people insure for thousands of dollars.

"Oh, umm, well thank you. So, you're Hank?"

"No, my name's Clint, but Hank's a friend of mine. Annie said she didn't remember my buddy until after you left yesterday. She knew you were coming back this morning but she's not working today so she wouldn't have a chance to tell you herself. I told him about you and he said he'd meet you if you came to his office. Now that I see you, I doubt it's the right guy, though. He's almost seventy. Much too old for you." He winks, drops his hands to his pockets and takes half a step back, as if inviting her to get out of the vehicle.

"It's not like that," Kathy tells him. This is promising: another Hank who is still alive, about the right age, and not a serial killer! *Clint is a good looking man despite his longish hair and bushy eyebrows,* she thinks. *Nicely dressed. Pleasant voice.*

But something in his body language sends up red flags. Despite his smile, he's tense, like her dog Chewie when he's waiting for the person with the ball to throw it. Why? Is it just that she's still spooked after last night?

She scans the lot and sees no people, only parked cars, a few semi trailers, and the windowless wall that's the back of the restaurant. She shrinks away from the door. *Not everyone wants to kill you Kathy,* she tells herself; still, when he reaches for the handle as if to open the door for her, she presses the lock button.

At the click of the door lock, a flicker of annoyance crosses his face. Did she really see that? She draws a deep breath, and asks, "Do you think he would he meet me here?"

"That would be asking a lot, don't you think?" Some emotion plays across his face. Anger? He covers it so quickly she thinks she might have imagined it and reminds herself that what she's feeling is the irrational fear her therapist says is a common result of post traumatic stress syndrome.

"I guess you're right. It wouldn't have to be today. If he's coming to town in the next day or two, I could meet him then. Or, if you give me his phone number—"

"Look," he cuts her off, "he doesn't want everyone and their dog phoning him. There's no point bothering him, trying to talk him into coming into town to meet you. He said he'd see you if you went to his office. I'm surprised he even agreed to that." Then he smiles the frown off his face and says, "as luck would have it, I'm meeting with him this morning. You can ride with me." He beckons to a low-slung black sports car.

"Umm, er, no, then I'd have to wait until your meeting was over and I'm meeting someone right now so I can't now and so I'd rather you gave me the address so I can go myself." She realizes she's babbling, and takes a breath. With those eyebrows bristling out over the tops of his wire-rimmed glasses, if he had a big nose and a moustache, he'd be a Groucho Marx look-alike. Well, if his eyebrows, moustache and glasses were black, anyway.

"I could use a coffee so I don't mind waiting until you're done with your friend. No use both of us driving all the way out there! I'd love to have company on the drive, especially the company of a pretty little thing like you. It would give us a chance to get to know each other. Besides, then you can tell all your friends you had a ride in a nice new Porsche 911R."

"Um, I don't really know anything about cars." She studies the car he pointed to, parked across the back lot a good distance from any other vehicles. "It's beautiful. Why'd you park it so far away?"

"It's a habit. I never park beside other cars. You've seen some of the beaters parked out front. Don't want some fat asshat hitting a four hundred thousand dollar work of art with the door of their five hundred dollar piece of shit."

It makes sense. Four hundred thousand! He must be well fixed to have a car like that. And he looks harmless. Maybe she should take him up on his offer to wait until she finishes up with the Danielsons.

"Come on. There aren't many Porsches around, you know. Beautiful woman like you should never be seen in anything less." His bushy eyebrows rise in the center in an expression of sincerity.

She reminds herself of the nice houses and expensive cars the guys at the head of The Children of Noah in Pillerton had. Those guys looked harmless too.

Besides, pretty, and now beautiful? Beware of flatterers! He's coming on strong, and she's learned from experience she needs to listen to her gut. "I can't, Clint. I'm more of a farm truck person anyway. So if you could give me the address?"

He shrugs and says, "suit yourself. I don't know the address, like the house number. I just know how to get there. There's no sign at the driveway, just a big carved bear at the gate, which you can't see from the road. It's a bit of a trip, way up Bear Mountain Haul Road."

"He has an office without a sign?

"His office is in his home. That's where he is most of the time."

"Wait a minute," Kathy says. She digs through her purse for something to write on "What's the name of that road again?"

"Bear Mountain Haul Road. It's an old logging road. A little tricky to find. Take the Hundred and Twenty Mile Road turnoff from the highway... You know what? Like I said, I can get a coffee while you meet with your friend, and then I have to go back there anyway. Why not follow me? Then you can leave as soon as you've talked to him."

Kathy shrugs. "Um, sure. That would be great, except I don't know how long I'm going to be, and I have other things to do after."

"If you're thinking to go out there unannounced, forget it. He's particular about who he opens the gate for. I have the code."

"Oh, okay. If I can just talk to him, I might not have to go at all. If you give me his number, I'll call. Might not take more than five minutes of his time and maybe that'll do it." Knowing she won't go to some remote location to meet the man, she lifts her phone and touches the screen, ready to enter a new contact.

Clint frowns as if deep in thought, pushes his glasses up and looks away, his eyes narrowing further. He gives his head a brief shake. Kathy thinks he's not going to give her the phone number, but then he looks back at her and smiles. "It'll piss him off if I give you his number, but you know what? For you, I'll do it. The number, umm … Jeez, just a minute. I have it in my phone. You know what that's like, right? Phone takes care of everything. I never learn a phone number anymore." He pats his shirt pocket, then both pants pockets. "Damn! Left it in the car. Walk over with me."

"Um, you know, I'll just go inside, and you can give it to me when you come in for that coffee."

He glances at his watch, then frowns and says, "Jeez, I see I'm running late. I'll have to forget about coffee. Come to my car and I'll give you the number."

"If you could just text it to me, that would be great," Kathy says, and rattles off her number. She powers up the window to cut off further conversation and backs out of the parking space, leaving Clint watching with an unreadable expression.

What made her do that? What was it was about him that made her reluctant to get out of the SUV? He looks so ordinary, so pleasant, and imagining him as Groucho Marx should have made him seem unthreatening, but instead something triggered her flight response. She must still be spooked from yesterday. The feeling of being watched and then the patio door unlocked. And all the talk of serial killers. Whatever it was, she breathes a sigh of relief at being away from him.

With luck, the man who dumped his briefcase is gone so she can park in front where there's traffic going by and people watching out the window; otherwise she'll have to drive around once more, and she'd rather not see that Clint guy again.

As it turns out, she doesn't have to go all the way to the end of the row; a pickup is just backing out of a space and when it drives off, she pulls in, right in front of the windows. It isn't until she's parked she wonders if Clint would remember her number.

CLINT SCOWLS AND stands arms akimbo. What was that number she rattled off? Now he has to wait until she comes back outside, and since she hasn't come around back again, she must be parked in front where everyone will see the goings on. He'll have to convince her to willingly either follow or come with him. What are chances of that? She didn't open her window far enough for him to reach in to stick her, and when he went to open the door, she locked him out. He carefully reaches into his right front pants pocket to get the syringe out before he can accidentally stick himself, and puts the needle guard back on.

It's puzzling. Females younger than this one are usually easy conquests. If they're hesitant, the sight of the expensive car seals the deal. In case she had no clue, he mentioned the car's value, even inflating it. So what spooked her? Whatever it was, if she finds him waiting for her when she comes out, would she believe him if he said he'd had time for coffee after all, and come along voluntarily? Would another try at sweet-talking her do the trick? It might make matters worse. Then he realizes his son, Trent, is at the motel. A better idea would be to have him grab her along with her things.

Clint heads for his car. As he passes the dumpster, he beckons to the bald man, briefcase at his feet, standing half hidden between it and the propane tanks. He picks up the briefcase and comes to walk beside him.

"What happened? You don't have the girl?"

"Nothing gets past you, Des." Clint scowls and looks around to see if there's anyone near enough to have overheard. The two stride across the lot to the Porsche. Clint slides behind the wheel and picks his phone out of the console. There's voicemail, so he touches the numbers and listens to it. It's Trent. He scowls. Contingency? What's that supposed to mean? No matter. He says he's heading out. Should he call and tell him to go back and wait for Kathy? No. He'll take her himself.

Des is on the passenger side, putting the briefcase in the back. Clint tells him, "Don't bother getting in. You ain't stayin'."

"What? Why not?"

He pulls a roll of bills out of his pocket, peels off a couple, and hands them to the young man. "Change of plans. You won't be driving the Porsche today."

"Now how'm I supposed to get home?"

"Call a buddy. Or, there's a bus stop right across the street." Clint starts the engine, barely waiting for Des to close the door before driving off.

Des is a good looking kid despite being almost completely bald at twenty-seven. It makes sense for him to shave his head, but why Trent keeps his perfectly good head of hair shaved off is a mystery. Must be just because he wants to be like his big brother, as if he has no identity of his own. At least Des has a few smarts.

His ex did a shit job of parenting. Hard to believe he was ever attracted to her. Trent takes after her: dumb, and not quite right in the head besides. It's like he never matured past the age of eight, and impulse control? Forget it. He's not ready to write him off just yet, though.

He turns onto the road that runs along the vacant section of forest behind the motel and pulls his Porsche to the curb where he told Trent to park. Don't want the activity, and especially not an identifiable car like the Porsche, showing up in motel surveillance. He'll hike through the bushes. She's small. He'll be able to carry her back the same way even if she's unconscious. Convenient her room is at the end and the trail through the bushes comes out right beside it.

She'll be shocked when she discovers her things are gone and he's waiting inside. She's likely to put up a fight. A wrestling match with the little vixen will be fun. He feels a stirring and realizes he's tumescent.

He's humming to himself as he gets out of the car and trots along the short path through the trees.

THIRTEEN

MEET THE DANIELSONS

KATHY PUSHES THROUGH the door and stands next to the cashier desk. Franny is at the far end of the lunch counter; she looks up, smiles, and beckons. When Kathy reaches her, Franny says, "they're already here. I've put you in the meeting room next to the office. Right through here."

She follows Franny through the double swinging doors and past a large stainless steel island where prep cooks are at work, into the back room. There's a round table with a couple close to her age seated on the far side. The man stands as she comes in.

"Hello," the striking blonde woman says as she half rises to extend her hand across the table, "I'm Astrid."

"Hi. I'm Kathy."

"And I'm Denver." The man removes his cowboy hat and offers his hand for a quick shake before settling the hat back on his head and sitting again. He's fair haired and blue-eyed, same as Rick, and easily as tall, too.

"Have a seat," Franny says. "I thought I'd have time to have coffee with you but we've just gotten super busy. Maybe when you're done? But you guys go ahead and talk as long as you want. Can I bring anyone anything? Pie? Donut? Hot chocolate? Tea?"

"Just coffee would be great," Kathy says, noting Astrid and Denver already have mugs and there's a thermos carafe on the table.

"I'd love a slice of cherry pie," Denver says.

"Oh, I knew it. Warmed up, with a scoop of ice cream, I imagine?" Franny asks.

"Yes, please!"

"Pie and ice cream at ten in the morning, after the big breakfast he had," Astrid says. As Franny scoots off, she looks at Kathy and tells her, "that's what he ordered the day we met."

"Still order it pretty well every time I come in here," Denver says with a grin. "When you find something good, I say stay with it." He gives Astrid's shoulder a rub. Kathy doesn't miss the look of affection that passes between them.

She hangs her purse on the back of the nearest chair before sliding onto it and pulling up to the table. She asks, "was that a long time ago? I mean, have you been together for a long time?"

"No," Denver answers, "only about five years. I lived in Merritt and Astrid's from Vancouver Island. We had to come all the way up here to meet. What about you? Where are you from?"

"Well, Reader's Digest version? I grew up in Saskatchewan, a little town called Pillerton. Moved away right out of school, moved back about five years ago."

"Pillerton? I've never heard of it."

"It's pretty small. Barely half as big as Dark River. About forty-five minutes south of Regina."

"So, you're looking for your birth father," Astrid says, "but all you've got to go on is a first name. What makes you think he could be here, or that it could be Hank Hazen?"

"Believe me, I know finding him is a long shot," Kathy agrees with a sigh. "I found letters, old letters, from more than forty years ago. Turns out my father wasn't who I thought he was and I might have a sibling and even a living father…" She draws a deep breath and lets it out slowly. "If you have family, you might not understand. But all my life I envied people who have sisters and brothers. Aunts. Cousins. You know, big family gatherings at Thanksgiving and so on. After my father — the man I *thought* was my father — er, *disappeared*, all I had was my mother. And she's gone. So if I have a father that's still alive, or a brother or sister, I'd really like to connect."

"I think I understand," Astrid says. "I've got no family to speak of either. Or didn't, until Denver, so I know what you mean. But I really hope you aren't related to Hazens. What do you know about them?"

"Just what people have been telling me, and what I found on the internet. I hope I'm not related to them, that's for sure, so I guess now my quest is to prove I'm not. I thought I'd show you the letters and you can tell me if anything jumps out at you."

She pulls her purse into her lap and digs through, shuffling things around. "Damn! Meant to put them in here but I must've left them on the desk back at the motel." She pulls out her wallet, chequebook, a few rumpled till receipts, then stuffs everything back in and looks across at Denver and Astrid. "Yup. Left them behind. I'm such an idiot! Sorry. I really meant to bring them. But anyway, I can probably give you the gist. I've read them often enough I've almost got them memorized."

"Okay, shoot," Denver says.

Kathy smiles at Denver saying something so similar to the archaic phrase Rick uses to answer his phone. "So," she says, "Hank talks about working out in a camp. I guess that would be a logging camp, but I'm not a hundred percent sure, because he mentions being blown out. Maybe a mining camp? What else would blow up?"

"You said blown out? Not blown up? Blown out just means it was too windy to work in the bush. Ever heard the expression 'stay out of tall trees'?"

"No."

"Not many tall trees around Pillerton, I don't imagine," Denver says. "We don't have guys out in the bush when it's too windy. Too dangerous. So, what camp?"

"That's part of the problem, he doesn't name the camp or say where it is, but the letters are all postmarked Dark River, and he says he wants to find a rental here. Oh, and he mentions another guy in Dark River who was also from Pillerton. Umm. Barney... Gave his last name, too but damn! Right now I can't remember it."

Denver and Astrid exchange a look, and Astrid asks, "what about return addresses on the envelopes?"

"There aren't any. One looks like he started it but didn't finish, just a post office box number."

"Might be able to find records for that," Denver suggests.

"Worth a try," Astrid agrees. "We have a room full of old records at the mill. We took over about the time we got together, but I haven't done much more than look in there and back away, it's such a mess. We talked about getting that room cleaned out and all those old files burned, but haven't got to it yet. Maybe that's a good thing, for you, anyway. They go back decades, so there might be employee records for when he was here. If he or the other guy he mentioned worked in logging around here, they very likely worked at our company sometime and there'll be a record of it. We could start there, although I have to warn you, the records are pretty disorganized. But go on."

"Okay!" Kathy says. She squirms in her seat, then looks across the table, making eye contact with both Astrid and Denver before continuing. "So. He says he married the boss's daughter, but that she's ugly and a lot older. As for when, this was about the time my father, or the man I thought was my father, disappeared. I was five or six. He mentions 'our little girl' and that the man I thought was my father married my mother even though she was pregnant. Says she should leave me with him. He flipped out when he found out my mother killed him but said he wouldn't tell anyone. Besides that, my mother was pregnant again and Hank was the father of that one, too, so that's why I think I have a sibling. No one ever knew about it. Well, obviously, someone did. Hank said he would send someone to get the baby and that my mother better not tell his wife or anyone or he would tell the cops what she had in her furnace."

"Wow!" Astrid exclaims, "she killed her husband and put him in a furnace?"

"In pieces, I guess. Although now that I think about it, it was a big old coal furnace. The door was big enough to fit a body, but she would've had to have help to put him in, er, all in one piece. I never wanted to hear the details. That's where they found his remains. But not until after my mother was dead."

Denver utters a low whistle. "All those years, his body was right there in the house?"

"Yeah. Along with the blood-stained mattress she butchered him on. She never even got rid of that. Why keep such an incriminating piece of evidence? They say murderers sometimes like to keep souvenirs or visit the dump sites. She may have kept the mattress for that. Although why, when she could've looked in the furnace anytime, is anyone's guess. And everything he owned was in boxes in the attic.

"I wasn't allowed in either the attic or the basement. I didn't want to go in the basement anyway because she said there was a dirty man under the stairs waiting to grab my feet and pull me through, you know, the space between the steps, and then do horrible things to me. The only time I went down there was when she put me there as punishment, and believe me, I was terrified. Even after I was old enough to know there was no bogeyman, I never quite got over it! Until, umm, everything happened, I never understood why she spent so much time down there. Now I realize how insane she was."

Franny comes in with a third mug, another thermal carafe of coffee, and Denver's pie à la Mode. "How's it going, folks?" she asks. She places everything on the table and fills a mug for Kathy.

"Good," Astrid says.

"Anything else?" Franny asks.

"No thanks Franny," Astrid replies.

Franny nods and says, "Let me know if you need anything," then turns and leaves, closing the door behind her.

"Maybe Kathy wanted something, babe."

"Sorry," Astrid says. "I guess I got too involved in your story. It's like an episode of Psycho, but without the shower scene. Would you like something? I can go and let her know, if there is."

"It's okay. Not really the time of the day for pie but if *he's* okay with it, I admit I thought about it. It looks good, but probably not until dinner." Kathy shunts her purse off her lap and nibbles on her thumbnail; then realizing what she's doing, leans forward and tucks her hands between her thighs and the chair seat.

"They have muffins and donuts, too," Denver says.

"I had a coffee and a muffin at the hotel. Continental breakfast they call it. I thought that was supposed to be toast and coffee but it's way more than that."

"I've heard it's a good place to stay even if just for the breakfast spread."

Astrid leans her elbows on the table and holds her mug in both hands, her forehead creased in thought. She says,

"Hank Hazen could be the one who wrote the letters. He would be okay with what your mother did and he'd keep it a secret. It wouldn't bother him at all. You said he was pissed about it, though."

"Well, he wasn't pissed because she killed someone," Kathy says. She takes a careful sip of the hot coffee before continuing. "He was planning on her getting the house so they could sell it, and that ended it. Not just the house, there's a whole city block, all vacant lots except for the house. She was supposed to have the baby, divorce my father, and get the property in the settlement. Killing him when she did put a kibosh in that, and he didn't want her without the property. Dunno how he planned to marry her since he was already married. Maybe he really would've made good on his promise to get a divorce or maybe he'd just marry her without getting one. I didn't have the sense from his letters that he was a big believer in doing the right thing! Would you believe, they'd been having sex since my mother was thirteen?"

"I not only believe it, but I'd say that would be Hazen, all right." Astrid puts the mug down and sits back. "I think we should swing by the mill, grab some boxes of old records, and spend the afternoon at our place. We have plenty to talk about. We can yak while we dig through the paperwork."

"That would be great, but I really need to keep looking. I hear there's a guy at the Mister Lube named Hank, and he might be old enough. He wasn't at work when I phoned today and of course they wouldn't' give out his phone number. Also someone a ways out of town I don't have a last name or number for. I need to talk to them."

"When are you going home?"

"Not until Saturday."

"You could check those other two guys out tomorrow, then," Astrid says. "I have a feeling you're not going to have to, though, and you won't like what I have to tell you. Right off the top, the boss's daughter wasn't ugly and she wasn't older than Hank Senior. She was a cute little thing, and he seemed devoted to her. She looked a lot like you, actually. What did your mother look like?"

"Short. Dark hair and brown eyes. About like me, I guess."

"So, he liked small brunettes. So I wonder ... well. We'll talk some more but I believe he's the one you're looking for."

"And Hank Junior would be the baby, my sibling?"

"He may be your sibling, but he was too old to be that baby, if the timeline is correct. He was older than me, so he'd be forty-three, forty-four, now. How old are you?"

"Forty-three."

"Well, you look younger than that, but it still makes him too old to be the baby you're looking for. Do you mind if we go? We have a lot to talk about."

Denver looks up from his pie, studies Astrid, then says to Kathy, "You don't want to argue with her when she's got that look."

"We can swing by your room and get those letters on our way." Astrid lifts her mug and drains it, then gets to her feet.

"Okay!" Kathy drinks half her coffee at a go, then slides her chair back, preparing to stand.

"Think you gals could wait for me to finish my pie?"

"I'll go with Kathy. You can come home when you're done here. Why don't you go visit with Harvey and those guys out front?"

"Okay, I will." Denver shrugs. He gives them a warm smile and Kathy is again struck by his resemblance to Rick. "I won't be home right away, though. I got a few things to do out at the sort yard."

"We'll see you later, then."

Denver takes his wife's hand and gives it a squeeze. "Works for me," he says. "I'll take care of the bill."

"YOU MUST THINK I'm crazy," Kathy says as she steers the Sorrento out onto the main drag. "You know, having a crazy mother. Maybe some of it rubbed off. Like mother like daughter."

Astrid is quiet for a few moments, then says in barely more than a whisper, "Like father, like daughter."

"What?"

"I don't normally tell people this, Kathy. When I said I don't have family *to speak of,* I meant it literally. I have a living father but never tell anyone I do. Because he killed my mother."

"Oh, my god!"

"I was seventeen. He's in jail." Astrid has her hands in her lap and is studying them as she clasps and unclasps them.

"I'm sorry." Kathy tears up as she says, "Maybe that's worse! All I knew was that my father disappeared."

"But they found him, all those years later? In the furnace? I guess the furnace wasn't in use, but how did they find him?"

"No. I, uh, a guy..." Kathy chokes up and can't continue. She feels the weight of Astrid's intense stare. After a moment, she collects herself and says, "Anyway, they were looking for me and found him when they searched the house." Her throat constricts and she focuses her attention on driving for a moment. "I'm sorry. I still get too emotional to talk about it."

"I get it. I never tell anyone my, er, my life story either." She sniffs. "Have you tried counselling?"

"Yes. I'm down to once every few months now. You?"

"I quit. It was too gut-wrenching. I decided it was better not to have to keep talking about it even though Dr. Malone seems to think otherwise."

"You went for the, er, you went because of your mother?"

"No, I'm pretty well past that. Having the old bastard locked up was closure for me on that one. Hope he rots there! He got life with no chance of parole for twenty-five years, also ten years for a Ponzi scheme he was running, but of course this is Canada, the sentences were concurrent, and he'll be eligible for parole soon. I wouldn't put it past them to decide he's not a danger to society and let him out. As if a sixty-something asshole can't push anyone else off a cliff."

"Oh!"

"If I see him, I'll kill him. But then, I think of my daughters... And Denver... So I hope I never see him."

They drive along, not speaking, for a few blocks. Then Kathy asks, "But you were in counselling all these years later?"

Astrid sniffs again before replying, "Not for that, although that's part of it, I suppose. I was abducted."

They share a look.

"You were too?" Astrid asks.

"Well, sort of. There's more to it."

"There always is."

They arrive at the Riverview; Kathy turns into the lot and parks in front of the door to her room. They both get out and Kathy goes to the door, key card in hand. She pushes the door open and Astrid follows her inside. Once past the bathroom, Kathy puts her purse down on the bed and the door closes with a clunk behind them. The scent of her perfume is strong.

How could one quick spritz be that powerful, or hang around so long? It must be from housekeeping, she concludes, *but they didn't make the bed?*

"Wow," Astrid says, "Nice! Separate bedroom?"

"Yeah, I didn't need a room this big but—what was that? Did you hear something?" Kathy gets halfway into the sitting area and stops up short. "Oh, my god!"

The patio door is open and the drapes are still billowing out the door as if someone has just left. Her computer and the papers are missing from the desk. The pillows that should be on the bed are on the floor, their cases removed. One of the pillowcases is ripped to shreds; the other is nowhere to be seen. She brings both hands to her face, and cries, "No!"

"What's wrong?" Astrid asks as she comes up beside her. "What is it?"

"Someone's been in here! My laptop! The letters! They were on the desk and they're gone! And I didn't leave that door open!"

"Oh my god! Don't touch anything! We'll go to the desk and report this. I'll call the police!"

TWO MARKED POLICE cruisers are parked outside Room 110 when Denver turns into the parking lot. He sees Astrid and Kathy standing on the sidewalk talking to the cop he recognizes as Constable Villeneuve. *Sergeant* Villeneuve, he corrects his thought. There is a chubby man with a comb-over nearby as well.

He parks as near as he can, and joins them. "Hey! It's been a while," he says to the cop. He extends his hand and they shake.

"It has," Sergeant Villeneuve replies. "You playin' wid duh old timers again dis year?"

"Yup. You?"

"Yeah, me too."

"Us old dogs never learn I guess." Denver gives Astrid a quick hug and asks, "so what's going on? I came as quick as I could. What did you say happened? Someone cleaned out Kathy's room?"

"Yes. I think we surprised them," Astrid replies.

"I thought I heard something when we came in," Kathy tells him. "The drapes were still moving as if someone left in a hurry and the patio door was open."

"They took some of your things?"

"They took *all* my things. Even the stuff out of the bathroom. Well, except for my perfume, which is broken on the floor. Who steals toothpaste and deodorant?" Kathy's voice catches. "How did they even get in? I wonder if they have a master key or something because the other day the patio door wasn't locked when I came in, and I'm sure I locked it when I left and they said there's no surveillance cameras out the back only the front but there was nothing missing that time so ... and then they tore up one pillowcase and took the other?" This last comes out almost as a sob.

Astrid reaches for her arm, gives it a rub, and says, "You're okay. Take a breath."

"Why would anyone take a pillowcase?"

"Sometimes, dey take a pillowcase to carry stuff in," Sergeant Villeneuve explains. He turns to the comb-over man and asks, "So dere's no surveillance?"

"Not in the back. Just in front."

"We'll need to take a look at it anyway. Dey packed off enough stuff, likely had a vehicle. Could be dey parked in front here. We need to check."

"Well, umm, Kiersten is the one who knows how to run it."

"I'll talk to her, den."

"She's not here."

"She was here when I left," Kathy says.

"Umm, well, she left without telling anyone. Left us scrambling for someone to put on the desk. Thought she'd be right back because she left her purse under her desk."

"Does she do dat often? Just leave?" Sergeant Villeneuve asks.

"No. She's very dependable."

"And she hasn't come back to get her purse?"

"No."

The implications flood over her and Kathy feels a jolt of angst; the blood drains from her face and suddenly everything seems very far off. Astrid clasps her elbow.

Sergeant Villeneuve frowns as he studies Kathy's face. "Ms. Klein," he says, "you don't need to stay here. You have anywhere you can go for a couple hour until we're done wid your room? You could start making a list of everyting dat's missing. And if you would come to my office so we can take your statement."

"When does she have to do that, Jacques?" Denver asks. "Can she come home with us and maybe come to your office tomorrow?"

"Dat would be fine. I know where to find her." He turns to Kathy and says, "call me if dere's anyting else in the meantime."

"But Kiersten! What about Kiersten?"

"We'll look into it."

The second policeman comes to the open door and beckons to Sergeant Villeneuve, who says, "Excuse me folks," and follows the other cop inside.

"You can't stay here tonight, Kathy," Astrid says. "You can stay with us. I'll loan you some jammies."

Denver says, "Good idea. We have an extra bed and I bet we can find a toothbrush no one's used yet."

Kathy nods and murmurs, "thank you."

"How about I drive?" Astrid suggests. "You're very pale."

"I'm worried about Kiersten..."

"Yeah, me too."

"Ladies," Denver says, "let Villeneuve do his job. He's not only the best center in the Dark River Old Fart Beer League, but he's a good cop, too. We can check in with him later."

"I know it's early, but there's a box of Riesling in the fridge that's calling my name," Astrid says, and guides her to the Sorrento.

BEARON IS AT his desk when he's surprised by two short blasts of a car horn. He's not expecting anyone. He clicks the monitor to display the front gate, and sees a car he doesn't recognize. The driver rolls down the window, sticks his head out, and waves in the direction of the camera. Recognizing Trent, Bearon clicks the open gate command, and the gate starts to roll.

By the time the car is parked in front of the garage next to Annie's Honda, Bearon has pulled on a balaclava is standing at the door. Trent gets out of the car and trots up the steps.

"What the fuck are you doing here?" Bearon asks. "Didn't your dad tell you to take the stuff to the Dogwood Street house?"

"Well, yeah, but umm, a contingency," Trent says.

"A contingency? What's that supposed to mean? And whose car is that?"

"Like I said, a contingency, a contingency happened. Two contingencies! First, my car wouldn't start. Hadda boost one."

"You brought a stolen car here?"

"Had to otherwise I woulda been late."

"Je-sus! Get it the fuck outta here! I hope the hell no one saw you."

"But ..."

"But what?"

"A broad ..."

"What?"

"This broad came in when I was gettin' the stuff so I hadda bring her."

"What the fuck?"

"Couldn't take her to Dogwood Street in the middle of the day, could I? Don't worry, I ain't stupid. She's tied up and she didn't see nuthin'. I put a bag over her head." He holds his hand up to display bite marks in the fleshy mound at the base of his index finger and complains, "Fuckin' bitch bit me. Hurts like hell. Prob'ly gonna get infected."

"A contingency," Bearon snorts. "Never mind. It's done. Put everything including the girl in the garage. Then get the fuck outta here."

Trent says. "I need to put something on my hand. You got polishsporn?"

"It's just a little bite, for fuck's sake."

"Yeah, but Des says human bites are bad, all them germs. Maybe I need to get a tetnis shot."

"Tetanus—? Jesus fuckin' Christ! Get everything out of the car and get the fuck outta my sight."

"But.."

"But what?"

"My pay?"

"If it was up to me, you'd be lucky to even *get* paid, fucking up like this. Your father will settle with you."

"It wasn't my fault! What was I supposed to do?"

"You didn't think you could just tie her up and leave her there?"

"She saw my face! I hadda do *something* with her!"

Bearon draws quick, deep breaths, then relaxes with a shrug. Naturally he wouldn't wear a mask for a simple B and E when the woman was supposed to be gone for longer than it would take. Anyone seeing someone around the motel wearing a mask would be sure to report it.

"Okay. You're right. But your dad will pay you. As agreed." He steps inside and closes the door firmly before touching the pad to open the garage door, then watches from between the slats of the blinds.

Trent stands as if he's forgotten how to move his feet; his lips are moving and his fists are closing, opening, closing, opening. Bearon is reminded of the navigation system when he misses the turn: *recalculating*. Not that Trent is as smart as the nav system.

Finally, Trent spins and trots down the steps to the driveway. He gets a suitcase and a laptop out of the back seat and takes them into the garage. When he returns, he opens the car's trunk, leans in, and hauls the girl out. It's awkward; her hands are tied behind her and she has a white cloth bag over her head. She wobbles a bit but he has her by the arm and steadies her, then propels her into the garage.

When Trent gets back in the car and drives out, Bearon pushes the buttons to open, then close the gate, before going through the house to the man door into the garage.

He touches the control for the garage door; it trundles noisily along its tracks as he goes to stand beside the girl. She's sprawled on the concrete floor between the Range Rover and the man door, feet out in front of her, struggling to get up.

With a jolt, he sees she's wearing a Riverview Inn uniform jacket and her brass name tag reads "Kiersten".

Muffled cries come from the bag over her head. He can make out some of what she's saying: she won't tell anyone if they let her go, why is she here, where is she? And then she's sobbing. Bearon clicks his tongue, turns and goes back inside the house.

Annie comes into the kitchen with a rag in one hand and an aerosol can of Pledge in the other. "What's going on?" she asks. "Whose car was that?"

"Nobody's."

He picks up a kitchen chair, takes it into the garage and sets it down beside the girl. He paws through the cabinet over the workbench until he finds the roll of duct tape. Hoisting Kiersten to her feet, he pushes her down onto the chair and secures her ankles to the chair legs before releasing her hands from the cords. She flails her fists and one surprisingly hard punch stings his nub ear. He snorts in astonishment, then pins her with his knee while duct taping her wrists to the chair's arms.

When he opens the door to go back into the house, Annie is standing there as if she was just about to come out. She has a clear view of the girl in the chair. "Oh!" she exclaims.

Bearon pushes her inside and shuts the door. "Shut the fuck up! You don't want her to hear you. You know her, from church? And likely she goes to Dot's too? She'll recognize your voice."

"What? Who?"

"It's Kiersten."

"Oh my god! What are you doing? Let her go!"

"Not that simple, Annie. Don't worry, she's not hurt. I won't hurt her, but she has to stay put for a bit. I'll explain everything, but now is not the time."

"But she's—that's uncomfortable! Why—?"

"I said, I'll explain later." He gives her a quick kiss. "Don't *worry*. I have to make a few calls. After that, no reason we can't spend some fun time together before you have to leave." He loops an arm around her, pulls her to him, nuzzles her ear and whispers, "You know how much I love playin' with those big beautiful breasts of yours."

KIERSTEN IS HUSTLED out of Bearon's garage, pushed into the delivery van and hauled up onto the bench seat, pressed between two men. The van door closes. One of the men raps on the solid wall separating the front seats from the rear. The engine starts and they drive off.

"Let's have a look at what we got here," the man on her right says as he pulls the pillowcase off her head.

"Where are you taking me?" she asks.

"Wouldn't you like to know."

"We got a long drive ahead of us," the smaller man on her left says. "We got time. Let's get to know each other a little. Where're you from, honey?"

Kiersten brings her hands, duct-taped together at the wrist, to her face. "I have to pee," she sobs.

BEARON IS AT the head of the table, with Clint on his right and the others in their usual seats. There's an empty chair at the far end.

"Preacher's late again. Let's start without him," Brent says.

Just then they hear footsteps thumping up the staircase and the portly sixty-something Preacher appears in the doorway. "Hey," he says by way of greeting. He comes to stand behind the empty chair and looks around the table; his gaze settles on Clint. He asks, "why is *he* here?"

"Hello to you, too, asshole," Clint hisses.

"This concerns him," Bearon explains.

Preacher's eyes narrow but he nods, pulls the chair out and sinks onto it. "No appies? Nothing to drink?"

"Jesus! I know you're a bachelor now but you own a fuckin' restaurant! Didn't you eat supper?" Brent asks.

"Yeah, but..."

"Don't worry, we got a few items coming up soon."

"I thought we weren't going to meet here again," Kevin says.

"That's what I thought, too, didn't think we'd have the need before the Lodge was ready," Bearon tells them. "Wouldn't have, but a project went off the rails this morning."

"What project? I didn't hear about any project."

"Here's all you need to know, Kevin. All of you. Trent was supposed to clean out a room at the Riverview. Kiersten walked in, so to keep her from calling the cops, he tied her up and brought her to my place."

"So? Apologise and let her go."

"And tell her what? A guy B and E'd a motel room, kidnapped her and took her to Bearon's, but it's okay? Let her talk to the cops?" Clint asks.

Bearon gives Clint a sharp look, then says, "Look. It's too late for that. I had Parm and a couple of the guys move her to the basement at the Lodge. They sat with her in the van while they drove around for a while, talkin' tough. Enough to get the idea across that there's lots of us and we're people she doesn't want to cross. She said she had to pee so they kept drivin' around until she pissed herself. Took fuckin' hours. Jeez, you wouldn't think anyone could hold it so long! The upside is, she thinks they took her a long ways away from here. And then she was happy to get out of the van and into the room. They made her strip, shoved her in the shower and took her clothes. Then they made friends, gave her a sandwich and one of the bathrobes from the Grotto. But we can't keep her. She has to turn up at work tomorrow before your manager, Wally," he indicates the Preacher with a lift of his chin, "what's his name?"

"Passmore."

"Before Passmore gets worried."

"Why don't we have one of our members in that position, Wally?" Kevin asks.

"You think of someone suitable, let me know," Wally says.

"Doesn't matter. Besides Passmore," Bearon continues, "we also have to expect the woman to show up wanting her room, or to check out or something. The two of them were friendly enough to have coffee together a couple of times. She'll be wanting to know where Kiersten is, too. She'll ask Passmore, so he has to know she's okay. Best thing is if she's back at the desk. The problem is, how do we make sure this doesn't land on us."

"On you, you mean, land on *you*," Kevin says. "If this was, er, a *company* project we would've known about it before now. This 'need to know' policy of yours is starting to piss me off."

"God save me from fuckin' lawyers!" Bearon exclaims. "It's for your own good. All of you. The less you know, the better. That way…"

"Yeah, yeah, we know," Kevin interrupts. "If something goes wrong and the cops question one of us, yadda yadda. Okay. Does she know where she is? Did she see you? Did she see anything? Would she know where she's been, like your place and the Lodge?"

"No. She was blindfolded when she was being transferred in and out of the van. She never saw where they were or the guys' faces, neither, just big scary guys with balaclavas."

Like you, Kevin thinks. He says, "okay, then, take her somewhere and let her go."

"She's gonna report it, for sure, and she saw Trent's face. He doesn't think she recognized him, but she saw enough she could give a description. Plus he's got a record. She could I.D. him outta a photo array. And he mighta left prints."

"So she picks him outta a photo array, that's not enough to stick. But prints? Even Trent's not stupid enough to go in without gloves," Preacher says, scratching his goatee. "Everyone's seen enough CSI to know better than that."

"Preacher's right," Kevin agrees. "Take her somewhere that she'll be found, and let her go."

"I doubt he had gloves," Clint tells them.

"What? Why wouldn't he?" Kevin asks. "Didn't he learn anything when he was inside?"

"He wasn't expecting anyone to find out."

"Not find out? The person missing their things is bound to notice."

"Well…"

"*Aaaannd* the plot sickens," Kevin says. "You better bring us fully into the picture, Bearon."

Bearon takes a few deep breaths, looks around the table, and says, "Clint was gonna grab the woman at Dot's but he missed her. So when she got back to her room and found it emptied out, she called the cops."

"Like father, like son," Preacher says, glaring at Clint. "Fuck-ups. I just hope the fuck they didn't wreck the door. Last time it was a thousand dollar repair. You're gonna get the bill."

Clint's nostrils flare and his body stiffens. He says, "forget your fuckin' door! We had a plan that would've worked like a charm. She's a skittish little minx and wouldn't get out of the car. Wouldn't even roll down the window."

"Oh? Not such a great plan, then. I guess you should've waited until she was out of the car before you tried to jump her," Preacher says. "Like I said. A couple of first-rate fuck-ups."

"You think you could do better?" Clint snarls.

"Everyone's got twenty-twenty hindsight. No use blaming blame, it's done," Bearon growls. "Clint's right. You wanna take over Clint's job, give it a try."

"Don't be ridiculous," Brent interjects. "We all know it's not a job for Preacher. But what do you mean, grab her? What the fuck? We agreed not to take anyone from around here."

"That's right, we did," Kevin says.

"True. But this bitch shows up outta nowhere, sayin' she's Hank Hazen's daughter. Claims she's the rightful heir to his estate," Bearon explains. "It's a shakedown. Any of you think we should go along with that?"

"She'd have to prove it. Could take years," Kevin points out. "How does she have a claim against the estate? It was settled years ago and the probate lawyers would've contacted beneficiaries then. What cause could she have to challenge the will?" His eyes narrow as he frowns at Bearon. "Does she have something on you personally, Bearon? If she can actually make trouble, the logical course would be to pay her off. Why the fuck would you think it was a good idea to kidnap her? That's just guaranteed to bring heat down on us! You want cops swarming all over the Lodge?"

"She doesn't have nuthin' on me," Bearon scowls. "What could she *possibly* have on me? And no one would connect her disappearance to the Lodge. If the cops swarmed all over it as you suggest, they wouldn't find nuthin'. I don't want to give her nuthin', that's all. Pay her now, she'll keep coming back for more. You guys know that."

"What were you planning to do with her?" Brent asks.

"Take her to the Lodge."

"And keep her there, like forever?"

"Sure. Why not? We could take her into the congregation. She might even become a True Believer. Or, she's cute for her age. We could ship her with the next lot. End of problem, and it not only costs us nuthin', but makes us a few bucks as well. Didn't think I had to run this stuff past you guys. This is just business."

"I don't agree, but putting that aside for a moment, why are you telling us now?" Kevin asks.

"Whether you agree or not, she sprung the trap. So it's more complicated now. She has no way of knowing we're connected to her room being emptied, so we can still see about negotiating a settlement with her, if that's what we decide to do. That's why I wanted to talk you guys. I don't want to spend Lodge money without you guys agreeing."

"How much are you thinking of? Whatever you have in mind, it's not gonna be chump change. We'll need positive cash flow first and that won't happen until we've got a few more deals behind us," Evan says. "We've had a few sales, but we're in a bit of a negative cash flow situation right now."

"If you're all so anxious to pay her instead of just eliminating the problem, maybe we give her a percentage of the profits. And then the Lodge doesn't turn a profit? That might work, but think about it. She'd be entitled to snoop around and I'm sure all of you can agree no good could come of that!"

"She could snoop around forever and she'd never find the Basement any more than the cops would. No one would."

Bearon scratches his nose and then gives his head a brief shake. "Anyhow, that's not our problem right now. Kiersten is."

"She can go to the Lodge," Evan suggests. "If this other woman you're talking about could stay there, Kiersten can too."

"Kiersten attends services. She's already a Believer. Why don't we just bump her up to True Believer status and tell her we need to protect her boyfriend's asshole son. Don't want him to go back inside, he's one of our own, he made a mistake, he's young, blah blah," Preacher suggests

"Doubt she'd care about that, since she was kidnapped," Kevin opines. "That trumps a few years in jail. Any sane person would think he deserves to go back inside."

"Give her some added incentive, then," Brent suggests. "Like maybe her boyfriend disappears if she talks."

"Maybe the True Believer status is the better way to go. Make her an Acolyte, even," Kevin suggests. "We need one anyway."

"She hasn't even been to a Communion Ceremony yet and she's never fucked no one but Clint so far." Bearon turns to Clint and asks, "you think she's ready?"

All eyes are on Clint as he blows out a breath, shakes his head and says, "I doubt it."

"Why haven't you brought her into the fucking pool, Clint? You been balls deep in her plenty of times now. Time to share the wealth."

"I know, but she's so naïve. And she thinks we're, like, exclusive. You know we've only been to Sunday services a few times. Dunno if she's into it enough that she'd go if I didn't take her. Didn't think there was any hurry."

"Yeah, you know, I've been wondering why you brought her up here in the first place," Preacher interrupts. "Was it dark when you picked her up?"

"Whaddya mean?"

"Well, you have to admit she's nothin' to look at. Skinny. Kinda plain."

"You think she's plain just because she's not blonde? You wanna fuck a fat gash with bleach blonde hair and big sagging tits, go fuck Annie," Clint snarls.

"All right, all right! Let's not get off task," Bearon says. Clint's emotional outburst in defence of Kiersten has given him an idea. "About Kiersten—"

"Kiersten's not the only problem," Kevin cuts in. "We have to get rid of Trent."

"Whaddaya mean, get rid of Trent?" Clint demands.

"Relax, Clint," Kevin says. "I'm not suggesting a permanent solution. But think about it. Just convincing Kiersten not to charge him, even if we could, isn't enough. Sooner or later she'll recognize him. Even if she doesn't press charges, by now the cops've gone over the room, they'll have his prints, they'll get him for the B and E and he'll go back to finish his sentence, with something tacked on for this."

"Yeah, that's a good point. And I don't trust him not to sing. Might think he can trade information for a deal. He has to disappear," Bearon says. As he drums his fingers on the table he makes a mental note of Kevin interrupting him, and that when he looks at him, although he can't control the look of distaste on his face, he doesn't look away. Kevin has criticized the balaclava several times. It's tempting to pull it off and see what kind of face he makes then! He stows the thought and says, "send him to the Lodge, Clint, and keep him there. Evan can take him to Pillerton with him. How soon are you leaving, Evan? You're pretty well done here, right?"

"Right. I don't have to be here full time now. I'm going back right after Communion."

"Good. Get him some new ID and he goes to live in Pillerton. Make sure he knows the consequences if he doesn't stay there."

"And Kiersten?"

"Don't worry about it. Like I said, I have an idea. Clint brought her here in the first place and she thinks he's her boyfriend. Now he can be her hero and rescue her." He turns to Clint and says, "I'll fill you in on the details later, Clint. We got other business to discuss. Go wait downstairs."

RICK WALKS INTO the airport terminal and has no trouble spotting the man he's meeting. There aren't a lot of people waiting for passengers, and he's the only one in a cowboy hat.

"You must be Denver," he says as they shake hands.

"And you must be Rick," Denver says. "Glad to meet you. I'm surprised you could get here so fast."

"It was a near thing, I got the plane with ten minutes to spare. Only two flights a week, Regina to Dark River. Lucky Kathy called when she did or I'd have missed it. She said I didn't have to come. Lousy timing, we're harvesting lentils right now, problems with the swather. You know how it goes."

"Ay-yuh, been there myself."

"Thought so. Anyway, I told her to come home. She would've had to get on the flight I just came on, but I guess the cops still need her here."

"Yeah, the cops want her to come in to give a statement, although it might've been possible to do that over the phone. She was pretty shaken up this morning, so when the cop said she could do it tomorrow, we thought we'd take her home with us, give her time to settle down. Didn't even think about her going straight home. And she's hoping to get her things back. Mostly her pendant. Said she forgot to put it on this morning and she's cursing herself for taking it off last night."

"Yeah, well, she always does, it's pretty heavy. I guess it's probably gone for good even if the cops find the rest of her things."

"Unfortunate. Sounds pretty unique." Denver turns to scan the arrivals area. There are a few people at the conveyor waiting for the baggage cart. "Do we need to wait for a suitcase?"

"Nope, I've just got this carry-on. Mostly full of Kathy's clothes. Hope I brought the right stuff."

Denver chuckles. "What're chances of that?"

"Slim to none."

They exchange a knowing nod, then walk outside into the late afternoon sun and head for Denver's truck.

"Well, your wife will be real happy you're here, whatever she might've told you. It's been a shock for her.

For Astrid, too. The robbery was bad enough, but the hotel clerk going missing…" He lets out a long breath.

"Astrid knew her?"

"No, but she, umm, had a similar experience to Kathy's, not this robbery but from before. She was abducted too. She doesn't want me tellin' people, so don't let on I said anything and for god's sake don't tell Kathy I know some of what happened to her! I'm just tellin' you so you understand. This missing woman—well, it must stir up bad memories, for both of them."

"You know about Kathy? What happened to her?"

"She talked about it a little. Just to Astrid, and in confidence. Astrid hasn't blabbed to me, just told me they've had similar experiences. They haven't had a chance to compare notes yet, but if they spend more time together, they might tell each other everything. Astrid still has trouble talking about what happened to her. Quit going to counselling. Says it's was too gut-wrenching to keep going over it. I think it might be good for the two of them, you know, talking to someone who's had the same experience. Their own support group of two."

As they approach the truck, Denver clicks the remote to unlock the doors. Rick tosses his suitcase in the back seat, and both men climb in.

Once they're underway, Denver picks up the thread of the conversation. "I'm glad she's gonna stay, you guys are gonna stay, at least for a bit, for selfish reasons. I'm hopin' talkin' to your wife will help Astrid."

"Kathy doesn't talk about her experience, either. She's only told me tiny bits. It comes out in dribs and drabs.

She's been in counselling, too, but doesn't go often anymore."

"I went with Astrid to a couple of sessions. PTSS, Dr. Malone says. Used to be PTSD but they call it a syndrome instead of a disorder these days. Apparently it can take years to get over. Can change personalities, sometimes so much it's like they're a different person. I wouldn't say Astrid is completely different, but I'd sure like to have the old one back."

"Kathy's definitely changed," Rick tells him. "She was always shy, but now she never wants to go anywhere." He clicks his tongue and shakes his head. "Talk about paranoid."

Denver frowns and gives him a quick sideways glance.

"Then," Rick continues, "if someone pisses her off, it's like a switch flips and she turns into a pit bull. But that's unusual. I'm amazed she came here, knowing she would have to talk to strange men. In all honesty, I didn't think she should've come."

"Hmmm. Well, it must've seemed like a wild goose chase, but it looks like she'd be a fine detective. She found us, after all. And Astrid's anxious about anything out of her routine, too. She used to love running the trails through the forest and now even taking the trail from our place to the other property, where our barn is, un-nerves her. She runs on the treadmill instead. Must be awful." He shakes his head. "I'm beginning to think she's never going to get over it."

"Yeah. I worry about that, too. It's no way to live."

KATHY AND ASTRID are on the patio behind the log house, enjoying the last of the day's sunshine. Documents overflow the box on the concrete next to the empty one. A large, very furry black dog and a smaller black and white one are sprawled out, sleeping in the shade under their chairs.

"Nothing here. Looks like we need to get the next box," Astrid observes. She tosses a bundle of time cards on the discard pile. "Maybe that's enough for tonight, though. These are all starting to look the same."

"Yeah, it's been a long day."

"A long, *stressful* day."

"For sure. I'm not at my best by this time of day anyway. Plus, the wine!" Kathy says. She leans back in her chair and stretches. She scans the house, two stories with a wide balcony the full length of the second story overhanging the patio. "Your house is awesome! How on earth do they build with those big logs?"

"There's a company in town that specializes in it. They use a crane. Heather's House, the women's shelter next door where our barn is, it's a log house, too, and about twice as big. That's where Hazens lived, and of course I lived there too when I was working for them. I wasn't sure we should do log, but Denver likes it. It suits the property, and of course we have lots of our own logs."

"It really does suit the property. Sure is different than home! There's a shelter belt around the old yard with decent-sized trees, but when we built the new house, Rick's house, behind the old yard, we had to plant our own trees and they're still pretty small. Nothing like this!" She waves at the old growth forest that surrounds them. "It's

Rick's family's farm. They've owned it for about a hundred years, bald ass open prairie so flat you can see the Blue Hills about, I don't know, a couple hundred kilometers away. His mother still lives in the old farmhouse."

"A hundred year family farm! Do you grow grain or raise cattle?"

"In the beginning the Schoenfelds did both but we sold the cattle a few years ago. Just have a couple of old cows now and we grow hay mostly, and some lentils. Sometimes canola. The family farm has almost gone the way of the dinosaur. We're surrounded by huge corporate farms. The old farmhouses are abandoned. Sometimes I think we should do likewise. Well, we'd keep the home quarter and sell the rest."

"Denver's family were ranchers. Like Rick, he was third or fourth generation on that ranch. But he didn't really like the cattle business. It's one reason he was happy to sell the family ranch. Now we just raise a few horses. The mill keeps us plenty busy."

"You said before you had no family until Denver. Does he have siblings? Are you close to them?"

"Siblings, yes. Close, no. He had a falling out with his brother. He's in Arizona, trains cutting horses down there. His sister and her wife are in Vancouver. Closest thing we've got to family is Wilson. He started working for Den's father when he was sixteen."

"Well, Wilson is great. Seems like he's big help, too. Did you ever wish for a sister, though?"

"Umm, no, not really. I guess I wondered why all my friends had siblings and I didn't. That's about all. You wanted a sister?"

"When I was little, I did. I thought a baby sister, or a brother even, would be wonderful. I guess I asked my mother about it too many times. She, umm, you could say she never took it well. Since I got those letters, I realize maybe me bugging her about it made her feel bad about the baby she gave away, although I'd be surprised if she ever cared that much. She was pretty willing to leave me behind when she thought she was going to move here to be with Hank. Anyway, I finally quit asking. When I got older, I realized it was just as well. And now I have Rick's sister, Jeanie. His daughter, mom, all his cousins and so on."

"Hmmm." Astrid sits back and looks off across the patio. After a moment, she says, "You know, I might not have come here if I had any family. No close friends, either. You've been divorced, maybe you know how it is. The friends you have as a couple go with either the wife or the husband when you split. I don't think it's a conscious thing. In my case, when I left, I moved across town. I guess there's a boundary, like a containment field, about twenty minutes out. Or maybe they just never really liked me as much as they liked him. Anyway, now I have Franny. She's great, but since...well, there's always this...I don't know, this *distance*. Almost like she blames me for what happened. Maybe that's a big part of the reason I don't tell anyone about, er, what happened."

"I know what you mean," Kathy says. "I still have a very good friend from childhood, Penny. She lives in

Vancouver, so since I moved halfway across the country—way outside the twenty minute containment field!—we're more like pen pals, or should I say email pals? People I know through work are friendly and all, like you'd expect in a small town. I don't know if I'm imagining it, but I always think when they look at me, they're thinking, *you're that woman.* Know what I mean?"

"Yeah. It's a wall between Franny and me, too. She says things that make me wonder if she's jealous. Because I inherited this." Astrid wobbles slightly as she waves her arm around. "Believe me, she has no idea. There's nothing, no amount of money or property, that could possibly..."

They're both fall quiet for a few moments. Kathy sips her wine, then says, "I wish no one knew. But, well, having this," she holds out her hand with its index finger amputated at the first knuckle. "And this," she pulls her hair back to show her ear with its missing lobe. "People always look and if they don't know my story, I know they're dying to ask what happened. You are, too, aren't you?"

"I'm sorry, Kathy, but, yeah."

"The guy who tried to kill me did it."

"Oh! My god!"

"Thankfully I was unconscious at the time."

"Oh! I'm *so* sorry!" Astrid's face twists and her eyes fill. She takes a couple of deep breaths. "I can't even tell you how sorry I am! I...I...My experience was bad but yours..." She chokes up and can't continue.

Kathy lowers her head and chews at the hangnail on her thumb, swallowing several times to get rid of the lump that still materializes in her throat when she talks about it. After a few moments, she looks up at Astrid and says, "I can't believe I'm telling you this! Maybe it's because you've been through it too. About the same time, too. Like parallel, or like we're twins."

"Sure. And then there's the physical resemblance," Astrid smiles and wipes her eyes with her hand.

"Well, obviously! If it wasn't for a six inch height difference, black-turning-grey hair instead of blonde, brown eyes instead of blue, we'd be identical! And we both live on a ranch and have cattle dogs! Ours isn't a Border Collie, though. He's an Australian Cattle Dog, they call them heelers. Ours is a red one, Chewie. He's a good old dog. When Rick wants the horses to come in, if they're too far away to hear him call, he sends Chewie. The horses start coming toward the barn as soon as they see him heading their way."

She realizes she's close to babbling, but it's moving the subject safely off her abduction, so she continues: "Rick's always had a heeler, ever since he was little, so now that Chewie's getting older, he wants to get another puppy. I say we should get a dog from a rescue. He argues you never know what their temperaments will be like, but if you get a purebred, you're pretty much guaranteed."

"Yeah," Astrid sniffs and wipes her eyes again. "You're guaranteed, all right! I think heelers are like Border Collies, working dogs, so you're guaranteed that they'll be busy all day and go herd the horses around if they get bored. Sounds like yours at least has a job. Our relentless horse herder, tireless ball chaser and talented frisbee catcher is Tippy the Third."

The black and white dog raises her head at the mention of her name and thumps her tail.

"Buster's getting long in the tooth, too," Astrid continues. "He's diabetic. I have to give him insulin injections twice a day and that ain't easy with his thick coat! At least he's good about it. He has to pee so often we can't leave him in the house overnight anymore but then he barks his head off half the night because he hates raccoons and of course they're nocturnal. Sometimes I think he's senile, the way he'll go running off into the bush and then stand and bark at nothing. If he trees a raccoon, forget calling him off, he'll bark at the tree for half an hour before he gives up. He slobbers and sheds so bad he was never a good house dog. And yet he's such a sweet guy I dread the day we have to euthanize him. I wish they didn't have such short lives. He's only eight and you've seen how he moves, he looks like an ancient dog. He used to be so tidy, always going out into the bush to poop, and now he just does it anywhere he happens to be, so watch out for land mines! They're everywhere! The only good thing is that he sticks around home more than he used to."

"Is there something you can give him to help? We have Chewie on Previcox. It seems to help."

"Did. He won't eat it now, though. No matter how carefully I hide the pill."

"Yeah, our old horse is on Previcox too, and she's like that," Kathy says. "Was like that, I mean."

"Was?"

"She, um, colicked yesterday and had to be put down."

"Oh. I'm sorry."

"She was pushing thirty so she had a good long life, but she was really Rick's horse. You know, I told him he didn't need to come, but I'm glad he is. He had that horse since she was a foal. I was sorry I couldn't be with him when he had to put her down. He wouldn't say so, but I think it tore him up. It'll be good for him to get away for a couple of days."

"He sounds like a guy with a tough shell and a marshmallow filling."

"You know, that's a good description of him."

"He'll get along real well with Denver, then." Astrid lifts the box of wine and refills Kathy's glass before topping up her own. "Lucky thing Denver's picking up more of this," she says, waving the box back and forth to show it's getting empty.

"I think I've had enough."

"We haven't drank all that much really. It wasn't full when we started, you know."

"But I'm already tipsy."

Tippy looks up and thumps her tail again.

"She said *tipsy*, not *Tippy*!" Astrid scolds the dog. Tippy pants and lolls her tongue; she looks like she's smiling as she rolls over exposing her belly, her tail wagging her entire back end.

The dog looks so funny, Kathy giggles. Astrid joins in. It's cathartic, and soon they're laughing so hard they don't hear the truck drive in. The dogs do, though; Tippy leaps to her feet and runs off, with Buster in pursuit.

Soon, the two men come out through the patio doors and join the women, who are still chuckling. Kathy wipes tears from her eyes as she gets unsteadily to her feet and goes to hug Rick.

"What's so funny?" Denver asks.

"Nothing, really," Astrid answers, "I guess we just needed a good laugh."

"Doesn't hurt that the two of you've got your shines on, neither," Denver says. He strokes her shoulder and gives it a squeeze. He introduces Rick to Astrid, then says, "looks like you had a few since I left. I'll get us some beers and we'll get started catchin' up, hey Rick?"

"He's probably hungry. There's a burger patty left over you can nuke," Astrid says. "Thank Kathy for that. All she ate was salad, beans and a bun."

"Wilson's got it covered," Denver says. "We're gonna grab somethin' and after a beer, take a run over to the other place. Turns out Rick's lookin' for a horse or two so I'd like to show him what we got for sale."

"We'll go with you," Astrid says. "Whaddaya think, Kathy? Up for a ride through the bush on an ATV?"

"Hell, yeah!"

"We've only got three ATV's so someone will have to double up."

"Nice you want to go with us," Denver says. "Tell you what, though, neither one of you's gonna drive."

FOURTEEN

THE EXCHANGE

IT'S FULL DARK AND the moon hasn't yet risen when Clint turns his Porsche up the Bear Mountain Haul Road. He drives slowly, watching for the turn onto the side road. Not easy to spot at the best of times, it's next to impossible in the dark, and it's especially dark under the canopy of native firs and cedars. The road is seldom used, and bushes crowd the roadway. At last he sees it, nothing more than a wide space in the bushes, and turns in.

He scowls and wonders why this couldn't've been done on the Haul Road. Hardly any traffic anytime and none at this time of night. "Couldn't they pick someplace that wouldn't ruin my paint?" he mutters, cursing as branches sweep down the sides of his car.

At least the meeting site isn't much further along, in a cleared area wide enough to turn around. Moonlight floods the area. He stops about fifty meters from the van that's parked facing him and gets out to stand in front of his car.

He takes a lungful of the night air, noticing there's still a hint of the smoke from the fire that came within a kilometer of the highway, and this road. Crews are still putting out hot spots.

Not for the first time, he wonders what forces protect Bearon. Even forest fires stop a safe distance from his cabin. And that bear! Clint has often wondered why Bearon always wears that balaclava and always, long-sleeved shirts. It must be to hide something, like one of those huge raised red birthmarks or some horrible birth defect. Or maybe some gruesome disfigurement that was the price he paid for a deal with the devil.

At that thought, a chill courses through him despite the evening being warm. Clint quickly crosses himself, and thinks, *fuck me! Hope those guys didn't see that! The Children of Noah creed doesn't recognize the New Testament and True Believers certainly never cross themselves.*

As caustic as Bearon can be, Clint counts himself lucky to be his go-to guy. That he keeps secrets from the rest of the council doesn't bother him, although more and more often lately he's found it irksome to be treated like an errand boy. Then he reminds himself he's privy to plenty the council isn't, and the perks of the job make up for a lot. So far, anyway.

The van's headlights go on and a dark figure slides out of the passenger seat, raising a hand in greeting before going to the side. Clint hears the door slide open. After a moment, the man appears in front of the van, backlit by the headlights, pushing a white-robed figure who stumbles along, arms shackled behind her back and a bag on her head.

Clint meets them halfway, catching Kiersten in a hug as she is shoved hard toward him. No words are exchanged. The hooded figure gives a nod; there's enough moonlight to see his grin and thumbs up before he turns and jogs back to the van. In moments the door slides shut, the engine starts, and the van pulls away. It passes them, goes around the Porsche, and disappears into the bushes.

"Are you okay, baby?" Clint asks as he pulls the bag off her head. "Did they hurt you?"

"N... no! A little... But I... Oh, Clint!" she sobs, "I was so scared!" Her knees buckle and she collapses into Clint's arms. He steadies her, then digs his Swiss Army knife out of his pocket, opens it, and turns her to cut the zap straps and free her hands. Then he holds her until her sobbing stops.

"They took my clothes! Who are they? How did you find me?"

"I put some feelers out. They gave you up pretty easily. I guess they didn't mean to take you."

"No, I just went to see Kathy and...Clint! That man! That awful man! He pushed me down and he hit muh-muh-me!"

"Shh! You're okay now. You're safe." He rubs her back and says softly, "you've been through a terrible ordeal and I'm sure you're exhausted. Let's get outta here."

He leads her to the passenger door, opens it, and closes it behind her once she's settled in. He gets in the driver's seat and starts the engine, driving carefully over the rough ground to turn back. Once they're heading along the roadway, he takes her hand. "I'm so glad you're okay, baby! You don't know how worried I was! But the deal I had to make to get you back—besides the money, I had to make a deal. You understand?"

Kiersten cocks her head, wipes her eyes, then nods. "I guess."

"There's a couple strings attached. You can't tell anyone. I don't know who these guys are, but there's a lot of them, and they said if you—we—go to the cops, or tell anyone, they'll get you again and next time—oh, God! I don't want to think about it!"

"They asked me about my sister, Clint! Wanted to know how long my niece has bu-bu-been taking dance at Calisto!" Kiersten starts crying again.

"It's okay, baby."

"But how would they know?"

"I don't know, baby."

"But they're in Vancouver! Lorraine and Kimmie, they're in Vancouver! How would they know about them?"

"They're a big operation. Got people everywhere. It's just lucky I knew who to reach out to. We don't need to tell anyone."

"I...uhh..."

"We don't."

"But my work!" she sobs. "Mr. Passmore is gonna be pissed at me if I just show up with no explanation for leaving like that! And they kept my clothes. My name badge."

"You have another work outfit, don't you?"

"Yes, but I need more than one. Mr. Passmore will be pissed that I lost one."

"I fixed it with him. You leaving like you did. I can fix the missing clothes thing, too."

"He's gonna fire me!"

"He won't. I told him you called me because you had an, er, anxiety attack and I took you to the doctor. Emergency. You know I have pull. I went right over Passmore's head to the owner. Got you that job in the first place, didn't I?"

She nods. Sniffs and wipes at her eyes.

"There's napkins in the glove box."

She digs them out and blows her nose. The glow from the dashboard lights illuminates her tear- and snot-streaked face and Clint feels a tug of empathy. He was on script when he said she'd been through a terrible ordeal, but now he realizes the truth of it. He says, "don't worry, baby, you'll be okay. As long as you stick with the story. You were on your break, right? You were on the phone with me when you had an anxiety attack. You don't know anything about any break-in. Okay?"

"Okay."

After a moment, he says quietly, "remember, they know where your sister and her little girl live. They know where you live, too. So this is important."

This sets off fresh tears. "They're not safe. They'll have to move. I have to move too," she sobs.

"They don't have to move. They could find them if they moved, anyway. They're perfectly safe as long as we don't tell anyone about this. So are you." He gives her forearm a rub.

"You're staying at my place tonight, for sure," he continues, now taking her hand and squeezing it. As per script, says, "We can talk about you moving in with me, too. I love you."

"Ohhh, Clint! I love you, too," Kiersten cries, and gives him a tremulous smile. She climbs partway over the console to push up against him and kiss his neck.

"I was scared, too, baby. I'd have done anything to get you back! But sit down and buckle in. This road's tricky. I wouldn't want you to get killed if we go off it. Pretty steep on that side I think." After a suitable pause, he continues, "I don't get it. Why that room? Whose room was it?"

"Umm, Kathy. I don't remember her last name."

"The gal you said you had coffee with a couple times?"

"Uh-huh," she nods and wipes her nose again.

"What would she have that anyone would be after?"

"Nothing that I know of. She's just a normal, ordinary person. Very sweet, just, um, ordinary."

He doesn't love Kiersten, of course, but saying he does and suggesting she could stay with him, possibly even move in, has the desired effect of getting her mind off being snatched. He watches as she sits up straighter and takes a deep breath that opens the front of the robe slightly and lifts her breasts. They're small, too small to make more than a slight bump in the thick robe. Still, the peek inside the robe is alluring.

"She's looking for her birth father," Kiersten continues, wiping her eyes with a fresh napkin. "That's all I know. Someone by the name of Hank. She doesn't even know his last name. Don't you remember? I asked you about it, and I gave you her phone number."

"Oh, right. That was her? I remember now. I called but didn't get an answer."

"She didn't call back?"

"Well, you know I don't leave messages, and my number's blocked."

"Well anyway, to me it seems like a crazy idea, coming all this way when it's so unlikely she'd be able to find him."

"So, she came a long way? Where's she from?"

"Well, not that far away, I guess, like not another country or anything. Some little town in Saskatchewan. I can get you her name and address, if you need it."

"Oh yeah? Sure, might as well," Clint says. But he thinks, *the probate lawyers, the financiers, and even the project manager Evan Briggs—all from Pillerton, nothing but an obscure little town in Saskatchewan, its only claim to fame being the headquarters of The Children of Noah. Bearon has been there. Kevin was wondering how that woman Bearon is so worried about could have a claim on Hazen's estate...*

The pieces are starting to come together. If her birth father is Hazen, maybe she has a legitimate claim on the Hazen estate or more important, the Lodge. But like Kevin said, it could take years to go through the courts. Irritating but not a big balls deal. So why is Bearon so secretive about it? There must be more to it. Something even Briggs doesn't know. *Bearon is hiding something. Something he doesn't even want me, his right hand man, his fixer, to know about.*

Kevin is not the only one who's tired of Bearon's 'need to know' policy. But everyone has secrets. So he phoned her? He'll have her number in his recent call log, and that'll be his secret. He groans inwardly when he thinks what Bearon would do if he found out Clint had her number days ago. That he could have set up a meet at a time and place that would be easy to grab her but didn't follow through on it. He wouldn't care that at the time, Clint had no way of knowing she was the target.

"Do me a favour, baby?"

"Of course! Anything!"

"Don't tell anyone else about, you know, you and me talking about this. Or that you had her number and gave it to me."

ASTRID COMES OUT the sliding doors and across the patio with a pink camo hoodie. "The kids are finally asleep, little stinkers!" she says. "Well, Kylie's been out like a light since before we came out here, but Elise! She was building a pillow fort under her bed. When I say little stinker, it's mostly her I'm talking about."

"Hiding from the Bear Man again?" Denver asks.

"Yeah. I thought she'd forgotten about him." Astrid hands the hoodie to Kathy and says, "we could go inside."

"No, not unless everyone else wants to," Kathy replies, "it's nice out here. I love the smell of the forest. So different from where we live. As long as the bears all stay on Bear Mountain."

"Well, we got bears around here," Denver tells them. "They follow the river valley. But don't worry. They're diurnal. Asleep by now and if they aren't, the fire keeps them away. The Bear Man, though…"

"Denver!" Astrid exclaims, "you're no help!"

"It's a monster?" Kathy asks.

"Yeah," Astrid replies, "she started talking about the Bear Man around the same time as she 'met' an invisible friend. Funny, but her invisible friend's name is Heather, like the little girl who drowned here decades ago. Heather's House is named for her."

"Don't worry, Kathy," Denver says, "I doubt there's actually a Bear Man, but if there is, you'll be fine. Unless you're the slowest runner. Think you can outrun Wilson?"

"I wouldn't bet on it," Wilson says.

"Ha ha!" Kathy chuckles humourlessly. "It's not funny. A Bear Man or Boogeyman can be very real to a five-year-old. Terrifying! I feel for Elise. And I don't think they're afraid of fire so that won't keep them away."

"Good thing you're not still five years old," Rick tells her. Then he turns to Astrid and says, "by the way, thanks for puttin' us up or puttin' up with us. We'll go back to the motel tomorrow and get them to move us to a second floor room for tomorrow night. After we take a spin on those two geldings of yours, of course."

The fire in the pit emits a loud ker-rack! and a shower of sparks flies up. "Guess I better put the screen over that." Denver gets up, takes the screen from beside the patio and sets it on the fire pit's perimeter blocks. "Don't think these small sparks would still be live by the time they landed on something but I don't wanna take a chance, with everything so dry."

"They said that fire over on the far side of Bear Mountain was started by sparks from some guy off-roading," Wilson tells them. "Hot muffler, I heard. So they closed the Denton Creek Haul Road."

"That's why we're on early shift for fire season," Astrid says. "Still see stupid people tossing cigarette butts out their car windows. Started a grass fire right in town. Never thought I'd say it but I miss the rain. Aside from crews not being able to work in the bush, we're having to feed hay, the pasture's so poor. I'll be glad when the fall rains start."

"Lucky for you, you know a guy who has lots of hay," Rick says with a grin. "Maybe we can make a trade for those colts."

"Funny, but I met Astrid because I brought that stud horse here. Hazen paid me in hay." Denver flips the cooler lid open, pulls out a fresh beer, and hands it to Rick. "Wilson?"

"Nope," Wilson replies, "I'm headin' inside. Past my bedtime. Good night, folks." He gets up and stretches. Everyone says their good-nights as he heads to the house.

Denver opens a beer for himself. "Lookin' at the hayfields now, it's hard to believe Hazen had hay to spare," he says.

"So you not only got the girl, but the ranch, too," Rick observes.

"Well, Astrid owns it, actually. Inheritance."

"Oh yeah, I remember Franny saying something about how lucky you were he left this to you," Kathy says.

"I wouldn't call it luck," Astrid says. She sees the puzzled expression on Rick's face, and hurries on in a brighter tone. "You know, I just realized, if Hank Hazen was your father, he would have left you something in his will."

"How do you know he didn't?" Denver asks. "Leave her something, I mean."

"Someone would've contacted her if she inherited something."

"True," Denver agrees.

"What if they couldn't find her? She got married."

"Didn't change my name, though," Kathy says. "They might not have been able to find me if I was still in Vancouver but I was back in Pillerton when he died. Hey! It proves he wasn't my father!"

"Or it just proves he didn't want to leave you anything," Rick points out.

"Well, I think you should get in touch with those lawyers who looked after the will, just to find out for sure," Astrid suggests. "Put an end to the question once and for all, even if it means you have no more leads about your family. I have contact information for the lawyers somewhere. I'll dig it out tomorrow."

"Sure," Kathy agrees, "good idea. Meantime, maybe we could check out the guy that creep at Dot's told me about. He didn't know the address, but said there's a big carved bear to mark the driveway. Do you know where Bear Mountain Road is?"

"Bear Mountain Haul Road. Must be pretty far up," Denver offers, "at least, I've never seen a carved bear, and I've gone right to where it peters out into a single lane trail through the bush. That haul road isn't on one of our properties, and I haven't been up there in a while."

Kathy turns to her husband and asks, "Can we go tomorrow, Rick?"

"I guess. But I really want to try out those horses, and there's the youngsters over on that other place we didn't see yet. Maybe you could go to the motel and get the room thing sorted out while I do that?"

"We could go after you do that, though."

"Don't forget, you're supposed to see that cop, too. Dunno how long that might take, and I think we need to get the rooms changed around before eleven o'clock check out time. On top of that, I think it's about a forty-five minute drive back to town. Right, Denver?"

"Yup," Denver agrees, "and then back out here, because Bear Mountain Haul Road is past our place, off Mill Road. It's a fair distance off the highway."

"I don't want to put off the horse thing," Rick says.

"You don't have to," Astrid says. "You stay here again tomorrow night. Tomorrow while you guys do your horse business, I'll dig out that paperwork and we'll put in a call to the lawyer, then Kathy and I can zip into town so she can check out. We'll go see Sergeant Villeneuve, and then from there we can go up the Haul Road and find that carved bear. Then we come back here and we'll have the rest of the afternoon and Saturday morning, too, for you guys to try any of the horses Rick thinks would be suitable."

"That's a great idea, babe," Denver says, "as long as you're okay going out to that guy's place on your own."

"You know Kathy's been going around by herself all week."

"Yeah, but to places in town. Any visits to remote addresses? Where there were no neighbours?"

Kathy shakes her head.

"The bad guys are all dead, remember, Denver?" Astrid says. Pushing away her mounting qualms, she draws a deep breath.

"Can you really do this, babe? Go out into a remote area of the forest alone?

"I won't be alone," Astrid says, "there's two of us. Right, Kathy?"

"Yes! That's right!"

"We'll be fine."

"Okay, if you're sure," Denver agrees.

"We're sure," Astrid and Kathy say, almost at the same time. They exchange a look, and smile.

"How about you swing by here before you head up there, though, and pick up the dogs. And be sure and let them out as soon as you're out of the vehicle."

CLINT AND KIERSTEN are skin on skin, enjoying the afterglow of a steamy, athletic sexual romp. He pulls her close and kisses her temple. "That was great, baby," he whispers. "Was it good for you?"

She nods and murmurs, "More than just good."

"It's a nice thank you for being rescued, eh?"

"Oh, Clint," Kiersten pulls away slightly so they can make eye contact. "You know it's not, er, wasn't to pay you back!"

"I know." He pulls her in close again and nuzzles her hair. After a moment, he says, "You know I love you?"

"I love you, too. I think I loved you from the first week. My hero. My prince!"

Clint wonders at the anxiety swirling in his innards, and wishes he didn't have to go on. More minutes pass and Kiersten is so quiet he wonders if she's dozed off. He takes a deep breath and says, "Remember I said that in order to get you back from those bad people, I had to make a deal?"

"Umm, yeah. We can't tell anyone."

"Well, there's another part to the deal. A part I hate." He pulls away from her, lays back and throws his forearm over his eyes. "I wouldn't have agreed to it if it wasn't... if there was any other way."

"What?"

"I don't even know how to tell you. You'll hate me."

"I could never hate you, sweetie! How can you think that? I love you!"

"Well, the guy who put up the money—and it was a lot, believe me, a lot more than I had—fuck! I can't even say it!"

"What? You can't say what?"

"I, uh... Well, he, uh... He wants to have sex with you."

"Oh my god! What a creep!"

"I know! I'll tell him that's not going to happen. I can do that, tell him to take a hike, now that you're safe. I'll pay him back somehow. Maybe sell this place. Or my car."

"Oh my god! You can't do that!"

"I'll have to. I don't want some other guy..."

"But that's crazy!"

"I should never have said I'd go along with it. It was just—I didn't want them to have you for the time it would take for me to get the money and he—"

"I can't believe you would do that for me," Kiersten says. "No one's ever been so good to me." Her voice catches in a sob.

Clint pulls her in close and tucks her head in against his shoulder. "I didn't have any choice. He's a powerful man. I wish I hadn't told him you were missing, that I needed money to get you back, but I didn't know where else to turn! If I don't pay him back, there's no place I could hide that he won't find me. Er, find *us*. I'll have to pay him back, no question of that."

"It's that guy you work for, isn't it?"

"Yeah."

Kiersten takes several deep breaths, then says quietly, "I'll do it."

"Are you sure, baby? Oh my god, you're the best!" He covers her face with kisses and then kisses her mouth. "You have no idea how I worried about this!" He gets out of bed and goes out to the living room to his phone. In minutes, he returns.

"Let's have a shower, baby. Get you freshened up. He'll be here in about an hour."

"Oh! Tonight? But it's already so late!"

"Tonight." He turns away and heads for the bathroom, where he starts the water in the shower. Kiersten must never doubt he was willing to part with his house and his car, even though that was never going to happen. Bearon already owns the house, and the leasing company owns the car. And there was never any money exchanged in any case. This is just the first step in indoctrinating Kiersten into the fucking pool. The first step in her becoming available to anyone Bearon decides to give her to. Business as usual.

She's a sweet girl and it's a shitty thing to do to her. She's agreed to fuck Bearon once. Wait until she finds out it's going to be more than once. A lot more. And there will be a lot of other guys. But before that happens, maybe there's an upside. Maybe if she spends enough time fucking Bearon before the other guys want in, she can find out why he's so worried about that woman from Saskatchewan. I just hope, after what she's been through, she can get used to fucking a guy in a balaclava.

FIFTEEN

BRIGGS

BEARON PULLS UP to the Lodge gate and punches button above the windshield that opens it. As he waits for the gates to roll wide, he notices with approval the landscaping is progressing nicely. Carpenters are working on the deck over the end of the pond and the trenching machine with the crew putting in the irrigation is raising dust. The flatbed truck with Reid Bros. Turf Farm logo is at the far side of what will be lawn, the Hiab offloading the last pallets of rolled turf; already a couple of guys are laying an island of fresh green in the middle of the parched landscape.

Everything inside the building is complete and the grounds should be finished up by tomorrow, well ahead of the Pillerton people arriving. They should be impressed!

When the gates open, he drives the half kilometer to the parking lot and parks at the main entrance. He walks around the corner and along the narrow lane that leads to his private entrance. He slides his key card into the slot. When the lock clicks, he opens the door, steps inside and closes it behind him. There's a short hallway with a bathroom and his office opening off it. When he opens the inner office door, he's startled to find Evan Briggs in his chair, just closing the bottom drawer of his desk.

Briggs looks up and says, "good. You're here. Saves me going to your place."

"Didn't notice your car in the lot, Briggs," Bearon says. He feels naked without his balaclava, but Briggs is used to what he looks like. Maybe looking frightful works in his favour.

Still, he hadn't expected anyone to be here. The transfer was done hours ago. What reason does Briggs have to be in his office once the cash is in the safe? Was he snooping through his private files? He'd love to call him on it, but if he does, will he look suspicious? As if he has something to hide? The second set of books is in his home office, so he decides to ignore the intrusion for now. He makes a mental note to lock the desk drawers from now on.

He narrows his eyes, draws a deep breath, then asks, "Why were you going to my place?"

"I told you before, I want the Range Rover."

"What's wrong with your car?"

"I should pick up the top brass in a Camry? You haven't forgotten who owns the Range Rover, have you?" Evan gives him a questioning frown. He waits for Bearon's head shake before continuing. "More to the point, what're you doing here? If you came to get your weasel greased, you're too late. Unless you want Trent."

"No, I don't want Trent, asshole!"

"Don't get your panties in a bunch. It was a joke."

Bearon scowls, wondering why Evan thinks he can treat him like he's one of the guys. Like they're friends. Must be the familiarity breeds contempt effect. On top of that, the Range Rover technically belongs to The Children of Noah, but he's the one it was given to. What makes Evan think he can borrow it whenever he wants to?

Evan makes no move to get out of his chair, so Bearon takes the armchair across from him. He sucks in a deep breath of new building smell. As enjoyable as that is, it still takes all of Bearon's willpower not to tell this asshole to get the fuck out of his chair. *Be nice. Don't want him getting pissy and putting the brakes on the insurance funds. Maybe taking too close a look at some of the invoices. At least until after the last draw down, you need this guy.*

Evan swivels around to the credenza behind the desk, turns two stubby glasses upright, opens the bottle and pours a splash of Crown Royal into each glass. He swivels back and slides one glass across to Bearon. They clink glasses, and Evan says, "they tell you the transfer went good? Would've had room for Kiersten, though."

"Yeah. Adding the extra soundproofing didn't take too much space away, then?"

"Nope."

"Reardon better get his ass in gear. No use sending the truck only partly full."

"Like I said, we had room for Kiersten. Maybe didn't need to do all that pussyfooting around, the drama of that fake kidnap exchange."

"Of course we did! You think the cops wouldn't be looking for her if she hadn't showed up at work the next day? Pfft!" He blows out a long breath and wonders how someone so smart in some ways can be so stupid in others. Bearon gives his head a slight shake, then says, "we won't be sending her anywhere. She's going into the Congregation. At least she's a decent fuck."

"Yeah?"

"Yeah. Very grateful for being rescued." He takes a swig of rye. "And it was a good reminder to Reardon that he has to share the wealth."

"Good thing," Evan agrees. "Meanwhile, that fucking Trent! Yells his head off every time someone comes near. Should've heard him when we took the girls out. I guess he thought we'd let him out then too."

"He's in the Basement?"

"Asshole kept trying to leave. Had to haul him back in once. He nearly made it to the gate. Good thing Brent was here, little fucker's tough and enough bigger than me I don't know if I could've done it alone. That got some strange looks from the landscapers."

"Fuck, and they're locals! Don't need that kind of talk around town."

"So you see why I had to lock him up. Lucky the soundproofing's good. When he's not yelling, he's crying or choking his chicken."

"Can't blame a guy for being horny, but crying? Ugly and retarded too?"

Evan gives him an odd look before saying, "Supposed to call it mentally challenged now. Anyway, I wouldn't call him retarded, just not too bright. And if you can believe him, he's got a girlfriend."

"Really? Shit, that's a loose end," Bearon says as he scratches at his ear nub. "You know who she is?"

"No."

"Maybe Reardon knows, or at least can find out."

"What do we do if he doesn't cooperate? Sending him to Pillerton won't help. He can still call her as soon as he gets near a phone. And he'll have to have a phone."

"It's a problem," Bearon says. He swirls the rye around the glass and takes a sip. "She might be willing to relocate. Or we could fix him up with something in Pillerton to take his mind off this one. Maybe there's someone in the Pillerton congregation stupid enough."

"Doubtful. That kid's a pain in the ass," Evan says, and empties his glass. "Maybe we just let him go. He doesn't know anything other than he grabbed up Kiersten. He wouldn't want to go blabbing that around."

"You obviously haven't been around him much. He yammers like an old woman. And he's stupid enough to be proud of it. And you call him a kid? He's at least mid-twenties. Did three years for that assault, remember? Cops will be looking for him for the B and E too, don't forget. And now that he's been downstairs, he knows a lot more. Wish you hadn't of done that. Now he's a Grade A Large problem. He's gonna hafta go with you."

They quietly sip their rye for a minute, then Evan says, "aside from that, we got cash to wash. I'll funnel it through Corporate of course, but we should buy a couple more houses."

"Maybe. How about the old house Kevin was talking about? He should be able to get the keys and I'll go check it out next week. The guy who inherited it looks pretty clean so far. May have to just buy it from him."

"Not ideal."

"No. But we'll rent it to the church, so we'll get clean money that way. And we'll be able to attract new members once we look legit."

"Yup." Evan leans back and drains his drink. "Now we're set up here, we can phase out Dogwood and sell that. More clean money that can go right into the Lodge account. Gonna need to fund the payroll account and fill the ATM at the Lodge."

"Don't need washed money for the ATM," Bearon reminds him.

"Oh yeah," Briggs says with a nod. "We should get some more."

"They're hard to come by. But we'll talk about it."

"Of course there's commissions to think about, too. Everyone's gonna have their hand out. Amazing how their ears perk up minutes after a shipment. But before we do anything, we have to take it to the Council."

"Yeah. The fuckin' Council." Bearon finishes his rye and pushes the glass across the table to be refilled while Evan is pouring another for himself.

"Yeah, the fuckin' council! Don't forget how important they were getting this whole thing going."

Bearon lets out a derisive snort.

"So, about the Communion Ceremony," Evan says as he pours, "the Pillerton guys confirm they're flying in tomorrow. How many of our members are in?"

"Ten? Maybe twelve? I don't know. You'll have to ask Preach."

"I will. I think you're right though. Probably no more than a dozen. Would've been nice to start off bigger." Evan knocks the last of his whiskey back, puts his glass down with a thump, and gets to his feet. "I'm taking off. Your keys?"

Bearon digs his keys out of his pocket, clicks his personal keys off the ring, and tosses the remote fob on the desk.

"Thanks," Evan says, and scoops it up.

"Fill it before you give it back."

"Sure. Happy hour is in the lounge at five tomorrow. The flight comes in at three-something so we should be here in good time. I'll see you then. Oh, and get those floor cushions unpacked. Don't want to be messing around with that shit tomorrow." Evan gives Bearon a nod and strides out the door.

Bearon watches the monitors, the working of his jaw and flaring nostrils giving the lie to his outward calm.

When the main door closes behind Briggs, Bearon leaps to his feet and takes several strides around the office. *Gimme the Range Rover, like it's fuckin' his? Sit in my chair like it's fuckin' his? Get the floor cushions unpacked? Like I'm his flunky?* He punches the log wall repeatedly until his fist won't take any more.

He strides to the chair Evan just vacated and throws himself into it. The monitor shows the Autobiography leaving the parking area and heading down the driveway. "You forget," he says as he watches the monitor, "this ain't Pillerton, and you are only the bag man here, *asshole*."

Will Evan ever quit reminding him he's the one who pulled him out of the snowbank and got him to the doctor? He snorts. Doctor? Goddamn veterinarian. No actual doctor would leave him like he is. And that gives him the right to jerk him around? Maybe he needs to meet Silverface. The only person who knows who he is, not bound by solicitor-client privilege, gone. It would be a good thing.

Then he reminds himself Evan will go home in a few days. The Range Rover—can't get too pissed off about that, since it does technically belong to The Children of Noah, and Evan is the Exalted Leader of the First Congregation—but still, that only makes him third in command, whereas Bearon is Imperial Leader of the Second Congregation. Where does he get off ordering him around? Maybe some distance will give him the opportunity to remember whose money he's been playing with.

Goddamn the old man for setting everything up through Prairie Equity and Wealth Management so that arrogant little prick holds the purse strings! *Goddamn* the old man for leaving the last five million up for grabs!

His fist is throbbing now. He checks the monitors to make sure there's no one else in the building, gets up and heads for the ice machine in its nook next to the kitchen. He fills one of the plastic buckets and brings it back into his office. Seated again, he tosses a couple of cubes into his glass and tops up the Chivas, then sticks his fist into the ice bucket and studies the monitors as he scrolls through the various camera views: front gate; parking area; upper floor hall; grotto; ladies change room; billiard room; the underground parking and adjacent ceremony room where boxes of cushions await unpacking; and finally, the sub-basement.

The first five cells are empty. The sixth and furthest from the elevator is Trent's; he is on his bunk with a Playboy, masturbating. Bearon watches for a minute or two; when Trent starts moaning and thrashing around, he considers giving him a blast over the intercom just to see if he leaps to his feet mid-stroke. But if Trent is too stupid to realize there's surveillance, it's probably better to keep him ignorant.

When the ice on his fist gets too cold to tolerate, he'll go down and speak to him. Maybe take him some massage oil and a new stroke book or two, payment for unpacking and setting out the cushions. He can launder the sheets from the other rooms while he's at it.

But that can wait. Watching Trent fuck his hand is oddly stimulating. Annie should be at his place by now. He'll go home and spend an hour with her.

It dawns on him Evan didn't give him the keys to his car. If they're not in the ignition, he'll have no way home but the Kubota UTV. He gets a balaclava from the closet behind his desk, pulls it on, and hurries out to where the Camry is parked next to one of the worker's trucks. Windows up. Doors locked.

He's tempted to break a window, but doubts it could be hot-wired. It would set off the alarm and probably refuse to move in any case. Maybe he should do it just to get back at Briggs. No. He'll find some other way.

SIXTEEN

AUTOBIOGRAPHY

DENVER AND RICK are on the highway heading for the ranch where Denver has leased pasture for his young horses, when the gunmetal grey Range Rover with blacked-out windows speeds past them in the opposite direction.

"Damn!" Denver exclaims. He swivels his head then watches it retreating in his rear view. "I've been wonderin' who owns that thing! Those black windows are illegal. Wonder why the cops never pulled him over for it!"

"They're illegal?"

"Yeah. Well, the front ones are. Cops like to see who they're comin' up on, I guess. I'm half-ways tempted to turn around and follow the guy to see where he goes."

"Oh yeah?"

"Yeah. I'm curious about who, around here, has the wherewithal to buy a $200K Range Rover. And who wants the windows blacked out. Who does that to a vehicle like that?

"Drug dealers or movie stars," Rick says. "Used to be an Autobiography in Pillerton. Elder Reeves, the guy that was the Grand Poobah of The Children of Noah, owned it. Crashed it."

"Children of Noah—that's the cult Kathy's mother belonged to? Must be some big bucks in the cult business! What an expensive claim that would be!"

"Dunno if it got replaced. Never saw another one around town."

"The Poobah or whatever you called him must not have liked it, then. From what I've heard they've got big powerful engines but handle like pigs."

Rick shrugs. "I wouldn't know about that, but the reason he didn't replace it was that he had no need for it. He crashed it because he had bullet holes in him."

"What? A murder in a town half the size of Dark River?"

"Yeah." Rick sighs and rubs his neck before continuing. "Five murders in the span of a few days that summer."

"Oh, I think I remember hearin' 'bout that. Were they all connected?"

"Not officially. We think they were, though. Kathy was almost the sixth."

Denver gives Rick a quick glance.

"Yeah. She was attacked by one of the guys who was later murdered. That cult was the common denominator." Rick squirms and heaves a sigh. "I shouldn't be telling you this. Kathy thinks if people know, they'll see her as a victim and she doesn't want that. But I want you to know why I'm puzzled that she came here. She's so paranoid about strangers. I never would've believed she'd come here on her own in the first place, and now she feels safe enough to go out to some remote location to look for a man she knows nothing about? She must really think a lot of Astrid."

Denver slows the truck as they approach a wide, cleared field with a rancher set well back from the highway and a run of white plank fencing. He turns into the driveway. "I'm surprised at Astrid suggestin' it, too. Like I told you, she hasn't ventured out into the bush since...well. Strength in numbers, I guess, but—no disrespect—how much help could Kathy be? She's barely tall enough to reach the pedals on that SUV."

"Yeah. She always says her legs aren't long but at least they reach the ground. But you haven't seen her when she goes pit bull." Rick chews his lower lip for a moment, then asks, "the guy who abducted Astrid was one of them, wasn't he? One of the serial killers?"

"Yeah, she lived with them and then they, er, locked her up. Those two and their compadres deserved what they got. Blown to smithereens."

"No one could've survived?"

"Nope. They were practically vaporized. Hardly enough left to bury. Anyone who did survive would've froze to death 'cause it was a blizzard and no one found out about the blast for days. A couple of the guys, all they found were parts. Must be tough on people doing the recovery. Imagine findin' part of a hand! So anyway, missin' and presumed dead was the best they could do."

Denver drives slowly through the farmyard, past the barn, and parks next to corrals at the back. There's a woman on a Gator in a field further down the pathway putting hay into paddocks; she looks up and waves as the men get out of the truck. In the pen in front of them, half a dozen pinto horses laze around a hayrick.

"That little one, the sorrel filly with all the white? She's an own daughter of Rocky Duster, so she's well bred. But she's on the small side, just a pony, really. Should mature around fourteen-one or -two. She'd be a good size for Kathy. Might be better for her than that big gelding, and cheaper bein' as she's not started yet."

"I kinda like that big gelding for myself. I'm not much of a cowboy, hardly rode since I was a kid. Pretty well quit once I got the ATV to run out around the pasture. I wouldn't be getting another horse but Kathy's got the bug and I might ride out with her once in a while. He's big enough for me and quiet's good for my skill, which is no skill at all really."

"Naw, you rode fine last night. But I know what you're sayin'."

"You're too kind. But that filly's pretty," Rick observes. "Kathy would like her. She's just halter broke?"

"Yup, that's all. Do her feet on schedule and she's good about that. Good for the vet. Had a saddle on her, ran her around the round pen wearin' it and she took to that fine, but that's all. She's just three and I don't like startin' them until they're four, sometimes five if they're immature."

"Well, I'm no cowboy and no trainer neither."

"They're all straightforward. Never had one that bucked or bolted, and this one's real quiet. But if you don't want to start her yourself, you must have someone you could send her to in the spring to put two or three months on her? And Kathy would have a real nice horse."

"We'll definitely talk," Rick nods. After a few minutes of watching the horses moving listlessly around their paddock as if preparing for their morning nap, Rick asks, "About that explosion—that bunch of guys—all killers, I guess?"

"We'll never know for sure. We know the two Hanks were, from DNA on some of the trophies, but the rest of the guys? At the very least, they went along with it."

"No one else could've been involved? Someone who wasn't there when it blew, maybe?"

"We-l-l," Denver drawls, "I have heard a rumour 'bout the new lodge pickin' up where the old one left off. I never gave it much credence, though. Put it down to fear mongerin'. You know how folks love to talk! Doesn't help, that crazy woman claimin' Heather's House is kidnappin' girls."

"What? What's that about?"

"It was a worry for us for a time. The woman claimed to hear voices in the laundry truck. Cries for help. Cops checked it out, found nothin'. Turns out she had a history of hearin' voices. She should've been at Nechako instead of Heather's because it turns out the husband she claimed to be runnin' away from didn't exist. Paranoid delusions, always phonin' the cops claimin' she was being stalked. I wouldn't know all this except I play hockey with Sergeant Villeneuve, so it's on the QT, you know?"

"Oh yeah? A buddy of mine is the NCO in Charge at the Pillerton Detachment. He's the center on the old fart's team I play on."

"That's crazy! Villeneuve plays center, too! Handy havin' an in with the cops. Hockey's good for more than a beer or two and the odd pulled muscle, eh?"

He waits for Rick's nod of agreement before continuing. "Anyway, she'd been institutionalized before. She's back in the psych ward now, but the damage is done. Shitty thing is, we had to discontinue the laundry service. You know what it's like when you're on a well and septic. Real nice havin' that all done off site so you're not using your own water and fillin' up your own septic tank. Free, too; great for a non-profit, all they wanted was a donation receipt. But we quit, just for optics." Denver lifts his hat and gives his head a scratch before continuing. "Don't worry, Rick. I wouldn't let them go if I thought there was any danger." He looks up the pathway where the Gator is raising a plume of dust as it races toward them. "You'll like Shirley. She was born on this ranch. Gotta be pushin' seventy, and has been runnin' it on her own since her husband died twenty years ago."

The Gator pulls up in a cloud of dust a few meters off. "Good morning! Sorry 'bout the dust. I should've stopped further away," the driver says as she turns the engine off and climbs out.

"I think we're used to it by now," Denver tells her.

"Come to check on your babies?"

"Gettin' to be pretty big babies," Denver replies, "Time they all got jobs! Any problems?"

"Nuthin's changed since you were here last, Den." the woman replies. Her wide smile crinkles her eyes. She removes her worn work gloves and tosses them on the driver's seat, then comes to the fence where the men stand.

"They're fine. Their appetites are sure fine, anyway. Pasture's just about done so they're hangin' around here eatin' hay most of the time. You're gonna hafta bring some more over in another week or so."

"Ay-yuh, same as at our place. Sucks we have to supplement pasture this early in the year. Too many horses and not enough feed. Damn drought!" Denver clucks. "Shirley, meet Rick."

"Pleased to meet you," Shirley says, and reaches for a quick shake of Rick's hand.

"Pleased to meet you, Shirley," Rick says. "I can't do nuthin' 'bout the drought but I think I'll be able to help Mr. Danielson with his other two problems."

KATHY PUSHES THE lobby doors open and is relieved to see Kiersten behind the reception desk, busy with a white-haired couple. "Oh my god, it's Kiersten!"

When she's done checking the couple in and they're rolling their suitcases toward the elevator, Kiersten smiles and says, "Hi Kathy!"

"Hi," Kathy responds. She indicates Astrid, and says to Kiersten, "This is my new friend, Astrid."

"Pleased to meet you, Astrid," Kiersten says.

"You, too," Astrid replies.'

"Are you okay?" Kathy asks.

"Okay? Yeah. Why?"

Kathy scans the area to make sure no one else is near enough to overhear before continuing. "Yesterday the manager said you left suddenly without telling anyone."

"Well that's—he's wrong. I wouldn't leave without telling him."

"But when my room got robbed, the cops wanted to talk to you but they, or he, your boss I guess, said you were missing!"

"Oh, no, I wasn't missing!" Kiersten squirms and looks away for a second before continuing, "I heard about your room being robbed. Sorry about that! Must've been spooky staying after that!"

"Um, no, Astrid let me stay at her place." Kathy frowns, then takes a deep breath. "Kiersten, I'm sorry, but I don't understand why he, your boss that is, would say you were missing if you weren't."

Kiersten's face flushes; she shuffles a little pile of papers, and says, "I, uh, well, yeah," she looks away again, as if something across the room has attracted her attention. Kathy turns to see what it is but sees nothing but the couple that just checked in entering the elevator.

"Yeah." Kiersten picks up her mug and takes a sip of coffee before continuing, "I, ahh, I get these panic attacks. I was on the phone with my boyfriend when I felt an attack coming on. He came right away and took me to the hospital."

"To the hospital?" Kathy studies Kiersten's face. A panic attack is nothing to be ashamed of, but talking about it seems to be making her uncomfortable. She takes a breath and says in what she hopes is a comforting tone, "I've heard they can be bad."

"Sometimes." Kiersten takes another sip of coffee, this time holding the mug in both hands as if to cover half her face. "I thought I was having a heart attack." Kiersten puts the mug down and busies herself with the little pile of paper again before looking back up; when their eyes meet, she looks away. "I wasn't, of course and I didn't really need to go to the hospital. My boyfriend is just over-protective."

"Can't fault him for that," Astrid says.

"Oh, it must be awful," Kathy says. "How long have you had these, er, attacks?"

"Umm, not long."

There's an awkward lull in the conversation. Finally, Kathy says, "well, anyway, we're both glad you're back." Then her gaze falls on Kiersten's plain white coffee mug. "Hey, where's your favourite mug?" she asks.

"My mug? Oh, I lost it," Kiersten explains, then rushes on, "so. How can I help you? I understand why you wouldn't want to stay in that room tonight. I have a couple of other rooms I could put you in for the rest of your stay. Sorry, I can't upgrade you because that's one of our best rooms already, but I can put you in one on the second floor, access only from the inside hallway, but with a balcony, closer to the river. Still has a nice view of the river. Or if you want I can put you close to the pool. But you said before you'd like to be upstairs, I guess so no one could...well you know..."

"Umm, no thanks, Kiersten. I just want to check out. It's a day early, but ..."

"I totally don't blame you."

"The deal we made was for a week, though."

"I don't think the manager will hold you to that! Umm, you know, in light of what happened, I think we can refund you for last night and cancel the extra night no charge but I'll have to check with him and see. I'll go find out!" She jumps to her feet, spins and strides off, pushing through the doorway and letting it slam shut behind her.

"Well," Astrid says.

Kathy turns to Astrid and says, "she's sure acting weird."

"I guess she's embarrassed."

"About having an illness?"

"Lots of people are private about stuff like that," Astrid says.

After a brief wait, Kiersten comes through the door behind the reception desk with the manager right behind her. "Good day, ladies," he says.

"Hello, Mr. er, Passmore." Kathy responds.

"Kiersten tells me you'd like to check out early, Ms. Klein?"

Kathy nods, "Yes."

"I understand. We'll just check you out, minus two days."

"I, well, it's only really one day."

"You couldn't stay last night so of course no charge for that, and no charge for today. We'll comp you for an extra day as well," he says, and pushes the paperwork across the countertop. "Hope you don't think badly of us."

"It wasn't your fault. I don't blame you."

"Well, it's kind of a thank you. If you hadn't scared them off, they might've gone on to the next room, maybe down the whole row. Don't need that on our Yelp review! We're going to beef up our security system and have a locksmith do something about those patio doors so they can't be pried open. Please accept our apologies."

"Apology accepted, and thank you. This is more than generous," Kathy says, folding the papers and tucking them in her purse.

"You're welcome." He turns and leaves.

Kiersten settles into her chair and fusses with the keyboard, then looks up at Kathy and says, "I feel responsible. I now know why you didn't want a room on the ground floor. I mean, with the door to the outside. I never would have thought about it. But it turned out okay, didn't it?"

It's not okay, of course; Kathy is surprised at how violated she feels, thinking about someone pawing through her things, not to mention the loss of the valuable pendant. Definitely not okay. It's not Kiersten's fault, though. "Well, nobody died," Kathy says. It's the best response she can come up with. "It's not your fault. It was the last room. What could you do?"

"I know, but I feel bad. Could I treat you to lunch, or maybe dinner, tomorrow? I'd say tonight but my boyfriend is going out of town tomorrow and we're having a special date tonight."

"It's okay, Kiersten. We're flying out tomorrow. But that's a nice offer. Thanks! You've been great. It's been nice meeting you."

"You too," Kiersten says, biting her lip.

As Kathy and Astrid head back outside, Astrid says, "Kiersten seems nice. She looked downright mournful you're leaving."

"Maybe she's lonely."

"But she has a boyfriend."

"You don't think a person in a relationship can be lonely?" Kathy clicks the button on the remote to unlock the doors and they both take their seats in the SUV. Kathy sits quietly for a moment, then shakes her head.

"Yeah, it can be tough to make friends," Astrid says.

"Some people need them more than others," Kathy agrees, and starts the engine. "I've always been more of a loner. I guess I learned how to be alone, growing up." She backs out of the parking stall, then shifts into drive and heads the Sorrento to the exit. "To the cop shop now I guess. Where is it?"

"Just go back out to the highway. You know how to get to Dot's. It's a little past that, across the road from The Plaza Bowling Alley."

"Hope it doesn't take too long."

"THE SMELL OF PERFUME was so strong. It turned out the bottle was on the bathroom floor, broken. He must've dropped it. And then I thought I heard something, and saw the patio door was open. Whoever it was, we interrupted them. I don't remember seeing a car, like, parked in front. I don't think there was one. I parked right in front of my door. So that's all I know," Kathy tells Sergeant Villeneuve. "Not much, is it? Astrid was behind me so she saw even less. You didn't notice a car parked out in front, did you, Astrid?"

"Well, there were a few cars in the lot, about what you'd expect, same as when you got there," Astrid tells the Sergeant. "That's all."

"We were just at the Riverview to check out, and saw Kiersten," Kathy continues. "She explained why she left suddenly, like I told you, so she isn't the thief. I thought she might be when she disappeared like that. I hated myself for even thinking that, when it seemed more likely she was abducted. I'm glad I was wrong, on both counts! So, I guess that's it." Kathy leans back with a shrug. "Do you think you might get my things back?"

"Dat's a long shot," Sergeant Villeneuve says. He reads the list Kathy handed him, and lets out a low whistle. "Some special pendant, eh?"

"Yeah. An American Double Eagle gold coin. A keepsake."

"Dat's a shame." He's tapping at his keyboard, studying the monitor. "You have a photo of it, by any chance?"

"Umm, yeah, actually, I do, but it's in my insurance papers at home. I can email it to you when I'm back there."

"Good. Lots of prints in the room like you'd expect, but we did get a hit on one. We got a BOLO out on him." He turns his monitor so the women can see the mug shot. "Dis guy, he look familiar? Like you seen him around maybe?"

Kathy and Astrid study the monitor, then both shake their heads. "Sorry, no," Kathy says, "I haven't."

"I don't know—maybe I've seen him around town but a lot of young guys look like that now. That tattoo on his neck, though..." Astrid sighs. "I really don't know."

Sergeant Villeneuve shrugs and turns the monitor back. "Okay. If he tosses your suitcase somewhere, we might get your clothes back, but your laptop and dat necklace—real easy to get rid of. He probably had a big party and dat's duh end of dat."

"Could he find a buyer for a $5,000 necklace so quickly?"

"Doubt he knew what it was."

"Surely he'd know it was gold! It's so heavy! That's why I take it off at night. Grrr! Wish I'd remembered to put it on yesterday morning! Better yet, I wish I'd left it at home."

"He might not realize it was real. He could fence it for fifty bucks or just trade it for drugs. Likely some drug dealer's wearing it now." Sergeant Villeneuve clicks his tongue. "Oh, while you're here. Dis broken mug…" he makes a couple of clicks on his keyboard and swings the monitor toward Kathy again. "Found it in pieces just outside the patio door. Yours?"

Kathy shakes her head. She studies it carefully, noticing it's got some lettering on it: 'FT' and below that, a large, slanted 'T'. "What's printed on it?"

"I don't know. Maybe advertising. Why?"

"Well it could be nothing, but this morning when we were at the motel to check out, I noticed Kiersten didn't have her favourite mug, the one that said, 'I have one nerve left and you're on it'. I asked where it was and she said she lost it. That looks like it could be hers."

"Hmmm." Sergeant Villeneuve leans back, crosses his arms, and swivels his chair for a heartbeat. "I talked to her dis morning. I'll check wid her again and see if she can identify it."

"I'll need the police file number for my insurance claim," Kathy says.

"Sure." He takes one of his cards from the little holder on his desk, and checking with the computer monitor, jots a number on the back before handing it to her.

"Thank you," Kathy says; she and Astrid exchange glances, then both stand. "So, that's it then?"

"Yup," Sergeant Villeneuve gets up, walks them to the door and pushes the buzzer to let them out. "I'll let you know if we find anyting."

Back in the Sorrento, Kathy starts the engine, turns the fan up to its highest setting to blast the hot air out, then backs out of the parking stall and drives to the exit. "Okay, two things done," she says. "I'm getting hungry. Lunch? At Dot's, maybe?"

"I don't know," Astrid says, "it's fast service there but it would still kill another hour at least. I'd rather not be in town that long, would you?"

"Not really. I'm looking forward to checking out that place up on Bear Mountain Haul Road, so we can get back to your place and ride some horses."

"I'm with you!"

Astrid says. "Do you find this? I hardly ever go to town, and when I do, after an hour I can't wait to get back home."

"Me, too. Although it's different for me, I go to town every day." She turns to glance at Astrid and says, "you might think this is corny, but I miss Rick, even when we're only apart for a short while."

"Do you really?"

"Yeah. After five years. I told you you'd think it was corny."

"No, not corny. I'd say you're lucky."

"Don't you miss Denver?"

"I, uh, not when he's only gone for an hour. When he's away for weeks judging horse shows, yes. And I've seen all the gorgeous girls on the show circuit. I suppose I worry a bit." She takes a deep breath.

"I know. It's hard to trust, isn't it? Rick was, well, to put it plainly, a total asshole when we dated in high school. I know he's changed, but... Anyhow. Enough of that! A person's got to eat. How about A & W?"

"A & W it is. And if you can eat and drive at the same time, we won't even have to go in."

"I eat half my breakfasts while I'm driving to work! Beyond Meat Burger, here we come!" Kathy says, driving past Dot's and heading for the main drag, and the A & W.

SEVENTEEN

MEET SILVERFACE

KATHY DRIVES THE Sorrento as far as she dares onto the dry weeds at the side of the gravel road and shifts into park. "Are you sure we're on the right road? Maybe we missed a turnoff somewhere."

"I don't think so."

"Well it looks like this is the end of the line, and no carved bear anywhere."

"There's that track there, though," Astrid says, pointing to a road access overgrown with weeds and grass.

"Not much of a track. And there's that," Kathy says, and points out a sign three meters up the trunk of a native fir.

"No trespassing. Oh. But if you're looking for someone, looking for their house, it's not really trespassing is it? And that could be the driveway. It's overgrown but it *is* gravel."

"Hmm. I don't know. Doesn't look like it gets much traffic but I guess since we've come this far, we might as well have a look. Maybe we should walk in, though. Just in case there's no place to turn around."

"Good plan. Buster needs to pee so the sooner I let him out, the better."

"That's why he's been whining for the last ten minutes?"

"Yup, that's why. I was gonna hafta ask you to pull over pretty quick anyway so this is just as well. I really don't know why Denver insisted we take the dogs along."

"Made him feel better, I guess. Buster is protective of you. He's such a sweet old guy I don't know if he'd actually do anything, but he looks formidable enough to keep the bad guys away," Kathy says.

"Sure. All I have to do is remember to let him out as soon as I get out, and if he runs off after a raccoon we'll just ask the bad guy to wait until he gets back!"

"Not funny."

"Nope. Not funny at all."

Kathy powers the windows down a couple of inches, turns the engine off and they both get out. Astrid opens the back to let the dogs out.

Buster shuffles a couple of meters away before squatting and peeing. "You've gotten so decrepit you can't even lift your leg without falling over, can you, old man?" Astrid says, giving his ears an affectionate rub. "Now let's see if this trail leads to anything."

With the dogs going ahead sniffing everything and stirring clouds of grasshoppers out of the sere grass, they set off. About a hundred meters into the trees, the trail curves and they come to a cleared area with a log house at the far edge. The wide open area around the house is surrounded by chain link fence. Three large black tanks stand in the shade at the side of the garage, and there's a tall, free-standing antenna tower on the rise on the opposite end of the house. A small grey sedan, its rear window winking in the sun, sits on the paved area in front of the garage door. On a mound just inside the gate is a chainsaw sculpture of a bear.

"This is it!" Kathy exclaims. "That guy did say you couldn't see the house from the road."

As they near the gate they see a sign with the words "Caution! Electrified Fence!" above an image of a person being struck down by a zig-zag bolt of energy.

"Jeez! Electrified?" Kathy says. "Can't touch the gate, then. How do we get to the door?"

"There's an intercom." Astrid goes to it, pushes the button, waits, then pushes it again.

A woman's voice answers, "yes?"

"Hi, umm, we're looking for Hank…"

"No one by that name here." Click.

"Nice woman," Kathy says. "Stuck way out here, you'd think she'd welcome company."

"I don't think anyone who puts up a barricade like this is interested in having visitors. It's like prison fencing."

"Survivalists?" Kathy suggests.

"Maybe. Yeah, maybe. That's the only thing that makes sense. Looks like those tanks collect rainwater from the roof, and the antenna might be for a ham radio? But there's overhead wires from the road to the house."

"And a satellite TV dish on that tower. I guess even survivalists take advantage of modern conveniences, at least until Armageddon or whatever it is they're worried about wipes them out."

"Yeah. There's crazies everywhere, looks like. Anyhow, what do you want to do now?"

"If we can't even talk to that woman, we might as well go back to your place," Kathy says. "I almost wish I had gone with that guy who waylaid me outside Dot's yesterday. He said this guy was his friend and that he has the code for the gate. I wonder how I could find him…contact him again."

"I have no idea how we could find out. Maybe Sergeant Villeneuve?"

"But he wouldn't give out information like that even if he had access to it. Not unless there was a reason, like a legal reason," Kathy concludes. "But he did say Annie told him I was looking for Hank. We can ask Annie!"

"Back to Dot's?"

"She might not be at work today. How about we phone? You have your phone on you?"

"Yup." She pulls it out of her pocket and turns it on. "Okay, can't call from here. No cell service. We'll have to head back down the road."

By this time, the dogs have disappeared into the bush. Astrid calls them back. Tippy comes bounding out through the underbrush, but Buster doesn't follow. After a few minutes of calling, Astrid says, "Damn it! That dog! He is so bad for running off! Can you keep a hold of Tippy while I go after him?"

"We agreed we wouldn't split up."

"It's okay. Don't think he's gone far, probably just over that rise. If you can just keep her here, I'll get him and be back in two minutes."

But before Kathy gets a hold on Tippy's collar, Buster's booming *woo-wooo-wooof!* shatters the calm. Tippy spins and dashes off.

"Now I suppose he's found a raccoon, and of course Tippy has to join the fun. I'll have to go get him and drag him back."

They start off in the direction of the barking, single file through the tall grass and weeds in the cleared area, staying a safe distance from the fence.

Besides barking, there's snarling and growling, and then something roars. "My god, that's no raccoon!" Astrid cries. She starts running toward the sound, with Kathy right on her heels. They run up a slight incline, skirt a rocky outcropping, and stop in their tracks.

In a wider cleared area where another trail, this one leading further into the forest, begins, Buster is face to face with a huge bear. Hair on the bear's hump is silvery, and when he turns his head, a white patch the size of a handprint gleams in the sunlight. He rears and bellows out a series of ear-splitting, percussive roars before dropping back down on all fours and lunging at Buster. Bear and dogs are all growling; Buster and Tippy snarl and bark while the bear's gruffly squeals are almost pig-like. Buster lunges in to attack and then scurries back out of reach of the bear's massive front paws while Tippy circles behind, nipping at his hocks.

"No!" Astrid screams. "Buster! Heel! Buster! Tippy! Heel!"

Buster gives no sign of hearing much less obeying, and even the usually compliant Tippy pays no heed. With a throaty snarl Buster lunges at the bear again, and this time succeeds in clamping onto his face. The bear partly rears and shakes his huge head but Buster doesn't let go. Tippy barks and worries the bear's back legs. The bear swings his head side to side, then gives another toss, breaking Buster's hold.

Buster falls and rolls away; he struggles to get up but before he can gain his feet the bear pounces and fastens his jaws around the dog's neck. Buster yelps and then is silent as the bear lifts him and shakes him as easily as a terrier shakes a rat. Bright arterial blood sprays from his neck when the bear flings him away. He lands with a thud and lies still.

Now the bear turns his attention to Tippy, who lunges at his back leg for another bite. One huge paw swats her. She utters a series of yips as she rolls into the bush but instantly leaps to her feet and comes back at him. He swats her away again and this time she lies still.

The bear rears and sniffs the air. When he was on all fours he looked big even compared to Buster, but upright, he looks massive. When he fixes his gaze on the two women just a few hundred meters away, Kathy, seconds earlier paralyzed into inaction, turns to run. Astrid grips her arm and hisses, "Don't move! If you run, you'll trigger his prey response!"

Kathy draws several deep breaths and stands, quaking, despite every instinct telling her to run. Birds, silent or at least unnoticed moments before, begin singing again, the cheerful sound incompatible with the tense drama still playing out.

"Stay close and don't make eye contact," Astrid says quietly. "We'll just back slowly away." She starts taking small steps backward while facing the ground, looking up under her brows at the bear. He drops back on all fours and makes a lunging dash toward them, but holds up after just a couple of meters. Astrid blows out a sharp breath while Kathy begins sobbing.

They hear an engine off in the distance and a loud *BOOM*! breaks the quiet; almost the same instant there's a *ZING!* and a small explosion in the rocks near the bear kicks up dust. The bear drops down on all fours and sprints toward them. A second *BOOM!* and a hunk of bark flies off a fir just meters away. The bear changes course and runs off further into the forest. Another gunshot. The bear bounds through the underbrush and over a deadfall as if it wasn't there. A fourth gunshot, another miss. The bear disappears from sight.

Kathy moans and collapses to the ground.

"You okay, Kathy?" Astrid demands as she hovers over her friend. "The bear's gone...You okay? I'm sorry! We should've run the other way while he was busy with the dogs. I was stupid! Just stupid! I could've gotten you killed! I'm sorry! Are you okay?"

Kathy nods several times, gasps and gets to her feet. "I'm not hurt. Just need a minute." She bends forward, hands on knees, and takes several deep breaths before straightening and asking, "who shot at us?"

"They must've been shooting at the bear but damn careless, shooting in our direction!" Seeing Kathy is all right, Astrid turns and rushes to the dogs with Kathy close behind. Kathy goes to Tippy while Astrid falls to her knees at Buster's head and tries to staunch the flow of blood from his neck with her hands. "Buster! Stay with me buddy!" Astrid pleads. He looks up at her for a second, gives his tail a half wag, then exhales a long breath and dies.

"Agggh!" Astrid wails. She encircles his huge grizzled head in her arms and rocks back and forth, keening in grief.

Tippy raises her head and whimpers quietly as Kathy approaches. "Tippy's alive! Hurt, but alive!" She calls out as she drops to her knees next to the dog. The fur on her side is saturated with blood. Kathy carefully probes the bloody fur to expose four parallel claw marks running from just behind her foreleg on her underside up nearly to her back; deep, wicked gashes tapering to superficial scratches.

The engine noise grows louder and a small black and orange truck-like vehicle comes out of the bush, stopping a dozen meters away. The driver turns the engine off and sits watching the women, silent.

"Hello!" Astrid calls out. She stands and turns her tear-steaked face toward the new arrival. The man in the UTV doesn't respond. She squares her shoulders, watches him and waits.

At last he gets out of the cab, his rifle cradled muzzle down under his arm. He barks, "this is private property. You shouldn't of came here."

In camo cargo pants and ankle-high boots, wearing a black T-shirt and a balaclava-like mask that covers most of his face, he'd be an imposing figure even without the wrap-around sunglasses. All it would take would be some type of helmet and a vest bulging with extra magazines for his rifle, and he'd be the picture of a combat soldier. When Astrid realizes this, and that it's not out of character for a survivalist, she relaxes somewhat.

"Well? What the fuck're you doing here?" he demands.

"I—we—are looking for Hank."

"You think you're gonna find some guy named Hank out here?" He comes around to the front of the UTV, rifle still at the ready.

"N-no," Astrid says. His tense body language drives her flight instinct into high gear. She commands her feet to stay where they are, and replies, "we asked at the house but then my d-d-dogs ran off—and then the *b-b-bear!*"

"We were told Hank lives there." Kathy gets to her feet, steps in front of Astrid, and waves an arm back to indicate the log house on the rise inside the fence.

The man snorts and shuffles his feet. "Well, he don't. No trespassing sign's there for a reason. Now for your stupidity you got two dead dogs. You could of been next."

"Thanks to you, we're not! But this dog is still alive..."

"I n-n-need to get her to a vet and I need to take him home," Astrid says, pointing at Buster. "Can you help me get them to our car?"

"Leave him there."

"What?" Astrid shakes her head. "No! I n-n-need to.."

"How're you gonna take him home? Carry him? Big dog like that?"

"If you could help?"

"No."

"I'll pay you."

"I said, no."

Astrid frowns and cocks her head, then turns to Kathy and mutters under her breath, "we don't have time to argue with this f-f-fucking idiot. I'll have to leave Buster, but do you think between the two of us we can take Tippy to your car?"

"We can make a sling," Kathy says. She draws herself up to her full five foot two inches, raises her chin and fixing the strange man with a defiant glare, reefs on her shirt tails to open all the snaps. She quickly pulls the shirt off and now topless except for her sports bra, goes to Tippy.

"Here," she says to Astrid, "help me get this under her. Her main injury is on her side, here. We can wrap it around her and hopefully, we should be able to carry her and stop the bleeding at the same time." They work the shirt under Tippy as carefully as possible. "He might've heard what you said. I don't think it's a good idea to provoke him," Kathy whispers. "What *is* he wearing?"

"I think it's like militia, or combat stuff like Fletch wore sometimes."

"Fletch?"

"John Fletcher. He worked for Hazens when I did. Long story," Astrid whispers, then sobs. "What the fuck? We have to leave Buster here?" Silent tears run down her face as she concentrates on fastening the blouse at Tippy's back. "Would it kill him to put him in the back of that ATV?"

"No. But he's holding a gun. We know he's not afraid to shoot at us and we don't know what else he's capable of."

"Goddamn fuckin' lunatic!" Astrid hisses under her breath.

Kathy looks up under her lashes to see if the man reacted, but if he heard, he shows no sign. He stands unmoving, feet apart, watching.

Tippy lets out a yelp, then whines. Moving her as they must to get the blouse around her is painful but she but seems to know they're trying to help, and keeps still. Finally they pull the sleeves together over her back and knot them there.

"I think that'll do it," Astrid says, sitting back on her haunches. "I hate to move her in case she has other injuries, but what choice do we have?"

"None," Kathy says.

They stand one on each side of the dog, each with a hand near the knot in the blouse, and tentatively lift. Tippy yelps again.

"Hold it!" the man calls out. "There's cell service just up at the top of the hill behind me. Call your husband to come."

"If my husband didn't have other things to do, he would've come with us. I can't waste time waiting for him to come now, while my dog is *dying*!" She sobs, then nods to Kathy and they start back toward the road. The dog weighs under thirty kilos but even shared, it's a load. With Kathy so much shorter, it's a challenge keeping the dog's legs from dragging in the tall weeds and grass, especially with the ground sloping down toward the fence.

"You doin' okay?" Astrid asks.

"I'll manage. But maybe I should be on the higher side?"

Before they can change places, the UTV coughs to life, roars past them and stops, blocking their path. "Get in the back," the man barks.

"What about my other dog?"

The man says, "let the bear have him."

A shudder courses through Astrid's body as she visualizes sweet Buster being torn to pieces, and fresh tears spring to her eyes. Would Denver come and get him? Would it even be safe? Maybe not. Besides the bear, there's this crazy man patrolling the woods.

They ease Tippy into the box, then hop up to sit beside her, their lower legs dangling off the back. Astrid is just pulling the dog's head onto her lap when the vehicle starts off at speed, bouncing along through the rough going, the dog whimpering with every bump. When they reach the gate and turn up the driveway, the ride is smoother but the speed increases. Thankfully it's not far to the road. The vehicle pulls up behind the Sorento and stops; they barely get their feet on the ground and lift Tippy before he races off.

"Well, that was a wild ride," Astrid says.

"Can't even imagine what his wife has to put up with," Kathy says as she digs the keys out of her pocket and clicks the button on the remote to open the tailgate. "No wonder she was so cranky."

"You think he lives in that house?"

"Oh, I just assumed...I guess not necessarily."

They carefully settle Tippy inside and Astrid climbs in with her to cradle her head in her lap. "What an asshole! What a *fucking* asshole!"

"But he did save our lives." Kathy closes the hatch and hurries to the driver's seat. She starts the engine, negotiates a three-point turn on the narrow roadway and accelerates away. "Should we go straight to the vet?"

"No. We have to go right past our place anyway. Just swing in there and Den can take over driving. I'll call him as soon as we're back in cellphone range."

"That would take time. Maybe we should go straight to the vet!"

"No, it won't delay us more than a minute or two and you're half naked and covered in blood."

"So are you! Well, not naked but you have more blood on you than I do. You'll scare the shit outta anyone..."

"I don't care! I'm not going to take the time to clean up, and I'm not leaving her." The dog's eyes are closed but as Astrid rubs her ears and says, "I won't leave you, sweetie," she thumps her tail.

FROM HIS VANTAGE point on the rocky outcropping, Bearon watches the SUV speed away in a plume of dust. He goes to the Kubota, starts the engine and pilots it back to the trailhead where his father's old dog lies dead.

Pity, he thinks as he looks down at it. Blood is congealing in a pool at his neck, and flies are already gathering. *Nice old dog, life cut short by Silverface because of those stupid women! But I suppose dying a warrior is a better end than fading away until the vet puts a needle in you, eh Buster? You won't be forgotten.*

He pulls his skinning knife out of the sheath on his belt and quickly slits the dog's belly. The visceral sac containing the intestines spills out. It's messy work and the pungent, metallic smell of blood and slaughter wafts up around him. A few more quick slashes and the innards are in a heap on the ground.

He read somewhere bears have the best sense of smell of any animal in the world, two or three thousand times better than humans, and that they can smell food from several kilometers away. In the unlikely event Silverface has forgotten about the kill, it's a sure bet he smells this butchery and is on his way back. In fact, he could be watching right now, maybe only a few hundred meters away. Silverface can have the guts, and later, the rest of the dog, but he'll finish skinning it inside the bear-proof fence. It's surprising the gunshots scared him off. He won't press his luck by staying near the kill any longer than he has to.

He picks up the carcass by its fur. Even gutless, it's surprisingly heavy; with an effort, he uses his good leg to help heave it into the back of the Kubota. He climbs into the cab and starts back to the gate.

If he had recognized those women before he scared the bear off, he might have let Silverface take care of them. Or, once he realized who they were, he could have shot Kathy and said it was an accident. He was trying to save her from the bear.

The first scenario would have been the better one, although either would have meant an investigation and this place would swarm with cops and forensics and possibly goddamn snoopy reporters. He'd be interrogated. There would be lawyers. They could find out who he is. They may even discover his motive.

The only way around all that would be to "disappear" both of those women without a trace. It crossed his mind. He had the rifle at the ready. But then Astrid's husband! Goddamn Danielson knew they were coming here. He knows from experience he would come looking and he wouldn't give up easily. He's seen Kathy's husband in action, too. The two of them teamed up? Tough combination.

The last time he was in Pillerton he saw Rick and Kathy together. Goddamn it! Does he have to take Rick's wife away from him? Yes. But it's not his fault, it's hers. She should have stayed in Pillerton.

Astrid and Kathy. Together. It's given Astrid has told her about the will, so why is she still sniffing around? It can't be because she actually wants to meet her father since she must know he's dead. So why hasn't she gone home? This hasn't made sense from the beginning.

Goddamn Hayward, telling Danielson Kathy was here! He knew I didn't want it spread around, he thinks.

Hayward is almost as bad as Briggs, getting an over-sized opinion of himself since being anointed Regal Leader. Second in command of the Second Congregation. The other two are just as bad. Even Clint is starting to have an opinion about everything. Time they all were reminded where the money comes from, that they're only involved in this lucrative enterprise thanks to him, and show the proper respect. Otherwise, he'll have to cut ties. But can he trust them to keep their mouths shut if they aren't sharing the wealth? No. He'll have to figure out a way to silence them permanently. Maybe Clint's idiot son too. He's so fucking stupid, he'd brag about...

Then it hits him: he doesn't have to do anything about Kathy, not in Dark River, anyway. She can't stay here forever. Trent's shipping out with Evan in a few days. Get him to do the job in Pillerton. Tell him it's an initiation to the inner rankings. Then all he has to do is convince the Big Guys Trent has to be shut up permanently. They're good at disappearing people. And there will be no possible way to connect a man with no past living in the wilds on Bear Mountain to a couple of murders two thousand kilometers away in Shithole, Saskatchewan. It's perfect!

He's at the gate punching in the code to open it when movement in the bush catches his eye. It's the bear, and as expected, he's on his way back to the kill. Something stains the fur on his hip. Blood! He's injured. *I didn't mean to hit him! That first bullet must've ricocheted. No wonder he ran off. He'll be meaner than ever now. Goddammit!*

Or is that a good thing?

"YOU SHOULD HAVE seen Kathy face that creep down!" Astrid tells them. "I swear, she grew about six inches, just glared as if to say, 'go ahead and watch, you creepy bastard' as she took off her shirt! Thank *dog* she was wearing a button-up shirt with sleeves. My t-shirt wouldn't have done the job."

"I'm just glad I was wearing a bra. Nearly didn't put it on this morning!" Kathy says. "On the upside, I was so hot and sweaty it felt kinda good to take my shirt off."

"Well, there's a glass half full comment if I ever heard one! I think usin' your shirt for a field dressing probably saved Tippy's life," Denver says. "Thank you!"

"I, er, well, you're welcome, but I wasn't really thinking, just reacting. I know that creep saved us, but I was totally pissed! What a mean, arrogant bastard! I guess I was coming down from an adrenalin rush. When I think about it, I could've been literally pissed. I think I almost peed my pants when that bear started toward us." She giggles, then takes another deep drink of her wine before continuing: "I wanted to run but Astrid wouldn't let me."

"She was right about that," Wilson says.

"She's also right when she says you two should've beat feet outta there while the bear was busy with the dogs!" Denver opines. "Astrid, what were you thinkin', callin' the bear's attention to you by callin' the dogs? You *know* you can never call Buster off and if he had come to you, don't you think the bear would've been right behind?"

"I know, it was stupid. I guess I wasn't thinking."

"She thought if she could call the dogs off, the bear would go away and the dogs wouldn't be hurt! That's what she was thinking!" Kathy declares.

"My heart, you girls!" Denver exclaims. "You so easily could've been that bear's supper and we'd be sittin' here wonderin' where the hell you were and cursin' you for bein' late! As miserable as that guy was, I should go up there and kiss him! I owe him a bottle of Chivas."

"Yes! We could get Buster, er, Buster's remains while we're at it," Kathy says. "Bring him back to bury him here, where he belongs. Right, Astrid?"

"Right!" Astrid agrees and nods emphatically. The men exchange uneasy glances.

"I don't think he meant it, Runty," Rick says. "We're not going, but even if we did, no way we'd take you with us."

"Doubt there's still remains to be got by now," Wilson points out, giving voice to what the other two men were thinking. "That bear would not have gone far. Suppose you was foolhardy enough to go try and fetch Buster, you think you could take a meal away from a bear?"

"No. I guess not," Kathy admits.

Denver gets up and goes to the kitchen, coming back with the box of wine in one hand and three more beers held between his arm and his torso. He puts everything on the coffee table, then passes the beers around before picking up the wine box again. He gives it a jiggle back-and-forth to judge the contents, and says, "We're gonna have to make a wine run."

"You got two boxes yesterday," Astrid says. "The other's in the fridge downstairs. You don't really think we drank that much, do you?"

"Never know," Denver says with a wink at Kathy. He sets the nearly empty box on the coffee table.

"I'll just leave this where you girls can reach it." He goes back to his recliner and opens his beer, taking a deep draft. "I was just thinkin', Rick. You know how two dogs is a pack? Like they're more than the sum of their parts? I think Astrid and Kathy is a pack."

"I think you're right. Dangerous combination," Rick says. He nods and opens his beer with a *pop!*

"Like Buster and Tippy. Buster was getting senile, but he might've had sense enough to run away instead of confronting the bear if he didn't have Tippy for back-up." Denver seems deep in thought. "I wonder. Maybe we should call Wildlife Conservation and report that bear. Seems like he's aggressive. Shouldn't he have been more likely to just stay away? No way he didn't know you guys were coming and he should've just hid somewhere to watch. It was no accident he came face to face with Buster. You said it was right out in the open. Big dog like that wouldn't normally trigger a prey response I don't think. What do you think, Wilson? Any of your buddies at the Fisherman's ever mentioned it?"

"A while ago someone talked about seein' a giant bear with a white face...think it was Carson. He never seen it himself, someone else who told someone else who told him. Can't believe nuthin' Carson says, he's so fulla shit. A white-faced bear? Sounded like a tall tale."

"Well, looks like he was right this time," Astrid says. "Maybe this bear wasn't a giant but he was definitely big, right Kathy?"

"Looked like a giant to me! But maybe that's just the size of a regular grizzly?"

"You'll have quite a tale to tell at the next meeting of the Problem Solvers of the World, Fisherman's Chapter, Wilson," Astrid says. She's smiling, but despite the warm evening, she shivers.

"Now I gotta tell 'em all Carson was right. Goddammit! That sticks in my craw!"

"Well, your story sure beats the hell outta anything I've heard in a while," Denver says. "What's that Arabic or Chinese curse? 'May you live in interesting times'?"

"I could live without interesting times." Kathy sits back and sips wine while everyone seems to be mentally reviewing the bear story. Then she exclaims, "Hey! Where do you keep your Medicare card, Astrid?"

"Medicare card?"

Rick says, "Okay, everyone, switch gears. I know Kathy well enough to be sure there's a lead-in to Medicare cards somehow. What is it, Runty?"

"Well, I was just thinking how easily that bear lifted Buster, and how Buster weighs more than me. If that guy hadn't come along, we really could have been hurt as Denver pointed out, and I was just wondering where my Medicare card is. Is it with my things, you know, was it stolen from my hotel room?"

"I think if that bear got you, you wouldn't have to worry about going to the hospital. Or anything else," Rick says.

"I know, and it's stupid to waste time thinking of that when I didn't need it anyway, but you know how your thoughts can swirl around. I remembered since I renewed my driver's licence last year, it's included on that," Kathy explains.

"Mine too," Astrid says.

"Everyone's is, likely," Denver says. "Good thing we've settled that question."

"And most likely Kiersten's is on her licence, too, and everyone keeps those in their wallets, right?" Kathy looks around the group. Everyone murmurs agreement.

"So, men usually keep their wallets in their pocket. But women keep them..."

"In their purse!" Astrid exclaims.

"So, can we all agree everyone's care card is in their wallet?" Denver asks. He shrugs and looks at Rick, lifting his hands in a gesture of confusion.

"Well, remember when we were at the Riverview, when the cops came and the manager, Mr. Passmore, explained why they couldn't interview Kiersten?'

"And he said she left without telling anyone!" Astrid sits up straight and nods at Kathy.

"I still don't get it," Rick says.

"He said she left *without her purse!* When Mr. Passmore mentioned it, it just went over my head. I guess I thought wow, she must really have left in a hurry. Then this morning she said her boyfriend took her to the hospital," Kathy says. "Not just to her doctor, or, I don't know where else, but to the hospital..."

"Ahhh! So she would've needed her card," Denver concludes.

"Now that you mention it, what woman goes anywhere without her purse, anyway?" Rick asks. "If that gal is anything like my wife, she would've been sitting with her purse on her lap, likely tapping her toe, waiting for her boyfriend to show up."

"Why did she lie?" Kathy wonders. "And that coffee mug—I asked her where her favourite mug was and she said she lost it—I bet the broken mug Sergeant Villeneuve showed us the picture of is hers."

"Another lie?" Astrid asks.

"Yeah, unless someone stole it and then dropped it by the patio door. What are chances of that? I think it's more likely she took it to my patio and she's the one who dropped it. But why wouldn't she say so? It doesn't make sense."

"And why wouldn't she have picked up the pieces?"

"It only makes sense if she saw the guy, dropped it, and ran," Denver suggests.

"But then she would tell someone," Kathy says.

"Maybe that's what caused her panic attack," April says.

"She still would've told someone."

"How severe are these panic attacks, anyway?" Rick wonders. "So bad she can't even tell her boss she's leaving, or ask her boyfriend to tell him? And forgets to take her purse? Anyone buy that?"

They're all quiet, digesting this. Finally Astrid says, "She knows something and she's not talking."

"I think I need to have another chat with Sergeant Villeneuve," Denver says, getting to his feet and pulling his phone out of his pocket.

Wilson says, "Meantime, anybody innerested in some grub? Chilli's ready anytime, and I got cornbread ready to come outta the oven. It's not vegan, just vegetarian, hope that's okay. Made a pot of vegan chilli, too."

"Aww, Wilson, thank you!" Kathy gushes. "Why didn't some woman snap you up years ago?"

"Because he's so busy arguing with Carson and the rest of his cronies he doesn't even notice when a lady is giving him the come on," Denver says. He walks out onto the deck, dials a number and puts his phone to his ear.

Wilson's ears turn red but he says nothing, just shrugs and gets to his feet.

"Well, it sure does smell good," Astrid says. "I'll go get the girls."

THE DARK RIVER airport Departure Lounge is bustling with people waiting to depart, while the full load of passengers deplanes. There are separate doors for departures and arrivals, but no segregation inside.

Kathy and Rick have checked in and are standing with Astrid and Denver, trying to stay out of the way of the arrivals collecting their luggage, while they wait for their boarding call.

"I'm glad to be heading home, but sorry to leave all the same," Kathy tells Astrid.

"Sorry you didn't find your family," Astrid says, "or at least, um, a different family. Not Hazens. You know what I mean."

"Yeah, I do, and I haven't given up. I still have that sliver of hope."

"You sure seem too normal to be related to, er, *them*," Denver says.

"Hazens, at least Hank Senior, seemed completely normal too, though," Astrid says. "Junior was an ass but he could sure turn on the charm, and no one ever saw him act like a crazy person. At least no one who lived to tell."

"Don't forget, there's no doubt who Runty's mother was and she was bat shit crazy," Rick points out. "Difference is, everyone knew she was."

"Rick!"

"Sorry, Runty. Just wanted to make sure everyone knows that you could be related to the Bad Hanks and still be your sweet li'l self."

"Anyway, we'll be back! Even if just to visit you guys," Kathy says. "I can't tell you how nice it's been, getting to know you. We have so much in common, and now we're even going to have two of your beautiful Paints! I hope you know we'd love to have you guys come to our place for a visit, too."

"Denver still judges horse shows, and there's a big Paint-O-Rama in Swift Current every year. Four judges?" Astrid looks to Denver for confirmation. Seeing his nod, she continues, "four judges. If he's not judging, we could take horses to that. It's not too far from Pillerton, is it?"

"About three hours," Kathy responds. "We'd definitely meet you there!"

"Wouldn't that be cool!"

"It sure would! Of course, it'll be a while before I'm ready to actually take Mindy to a show."

"Maybe not so long. By next summer you'll be able to enter a halter class, if nothing else. Nice to get some halter points and start working on her championship."

"Championship? That doesn't seem likely. But it might be fun to do the halter thing, and an excuse to see you guys at a show!"

"I'll start teachin' Mindy to stand up before I deliver her, and I can give you a couple of showmanship lessons when I bring the horses," Denver offers.

"Oh? She has to be taught to stand? And showmanship?"

"There's a lot of prep: grooming, feeding, lunging so she's fit and so on. There's a knack to it. Not as simple as just leading your horse in and standing there."

"I suppose nothing is ever as easy as it looks."

"You got that right!" Astrid says. "And you'll need to start putting together a nice showmanship outfit. Check it out on the internet! Anyway, we'll keep in touch."

Denver says, "I'll let you know what Sergeant Villeneuve has to say once he interviews Kiersten again."

"That would be great, thanks."

"Will you update me once you've met with the probate lawyers?" Astrid asks. "I know it's none of my business..."

"Well, it is, though, since I wouldn't have even known about it if not for you."

"I admit, I'm intrigued," Astrid says. "If Kiersten doesn't tell Sergeant Villeneuve anything, I'm going to cozy up to her. Maybe I will anyway. I've already met her, so it wouldn't be crazy for me to invite her for coffee, for starters. I'm sure she's hiding something. If she knows who took your pendant..."

"Oh, Astrid, be careful!"

"Don't *wowwy*, I'll be *vewy vewy caweful,*" she says in the funny voice she sometimes speaks to her kids with, bringing a smile to Kathy's face.

"I'll get trucking arranged for your hay, and give you a call when I've connected with that horse hauler you were talking about," Rick tells Denver.

"Sure," Denver agrees. "I've been thinking, though. Might work out better for me to bring 'em down in the stock trailer. I could load the trailer with hay for the run back, too."

"Well, that sounds like a good idea, if you think you'll need more than a semi load."

"Hell, yeah. Good alfalfa mix hay at the price you're askin'? I'll take as much as you'll sell me. 'Specially since you agreed to take lumber for your new corrals to cover the shortfall between the price of the horses and the hay."

"I think we got a helluva deal on those horses, Denver."

"Maybe we could have asked more, but knowing they're going to a good home is important," Astrid says.

"Works for both of us, for sure," Rick says. "No sense the hay truck comin' back empty. It does mean I've got a lot of work ahead of me, though."

"Pfft," Kathy says, "you'll have Ryan doing most of it."

"What? You know Ryan can't build corrals by himself! Someone has to sit on the tractor running the auger."

"Of course," Astrid agrees.

"Isn't it an awful long time in the trailer for the horses, though?" Kathy asks.

"Ay-yuh," Denver says, "but a buddy of mine, a Paint breeder, his place is just outside of Calgary. I can overnight there. If we can deduct the cost of the gas from whatever a stock trailer full of alfalfa costs I'd be happy to do it."

"Hey!" Astrid exclaims, "if Den delivers the horses, the girls and I can come along!"

"That would be awesome! Meantime, keep us posted on how Tippy is doing," Kathy says. "I hope she'll be okay."

"I'm sure the vet wouldn't be letting us pick her up this afternoon if she was still in danger."

Just then Rick glances at the arrivals area. The crowd is thinning as the last few passengers retrieve luggage from the conveyor. His attention is drawn to a group just walking out the door to the parking lot: four men and a woman with blonde hair drawn back in a ponytail.

"Rick," Kathy says as she points at their departing backs.

"Yeah, Runty, I see them. That sure looks like Tina."

"I was just going to say that. Kind of looks like Carl, too."

"Can't be sure from the back but it sure did look like them. Wisht I'da noticed them sooner."

"Who's that?" Denver asks, turning to look.

"A couple of people we know from home," Kathy explains. "The guy who owns Big Al's, which is Rick's favourite hangout, and Rick's ex-wife."

"It doesn't make sense," Rick says. "What would they come here for? I don't mean to dis your town, guys, but before Runty's letters, I'd never even heard of Dark River. What are chances of what, five? Six? People from a town as small as Pillerton being at the airport here at the same time? It would be a helluva coincidence."

"It can't be them," Kathy concludes.

The boarding call comes over the loudspeakers.

"Guess that's us," Rick says.

The men shake hands as Astrid and Kathy hug each other. Rick picks up the carry-on and they join the queue at the departure gate, with Kathy turning to give a final wave before going out the door.

AS HE AND Astrid head back to their truck, Denver spots the Autobiography in the parking lot. Four men are stashing luggage in the back; a woman with a long blonde ponytail stands by. "That's the woman Kathy said she thought was Rick's ex," he says.

"Yeah? I didn't see them."

"They were on their way out, so we just saw their backs. The ponytail, though…"

"Wanna go introduce yourself?"

"Nope!" He pulls his phone out of his pocket and takes photos of the group. "I'll send Rick some pictures, though."

"Why do you care?"

"It's just another curious thing. You know I've been wondering about that vehicle, and three days ago I'd never even heard of Pillerton. And now a group of people from a town not much bigger than a shit stain a couple thousand kilometers away, is climbing into it?" His thoughts trail off as he stands watching the Autobiography until it drives out onto the highway and speeds off.

"You ever hear the expression: 'it's a small world'? And I doubt Rick and Kathy would appreciate you calling their hometown a shit stain," Astrid tells him when he finally climbs into the truck.

"Where d'ya think I got it from?"

It isn't until he's reviewing the photos later Denver recognizes one of the men. "Whoever they are, Briggs knows them," he mutters under his breath. Briggs is from Saskatchewan but didn't he say he lives in Regina? But Pillerton isn't that far from Regina. He makes a mental note to ask Evan who these people are the next time he sees him.

EIGHTEEN

DON'T BE SILLY

"JUST SO YOU know, I won't be coming out here again."
Annie puts her phone in her purse as she picks it up, turns
her back to Bearon, and starts walking toward the door.

"What? What do you mean?"

"Just what I said. I'm not coming back," she says over
her shoulder.

"Don't be silly."

"See? You call me silly. I'm not being silly!" She turns
to face him, lower lip trembling. "Why do you think me
calling an end to this—this—this *thankless*, one-sided
relationship is me being silly?"

Bearon gets up from his lounger and comes to her,
cupping her shoulders as he draws her to him to kiss her.
She remains rigid and although she allows the kiss, she
doesn't kiss him back.

"What's this all about?" he asks quietly. "What's
wrong?"

"As if you don't know!" This comes out as a near-sob;
Annie shrugs his hands off her shoulders and pulls away.

"No, sweetheart, I don't know." He reaches for her hand
but she snatches it away.

"Now I'm *sweetheart*?"

"Of course, you're sweetheart. You're *my* sweetheart. You know that."

"No, I don't know that, because that's the first time you've ever called me that."

"Naw, that's not true!" He takes her hand again and this time she draws a couple of deep breaths but doesn't pull away.

"I'm sorry, sweetheart, I always think of you as my sweetheart. If I haven't told you that before, I should have." He pulls her close and puts both arms around her. She doesn't return the hug and leaves her arms hanging by her sides, but doesn't move away.

"You're feeling bad about something. Let's sit down and talk about it."

She allows him to lead her to the couch in the living room and when they're both sitting, he pulls her close again. "Tell me about it, Annie," he whispers. "Come on. I hate to see you feeling bad but help me out here, sweetheart. I really don't know what's bothering you."

She's quiet for a couple of minutes while he strokes her hair, then says, "Do you think I like being passed around to your friends? I only do it as a favour to you. Because you say it helps you out. But I *hate* it! I'm sure they all think I'm a slut."

"Naw..."

"Yeah, they do! They don't have no respect for me! And now this week-end, with that...that *ritual*! All those people will remember me when they come in to Dot's...and those *strangers*...!" This last comes out as a sob.

"They'll remember how awesome you are, and you'll remember them, too," Bearon reminds her. He holds her tight, tucking her head in and kissing the back of her neck, letting her cry. *Goddammit,* he thinks, *she can't walk! How will I replace her? Maybe Kiersten? She is a good fuck, but would she even get wet if she saw me in the daylight? Annie's the only person around here who has seen me without my hood. She's gotten used to what I look like but it took a while. No, better do something to keep her.*

When her sobs abate, he says, "sweetheart, you know the teachings. Now you're not only a True Believer, but you're also Purified and a Ceremonial Wife! You're *my* Cere-monial Wife!"

"I'm *everyone's* Ceremonial Wife!"

"And all the men are your Ceremonial Husbands. And no one thinks less of you, in fact everyone loves you. Everyone loves everyone. Like it's meant to be. You've read the bible. Men always had many wives, even among their brothers' wives and their own daughters. It's only when the False Religions got powerful that it changed. It's the natural way of things. Like a pride of lions. Two or three males looking after any number of females. Humans are not meant to be any different."

He strokes her hair, then holds her away a bit and says, "You know, I have something for you. I got it for your birthday but I think I'll give it to you now. I was having a hard time keeping it secret anyway. I've been fantasizing how it will look on you."

He pushes away from her and gets slowly to his feet, turning his face away from her so she can't see him clenching his jaw against the needles of pain in his hip.

"You stay right here. I'll be back in a minute."

He goes to his office and slumps down in the chair and opens the pencil drawer. There's a bottle of Oxycontin, and he dry swallows a couple of tablets, then closes that drawer and opens the file drawer. Behind the last file is a small box. He comes back to sit next to Annie and hands it to her.

"Here, sweetheart. Open it."

She takes the lid off the box to expose a sturdy gold chain with a large round pendant, and gasps. "Oh my god!" She lifts the pendant and examines it closely. "Is it a coin? Some kind of actual coin?"

"Yeah, a real old one. You like it?"

"Oh, I do! I do! But it must've been expensive."

"Yeah, it's expensive. I wouldn't insult you by giving you something cheap, sweetheart. I wanted to prove how much I value you." He kisses her, and coaxes, "put it on. The chain should be long enough to fit over your head so you don't have to undo it. Here," he takes it from her and holds it up to her forehead.

She ducks her chin and Bearon works the chain over her hair until it's around her neck. He opens the top buttons on her Dot's Diner shirt and lets the coin slip inside to nestle in her cleavage.

"Beautiful," he whispers huskily, and plants kisses around it. Then he tells her, "I, er, there's another reason I didn't give it to you sooner. I worry—I've been worrying. I don't think you should let anyone see it. It's worth quite a bit. Some of those guys at Dot's see it on you—you know the guys I mean—if one of them realizes how much it's worth, they might hurt you to get it. I'd feel awful if you got hurt."

Annie's eyes fill. "Oh sweetie! Thank you!"

"Maybe you should leave it here and just wear it for me when we're making love."

"No, I'll be careful. I'm sorry I was so…"

"Don't say another word. Just be sure to keep it tucked in outta sight, then," he says.

"I will!"

He works his hands into her bra to scoop her breasts out and pushes his face into her cleavage.

"Bear, I have to go…"

"This won't take long," he murmurs. "You know how hot you make me." He pushes his erection against her thigh.

She slides down to kneel on the floor and turns to him, working her hands into his sweatpants. "Here, baby, let me take care of that for you."

Her hot mouth with its busy tongue feels wonderful; he lets out a husky groan. Is the Oxy kicking in already or is it Annie's attentions that makes him forget his aching hip? He collapses back to enjoy it. But he's thinking, *goddamn fuckin' shit! That necklace must be worth thousands. Now how am I going to get it back?*

And then he's surprised by the realization he is fond of Annie. Fond enough to let her keep the pendant. It's a small price to pay for all she does for him. Anyway, it's only money, and he'll soon have a lot more of that.

NINETEEN

UNDERCOVER

CLINT SLOUCHES BACK on the sofa after draining his beer. The room is illuminated only by the reruns of Law and Order, Special Victims Unit on the sixty inch flat screen TV. It's nearly three a.m., and he should be sleeping. He can't, though, because his bedroom is occupied, and he's trying hard not to listen to the sounds coming from it. Sounds that are getting louder.

He takes the remote for the TV, punches up the volume, and reminds himself he shouldn't be pissed that she's so loud. It's not her fault she's with him, after all, and he did tell her she should always fake an orgasm and make sure it's convincing.

"Doesn't have to make it *that* fuckin' convincing," he mutters.

The sounds coming from the bedroom stop, but it isn't until a full nineteen minutes by his watch that he hears the shower running. He thinks, *what the hell? Were they cuddling?*

Finally Bearon comes out into the living room. "Thanks, Clint," he says. "You know, we wouldn't have to kick you out of your bed if you put some furniture in the other bedroom. Why don't I send something? Excess from the Lodge."

"Sure. Or maybe I should just send her to your place and she can come back in the morning."

"All kinds of reasons why that won't work. Not open for discussion. Best thing you can do is to get her True Believer status."

"Workin' on it," Clint says. He stands, clicks the TV off, and tosses the remote on the coffee table.

"Good." Bearon goes out the door, letting it slam behind him.

Clint watches out the window as the Range Rover leaves, then locks the door and goes back to the bedroom. The light in the ensuite is on, and Kiersten is in the shower. He debates joining her but thinks better of it, drops his boxers and climbs into the still-warm bed instead. With his head on the pillow, his senses are assaulted by the smell of the other man, and sex. He gets up, pulls on sweat pants, and goes back to the living room.

Finally he hears the water stop running, and in moments, Kiersten comes into the living room, one towel wrapped around her torso and another turban-like on her head.

"Oh, here you are," she says. "Coming to bed?"

"No."

"But it's the middle of the night."

"No. Really?"

She eases down onto the sofa beside him and takes his hand. "Bothers you?"

"What do you think?"

"Clint, baby, I…"

"I know. It's not your fault." He blows out a long breath.

They sit quietly for the passing of several minutes, then Clint pulls her into a hug and says. "Really. I know it's not your fault. You're a trooper, doing it just for me. Tell me something, though. You fantasize it's me when he's in you?"

"I told you I do."

"Is he better than me? Bigger?"

"Clint, don't..."

"Forget I asked!" Clint pushes her away and stands. "I'm just going to shower and then hit the road."

"Oh? So early?"

"Yeah, nice to get an early start."

"When are you back?"

"Dunno for sure. Sometime next week. Don't worry. You won't be lonely. He's coming back again tomorrow night and the way things are going, maybe all this week again. You'll hardly have time to even think about me. I might as well move out."

"Baby, you don't mean that! You can't move out. And I think of you all the time. I love you!"

"Yeah," Clint says, and reminds himself she's not a real girlfriend, just another ho getting softened up to join the fucking pool. "Tell you what. Why don't you get your things moved in here while I'm away? Des must have a buddy with a pickup. He can help you move."

"Oh, Clint," Kiersten exclaims, "thank you, baby! I'll have everything all nice when you get back!"

"Sure." Clint gives her a quick kiss, then gets up and goes to the linen closet at the end of the hall for fresh towels. He heads through the bedroom and into the ensuite, where he starts the shower just vacated by Kiersten. Moments after he climbs in, Kiersten comes in, drops her towels, and joins him. She squirts shower gel into her hand and begins lathering his genitals. As water pelts down on them she looks up and says, "by the way, the Vampire said something interesting. He's coming into a lot of money soon."

"Yeah, I know. He's always coming into a lot of money soon. He loves to brag about the business. That the business…is…booming."

"Not business. Something else."

"What?"

"I don't know. Just that it's nothing to do with anything else. And it's a lot of money."

"Oh?"

"Want me to try and find out what it's about? You know, if there's a next time?"

"Whenever you can, baby. Make sure he doesn't get suspicious, though."

"I won't. He likes to talk. Maybe he has no one else to talk to.

"I don't think that's it. He's got plenty of people begging to suck his dick."

"You mean figuratively. And I'll bet they're all men, and you know men never talk about anything important. They tell women things they'd never talk about with other men."

"More likely it's because you're such a good listener. And you must be putting on a convincing act in the sack or he wouldn't keep coming back for more."

He wishes he could convince himself it's just an act. Another thing Bearon brags about besides all the money he has or is going to have, is the size of his dick.

He thinks, *I'll have to get used to him using her. What he doesn't know is that I'm using him. She's my asset. My undercover agent. Literally under cover.*

Between that thought and the attention she's paying to his erection, he forgets he's resentful.

TWENTY

NEWS HOUR

ASTRID TURNS INTO the cul-de-sac and scans the houses
for the green rancher with number 117 above the garage
doors. It's at the end, set back further than its neighbours
behind a tidy lawn and surrounded by low shrubs. She pulls
into the driveway and turns off the engine.

Kiersten comes out the front door and locks it behind
her, then trots down the steps and comes to the passenger
door.

"Hi, Astrid," she says as she pulls the door open and
climbs in. "Thanks for picking me up!"

"You're welcome," Astrid responds. "So. Where should
we go? It's such a nice day maybe we should sit outside
somewhere. Riverview has a nice patio."

"Yeah, but you know, I'm there so much. Could we go
somewhere else?"

"Sure. Let's see…how about Cherry Creek? I think they
have a patio."

"They do. I've been there with Clint. It's nice."

"Cherry Creek it is, then," Astrid agrees, and backs out
of the driveway.

At the pub, Kiersten leads the way to the patio at the back. As they're passing through the restaurant, a server says, "sit wherever you want. I'll be right with you."

Once seated under an umbrella next to the planter and rail structure that encloses the patio, Kiersten says, "you have no idea how happy I was to hear from you, Astrid! I miss having a girl friend. I've been in town since April and haven't managed to make any friends yet."

"Well, at last we found a time that worked for both of us to actually get together and not just gab on the phone," Astrid says. "I'm not really social myself, but I thought you'd have lots of friends by now. Working the desk at the Riverview, you meet lots of people, like Kathy."

"She lives so far away, though. That's the problem with meeting people through my job. They're always just passing through. Kathy and I were just getting to know each other."

"But your boyfriend, he must have friends you all hang out with."

The server appears and puts menus on the table. She asks, "can I get you something while you're deciding what you want?"

"Just coffee for now," Astrid tells her.

"I'll have a glass of house red," Kiersten says.

"Sure thing." The server bustles away.

"Since you're driving, I might as well take advantage of the opportunity to have wine with lunch," Kiersten says. "Do you like nachos? They make a great sharing size here."

"Sure! Let's have that," Astrid agrees. "I guess you're the designated driver when you go out?"

"Yeah, of course. Isn't that how it works for every couple?"

"Well, my husband never has more than one or two beers when we go out. Which isn't very often. He's a big guy so it's not enough that he's even close to the limit. Good thing, because sometimes all it takes for me to get a buzz is one glass!"

"I know, hey? Me too! Funny how that works!"

"So, your boyfriend. He must have friends who have girlfriends. None of them you could be friends with?"

"He's got friends, but we don't hang with them. Clint has only been living here a few years, and he's on the road a lot. His friends are guys he works with. He says when he's home, the last thing he wants to do is spend his time with them!" Kiersten chuckles. "I've only met one. And we don't socialize with *him*."

"No?"

"No. He's a big, creepy guy. I call him the Vampire because I've never seen him except in the dark. I told Clint I think he can't come out until the sun goes down but Clint says he's got lots of friends and we're lucky he spends any time with us, but socialize? *Eww.* I don't think so. It surprises me anyone would want to hang out with him. But he's the boss, so..."

"Where does your boyfriend—what's his name? Clint?—where does he work?"

"I don't know the name of the company, but he's a scout, like a talent scout. I think he's a freelancer, actually. Like I said, he's on the road a lot. When he's home, he doesn't talk about work. He doesn't have, like, a nine-to-five or anything. I guess it's commission. All I know is the pay must be good. You saw his house."

"It looks nice," Astrid says.

"Yeah. And he's also got an expensive sports car and a watch, a Rolex he says set him back over ten thousand dollars. Imagine!"

"Man, really? That's kinda crazy! How many people even wear watches anymore?"

"I know! Mostly Baby Boomers. I look at my phone when I want to know what time it is. Or did, before I got this." She reaches her arm out to show Astrid her watch.

"Oh, is it a FitBit?"

"It's an Apple Watch, actually, but it counts steps like a FitBit. I don't know half the things it does, I just use it like a watch. Clint gave it to me."

"So, lookit that, it's got a heart rate monitor. Does it help with your, er, you know..."

"Help with what?"

"Your panic attacks. So you know when..."

"I, um," Kiersten cocks her head and looks away for a second and studies the menu card for a moment before continuing. "I, er, that is, that's why Clint gave it to me."

Astrid watches Kiersten's face, notes her squirming, and says, "well, those things are expensive."

"Yeah, it's an expensive gift," Kiersten says, and brightens. "He's the best thing that ever happened to me. I'm not so crazy about his religion. He's mostly away on week-ends and services are Sunday so we don't have to go very often. I'm an atheist, so we don't talk about it."

"That's probably wise," Astrid opines, thinking how difficult it must be to sit through church services when you don't believe any of it. She decides against suggesting Kiersten tell the guy he can go alone, and instead changes the subject. "So, have you heard about the big fancy dinner they're putting on for the grand opening of the Bear Mountain Lodge?"

"Sure. I think everyone has."

"Maybe you and Clint could come with my husband and me."

"Oh, thanks, but we can't. Clint's out of town."

"That's too bad. It would be nice to have company. You could come with us, though."

"I, er, thanks, but I'm working too."

The server arrives with their drinks and asks if they're ready to order.

"Yes," Astrid tells her, "we'll have the share size nachos."

When the server has moved on, Kiersten asks, "what about you? I know you're married, and that you own the mill. Do you have kids?"

"Yup! Two kids, a dog and horses too. I guess that's why I don't socialize more."

"Hey, your mill is right across the road from Heather's House, isn't it?"

"Yeah, and we live next door."

"Oh, wow! Do you think it's true that they kidnap girls?"

"No, it's not true!" Astrid snaps, then takes a deep breath, shakes her head and sits back. "That's our foundation, you know."

"Oh! I'm sorry! I didn't know."

"All it takes is one crazy person to start a vicious rumour. Fact is, women that end up in Heather's House are often transient to start with. It's true they sometimes just disappear without letting us know they're leaving, but we sure as *hell* don't kidnap them!"

"I didn't mean to suggest...it's just that I know..."

"You know what, exactly?"

"Nothing. Forget I said anything."

"No, really. I want to know."

Kiersten shrinks into the back of her chair, her face twisted in anguish.

Astrid sighs and says, "I'm sorry. I didn't mean to jump on you like that, but it's a sore point. We've had government people all over us and it even looked for a while like we might be shut down. We don't get anything out of it, I mean, financially, and it's a pain in the ass to be involved at the best of times without being treated like criminals. Sometimes I think we *should* shut it down. It seemed to be such a good idea at the beginning and now, honestly, I'd be glad to be out of it. But the need is so great! To think we might be shut down because of what one crazy person..." She sits back and is relieved when the server provides a break in the conversation by bringing the nachos.

"But Astrid," Kiersten says when the server has moved on, "I think there might be something to it. I mean, not you guys, but that *someone* is taking girls."

"Are you talking about the new Bear Mountain Lodge being just like the old Spirit Bear Lodge?"

"Is that what it was called? But yeah, that's it. Some of the girls at work were talking about it in the break room.

One of them said she thinks the girls from Heather's House are scooped up and taken to the Lodge so it can just keep on like before. A gentleman's club, they call it. You wouldn't believe how many tourists ask about it."

"Great thing for the town to be famous for, eh? But I, uh, I've thought about it, too. Not about Heather's supplying the girls, but there's other places they can get them from. My husband tells me it's a crazy thought, as if there could be a rape-murder club continuing on from before. He reminds me that all the guys were killed in the explosion."

"They were all killed? Who was all killed?"

"The previous owners, or the members too, I guess, of the old lodge. It was right about the time I moved here, so a few years before you came. There was a prominent businessman, the mill owner, and even the pastor of one of the churches here in Dark River."

"No! Really? A pastor?"

"Yeah. And the businessman in question owned a bunch of restaurants including Dot's, which my friend Franny bought through a court ordered sale after he was killed. After they were all killed."

"Wow." Kiersten sits quietly for a moment as if trying to make sense of it. Then she says, "I think there might be something to it, though."

"Why? I mean, why do you think that?"

Kiersten leans forward and whispers, "I can't tell you. Just believe me when I say that it's possible. And I have, er, that I know... That is, I have reason to—oh! You can't tell anyone! Please don't tell anyone I said anything!" She looks anxiously around, her forehead creased and lower lip trembling.

"I won't," Astrid agrees, "don't worry." But her mind races. She was right, Kiersten knows more than she told the cops. Should she press her on it? But she looks so anxious. Maybe it's best to change the subject in hopes she might confide more over time.

"Well, we all have secrets. There's lots I wouldn't want anyone to know about, either." When she sees Kiersten nod and her expression brighten, she continues, "so, do you have any kids? Pets? Hobbies?"

As Kiersten babbles about the cat she adopted from a rescue after moving in with Clint, Astrid thinks ahead to the video call she'll have later with Kathy. She feels uneasy, pretending to befriend Kiersten to get information from her. But there's more to the story. If the break-in to Kathy's room wasn't to steal her belongings but to grab her, like if the bastard only got scared off when she didn't come in alone, and if Kiersten is part of that, then other girls are at risk.

The cops have already lost interest in what they say was a random break and enter. She can't go to Jacques and ask him to look into it again on the basis of an ambiguous remark and because Astrid thinks Kiersten is nervous about something. The end, as they say, justifies the means.

LATER THAT NIGHT, at the end of the second period of the Canuck's game, Wilson announces he's going to go do night check at the barn.

"Why?" Astrid asks. "Jake not here tonight?"

"Ay-yuh, he's here."

"So…?"

Wilson says, "somethin' 'bout that guy bothers me. Prob'ly nuthin'."

"I'll go with you," Denver says.

"No need. I'll be back before puck drop." Wilson heads out the back door; in minutes, they hear an engine start and the ATV roars away.

With Wilson gone, Astrid tells Denver about lunch, and her fears Kiersten knows something about the Lodge and the kidnapping of girls.

"She heard Heather's House was where they got the girls from."

"I hope you straightened her out about that."

"Yeah, well, about Heather's House, anyway."

"You're still suspicious of the Lodge?"

"I am. Not just the Lodge, but that there's still some of the old club members around, up to no good again," Astrid admits. "And I'm sure Kiersten knows more than she lets on. She said she *knows*, not *thinks*, and that she has *good reason,* but she wouldn't say more and got really worried, looking around like someone might be watching. Made me promise not to tell anyone she said anything. And not only that, her boyfriend is a talent scout, for Pete's sake. What's a talent scout doing out here? And that his boss is a creepy guy. A vampire. Says he can't go out in sunlight or at least he only goes out after dark."

"Well, it's starting sound like she belongs in a padded room at Nechako Manor."

"What if she's not crazy, though. What if there's something to it?"

"Hmmm." Denver thinks for a moment, then says, "well then, you and Kathy better quit nosin' around."

"But what if we're the only ones who can stop it? You know Jacques has taken it as far as he can. What would it take for the RCMP to re-open the case as an attempted abduction instead of a B and E?"

"Hmm. I don't know."

"Do they have to wait until someone, another woman, is abducted?"

"There really haven't been any missing girls or women from around here, though."

"That we know of, you mean. What if the women who left Heather's suddenly actually were abducted? And what if they're getting women from all over, not just Dark River? Do the cops have any way of finding out?"

"You mean a special unit, like in the Lower Mainland? I don't know if they have the resources. For sure the Dark River Detachment is already stretched too thin."

"And Kathy really wants answers. You heard what she said about wanting a family connection. Think how you'd feel if all your life you thought you had no family?"

"Babe," he says gently, "why don't you just tell her?"

Astrid bites her lower lip, studies her folded hands, and finally says, "I can't."

"She'd be overjoyed—"

"I can't!" Astrid shakes her head and looks off. "I just can't. We talked about this. You know why I can't tell her. Imagine growing up knowing your father was a serial killer."

"Okay. Well, we'll carry on, then. And just be careful. Maybe we should join the gun club. Dust off some of those guns you inherited, and learn how to use 'em."

Astrid jerks to attention at this suggestion and gives Denver a sharp look.

"Don't look at me like that! It's no crazier than thinkin' the murder club is still carrying on. In fact, if you're right and it is, it's downright sensible."

"I guess."

"And if I can think of a way to convince Jacques that you haven't gone off the deep end, I'll talk to him about it, too."

"Oh, that would be great!"

Denver gets up out of his recliner, goes into the kitchen and comes back with a fresh beer and a glass of wine for Astrid. He sets them on the coffee table and slides in next to her on the couch, pulling her into his arms. "Don't worry, babe. When I told you I'd take care of you, I meant it."

Halfway into third period, the Canucks, down by two, have just scored. There's a commercial break, and Denver looks at his watch. "Thought Wilson would've been back by now," he says.

At that moment, the text alert on Denver's phone chimes. He pulls away from Astrid to read it, then turns to her and says, "I have to go. There's a problem at the barn."

"What? Is someone...one of the horses...hurt?"

"Nope. Not a horse. Can't be sure about Jake, though. Looks like Wilson interrupted a drug buy." Denver gets up and hurries to the back door. "I'll keep you posted."

TWENTY-ONE

PILLERTON

KATHY IS AT her desk working through a backlog of email. Back at work for weeks, she still isn't caught up. She blames it on all the time she's had to spend dealing with the drama of Godzilla firing Pat while she was away, but in fairness, she didn't actually fire her, just shit on her enough that she walked out. That's only the most recent and most extreme episode of the Godzilla Show.

More and more often, Kathy wonders if buying into the agency was a mistake. It seemed like a great opportunity at first, but being a minority shareholder in a private company means even if you're the managing partner you have no control over the bookkeeping. The controlling partner can run all sorts of expenses through the company to make sure there's never any profit, ergo, no bonus cheque either, and if you resign, forget about getting a realistic valuation on your shares.

Just hang on, she tells herself. *Godzilla's going to retire.* But she keeps pushing her retirement date back and the price she wants for her share, up.

Kathy runs the place, doesn't get paid for the hours of overtime she works, and on top of it, has to put up with

Godzilla. Now instead of being happy, Godzilla is mad because Kathy smoothed Pat's ruffled feathers and got her to come back. It's not easy finding licenced agents anywhere, and virtually impossible in a town as small as Pillerton. And training a new agent takes months, years even, for someone to take the courses and pass the licencing test. Meanwhile, a licenced agent, in this case Kathy, has to pick up the slack.

I put in enough unpaid hours as it is, Kathy thinks. She sighs and leans against the back of the chair, working her shoulders back and forth to ease the stiffness. When she reaches for her coffee on its little electric warmer, she glances through her office door to see Millie at the counter, serving a bald customer. Millie's head is down as she explains something, probably how many claims-free years he'd have to have to qualify for the various levels of discounts. But the man isn't looking at the paperwork; instead, he's staring at Kathy. When their eyes meet, his brows draw together and his eyes narrow.

Kathy draws a sharp breath and a shudder passes through her. In a heartbeat, the man turns and strides out of the office, leaving Millie to watch his retreating back before clicking her tongue, gathering up the paperwork and returning to her desk.

Kathy gets up and goes to stand in the doorway to the outer office. "What was that all about, Millie?" she asks.

"I don't know," Millie says. "It was odd. He said he wanted car insurance but he didn't have any papers with him. Just moved here, doesn't have an address yet. So he wastes my time and then just walks out? Not even a thank you." She tosses the paperwork in the recycling bin and goes back to her chair.

"Jerk!" Pat pipes up from behind her monitor. "I hope he doesn't come back. Something about him gave me the creeps. Maybe all those tattoos."

"Lots of guys look like that these days," Kathy says. "Shave their heads and get those bulging muscles at the gym rather than working, like throwing bales. I think it's because they all want to look like MMA fighters."

"Oh, yeah," Millie agrees, "Mixed Martial Arts. I've seen it advertised on TV."

"I'll take our Pillerton farm boys any day! Oh, for the days when guys shaved their faces instead of their heads," Pat says. "And wore jeans that weren't a fart away from falling off."

A car pulls into the angle parking stall right outside the door. A small woman with short grey curls gets out from behind the wheel and stands with her phone to her ear, looking toward the office as if trying to see through the solar film on the windows. She's waving her free hand around as she yells into the phone loud enough to be heard inside the office.

"Looks like Godzilla's off her meds again," Pat says, and turns her attention to her monitor.

The woman puts the phone in her purse and comes toward the door, pushing her oversized sunglasses back up on her head as she steps into the shade and reaches for the door handle.

"Thought she wasn't coming in again this week," Millie says. "She does know we can see her even if she can't see us, doesn't she?"

"If she doesn't, I'm not going to tell her. In fact, I'm not going to talk to her at all." Pat opens a file and starts flipping papers, then picks up the telephone to make a call.

Kathy draws a deep breath and goes back into her office. Godzilla coming in today is a surprise. "What now?" she mutters under her breath as she takes her seat behind her desk.

She's really going to flip out when she learns I'm leaving early today. Maybe she's just come to raid the petty cash for the second time this week and will be gone again before Rick gets here to pick me up.

Godzilla storms through the front office without so much as acknowledging Pat or Millie. She doesn't pause at the door to Kathy's office to wait for an invitation, either, just strides to her desk, looms over it and slams a paper down.

"I just got this renewal notice in the mail. The premium on my Elm Street property has gone up again! Didn't I tell you to take care of that? I was on the phone with Madeline at the company just now. I told her it's your screw-up and that you will get in touch to straighten it out. She's expecting a call from you. Now!"

"Oh, hello Carol," Kathy says. Not for the first time, she thinks, *this is no way to live.*

TWENTY-TWO

HEAVYWEIGHT

EVAN LEANS BACK in his chair and swivels side to side a couple of times, studying the young man lounging in the armchair across the desk from him. He thinks, *goddamn, you don't have to be gay to appreciate how handsome Reardon is. How did he ever sire an ugly little rat like Trent?*

Well, he's not little; he's taller than Evan by enough that he has to look up to him, and likely outweighs him by twenty kilos, all of it muscle. Maybe he wouldn't be ugly if it wasn't for that flattened nose and those messed-up eyebrows. The missing tooth doesn't help, but then he doesn't smile often so it's not all that noticeable. Maybe he's just had his face beaten in a few too many times.

Coming to that conclusion, Evan turns his mind to the reason Trent is here, leans forward and says, "so, you got it done?"

"Uh, uh, no. Gotta have a plan, you know."

"Yeah, I know, but you've had weeks. What's the hold-up?"

"Well, I'm just makin' a plan."

"You know, I'm beginning to think you can't do it. I should get someone else."

"Whaddaya mean? I spent lots of time surveillancing her—"

"Lots of time for *surveillancing* when you weren't busy sucking Arnie's dick, was there?"

"Sucking...? No!" Trent frowns. "I ain't no cocksucker!"

"It's a figure of speech."

"Oh." He leans slightly forward and looks Evan in the eye. "Well, you told me to make friends with the bikers. That's what I done." He slouches back again and picks his right nostril with his thumb before continuing. "Anyhow, I learnt her habits, what time she goes where and all that kinda shit. You gotta surveillance, learn their routine, you know. Otherwise you fuck up and get caught! You think I just grab her in the parkin' lot or maybe outta her office? She's always got people around. Like I said. I been waitin' for a chance. When she's alone. And anyway, you promised to renumerate me. I'm countin' on that money."

"Dozens of guys can *surveillance* someone. It takes a heavyweight—"

"I'm a heavyweight! I told you, I can do it," Trent says. He looks around, and seeing no one near the glass surround of the office, leans forward. "I done it before."

"Oh yeah?"

"Yeah. 'Member last spring, them two dudes who nobody seen after they got off a fish boat in Port Hardy?"

"You did them, did you?"

"Yeah."

"Oh, yeah. I forgot, you're from Vancouver Island. So you offed those two guys? Hey, was it you did that dude in Nanaimo who ran that escort service?"

"N-no-no. Um, well, not that trip anyway." His eyes narrow and he squirms in his seat as he looks at the wall behind Evan's shoulder.

Evan notes the classic tell of a liar. It's an eyeroll moment; he has to force himself not to smile as he watches Trent's facial expressions change while he tries to figure out a way to claim responsibility for a third murder, one that didn't happen. After a moment, Evan continues, "so, how did you manage to take out two guys? That couldn't have been easy."

"Well, it wasn't just me, it was me and my brother, Des. But it was my job." Trent gives a sharp nod to punctuate his statement. "Them guys had their duffle bags stuffed with coke. Probably ten keys each. Pure, uncut, beautiful stuff."

"So you cut it and..."

"Well, no, we just delivered it. It was a contract, see?"

"So, what did you get paid for that job?"

"Same as your job, ten large. We each got ten large."

"What do you think the street value of that much blow was?"

"I, er, umm. Dunno, lots prob'ly," he says with a shrug.

"Yet you handed it all over for $20K."

"Suppose you think we shoulda kept it? Des says it's a fuckin' big deal, you know, cuttin' it, baggin' it, then you gotta have a way to distur...er, disturbute it. And you don't fuck with them guys, neither. Mrs. Reardon didn't raise no idiots! Better to each take our ten K and fuck off. Bought my car, drove up to Prince George, and then we partied for a week." He grins, showing his missing eye tooth. "*Fuck* I hated to leave my ride in Dark River."

"You got paid for it."

"Not fuckin' enough! It was a classic."

"That's the car that didn't start half the time, wasn't it? You were lucky to get anything."

"It just needed a little work," Trent shrugs and shakes his head, then says, "Anyhow. Point is, I done that dude. This little job of yours, this little twat, it'll be a cake walk."

"So, how did you do it?"

"Do what?"

"The dudes."

"Oh, the dudes. Mo'fuckers was hitchhikin'. Me and Des, we got tipped off when to expect 'em so we waited for 'em and picked 'em up. Should of heard 'em laughin', it was rainin' so they was happy as pigs in shit to get a ride so quick! We stopped for a piss just before the Majestic Grove. That's a park with fuckin' big trees. 'What're we stoppin' here for,' one of 'em said. 'Have to piss,' I told him. 'There's toilets at Majestic Grove,' he said. Lots of tourists, too, you know? So NFG for us, for our plans. Couldn't say that, a'course. So I called 'em a couple a pansies, can't piss in the bush, afraid of spiders maybe? And I told 'em we're stopping now and we ain't gonna stop again til we get to Duncan which is where they wanted to go. So if they thought they wouldn't have to piss for another five hours they could just wait in the car, I told 'em. 'Course if they had of, we would of had to of either did 'em in the car and I don't need *that* fuckin' mess, or drag 'em out and who knows how bad that might go what with cars passin' by. But they saved us the trouble, got out and went into the bush with us like good little fuckers. Wouldn't even leave their duffle bags in the car. Took 'em with 'em, as if *that* did 'em any good! I went up behind one guy and Des went behind the other, and *keeche*!" He gestures a slash across his neck, then shakes his head and chuckles. "Des hadn't done his guy yet, thought it would be fun to let him watch. Just had his arm wrenched up behind him and his big ol' pig sticker on his throat. Shoulda seen the fucker's eyes pop when he saw his friend's head flop, blood gushin' outta his neck, and figured out he was next!"

"Messy."

"Yeah, well, that's why you do it from behind, see? Anyhow, don't worry, we washed 'em up nice."

"Oh?"

"Yeah. I told you the reason we was stoppin' was to take a piss! I really did need to. We musta drank a dozen beers, waitin' on them to come along," he laughs louder this time. "By the time they got found, we was partyin' in Dark River. Perfect crime."

He leans back in the chair and slings one leg over the arm, giving his genitals a tug as he does so, the expression on his face smug. "Don't worry. The gash you want disappeared won't be breathin' this time tomorrow. I'll get her on her way home from work tonight. But I need the money now. Got to put a deposit on a place today or they're gonna rent it to someone else. Don't wanna keep livin' in a motel, cost of that mounts up, eh?"

"You really think I'll pay you before you do the job?"

"Well, um, okay. If not all, at least two K."

"What did you do with the money you got for the motel job? And for your car, for that matter?"

"Didn't get much for the motel job. The big guy blamed me for it goin' bad, which ain't fair, but anyhow, he's the boss. Hadda buy another ride. Hadda live somewhere once we got here too. Told you, a motel room ain't cheap. Hadda borrow money from my ol' man already."

Evan shrugs, "Okay. I'll give you five hundred. Come back at five tomorrow and I'll give you the rest. If the job's done."

Trent scowls and lets out a low grunt, but nods.

"Good," Evan says as he gets to his feet. "I'll be right back."

He goes out the door and into the outer office. "I need the cash box," he tells the secretary. She opens a desk drawer, pulls out the box and hands it to Evan. As he is counting out the bills, he glances up and notices Trent watching intently.

"Find another place for this," he says as he closes the box and puts it on the desk. "Maybe it should go in the safe overnight."

He returns to his office and when he doesn't go back to his seat, Trent stands. Evan hands him the money. "Okay then. See you here tomorrow."

"Tomorrow. Yeah."

"And Trent?"

"Yeah?"

"If you're thinking of coming back for the cash box, like after hours maybe, remember there's an alarm system and cameras."

"Ffftt! I wouldn't—"

"Good. Then we won't have a problem."

Trent glares at Evan for a moment, then gives the waistband of his jeans a hike before turning and striding through the outer office, past Tina's station at the reception desk, and out the glass doors.

There's a guy who should never play poker, Evan thinks. He goes around his desk and sinks into his chair, rocks back and tents his fingers. Is it really necessary to eliminate Trent? With Max gone, he might be useful.

The Children of Noah's relationship with the bikers is uneasy even though they returned half of that money. Nick would never have made a deal for a sixty-forty split, but once Nick was gone, the bikers swore that's what the deal was. Maybe they wouldn't have returned any of the money if not for another job coming along. That, and the promise of a continuing relationship. Still, trust hasn't been restored and the Triumvirate would rest easier if they didn't have to rely on the bikers for their security work.

The bikers were useful getting Trent set up with a vehicle, though. It would have been difficult for him to buy one legitimately, with transfer papers, registration, insurance—his fake I.D. might hold up, but it's better not to take a chance. Their auto salvage business comes in handy for more than just the crusher.

But Trent is no Max. Max had always known how to keep his mouth shut and you never knew what he was thinking. Trent runs his mouth non-stop and everything he thinks is written on his face. No doubt he has bragged about those murders before. Will he be able to keep his mouth shut about another one?

Besides, he's sloppy. He left prints in the hotel room, triggering Canada-wide warrants for his parole violation, and now he brags about leaving urine on a murder victim. He'd better hope it rained enough before the bodies were found that they couldn't get DNA out of it to I.D. him.

Evan warned him against doing anything to draw attention to himself: no bar fights, no speeding, no illegal U-turns, not even a parking ticket. If he has a run-in the cops for any reason, he'll be back in the slammer. The plates on the old Bronco the bikers pawned off on him came from who knows where, definitely not legit, the driver's licence won't stand close scrutiny and the scuzzy beard won't fool anyone. But he seemed to take the warning lightly.

Is that why Bearon wants Trent whacked? If he's so unreliable, why does he have to be the one to take care of that Kathy woman? The job could have been given to a more professional local. If Trent doesn't get it done by this time tomorrow, Evan will take him off the job.

Maybe the whole idea she has to be whacked needs more than just Bearon's say so. Trent, too. Decisions like that aren't made at the branch level. He needs to discuss it with Carl.

TWENTY-THREE

LAWYER GAMES

"HERE WE ARE." The perfectly coiffed and manicured lawyer stops flipping the pages of the document and folds it back to mark his place. Finally he looks up over his half-frame glasses at Kathy, on the other side of his desk, and says, "Yes, Ms. Klein, your name is here."

"Oh," Kathy utters a sigh. This destroys her last hope of not being related to the serial killers. Her shoulders slump.

Rick asks, "Can we assume he left her something?"

"Assume away, *Mister* Schoenfeld."

At the expression of malice on the lawyer's face, Kathy retreats back into her chair. Rick, far from being intimidated, leans forward, eyes narrowing. "So, what did she inherit?"

"Well, obviously I'm not going to tell you that until she can prove she is who she claims to be."

"Show *Mister* Robertson your I.D., Runty."

"It's not quite that simple," the lawyer says. He takes off his glasses and fusses with them as he frowns at Kathy. "Anybody could walk in here and claim to be Kathryn Klein."

Kathy straightens and leans forward. "But that's ridiculous. You know who I am."

"Yes, I do. That's the problem. Seems to me not that long ago you showed up out of nowhere and claimed to be another man's daughter. The daughter no one had seen for twenty years. Surely I don't need to remind you? And now here you are again, this time alleging you're the daughter of Henry Hazen, conveniently just months before the time to make a claim on his estate expires. If memory serves, you didn't claim to be the *adopted* daughter of Mr. Klein and your birth records showed him as your father. Obviously no one has two biological fathers." He sits back with a smug look. "You see the difficulty?"

"But all my life I thought Gerald Klein *was* my father. My *biological* father. I never had any reason to think otherwise. And then I got those letters—"

"Ah, yes, the letters. Somehow years later, letters turn up. Letters no one but you saw, and that you say were stolen."

"But it wasn't even us who found them. And they *were* stolen..."

"So," Rick intercedes, eyes narrowing, "I bet you have some hoops for us to jump through."

"I suppose you think I should tell you what you have to do to prove she's his daughter?"

"How about DNA?"

"Normally that would be a good idea," the lawyer agrees. He folds his reading glasses and carefully sets them on the marble base of his vintage pen set, then fiddles with the pens before looking up. "I would have suggested it, but since we don't have Mr. Hazen's DNA for comparison, Ms. Klein's DNA won't do any good."

"Astrid thinks there were other children. Kathy's siblings. We could get DNA from them to compare."

"Ahh, yes, your friend Astrid Ingebritson." He flips the pages over and stuffs the will back inside its folder. "If you can find these other children, and if they agree, that would be sufficient."

"But you know who they are."

"Yes, I do, and I can't divulge their names any more than I could contact you about your inheritance. Mr. Hazen gave explicit instructions. He didn't expect anyone to come forward and frankly, neither did I." With a self-satisfied smirk, he continues: "so if that's all...?" He stands and goes to the office door, opening it and standing aside. "I assume you can find your way out."

Kathy and Rick exchange a look, then get to their feet, push their chairs back and head for the door.

Rick stops beside the lawyer. He moves close, nearly standing over him, causing the much smaller man to bump the door back against the wall, and says, "I *assume* we'll hear from you once you've given the matter of what is acceptable proof your consideration, *Mister* Robertson."

He maintains eye contact with the lawyer for a second longer before following Kathy through the long hallway, passing a dozen other office doors and the reception desk until they are at the elevator.

Once they're out of the building and on the sidewalk in the late afternoon heat, Kathy says, "so, Mr. Big Balls hasn't improved with age."

"Nope. Once an asshole, always an asshole. Kept us waitin' half an hour and then rushes us out after ten minutes. Now it's too late to get to the bank. And for what? No way he was busy with clients. It's just a lawyer game, makin' people wait. I should've known he'd still be pissed about Penny and Reese gettin' the better of him. Thousand dollar suits and the teak-panelled corner office with a view of the lake and everyone should kiss his ass." Rick grins and draws her in for quick hug. "He had you goin' for a minute there, didn't he?" He releases her and they continue down the sidewalk along the storefronts to the parkade.

"You mean when he looked down his nose at us like we were a couple of worms?"

"Yeah. His mouth was puckered up like he was sucking on a lemon. With those drooping jowls, I thought for a second I missed seein' him turn around and drop his pants, I was so sure he was moonin' us and I was lookin' at his asshole."

Kathy giggles. "Did you see his face when you mentioned Astrid? That was a butt face if I ever saw one! And he puts me off for weeks and then acts like such a pompous ass!"

"I thought he would've left Robertson, Robertson McKinley et al to the second Robertson years ago and would be spending his days on the golf course by now. Since he doesn't seem to realize that he ought to be retired, someone needs to take him down a peg."

They turn into the parkade at the stairwell that leads to the third level, and climb the stairs single file.

When they're settled in the truck and driving out, Kathy says, "there's something I've been wondering about. Why would Hazen have a lawyer in Regina? Why not closer to home?"

"I've wondered that myself," Rick says. He slows to let another vehicle back out of its parking spot and follows it down the exit ramp.

"Those photos Den sent me. He recognized Briggs as the project manager for the rebuild of that lodge, and turns out we know him from when he was the bank manager in Pillerton. Before he replaced Donnie as the manager of Prairie Equity. And we know he was at the airport to meet Carl and Tina. Couldn't make out who the other two guys were but they were all travellin' together so odds are they're from around here too. Why would they all go to Dark River? And how'd a guy with no experience in construction, a banker for chrissakes, wind up bein' the project manager for a job that big? How'd Prairie Equity end up dolin' out the insurance funds? How do money managers make a deal with an insurance company like that? And the contractors, and now the lawyer, all from around here? What's the connection between Pillerton and Dark River?"

"Yeah, there's a lot of questions," Kathy agrees. "Maybe just ask Carl and Tina? I don't know why you haven't told Carl, at least, that we saw him in Dark River. You're in Big Al's every day."

"Not every day. It's not like it used to be. Hardly know anyone there anymore. And anyway, Carl hasn't been around much since he made Marge the manager." The car ahead of them turns out into the street, but Rick has to wait for traffic to clear. "Great," he mutters. "Now we're stuck in rush hour traffic. Another thing to thank Big Balls for."

"You could ask Tina, then," Kathy suggests.

"You *know* how that would go!" There's a break in traffic, so Rick eases the truck out into the flow.

"Well anyway, I need to talk to Penny and Reese. Too bad Reese moved out to Vancouver instead of Penny moving back here. It would be nice to have a lawyer we could trust to run things at this end. Plus it would be nice to have my friend closer. Reese still knows a lot of lawyers in Regina. She might be able to suggest someone. Robertson mentioned something about a time limit, the time for claiming running out soon? We might have to do some legal thing to make sure my claim doesn't just expire."

"Yeah, good point. And meantime, Mr. Big Balls thinks we have no way of proving your entitlement, and we'll just let him think that for the time being."

"But we don't, do we? Unless you've thought of something? You heard what he said about DNA. I don't see how we could ever locate the other, er, *my* siblings. They're probably like me, different names altogether, no adoption records, don't even know who their real father is. So that leaves us with Hank Senior and Junior. How would we get their DNA?"

"Not sure. Maybe Astrid still has something that belonged to them that might have DNA on it. What happened to their stuff outta the house? Maybe still around somewhere?"

"Maybe. Hank Senior's wife is still alive so it's possible Astrid stored it for when she gets out of the looney bin. Although she thinks she never will."

"It's a long shot. If they weren't cremated, we might be able to have them exhumed, but from what Denver says, there wasn't enough left to bury. Maybe some body parts? Another long shot, and a ghoulish thought at that, and something we might never be able to make happen," Rick agrees. "Do we have to go to your office to pick up your car? I don't mind taking you to work in the morning. Have to go to the bank tomorrow anyway since it's too late today."

"My car's okay in the lot overnight," Kathy says. "What time are you leaving tomorrow?"

"Six-thirty? Seven?"

"That's too early. Tomorrow's Friday and I'm on the late shift, so I don't have to go in until ten. I don't mind going in a little early but I'd rather not be there at seven. You don't want to be at the bank before it opens, surely?"

"No, I gotta swing by John Deere to pick up a part, and they're open early."

"We could go there now."

"Naw, I gotta go to the bank tomorrow anyway."

"It would be a lot more convenient if the farm accounts were at the bank in Pillerton."

"Sure it would, but they were impossible to deal with when Pops and I wanted that big farm loan. I'm still pissed about that. I won't deal there."

"That was decades ago!"

"I have a long memory."

"That's called biting off your nose to spite your face. They've been good to deal with for the insurance agency's accounts."

Rick shrugs. "Like I said, I got other things to do in town anyhow."

"But you wouldn't have if we went to the dealer now."

At the look he gives her, she throws up her hands and says, "I know what you're going to say. You have to go to the bank anyway. I give up! But that's too early for me to go to the office. So I'll need my car."

"Well, that means adding half an hour to our trip home."

"That's not much. Do you really have to go so early?"

"I do if I want to get back early. Don't want Ryan with his face hanging out waitin' for that part. Maybe him or Sarah could swing by and pick you up."

"I'll ask." She gets her phone out of her purse and sends a text, checks it for email, then puts it away and looks at Rick.

They listen to the five o'clock news for a few minutes, then Kathy says, "I was just thinking about some of the stuff Astrid and I talked about. She said she liked Hank's wife. Maybe she could get her to agree to exhume one of them."

"If they weren't cremated, and if the powers that be would accept an order or whatever is required from someone who's in the looney bin."

They ride along in silence for a couple of blocks. Then Kathy says, "I don't know why I didn't photocopy those letters!"

"I don't either, but don't beat yourself up over it. I doubt Mr. Big Balls would believe you are the little girl he mentioned anyway."

"Courts might, though."

"Yeah, but how would you prove the letters were from Hazen? They're gone, and there's no use worryin' about it. Robertson's going to make a battle out of it no matter what. Just like before. You'd think it was his money."

"Maybe he gets a share of whatever isn't claimed." Kathy roots through her purse and comes out with a pack of gum. She pops a stick in her mouth. "Want one?"

"No thanks."

"You know, sweetie, if it's going to be as big a hassle as last time, I wonder if it's even worth pursuing. It seems like it's going to be an awful lot of trouble."

"We don't know what's at stake, thanks to that pompous stuffed shirt not telling us, but from what Astrid says, it was a big estate. He wouldn't name you in the will just to give you a couple hundred bucks. Plus, I won't drop out and give Big Balls the win." He pilots the truck onto the onramp for Highway 19 and once merged, gives her a sideways look, then grins.

"What?"

"There's one other sibling, remember?"

"Of course. But I couldn't find that person before so where would I start looking now? Everyone's dead."

"Maybe not everyone. The Lodge has been rebuilt. Who would rebuild? The person who inherited it, right?"

"Well, that's who would be entitled to the insurance money. But maybe the land was sold and the insurance money went into the estate."

"Maybe. But if ol' Hank had other kids, don't you think he'd leave it to one of them?"

"Yes! You're right! But there's no chance Robertson will tell us who."

"Nope. No chance." He reaches over and takes her hand. "We might eventually have to make another trip to Dark River, but for now, why don't we get Penny to find out who the new owner is?"

"No flies on you, husband!"

"Meanwhile, I'm starvin'. Wanna stop at the Holiday Inn for that mushroom tortellini you like so much?"

"Yes, let's."

TWENTY-FOUR

BRONCO

A DOZEN KILOMETERS north of Pillerton, Rick turns off the highway onto the gravel road leading to their farm. He says, "Wonder if Mutti baked a cake today."

"I can't believe you're thinking of cake after that big meal."

"Wouldn't have to be a big piece of cake."

"I don't know why you aren't fat," Kathy says. Then she frowns as she looks down the road. "What's that?"

Acres of crops awaiting harvest stretch as far as the eye can see, waving in the breeze on both sides of the road. Aside from the scrub aspens that grow around the slough just past their farm, the only trees in sight are those the Schoenfeld family has planted over the decades: Colorado Blue Spruce and tall narrow Lombardy Poplars in the grove surrounding the old house, smaller versions around the new house at the back. Just before the Schoenfeld driveway, a vehicle with its hood up is stopped, half blocking the road.

"Car trouble," Rick says, slowing to a stop beside the Bondo-mottled Bronco. A bearded man wearing a ballcap and a grubby camo jacket is on the far side, bent over the fender as if tinkering with the engine. He looks up for a second, then tugs the bill of his cap to settle it further down his forehead, and without looking up again, waves them off.

Kathy powers her window down and calls out, "need help?"

"No," the man calls out. He slams the hood down, then scurries around the back to the driver's door, opens it, and climbs in. The engine coughs to life.

"Must be okay," Rick decides. He accelerates slowly away, then pulls into the driveway and stops. "I'll just wait and make sure he can roll."

They watch as the Bronco spews gravel and dust from its tires when the driver negotiates a U-turn and speeds back toward the highway.

"That's odd," Rick says with a frown. "I expected him to keep goin' in the direction he was parked. Although I dunno what he'd want to go further down this road for."

"Not what you'd call a friendly guy, pretty rude when someone's just asking if he needs help. A 'no thank you' wouldn't hurt. You know, something about him looked familiar."

"Oh yeah?"

"Hmmm. Can't place him, though. Maybe it's just that he reminded me of the weird guy who came into the office this morning. But he was bald. Of course with the ballcap and sunglasses... Anyway, neither of them look like they're from around here. Godzilla has new tenants in one of her rentals. Maybe that's one of them."

"With Regina growing out our way, our town is changin'. I go into Al's, half the time I don't know anyone." He shifts into drive and continues up to the house. "And anyway, what do guys from around here look like?"

"Well, clean shaven and not wearing jeans two sizes too big that leave you wondering if there's even an ass in there."

"Tell you what. When we get home, you can check to make sure my jeans have an ass in 'em."

"Your jeans fit fine."

"But a person can't be too sure. You should check."

"I'll take your word for it."

"No, I insist. And I'll check yours while we're at it."

"Oh, well, I wouldn't want you to go to any trouble."

"No trouble. It's the least I can do."

AT FIVE-THIRTY the next morning, Trent's cellphone alarm blasts. He's been tossing and turning for at least an hour so he didn't really need the alarm, but he's been called a fuck-up often enough that this morning going smoothly is really important. He had set it just to be sure he didn't sleep in.

His erection is pushing the sheets up. *No use trying to piss like this*, he thinks, and grabs it. Once he's squirted his jism he heads for the bathroom. He doesn't shower or brush his teeth, just takes a whiz, throws his clothes on and heads for the door.

He opens the door a few inches and seeing no one, carefully sticks his head out for a better look around. There's a van parked at the office. A guy gets a bundle of what looks like newspapers out of the side door and he takes them inside.

Trent waits until he returns empty-handed, gets back in the van and drives off. He's planned everything carefully. It wouldn't be good if someone saw him taking off so early. If things go bad and he needs an alibi, he wants to say he was here in bed because he likes to sleep in.

Things can't go bad, though, not with all the thought he's put into it. Des always says, you gotta plan for all the contingencies. His target coming home with a dude yesterday was definitely what Des would call a contingency.

First she's late, makes him wait out in the hot sun nearly two hours, then she shows up with a dude. Definitely a contingency. He hadn't planned for it. Who could? It's okay, though, because he figured out what to do and it'll all be fixed this morning.

He swings into the drive-through at Tim Hortons. There's a double line-up and cars backed out into the shopping center parking lot besides. It's frustratingly slow. *Why the fuck are so many people up this early?* Good thing he gave himself plenty of time. Planned for a contingency. He's finally at the window, picks up his coffee and a box of double chocolate donuts, then heads out to Highway 19 southbound holding the cup between his knees.

The first sip of coffee is too hot and burns his mouth. He curses. Maybe he should sue them for having their coffee too hot. He heard about some bitch getting millions from McDonalds that way.

At the first stop light, he pulls the liter of rye out from under his seat, takes the lid off the cup, and pours a little rye in. Not much, though, because it's still too full. And too hot. Maybe he should dump some out the window so he can add enough rye to make it cool enough to drink. But he doesn't want to drink it all right away anyhow, because he might have a bit of a wait.

The only downside to his vehicle is that it's too old to have cup holders. He puts the coffee back between his thighs, careful not to squeeze. Each time he has to clutch and shift gears, he picks up the cup with thumb and forefinger of his left hand and steers with the other three fingers while he works the shifter with his right hand. The Bronco is constantly pulling to the right, so he needs a better grip on the wheel. It's impossible not to keep the coffee from sloshing out the hole in the lid.

After a few blocks, he's sipped enough out that it won't splash over, and sets it on the box of donuts in the passenger seat. No stupid asshat better cut him off and make him brake hard! He'd regret it if he did! But then, he can't take the time to tune anyone up so there's no use thinking about it.

Once he's out on the highway at cruising speed, there's no problem. It comes to him there are cup holders you can stick on the dash, and gives himself a pat on the back for thinking of it. There's a Canadian Tire near the motel. He'll stop in there on his way home later and get one.

It's a forty-five minute drive from the motel to Pillerton if he stays right on the speed limit. Not for the first time, he's tempted to see what the big V-8 can do, what with this inviting, wide-open stretch of road in front of him. But he knows the cops cruise the highway often, plus there's a grove of trees around a farmhouse where he's seen the sneaky bastard cops hiding with their radar guns, so he's careful.

It sucks, though! Forty-five minutes on this flat, straight road through the endless featureless fields of some kind of crops, and he has to keep the needle at ninety! The sunrise is spectacular as only a prairie sunrise can be, but he barely notices. If he didn't have coffee, he'd likely fall asleep.

At last he reaches the turn-off to the gravel road leading to her house. He was waiting for her yesterday, but then the contingency happened. She came along in a truck instead of her hatchback, and of course, had a dude with her. He wouldn't have realized it was her in the truck because he was waiting for her car, but they stopped and she looked right at him. Mr. I'm So Fuckin' Smart Briggs never told him she was hooked up, and at no time when he was watching her did he see her with a dude. No matter, he'll get the blame for it anyway. Like he's a mind reader and should know about it even though he's never seen her with a dude before? It was totally not his fault. Anyway, he can still get the job done this morning, show up to collect his $9.5K at the appointed time and not have to explain yesterday's contingency.

He turns onto the sideroad slowly so as not to tip the coffee, and mutters, "God, please don't let her leave with that dude!" As he approaches the farmhouse, he slows to make sure he's not raising too much dust in case someone is watching; then he realizes he's going to go past their place so they wouldn't think anything of it anyway, just a vehicle driving by on the road. No cops on this road!

He boots the accelerator. The big engine emits a satisfying roar and the Bronco he's affectionately named The Beast fishtails in the loose gravel. For a tense moment he thinks he won't be able to get it under control; it slews in the gravel at the edge of the ditch, then grabs and shoots back onto the roadway. It's enough of a surprise that he eases back on the throttle. Of course the coffee tipped.

"Fuck! Fuck! Fuck fuck fuck!" He flicks the empty cup off the donut box onto the floor. If he had only thought about the need for a cup holder sooner! Can't blame The Beast for not having one.

Sure, the Beast needs work and it's a gas guzzler, but it's a classic: no plastic body parts on this beauty! Big chromed steel bumper. Powerful V-8 engine. He can fix it up and it'll be worth bags full of money. Surprising how old Broncos cost more than some much-newer cars. He pulled one over on those bikers, for sure, getting this off them for half what it's worth. No use having a vehicle that's pristine just to ding it up in case he can't just scare her off the road and has to crash into her, and no way she will be able to outrun him in her little four-banger.

When he's past the driveway to the farmhouse and just over the slight rise, he negotiates a U-turn and pulls the Beast into the ditch facing back the way he came, tucking it in behind some bushes. A beautiful thing about Saskatchewan is the wide, shallow ditches, not like the trenches on Vancouver Island. The going is a little rough but the Beast farts at terrain far worse than this.

He takes his bottle of rye, what's left of his donuts, and the binoculars and walks to the top of the rise. The big trees are on three sides of the farmhouse, none in front, as if they never wanted to block the view. A view of nothing but empty fields. Saskatchewan people must be idiots! It does mean he has full view of it but people in the farmhouse can see him, too, so he huddles in the tall grass at the edge of the road.

Satisfied he can't be seen, he gets another donut out of the box, and waits. If any cars come along, he'll just stand up and pretend to be taking a piss. Doesn't seem like that's going to happen, though. Times he's been on this road, there's never been any traffic. Why? Maybe this road doesn't go anywhere? If it doesn't, people might wonder what he's doing there.

"Don't be an idiot, Trent," he tells himself. "Mrs. Reardon didn't raise no idiots. They don't build roads that don't go nowhere."

He's drunk half the rye, polished off the donuts, smoked half a dozen cigarettes careful not to set the grass on fire, and actually does have to pee desperately before he sees the truck coming down the long driveway and out onto the road. A check with his binoculars confirms one person in it. One big person that has to be the dude. Then a second smaller head appears.

"Fuck me," he mutters. Then the head turns and bobs around. It's a dog! He breathes a sigh of relief. "A fuckin' dog!"

Now he just has to wait for her, and he can do that from the truck. He'll pull up onto the road, ready to go. If she looks to her right and sees him, it's just another vehicle and she won't think anything of it.

He gets up, wobbling a little. He's got a buzz from the rye. Good. Des always says it's a good idea to take the edge off your nerves before a job. He trots back to the Beast and stands just behind it to pee.

There's a grasshopper bigger than any he's ever seen before next to the tire, and he aims his urine stream at it. It launches at him, hits his thigh and clings there, startling him so he splashes piss on his boot.

"Goddamn fuckin' shit!" he yelps. He swats at the insect but it takes to the air again, this time spreading its red wings with a clattering sound. He regrets trying to piss on it. He should've let it alone so it wouldn't have grabbed on to his jeans with its clingy little feet and looked at him with its bulging demon eyes. This is a bad sign. He curses under his breath some more, cleans the urine off his boot by rubbing it on the back of his calf, and zips up.

It's at least half an hour before she usually leaves, but he wants to be ready. He slides in behind the wheel, starts the engine and pulls The Beast up onto the road, before turning it off to wait. Like Des says, hurry up and wait.

"Des says. Des ses. Dez sez. What sez Dez?" He sings tunelessly along with the radio, trying to organize his thoughts so he can plan what to do with all the money, but when he pushes the Dez sez out of his mind, his thoughts keep turning to the dog in the truck. He didn't know she had a dog. Didn't care anyway. What is it about the dog leaving with the dude that stirs his thoughts? Something is niggling at him. He can't quite make sense of it. Dez sez.

Then he experiences a eureka moment. He doesn't need to wait for her to take her sweet time coming out and then chase her down. He can do her in the house and be long gone before anyone even realizes she's missing! No car off the road with a body in it to get the cops going! She won't be missed at work until at least nine. That gives him plenty of time. It's totally fuckin' awesome luck the dude took the dog!

"Fuckin' Arnie should of gave me a gun," he mutters, "Could of just popped her. Would of solved all this bullshit."

But Arnie didn't, so he had to come up with something else and this is a better idea anyway. He'll grab her and take her out into a field because when she doesn't show up at work, her house is the first place they'll look and right away they'll know. If he does her out in a field it'll take them days to find her, if they ever do. The Beast will have no trouble going through a field. It farts at worse than that! Better a missing person than a dead person, Dez sez.

There's a shovel in the back with the tangled cables and that greasy old camo jacket and other crap the bikers didn't bother cleaning out. He can plant her right where he does her and no one will even miss her until long after he's gone, with $9.5K in his jeans.

In fact, there might even be time to have a little fun with her before he does her. Or after. Whatever. Imagining what he might do gives him a woody. He wishes he had time to rub one out, but what if she leaves the house while he's doing it? With some difficulty, he pushes the idea away.

Why didn't he think of this plan in the first place? Of course if he'd tried to grab her out of the house before he knew there was a dude, he would've been there. So God was looking after him yesterday when he showed Trent his target was living with someone! And again today, when he showed him the dog. Running into either a dude or a dog wouldn't be good! Maybe the incident with the grasshopper wasn't a bad sign, after all, when he thinks about the other favours God did for him. He clasps his hands together and raises them up as he says to the sky, "thank you, God!" He starts the engine, shifts into second gear, drives the short distance to the driveway and turns in.

Once in the farm yard, he parks at the gap in the hedge, turns the engine off, and gets out. He should have gloves. Those assholes called him a fuck up for leaving prints at the motel. Again, not his fault. How was he to know anyone would come along? But he won't make the same mistake again. He has no gloves now, of course, because he hadn't planned to go into her house. He'll just make sure not to touch anything.

He pulls his sleeve down over his hand and opens the gate, then trots the short sidewalk, up the steps and across the verandah to the door. With his sleeve still over his hand, he turns the knob. Locked.

"Fuck!" he grumbles under his breath. "Fuck fuck fuck fuck fuck!" He'll have to kick it in. It's not a great idea because it will make a loud noise and alert her, but he doesn't have a choice—or does he? Should he knock and wait for her to come to the door?

He stands puzzling it out for a moment. Would she open the door? She might look out that little window at the side of the door and decide not to let him in, and then he would have to kick it in anyway. Might as well just surprise her. Always have surprise on your side, Dez sez.

He rears back slightly and puts his boot to the door next to the knob as hard as he can. With a loud crack the jamb splinters and the door crashes back against the wall. He darts in. Where is she? Upstairs getting ready for work? He'll check out the main floor first.

He is scurrying along the short hall next to the staircase checking the rooms on either side, when a grey-haired woman in a bathrobe appears where the hall opens into what looks to be the kitchen. This is so unexpected he is momentarily paralyzed. Then she utters an ear-splitting scream.

"Shut up!" he yells, and sprints toward her. "Shut up and you won't get hurt!"

But the woman keeps screaming. He leaps to grab her but she's surprisingly quick and eludes his grasp, shrieking like a banshee the whole time, loud enough to split his brain. He makes another lunge but catches his foot on a chair leg, sending the chair skittering away. He gets a handful of her bathrobe. She pulls away, her loosened robe coming open. She's almost successful in shedding the robe as she makes a dash for the open door to the outside, but he catches her easily. She stumbles and they both fall to the floor. The old woman's head strikes the stove with a loud metallic bang and his hundred plus kilos landing on her expels the air out of her lungs with a whoosh. At least she quit her screeching.

Trent leaps to his feet, wondering how to tie her up while he searches for the target, but realizes it won't be necessary. The old lady is out cold. Is she hurt? He doesn't have time to worry about it. Another fuckin' contingency! He has to find the target, grab her and get out.

He confirms there's no one else on the main floor, then takes the stairs two at a time to the second storey.

No one there either. His forehead creases in a frown. Unless she left before he got there, like really early, she must be here. Did she hear the racket the old lady made, and hide? He's in no mood for hide and seek. He checks under the bed and in the tiny closet, then does the same in the other bedrooms. Nowhere to hide in the bathroom. "God *fuckin'* damn it!"

He races back downstairs and takes another look at the woman while he puzzles out what to do. She's still exactly as he left her, hairy legs, veiny and white, spread open immodestly. He averts his eyes from her holey panties and, careful not to touch the stove because that would leave fingerprints, pulls her away so her head flops down on the floor and she's lying flat.

He pokes at her neck, but can't feel a pulse. That's not surprising. He's never been able to find even his own pulse. He can't tell if she's breathing, either, but her eyes are closed so she's not dead, just unconscious. He's seen enough movies to know dead people have their eyes open, plus those dudes he and Des took out were staring at the sky. So she's okay even though she's in an uncomfortable position.

She's old, maybe as old as his grandmother. Old people shouldn't fall. Look what happened to his grandmother when she fell—broke her hip and was never the same again. But it's not his fault this old lady fell, it was her own stupidity. She shouldn't have kept on screaming like that, and if she hadn't tried to run away, he wouldn't have accidentally knocked her over.

He pulls her nightgown down so her old granny panties are covered and settles her arms across her body so she's more comfortable. It's okay. It's only hard things like doorknobs and furniture and such you have to worry about leaving prints on.

She will be out cold for a while, so she's not the problem. Where is the target? Not here, goddammit. He's going to have to go somewhere to figure out what went wrong, and the sooner the better before someone comes along. But there was that jewelry box on the old lady's dresser. Easy pickings. He might as well get something out of this.

He goes back upstairs and paws through the jewelry. It looks like there's some good stuff there, even a little bundle of bills, but he's not stupid enough to look at it now. He stuffs the cash in his jeans and will sort through the rest of the loot later.

He pulls the case off one of the pillows, dumps the jewelry into it and tosses the empty box on the bed. Using the end of the bedspread he wipes the jewelry box to get rid of fingerprints, then purses up the pillowcase, trots out into the hall and thunders down the stairs. He's out the door and back at his truck, by his estimation in less than five minutes since he got there.

But before he's settled in his seat, he's overcome with a desperate need to defecate. It's past his usual time for a dump or as Des calls it, a kip. Des explained it means a poop caused by coffee, or something like that. It doesn't really make sense because coffee doesn't start with a K but when he told Des that, Des just snorted and shook his head.

Coffee does seem to move things along in the morning, but besides that, he often has to kip when he's doing a job. Des razzes him about it and has even gone so far as to push him over when he's in the middle of it, but when they boosted the computers and stuff out of that lawyer's office, he joined him on the lawyer's desk, didn't he! They still laugh about that. Two steaming piles of shit right in the middle of the guy's desk! Wish they could've seen his face!

It's so urgent he's not sure he'll be able to hold it in. He's learned his lesson about that! Should he go back inside and use the toilet? What Des calls dropping the kids off at the pool? Or maybe just squat somewhere, like they did at the lawyer's office?

He looks around. There's no sign of movement anywhere. He remembers seeing a bathroom quite close to the door. He decides to drop the kids off at the pool and goes back into the house. Anyway, it's always better to give the ol' cornhole a nice wipe so you don't get skid marks in your shorts. In a matter of seconds it's done and he congratulates himself on remembering not to touch the flush handle.

He's back in his truck heading out to the highway, and still hasn't seen another vehicle. *This road must not go nowhere*, he thinks. *Why did they build a road that don't go nowhere?* He's almost at the intersection when a pick-up truck turns off the highway and onto the road heading his way. So the road does go somewhere. That makes sense.

But wondering about the road is only a stray thought, and his mind quickly turns to the folded bills in his pocket. He roots them out and holds them up on the steering wheel to riffle through them. Looks like foreign money mixed in, but even so, with the fifties and hundreds, this by itself is a good haul. And the heavy bag of jewelry! "Woot! Woot!" he hoots, and stuffs his new bankroll back in his pocket. He can get the target another day. No big hurry to get paid at least for a while, if that old jewelry is worth as much as he hopes.

It's puzzling the little twat wasn't in the house this morning, though. It's a contingency. Where did he go wrong? He's certain that's the driveway he's seen her go up, no mistaking that. He must have done something to piss God off, so he only gave him that little bit of help. He'll pray on it.

He was so sure she lived in that house. But maybe it's that dude's place and she lives somewhere else. Maybe she went home after he left off surveillancing. That must be it.

He'll need to put some thought into it and after his meeting with Mr. I'm So Fuckin' Smart Briggs this afternoon, he'll go back to her office at quitting time and follow her again. This time, he'll surveillance long enough to find out where she goes.

In the meantime, he'll call his new buddy Arnie at the auto wreckers and find out how to fence the old lady's jewellery. He's got all day to figure out how to explain to Mr. I'm So Fuckin' Smart Briggs what went wrong.

He wishes his brother was here. He's good at puzzling these things out. He grins, then laughs out loud. The old bag was a contingency, that's true, but it hasn't tanked the job and he made a big score out of it besides! If Des was here, he would tell him he's a genius and High Five him.

No sir, like Dez sez, Mrs. Reardon didn't raise no idiots.

TWENTY-FIVE

RUN-RUN-RUN

RYAN TURNS UP the driveway and drives through the yard, passing between the farmhouse and the horse barn to Rick and Kathy's house on the other side of the grove. He parks near the back door, turns the engine off and is about to go up to the door to see if Kathy is ready to go, when she comes out, her purse in one hand and a travel mug in the other.

"Good morning," Kathy says as she climbs into the truck and sets her coffee in the console cup holder.

"Good morning!"

"Clear skies this morning. Looks like it's going to be another hot one."

"Yup. Can't complain, though. Good harvest weather, and it'll be forty below before we know it."

"That's the truth. Hey, thanks for picking me up."

"No problem. It's practically on my way." Ryan starts the engine. "Maybe we should just check on Mutti, though," he says. "Her front door was open when I drove past. I didn't think anyone ever used that door."

"You're right, that's odd. We'll just nip in and see what's going on."

Ryan pilots the truck through the grove and back into the main yard to park at the gate in front of the farmhouse, where they both get out.

"Gate's open, too," Kathy says. "That's really unusual."

They go up on the verandah to the door. "Oh my god! She's had a break-in!" Kathy exclaims, pointing to the broken jamb and wood splinters on the floor. She darts forward but Ryan grabs her by the arm.

"Stay back," he commands as he pushes her behind him. "He might still be here."

He eases his way in, quietly making his way down the hall, glancing into the living room, dining room and bathroom on his way to the kitchen, with Kathy right behind him.

They find Mutti on the kitchen floor next to the stove. Kathy pushes past Ryan and rushes to her, dropping to her knees and clasping her hand. "Oh, my god! Mutti! Mutti!" She turns to Ryan and says, "She's so pale! Call 911!"

Ryan kneels down next to Kathy and pulls out his phone.

The operator answers with: "Nine One One, what's your emergency?"

"Someone broke in and there's an elderly woman unresponsive on the floor."

"Okay, sir. Where are you located?"

Ryan rattles off the address and adds his phone number. He says, "This is a cell phone but I'll stay here…"

"Good. Stay with me, sir. Just repeat your address for me please."

He does, and the operator says, "Okay. I'm dispatching ambulance and police now. Is she breathing?"

"I don't think so," Ryan says.

"Is there anyone there who knows CPR?"

"I might...I can give it a try." He sets the phone on the floor and tells Kathy to go out to the road to flag down the first responders, then pulls Mutti clear of the stove and begins chest compressions. He keeps at it, taking only a short break every few minutes, until he hears sirens and the paramedics come in. He sits back on his heels and tells them quietly, "I think she's dead."

THE YARD IS overflowing with vehicles: a Jeep with "CKCK NEWS" emblazoned on it; a cube van with the RCMP logo; several RCMP cruisers; a gray sedan marked "Coroner"; Jeanie and Sarah's cars and of course Ryan's truck; Rick's truck and an ambulance. When the ambulance pulls away, followed by one of the RCMP cruisers, Sergeant Neufeld comes to join the group clustered around the side yard of the farmhouse. "I told the news reporter you won't be speaking with her, and that it looks like a home invasion gone bad," he tells them. "Ryan, you didn't see anything? No vehicle?"

"No. Nothing. We wouldn't have gone in except when I drove into the yard I noticed the door was open. No one ever uses that door."

"What time was that?"

"Maybe nine? About nine, Kathy?"

Kathy says, "Yes, a few minutes before nine."

Sergeant Neufeld turns to Rick and says, "and you said you left a little after seven. Do you think you might have driven through the yard without noticing the front door was open?"

Rick's brow creases and after a moment, he says, "I don't think so. But I suppose it's possible."

"What about the dog. He didn't make any noise?"

"I took him with me." Rick covers his face with his hands for a moment, then gives it a brisk rub before dropping his hands to his hips. "Goddamn! If Chewie was at home—!"

Kathy loops her arm around his waist and tells him, "If Chewie was home, he'd sleep right through it." She faces Sergeant Neufeld and says, "you know Chewie, Ben. He's gotten so deaf, half the time he doesn't even wake up when you drive into our yard. He'd never hear anything over here."

Sergeant Neufeld clicks his tongue and blows out a breath. "She's right, Rick. Nothing you could've done. We'll see what the medical examiner says about time of death, but for now, I'm gonna say it was likely between seven and nine. No traffic on the road, I suppose?"

"I didn't see anyone," Rick says. "I never expect to. You know this road doesn't go anywhere now that they built the new connector to the Caledonia mine."

"I saw a truck," Ryan tells them. "Quite a ways from here, but heading to the highway in a hurry. Sometimes guys go in thinking the road connects up to the Moose Jaw highway and then they have to turn around at the old Caledonia gate, so I didn't think anything of it."

"I guess you didn't get the plate number, but do you remember anything else? Make? Model?" Sergeant Neufeld asks. "Colour?"

"Yeah, it was an old beater Bronco. Lots of Bondo. Dirty, but green, dark green, I think."

"Holy shit, Ben!" Rick exclaims, "that vehicle was parked out at the road just east of our driveway when we came home yesterday!"

"That can't be a coincidence."

"If that's him, I got a pretty good look at him," Kathy tells them. "I think I could describe him. Although with the ball cap and the sunglasses... Maybe not enough to be useful. And you know, I think the same guy was in my office yesterday."

"We'll get you with a sketch artist anyway. Do you have video surveillance at work?"

"Ben," Rick says, "this is Pillerton."

"I know. It's possible one of the other businesses on the street does, though. Wonder where else he's been. Maybe the cameras at the bank caught something. We'll check it out. Might be he's not involved but he could've seen something. At the very least we need to talk to the guy. I'll call it in." He closes his notebook and puts it in his pocket. "I'm going to tell the reporter to ask for anyone in the area this morning to come forward, and that we think the person driving the Bronco might have seen something that can help us."

He puts his hands on his hips and takes a few steps around before turning back to say, "I'm not sure how long the Evidence Recovery Team will need the house, Rick. They're confident they'll get prints and possibly DNA too, since it was likely him that forgot to flush. They'll let you know when they need you for elimination fingerprints. And Kathy, I'll let you know when the sketch artist can meet with you. Can you go to the Regina Detachment?"

"Yes, absolutely!"

"Good." He blows out a long breath. "Sorry for your loss, folks. I'll leave you to make your arrangements now. Call me if you think of anything else, and I'll keep you posted."

As Sergeant Neufeld's cruiser drives away, Kathy sinks to the verandah steps and says, "such horrible things have happened since I came back to Pillerton. I never should have come back." She dissolves into tears, and sobs, "If I hadn't come back, Mutti would still be alive!"

Rick sits next to her, chocking back his own sobs, and pulls her into his arms. "Runty, this isn't your fault. You coming here didn't cause this! I know you've been through a lot but this doesn't have anything to do with... It's just a coincidence."

"Come on, big brother," Jeanie says as she comes to stand over him and gives his shoulder a rub. "Let's all go to your house and wait until they're done collecting evidence. After that, we can go to my place. I'll make dinner or we can order pizza or something. Sarah and I can get started on that list of Mutti's jewelry that Ben wants, and we can see about funeral arrangements. We have to let Waltraud know." Her eyes fill. "How my god! How do you tell someone their sister's been murdered?"

"Oh my god! Auntie Waltraud!" Sarah cries, and breaks out in fresh sobs. Jeanie pulls her into an embrace and starts crying herself. Ryan comes to put his arms around both of them.

"Why don't you all go to Jeanie's now," Ryan suggests. "If the ERT people need you for anything, I'll give you a call. When they're done processing the house I'll cobble up a temporary repair of the door, and then join you there."

TRENT CRUISES THE main street, past the old curling rink, to its end at the cenotaph. There he pulls a U-turn so he's on the same side of the street as the Prairie Equity building and goes back the block and a half to park in front.

With wood beams much bigger than needed to support the narrow canopy and Prairie Equity spelled out in gleaming stainless steel letters, it's the only building in town that looks like anyone's done anything with it in fifty years. Except for Big Al's, with its illuminated bubble sign for the Al Capone Tunnels, that is. And of course the Co-Op put up a new awning.

One pub with one pool table, one store, one old bank, not even a traffic light. And they expect him to live here in Hicksville the rest of his life? It's worse than Dark River! No chance he's going to go along with that. Well, unless the bikers let him join. Arnie didn't say he'd sponsor him as a prospect, but he didn't say he wouldn't, either. If he does, maybe he'd sponsor Des, too, and then he would move here. Maybe there'll be more work coming from Mr. I'm So Fuckin' Smart Briggs. And Regina's not that bad. He could spend time with Arnie and the other guys in the clubhouse and not have to hang out in Pillerton at all.

As if he was a little kid, Mr. I'm So Fuckin' Smart Briggs gave him the big talking to about what not to do, including not to call Emmy. He's talked to her a few times anyway of course, coaxing her to move to Pillerton or at least Regina. Too cold in winter she says, as if it's any better in Prince George.

A couple of times she's mentioned a dude she met at the pub. He hit on her but she made it clear she has a boyfriend, she said. What was his name? Ken? Kevin? Just friends, she keeps telling him, although she did let it slip that he gave her a pair of earrings. Diamond studs. She must think he's stupid! A so-called friend gives her diamond earrings? Mrs. Reardon didn't raise no idiots! She's two-timing him and that's the real reason she wants to stay in Prince George. He needs to go back before it gets serious. He'll head out as soon as he gets the job done and has the rest of the money. He'll give her the gold earrings with the cluster of diamonds that he saved out of the old lady's jewelry. Three diamonds on each! That's gotta beat the ones Mr. I Need A Fuckin' Tune-up Ken gave her.

She'll come with him if she realizes he's got a good thing here: new friends at the auto wreckers; work, maybe not steady work but work; and a nice basement suite with furniture in it rented already. Or it will be soon. No use parting with the deposit until he gets the keys. With Emmy's experience bartending and serving and so on, she could get a good job no problem and they'd be cruisin' on Main Street, headin' for Easy Street! These thoughts put him in a good frame of mind for his meeting with Mr. I'm So Fuckin' Smart Briggs.

When he enters the reception area, he looks over the counter into Briggs's office and is surprised to see the owner of Big Al's sitting there. He says to the pretty receptionist, "I, er, Mr. Briggs is expecting me."

"Yeah, he is. You can go right in."

Mr. I'm So Fuckin' Smart Briggs looks up and waves him in.

As he's coming through the doorway, Evan says, "Trent, you know Carl?" He indicates the man in the chair across the desk from him.

"I, er, I seen him at the pub but I never met him. Howja do?" He sticks out his hand. Carl hesitates for a second, then leans forward enough to reach it for a quick shake. *Limp wrist,* Trent thinks. *How's a limp wrist own Big Al's?*

"Carl's a friend," Evan says. "Also an associate. Take a seat." He beckons to the empty chair.

Trent settles onto the chair, surprised there would be someone else in on this. The fewer people in on any job, the better, Dez sez. This limp wrist with his soft white hands can't be a player. Maybe he's just visiting Mr. I'm So Fuckin' Smart Briggs and will leave right away.

Carl says, "So, Trent, here to collect your pay, are you?"

"Well, um," Trent squirms, lifts his ballcap and scratches the stubble on his head as he realizes Carl is, in fact, in on it. "Still haven't got her alone," he says, "gonna hafta surveillance her some more."

"Sure," Evan says with a half-shrug and a nod. "By the way, did you hear about what happened out on the Old Caledonia Mine Road this morning? They're saying there was a home invasion. Not often we make the CKCK noon news."

"I, er—no, I—"

"Never mind lying, Trent," Evan says. "We know you didn't have to see it on TV. That was you, wasn't it?"

"Yeah, I, er, I went in, didn't find the woman, and left. Didn't touch nuthin' or do nuthin'."

"Didn't touch the old woman?" Carl asks.

"Nope! Just in, didn't find my target, and out. No one saw me."

"So, you didn't take anything?" Evan's eyes narrow as he fixes Trent with a glare. "Like maybe some jewelry?"

Trent swallows hard. How do they know about that? "Might as well, as long as I was there anyway. Smart thing to do. You know, since there was a contingency anyway."

"A contingency?"

"Yeah. The old woman being there and the young one not being there. But she never seen me. I never seen no one else around there when I was surveillancing. I seen her go up there last night, the young one I mean, and she never left this morning. Who the fuck knows how that could be? It's a contingency. But I always plan for contingencies, and I got a plan for this one."

"Oh yeah?"

"Yeah. I'll get her when she's on her way home after work tonight."

"Maybe that's not such a good idea."

"Why not?" Trent demands. He's had about enough of Mr. I'm So Fuckin' Smart Briggs. He thinks, *can't wait to blow this shitty little town.* He'd like to tell him what he thinks, but he doesn't have the money yet. Instead, he asks, "you got a better idea?"

Evan nods once and says, "yeah, as a matter of fact, I do. Lemme ask you something. If nobody saw you, why are they looking for a green Bronco?"

Trent takes a couple of deep breaths. His eyes dart back and forth between Evan and Carl. How can the cops be looking for his Bronco? No one saw him, he's certain of that. Unless... Is it because they saw him there yesterday?

But why would anyone think someone with car trouble the day before...

"So someone saw you," Evan continues, "and if you didn't touch anything, how do you explain the woman being murdered?"

"Murdered? No. She was alive when I left."

"So she fell over dead after you left?"

"No, I, er, she was okay, she just fell down..."

"You killed the wrong person, asshole. Someone saw your vehicle and now you park that piece of shit right in front of this office?" Evan growls. "It's gotta disappear. Take it to the wrecking yard. Arnie's expecting you, along with his share of the money from the jewelry you fenced. And that fuckin' wheezed-out old Bronco is going into the crusher."

"What? No!" They know he fenced the jewelry? Goddamn bikers must've squealed. "You can't...what about the job? There's still that job! You promised to renumerate me!"

"Don't press your luck," Carl says. "No remuneration for fuck-ups. Just be glad you're not going into the crusher with the Bronco."

"Get the fuck outta my sight," Evan demands. "In fact, stay outta everyone's sight and don't stick your head out again until I tell you to. Now go settle up with Arnie. And no pissin' around. I'm texting him to let him know you're on your way."

"But how will I get back...?"

"That's your problem. Maybe you can work something out with Arnie."

"Work something out? What's that supposed to mean?" Trent snorts and looks at Evan, then at Carl. Do they really expect him to give up The Beast and hand over more money for another vehicle that probably won't be as good? From their stern expressions, he realizes there's no use arguing with these two smug assholes.

He jumps to his feet and storms out. He settles in the driver's seat and thumps the steering wheel with the heel of his palm several times, hissing, "Fuck, fuck, fuck-fuck-fuck!"

He gives Prairie Equity the middle finger salute as he backs out of the parking slot, then burns rubber, fishtailing and spewing a cloud of blue-black exhaust. The Beast roars along at close to ninety KPH by the time he passes Big Al's, scaring a fat guy in coveralls back up onto the curb and turning the heads of the blue-haired old biddies clustered around the Co-Op entrance.

In a heartbeat, he's flying over the railroad crossing heading for the stop sign on Highway 19. There's no traffic so he barely slows, just cranks The Beast onto the highway; he opens it up until the needle hits 140, then backs off. It's a 90K zone. No use getting a cop on his tail even though they're taking The Beast away from him. He had such plans for it. A little tinkering is all the engine needs, and The Beast would look so gnarly with a camo paint job, which he could easily do with a few cans of spray paint. He'd cover the Bondo at the same time.

He's nearing the turn for the back road to the auto wreckers when an idea blasts into his brain. He doesn't have to give up The Beast and he doesn't have to give the bikers any money, either. The old bag had a lot of jewelry;

good stuff, too, and that bundle of cash alone turned out to be nearly a thousand dollars. He promised to give Arnie a taste. He wouldn't tell Arnie how much he got for the jewelry and he certainly would never have told him about the cash, but why should Arnie get anything at all, just for sending him to a friendly pawn shop? And then he rats to Mr. I'm So Fuckin' Smart Briggs about the jewelry? Is that any way to treat a new prospect? Fuck him!

He pulls off onto the shoulder, checks for traffic, and seeing none, negotiates a U-turn. He'll go back into Pillerton, just as far as the Co-Op, and get a couple of cans of black spray paint. Might as well grab some beer and a couple bottles of rye while he's at it. Half an hour or so to turn the paint on the Beast into camo just like he planned. He'll jack some different plates. Chances of finding another Bronco probably aren't great, so he may have to settle for plates off any old truck.

Then he'll get his things out of his motel room and book for the Trans Canada Highway heading west. He can always switch the plates again if he comes across another Bronco further on. Maybe in Alberta.

He's not stupid enough to go back to Dark River, which is too bad because he'd like to get in with the Children of Noah now that he's made that connection with their God. He's only been to one service and look what their God did for him already! Sure, not everything went perfect, but it's thanks to God he's got the money to tell those assholes to fuck right off.

No, he'll have to stay out of Dark River at least for a while, but he'll be in Prince George fucking Emmy's brains out by day after tomorrow. Des will hook him up with work there and Pillerton will be nothing but a rotten memory. It's a very smart plan. Fuckin' genius really.

They all think he's a fuck up? Someone they can treat like an idiot? If worse comes to worse and he gets arrested, which is a contingency he is smart enough to plan for, he's got an ace in the hole. A get out of jail free card.

They ought to be more careful with a guy who knows as much as he does. They'll shit themselves when they realize he's gone and they can't find him. *That* he would like to see. Who fucked up now?

No sir, like Dez sez, Mrs. Reardon didn't raise no idiots!

EVAN IS LOCKING the front door when three motorcycles roar up to the curb. He turns to see Arnie step off his bike and set his helmet on the seat. The other two bikers turn their engines off but remain on their bikes.

"Hey, Arnie," Evan greets him, "what's up?"

"Where is the stupid fucker?" Arnie demands as he steps up onto the sidewalk.

"You mean Trent? What do you want him for?"

"Didn't you say he was on his way a couple hours ago?"

"Yeah. Didn't he show up?"

"No, he fuckin' didn't."

Evan takes a deep breath and blows it out through his mouth. "Goddamn fuckin' stupid shit! He's on the run!"

"What do you care? He owe you money, too?"

"Five hundred bucks, I guess. But he's a loose end and more of a problem than a few hundred bucks."

"Besides my share of what he fenced, he still owes us on the Bronco," Arnie says. He puts his hands on his hips and takes a few steps around, looks at the other two bikers, then turns back to Evan and says, "well, we can take care of that problem for you. Where do we find him?"

"Yeah. Problem there. I don't know where he's been staying, except it's a motel. He was going to rent a place but I don't know where. Don't think he's moved yet anyway."

"Jesus fuckin' Christ. Wisht we'da gone to his place that time he invited us. Needle in a haystack now."

"Well, if he didn't go to your place, he's still got the Bronco and he's likely heading for Prince George. He's got a girlfriend there."

"Oh yeah? Dunno if that helps. If he's smart, he'll stay away from her."

"That's if he's smart."

"Yeah, you're right. He's probably gonna show up there. Any idea how to find her? Or how long it will take him to get there?"

"Three days, if he drives hard. We put someone on the girlfriend, just in case he tried this. We'll know when he gets there, if that's where he's headed. I can let you know. But you don't want to go that far…"

"Fuck no. It'd have to be more than a couple large to make the trip worthwhile. But we got people there that can give him our message, and yours, while they're at it."

TWENTY-SIX

THE LODGE

DENVER TURNS THE truck off Bear Mountain Haul Road onto the driveway that's little more than two wheel tracks through the forest, drives up to the gate and turns the engine off. He lets out a low whistle as he scans the clearing. "You weren't kidding," he says.

"I told you," Astrid says.

"They can store thousands of gallons of water in those tanks. What for? One would be plenty for a household, even if they had a few horses, but I don't see any livestock. Nice fence, though."

"Yeah, for a prison yard! Maybe we can put up an electrified fence around Heather's, too. Solve the problem of women running off without giving any notice."

"It would keep people in *and* out. I like that bear statue."

"Yeah, it's nice." Astrid fidgets uneasily in her seat. "Seen enough? Can we go before the live bear shows up?"

"Umm, you know... The neighbourly thing to do would be to introduce myself."

"Neighbourly? How are we neighbours?"

"Friendly, then."

"They're no friendlier than the bear. We'll be late for our reservation."

"This'll just take a minute," Denver promises; he unbuckles his seat belt and slides out of his seat. Although he doubts the bear is around, he can't quite convince himself of that and leaves the truck door open in case he needs to get back in fast. He goes to the intercom and buzzes a couple of times, but there's no answer, so he gets back behind the wheel, buckles up, and starts the engine. There's enough space at the left of the gate to turn around. He backs into it and is just about to put the shifter in drive when a flicker of movement in his peripheral vision attracts his attention. He stops for a moment to see if he can spot what moved. Was it the blinds on the big front window?

"This wasn't exactly just on our way." Astrid says, breaking into his thoughts. "It must be an hour from here to The Lodge."

"That's why we left home early enough for a side trip. Who lives like this?"

"Kathy and I figured he must be a survivalist. He had on the military combat balaclava thing and black wrap-around sunglasses like Fletch used to wear sometimes so all we could see was his nose, like we told you guys. Navy Seal-wannabe. Nut job."

"No arguin' that. Sane people don't hole up like they're waitin' for the livin' dead to come for them."

"Maybe they *are* the living dead. Maybe he's covered from head to toe to keep his body parts from falling off."

"Could be, all right!" Denver barks a laugh. "Tell you what, though, I dunno if he's thought it through. All those tall trees so close to the fence? A good windstorm and he'll be lucky if he doesn't have a dozen down on it. It won't keep anything out then."

"I'll be sure and tell him you think so next time I see him. Anyway, now you've seen it, can we please go?"

"Yeah." Denver's frown deepens as he scans the yard one more time. He clicks his tongue, puts the truck in gear and aims it up the driveway and back out onto the road. "I imagine every busybody in town will be at there, happy to spend many times the price of a Dot's Diner meal just to tell all their friends they were the first to eat at the Bear Mountain Lodge."

"*Dine*, not eat. And everyone's curious. Don't tell me you're not!"

"I am. I'm even more curious to know how they convinced otherwise sensible people like my wife to shell out two hundred bucks for supper."

"I told you, we're invited guests thanks to your buddy Evan Briggs, so for us, it's free. What sensible person would pass on that? And it's not supper, it's *dinner*. A set menu with wine pairings."

"S'pose that means I won't be able to get a beer."

"Probably no cherry pie with ice cream, either. Your redneck is positively glowing."

He gives her a sideways glance and says, "well, if nuthin' else, it gave you a reason to get all gussied up. I gotta say, you are an eyeful in that pretty dress." He reaches across to give her hand a squeeze, then tickles the back of her neck and from there, traces the scoop neckline of her dress. When his fingers begin working their way into her bra, she takes his hand.

"Hey! Keep your hands on the wheel and your eyes the road!"

"Five years and I still can't keep my hands off you." He pulls her hand into his crotch. "See what you do to me? How about we find a nice spot to pull over..."

"No!" Astrid laughs and pulls her hand away.

"Why not? For old times' sake."

"A couple of old married people getting it on in their truck out in the bush even if it means missing an expensive supper?"

"We could make it a quickie."

"No, absolutely not!" Her smile belies her stern refusal. "Not now, anyway. But how about on our way home?"

"Deal!"

"And just so you know, I'd rather it wasn't a quickie."

Just then her phone chimes and she pulls it out of her purse to see Kathy's face. "Oh, it's Kathy! Wait'll she hears where we're going." She touches accept and lifts the phone to her ear. "Hi, Kathy!"

She's quiet, and then says, "Oh my god!"

WHEN HE SEES the driver of the truck turn his head to look toward the house, Bearon quickly takes his hand off the blind. At this distance he can't be certain, but the cowboy hat makes him think it was Denver Danielson, the big shot hero of Dark River. The reason he is the way he is. And it's a sure bet the woman in the passenger seat was Astrid. What are the two of them doing here? Weren't their names on the reservation sheet? They should be at the

Lodge. But no, they had to come here first and snoop around.

First Kathy and Astrid, and now Astrid's husband, poking their noses in where they don't belong. Probably Kathy's husband too. He doesn't know much about Rick other than faded memories from when he was a little kid, but Danielson is like a terrier on a rat. He'll be tough to put off.

The pain in his back and hip has settled down to a dull ache radiating down his thigh and making his buttock feel tingly-numb. He has to be careful how he moves the leg or intense pain knifes through his hip. It's worse since the Buster debacle, heavy damn mutt even gutted, but he'll have a nice new fur on the wall next to Brutus. It's so big and furry, maybe it'll be nice on the floor in front of the fireplace. Whatever. It was worth the effort. It's a tribute. Roy Rogers had Trigger stuffed, didn't he?

Annie says keeping the dog's hide is morbid. She especially dislikes the head being left on. He wonders what Kiersten would think. She's a mouse, but soft-spoken and intelligent, the total opposite of Annie. He's beginning to understand what Clint sees in her.

He takes a few steps away from the window. One wrong step, and the pain is so intense he almost can't lift the leg. Communion didn't help, but that's always worth a little pain. Still, lately it seems to take less and less to fire it up. Thank god he doesn't have to climb the steps to the attic meeting room at The Fisherman's anymore. The hot tub helps, and that's where he was headed when Danielson showed up.

He hadn't planned to be anywhere near the Lodge when the fancy grand opening dinner was going on, but now he thinks he'll go, just to keep an eye on Mr. and Mrs. Danielson.

He goes to the bathroom, gets the Oxycontin out of the medicine cabinet, opens the bottle and tips two into his hand. On his way through the kitchen, he gets a glass of water and swallows the pills, then continues out to the back deck. He can spend ten minutes in the hot tub. With the pills, that should be enough to take the pain down to a dull roar. He'll take the shortcut and be in his office in front of the monitors before they get there.

DENVER BACKS THE truck into the last space in the row of cars, watching the screen for the back-up camera to avoid hitting the planter and to make sure he isn't blocking the lane that runs behind the building.

"I'm not sure I feel like dinner after all," Astrid says.

"Maybe it'll take our minds off it."

"Imagine killing an old woman! In her own home! Just to get her jewelry. A home invasion out in the country where things like that aren't supposed to happen!"

Denver reaches for her hand and gives it a squeeze. "It's awful, babe. But there's nothing we can do, so we might as well go inside and see if we can't enjoy that fancy meal, at least a little."

They both open their doors and slide out; as he does so, Denver glances along the back of the building, and frowns.

Astrid waits for him in front of the truck but when he seems engrossed in what he's looking at, asks, "What's so interesting back there?"

"Come look," he replies, and points back behind the building. "Is that what you saw Bear Man driving?"

"I wish you wouldn't call him that! Especially with Lisey..."

"She's not here."

"You'll forget yourself and say it when she's around. You know she doesn't miss anything." Astrid comes to stand next to him and sees the orange and black Kubota UTV parked beside a doorway.

"That's it!" she exclaims.

"Hmm. But there's more'n one of those around. They need it here for the yard work. You know how much we use our Gator," Denver says.

"There's the gunrack—with a rifle!—in the back window of the cab. They don't need that for yard work."

"No," Denver agrees, "but we are in bear territory. We get the odd bear in our pasture so it's possible they might come right up to the buildings here. I'd sure want a rifle handy in that case. But suppose it is the one you saw. I wonder if, or how, this place is connected to Bear Man."

She frowns at him; he gives her a wink. She clicks her tongue and says, "maybe he's the new owner. Look, there's a gate behind the garage there, right where you and Fletch cut the fence, and a trail into the forest. How much do you want to bet it comes out at that survivalist compound?" A shiver courses through her and the memory of the night the fence was cut comes unbidden.

"Possible," Denver says. He doesn't miss Astrid's pinched expression. Dilated nostrils and sudden rapid breathing. Quivering lower lip. The quaking of her entire body. "But we're not gunna prove it tonight. Let's get inside. I'm gettin' hungry and I can't wait to see how small they can make those medallions of capon you told me about. I'm thinkin' we might have to go for a cheeseburger after supper."

He pulls her close and hugs her until her trembling subsides. Then he gives her a quick kiss, takes her hand, and they go back through the parking lot to the front entrance. Once inside, they wait while another couple is seated ahead of them.

When she comes back, the hostess says, "Welcome to Bear Mountain Lodge. Your names, please?" When Astrid tells her, she checks the seating plan on the podium and says, "Right this way."

They follow the hostess into a large room with five meter high ceilings. There are huge peeled logs everywhere and a massive, full-height river rock fireplace in the middle of the room. The entire front wall is windows; a couple of them are sliding doors open onto a paving stone patio where a handful of people lounge under the umbrella at a horseshoe-shaped bar.

A silver-haired man in a tuxedo tinkles away on the grand piano at the far end of the room. Tables, each with a rose bowl on its white cloth, are set along the window wall, around the potted palm in the center of the room, and on both sides of the fireplace. There are servers and bus boys bustling everywhere.

They're lead to a table for two on the far side of the cleared area giving access to the patio exit and next to the window.

"Your server will be with you in a moment," the hostess tells them. "Enjoy your meal."

They thank her and Astrid hangs her purse on the back of her chair as she looks around. "Wow, nice table! Fresh air. No near neighbours. Almost like we're in a private room," she says. "But I really thought I'd see more people I recognized. You see anyone you know?"

"Jonesy from the Caterpillar dealer, over there." With a lift of his chin, he acknowledges a couple just being seated at a table next to the fireplace. "Guess that's his wife. That's about it. Lots who look familiar, though. Maybe there's more we know on the other side of the fireplace. Jeez, at two hundred a head, they're rakin' in thousands tonight."

A familiar figure is coming their way, and Astrid says, "oh, there's Annie!"

"Hey guys," Annie calls out as she approaches their table. "Saw your name on the reservations. Glad to see they put you in my section."

"Not working at Dot's tonight, obviously," Astrid comments.

"Nope! Pay's better here. Franny has been cutting back everyone's hours since tourist season is over, so she don't mind. I had to learn what all these high-falutin' menu items are, though! Nuthin' you'd ever see at Dot's, eh? Medallions of Capon! Can't they just call it chicken chunks?" She rolls her eyes and then grins. "Maybe it tastes better if you call it somethin' fancy. How're you guys doin'?"

"Well, we had some bad news," Denver tells her, "so I think we'll be startin' with a nice half liter of house white for my wife, if we can do that. And is it possible to get a beer?"

"Oh? What bad news?"

"Just a friend's mother was, er, a friend's mother passed away."

"Well, that's the shits! For your friends anyhow. Of course you can have whatever you want from the bar."

Astrid says, "he might think I need a liter to start with, but I think I'll just have a glass and wait to see what comes with the first course."

"Good enough." She rattles off the house wines and what's available for beer, and when Denver and Astrid have made their selections, hurries away.

"Good ol' Annie," Denver says. "I don't think she has an inside voice."

"That'll be Lisey if she doesn't outgrow it," Astrid says as she shakes her head. "She's a little rough around the edges but her heart's in the right place. She's the reason we met Kathy and Rick, after all. Besides, they might not've had a lot of applications for a one-time job way out here. I'm surprised I don't see more girls from Dot's. Looks like they recruited girls from Hooters."

"We got a Hooters in Dark River? How come I don't know about it?"

"I guess we should go straight there when we leave. They probably have cheeseburgers."

"Naw, it'll be too late," Denver says with a wink. "Don't forget about that other stop we have to make."

The hostess interrupts their conversation to serve their drinks. Right behind her, one of the young men drops off a basket with four small buns tucked inside a cloth, together with four butter curls on a side plate.

"One of these fancy little things for each bun, I guess," Denver says as he splits a bun and spears a butter curl with his knife. "If the rest of the servings are as small as these little gaffers, I really am gunna want a cheeseburger on the way home."

After appetizers of hot cheese-stuffed mushrooms and pancetta crisps with goat cheese and caramelized pear, there's gazpacho soup, then a wilted spinach salad with warm apple cider and bacon dressing. That done, they're served the medallions of capon with risotto and sage brown butter. There's wine, different and in a fresh glass, to go with each course. Annie explains the wines were chosen to complement each dish by someone who knows these things.

"If it was me, I'd have a beer with everything," she tells them.

"I like how you think," Denver says. "I have to admit, this is pretty nice, though. How the other half lives, eh?"

Boys in black pants and white shirts keep water goblets filled and used dishware taken away.

When Annie brings a small plate with a nugget of yellow sherbet the size of a golf ball resting on a mint leaf and flanked by a raspberry and a blueberry, Denver says, "I thought dessert was going to be in the Grotto."

"This ain't dessert. This is to *cleanse* your mouth before the main course," Annie explains.

"Oh?"

"Who knew your mouth needed to be cleansed, eh? I thought that's what Listerine was for!" Annie says, and laughs. "Roland has your espresso." She gestures to the young man hovering behind her, and hurries off.

When their tiny cups of espresso are in front of them, Astrid picks up the menu card. "The sherbet is the Intermezzo," she tells Denver. "Main course is slow braised short rib with garlic mustard pesto, a salmon filet in phyllo pastry with tarragon hollandaise, morel mushrooms and grilled asparagus, baby peas and a sweet carrot puree. Sounds delicious."

"I thought those three little chicken chunks were the main course. Maybe I'm not going to need that cheeseburger after all."

When she's finished the sherbet and the very strong espresso, Astrid says, "I need a bathroom break. I think the washrooms are near where we came in." She gets up and wends her way through the other tables, stopping for a moment to say hello to Jonesy and his wife and comment on what a nice evening it is.

"Fancy meal," Jonesy says. "Cold soup and warm salad. The wife's been doin' it wrong all these years!"

They chuckle, then Astrid suggests, "Come join us for a drink after."

When they agree, she carries on to the entrance foyer, where there's a sign indicating the washrooms are down the hall to her left. As she nears the ladies room, Annie, dishes in one hand, comes out a door at the end of the hall. She turns to face back into the room, listening to someone inside. The door is open wide enough for Astrid to get a glimpse of an array of monitors off to one side and a bald man at a desk.

When she turns and sees Astrid, Annie quickly pulls the door closed behind her. Cutlery clatters to the floor as she bobbles the dishes. She picks up the fallen items and hurries past Astrid with just a sideways glance and a nod.

When Astrid returns to the table, she says in an almost-whisper, "Annie was just coming out of an office back there. She was talking to someone inside, a bald man I think, unless there was someone else in there with him. When she saw me, she got flustered. Panicked, even."

"Panicked?"

"Yeah. She got a look of shock on her face when she saw me, and shut the door in such a hurry she dropped the cutlery off the plates she was carrying. I had a sense she was panicked about me being able to see in. Like maybe I shouldn't see the guy she was talking to."

"He's probably the boss. Maybe even the owner. You think that's his Kubota parked out back?"

"Umm. Would a survivalist own a fancy place like this? Put on a fancy dinner like this?"

"Why not? Makes sense, actually. They gotta have money. And then that trail you noticed, if it leads to his place, would be handy so he can just get in his UTV and be here, probably in a lot less time than it would take comin' in on that poor excuse for a road. Maybe he was on his way back from here when you, er, *met* him that day with Kathy. And he sure does set a store on his privacy so he might not want anyone lookin' into his office. Did he look familiar?"

"Hmm. No. I only got a quick glimpse of him. Now that I think about it, I'm not even sure he was bald. His head was—I don't know—shiny, or like the skin was puckered somehow. Must have been a skull cap like Muslims wear, or a yarmulke." Astrid closes her eyes, mentally reviewing what she saw, but can't bring the man into focus. She straightens, leans forward, and whispers, "I can't figure it. What if it's not that he *likes* privacy, but that he *needs* it? Because he's hiding something? After what Kiersten said at lunch—"

"Kiersten didn't really give you any details, though."

"No, but you didn't see the look on her face. She was horrified, or, er, more like panicked, when she realized she'd said something she shouldn't have. Something that might get her in trouble. She looked around like she was being watched or something. I was worried if I pushed her further I might send her into another panic attack. And that's odd too because I asked her if the heart monitor on her Apple watch helped her keep on top of the panic attacks, for a second I thought she didn't know what I was talking about."

She looks up and sees Annie coming toward them with two plates. "Oh, here comes Annie with our main course. I'll ask her who she was talking to back there."

"Probably better if you don't, babe. Don't want to embarrass her any more."

"I'll be diplomatic."

"Babe, if Kiersten's right and the new Lodge is just like the old one, she might be part of it. We don't want to tip her off."

"You believe me, then? Believe Kiersten? You must, because we unpacked Fletch's guns. You didn't do that just to shut me up, did you?"

"No. Maybe I don't believe it, but I don't disbelieve, either."

Astrid is mulling it over as Annie gets to them.

Denver leans back in his chair, loosens his belt buckle a notch, and fixes a smile on his face. "Gads, Annie! I'm startin' to hope the servings are small. Otherwise I don't know if I'll have room for dessert."

KEVIN IS ON the narrow deck outside the patio doors leading to his second-storey room at the Lodge, enjoying the fading rays of the day. Soon the sun will be blocked by the giant Douglas firs at the end of the cleared area just fifty meters away.

His room is not unpleasant, but it rankles that Hayward and Preacher got primo rooms on the front. Bigger, with morning sun and afternoon shade. A view of the water feature and tidy landscaping instead of the industrial-size propane tanks and remains of the construction debris out back and beyond that, nothing but forest. No hum from the heat pumps. No exhaust fans blasting out food and detergent smells from the kitchen and laundry.

Why are Hayward and Preacher even involved in this? Preacher can't preach worth a shit. Read the sermon at Communion. Hayward is even more useless. They don't have skin in the game and yet they're higher status than he is, just because they were left over after the explosion.

He paid nothing to get in either, but at least he contributes. Where else would they find a lawyer who would turn a blind eye to everything? And he does all their legal work with never so much as a thank you. If only the explosion had happened a day later! Hayward and Preacher would be gone with the rest of them. Instead, they're Elders and he's not, so he gets the room on the back side. *I get the backside,* he thinks. *Always the backside.*

He got the backside at communion, too. Nothing more than a smile and a quick squeeze from the hot Acolyte as she applied the scented oil, and during the Mingling, it was the three in the red robes the so-called Ceremonial Wives flocked around.

Once they got a look at Bearon's junk, it was almost over for Hayward and Preacher, too. Wonder if he'd still be so popular if they saw what's under the balaclava! He'd like to see it himself. The little bit that shows when he pulls the bottom flap of the balaclava down under his chin gives a hint of what a gnarly mess the rest must be. Like he was the victim of an acid attack or something.

Despite Bearon's assurances he'd get as much pussy as the Elders, it hasn't worked out that way. He complained to Bearon and got assigned to the Emmy project. She has the vocabulary of a grade schooler and is not much to look at, skinny as a crack ho, but he has to admit she makes up for it with youthful vigor in the sack. She's more than twenty years younger than he is, after all. He slipped her some folding stuff to pay for her score when they "accidentally" met at the pub and he's been enjoying her attentions regularly ever since.

Since he learned of her fondness for nose candy, he brings her a little something from the company stores each time he comes. He even gave her a pair of earrings he told her were diamonds. He gets lots of goodwill out of those! Until she tries to pawn them, anyway.

He can't complain, but it may not last much longer. Maybe this hide-away weekend is the last he'll see of her, what with Trent on his way back. Then again, maybe not. It depends on what they do with Trent. He doesn't know if he even wants it to continue. They ought to be able to hook him up with someone a little easier to look at.

Being treated as if he's on the same rung of the ladder as Clint stings, too. Bearon acted like giving him the Emmy project was a perk. Some perk! Does Bearon really think he's too stupid to realize he was the only choice for the assignment? Clint couldn't do it even if he was home since Emmy is his son's girlfriend. Clint wouldn't rat on his son even if he would fuck his girlfriend. No way Hayward or Preacher could do the job. Neither of them would ever get into Emmy's pants! Too old and too fat. The girl might be free with her favours but she wouldn't stoop to that! Well, not for a twenty dollar pair of earrings. Maybe for the drugs.

His phone chimes and he picks it up off the table to see it's from a blocked number. He touches the accept button and says, "Hey."

"Hey," Bearon responds, "those clients of yours that you didn't want to see you are here. You better keep out of sight."

"Don't worry. I plan to."

"Good. I just told Annie to take up a trolley with your meals. Meanwhile, any news?"

"Yeah. I'm taking her home first thing tomorrow."

"He'll be back in town so soon?"

"Tomorrow or Monday."

"Okay. Make sure she calls you as soon as he gets to her place."

"Yeah." He touches end call and hisses, "Fuck you!" Bearon presumes to micromanage *him*? Like he wouldn't know what to do otherwise? He drops the phone on the table next to his chair.

A reed thin woman in nothing but a lacy thong panty and full sleeve tattoos comes through the sliding glass door onto the deck, fresh drinks in hand, just as the phone clatters to the table. She puts the drinks on the table and sinks to the chair across from him. "Something wrong?" she asks.

"Nothing for you to worry about, baby," Kevin tells her. "They're bringing our meal up pretty quick."

He takes a long drink of the Cuba Libre Emmy just brought him as he ponders how to change the status quo.

Even if he wanted to get out, which he doesn't, they'd never allow him to go. Not knowing as much as he does. They've already quashed his suggestion they renegotiate their charter so they could have four Elders, so there won't be room at the top until an Elder dies.

Maybe there's a way to facilitate that.

TWENTY-SEVEN

THE KIERSTEN SHUFFLE

CLINT PULLS THE laundry truck up to the stanchion. The driver's seat is too high for him to reach the touch pad so he opens his door, slides out, and punches his code in. As the gates roll open, he climbs back behind the wheel and drives to the basement parkade entrance.

Bearon must have seen him on the monitors, as the overhead door is already rumbling up. He swings the truck around and slowly backs in past the row of empty stalls to the reserved spot at the end wall, turns the engine off, and gets out.

Several minutes pass before the elevator door opens and Bearon hobbles out.

"Shit, Bearon," Clint says, "what happened to you? Fall off your UTV? Couldn't you send someone who's in, er, a little better shape to help with this?"

"If I could, I would. I'm here alone tonight. Whatcha got?"

"Just two."

"Two? Thought you already had two three days ago."

"Goes like that sometimes. These two are prime, though."

"Okay. Well. Nuthin' we can do about that now." Bearon adjusts his balaclava to cover most of his face and points into the box. "Let's get after it. We can take 'em both at once. I got places to be and it's already midnight."

Clint opens the rear door and climbs into the box. Shoving aside the rolling bins heaped with sheets, he pulls metal shelving away from the back wall to expose a door. He flicks the light switch next to the door as he opens it. "Okay, girls, wakey wakey!"

Two girls huddle together on the lower bunk, squeezing as far into the corner as possible as he comes toward them. "Come on, honey, I'm gonna take you to a much more comfortable place," he tells them. He holds out his hand and says, "here. Take my hand. I'll help you."

When neither girl moves, he takes the nearest one by the upper arm and pulls her to her feet, propelling her out the small door and through the box to the rear door where Bearon waits.

When the girl sees the masked man in dark clothes, she sobs and shrinks back against Clint. "Don't worry," he tells her, "he can't bite with that thing over his mouth. That's why we make him wear it." He pushes her down onto the floor so Bearon can grab her, and goes back to get the other girl.

Bearon takes the girl by the hips and pulls her off the truck, then holds her firmly by the arm until Clint returns with the other girl. With both girls out of the truck, Clint hops down and corrals the two of them against the wall next to the truck while Bearon unlocks the door marked "Electrical".

Inside the small room is a bank of metal boxes. Wires of all sizes and colours stapled to the walls and ceiling feed in and out of the boxes. The back wall houses tall steel cabinets with knobs and dials and more wires feeding in and out. Clint goes to the center cabinet, turns the knob at the top, then pulls. The door swings open, revealing a narrow staircase descending into the dark. He flicks a switch. Lights come on and they go down. At the bottom, they come out into a windowless hallway with half a dozen doors down one side. Clint stops at the first door they come to.

"Next one," Bearon tells him. He has each girl by her upper arm and pushes them to the next door. Clint follows to unlock and open it. The room is not much bigger than a jail cell, with upper and lower bunks, a small table, two plastic chairs and a narrow door on the back wall.

When Bearon releases their arms, the girls scurry to the far end of the room and turn back to face the men. "Toilet and shower in the back," he tells them. "Someone will bring you breakfast in the morning." He closes the door and when he hears the lock click, gives it a tug just to be sure.

He turns to Clint, pulls the bottom of the balaclava down under his mouth, and says, "by the way, that comment about me biting wasn't funny."

"Oh? Sorry."

"You won't like what happens if you come out with a smart ass remark like that again," Bearon warns. He stands rigid, glaring at the smaller man.

"I said I'm sorry! It just came out. I'm tired. It's been a long trip. It won't happen again."

"It better not." After a moment, Bearon relaxes and asks, "where'd you get these two? A junior high school? They look like they're about eleven."

"Runaways. I picked 'em up west of Calgary. They claim to be nineteen and that they're singers, on their way to fame and fortune in Vancouver."

"Jesus. I doubt they're even sixteen."

"Well, they've got tits."

"The start of tits, you mean. Just babies."

"They don't think so. When I gave them the cash, grass or ass options of paying for the ride, guess what they chose."

"You fuck 'em?"

"What do you think? They weren't virgins, so, no harm, no foul." Clint's attention is drawn by thumping on the first door. "What the hell, Bearon? Someone else brought someone in?"

"Yeah. Not what you're thinking, though."

Bearon goes to the first door, unlocks it, and stands back, saying, "after you."

Clint pulls the door open to find Trent standing in front of him.

"Dad!" he sobs and lurches toward Clint, "look what they done to me!" He holds out his battered arms. His eyes are nearly swollen shut and his face is mottled with bruises and cuts under half a dozen butterfly band-aids.

Clint says nothing for a moment, then turns to Bearon. "What the fuck, Bearon?"

"He ran into some guys he should've known better than to fuck with. He's lucky he's still breathin'."

"What's he doin' here?"

"Ask him. Can't wait to hear what kind of excuse he's dreamed up. Just know he was given a job to do in Pillerton and he fucked up, killed an old woman while he was at it. He wasn't supposed to come back here, remember? Yet here he is. He stays here until I decide what to do with him." Bearon starts away but turns back to say, "Lock up when you leave, but don't hurry home. I've got a date with Kiersten." The door clanks shut behind him.

Clint clenches his teeth and stares at the closed door for the seconds it takes for a slow burn to work its way through his guts. Doesn't Bearon think maybe a guy who's been on the road for over a week would be anxious to get back to his own bed? The bastard has been swinging his dick more and more lately and there's no one to take him down a peg.

He needs to get home. Kiersten has been odd when he's called her, and her texts have been terse. She didn't answer when he tried FaceTime. Something's going on, and now he has to cool his heels somewhere instead of going home? Even if he's imagining things...even if there's nothing wrong and they get jiggy as soon as he's home, it'll be sloppy seconds thanks to Bearon.

"It wasn't my fault," Trent says, breaking into his thoughts.

"What?"

"I know it sounds bad, about the old lady, but it wasn't my fault!"

"Old lady? What old lady?"

"The one that croaked. It wasn't my fault."

Clint thinks, *whatever went wrong wasn't his fault. It never is his fault.* He's in no mood to find out more. He says, "I know, son."

"The fuckers really hurt me, Dad," he says with a sob. "I think they busted my ribs!"

"Did you get x-rays?"

"All they done was put these b-b-bandaids on me." He gingerly strokes the butterfly plasters on his brow and cheeks. "They n-n-never took me to no doctor. I tol' 'em I prob'ly need a tetnis shot but they w-w-wouldn't listen!"

"Is there anything, I mean *anything,* that might connect you to, um, that old lady?"

"No, I never done nuthin' to her! Besides, I know better. I never touched nuthin'."

"Nuthin' at all?"

"Well, a jewelry box, but I wiped that. And The Beast."

"The Beast?"

"My Bronco. Cops were lookin' for that. Someone seen it around the ol' lady's place I guess. But that's...there's no way they can tie that to me. It's in the made-up name they give me."

"Where is it now?"

"Dunno. The bikers took it off me. They've prob'ly got rid of it by now."

"Okay, then," Clint says, "I'll take you and get you checked out. After that, I'll stash you somewhere the boss won't find you. Maybe you can go to your mother's for a little while. It'll be okay"

"But he said..."

"I know what he said." He leaves his arm around Trent's shoulders as they walk toward the stairs. "Fuck him."

"A FOUR-HOUR wait in Emergency and all they can come up with is yeah, you got two broken ribs, but they don't do nuthin' about it, just tell you they'll heal on their own, and send you home? That's the best modern medicine can come up with?" Clint scowls. "Waste of fuckin' time."

He and Trent come out the emergency room doors into bright morning sunlight, take the sidewalk to the parking lot and head for the Porsche at the far end.

"They give me a pill for the pain and I can get more with the scrip he give me. Also, I got stitches. See?" He turns his head and leans in.

"Yeah, I see. Good to get 'em cleaned out so they don't get infected."

"The doc said he thinks the one on my cheek is gunna leave a scar."

"Well, you're gunna be one tough-lookin' hombre for sure," Clint tells him. He doesn't think a few more scars are going to matter. Poor kid was never going to win any prizes for his looks.

"Dad, I don't think the doctor believed me that I fell into a ditch. He told me to be sure and watch where I was goin from now on."

"Whether he believed you or not doesn't matter," Clint tells him. He notices two marked RCMP cruisers in the designated ambulance parking, but inside, there was a bloodied guy handcuffed to a gurney with a couple of cops hanging around chatting up the nurses, so he thinks nothing of it.

As they walk up beside the first cruiser, Clint is surprised to see there's a cop in it. In fact, the second cruiser is occupied, too. Two cops per cruiser?

Trent notices it at about the same time, and says urgently, "Dad!"

"Nuthin' to worry about, son. They're just fuckin' the dog while their partners are inside with the..."

At that moment the driver's doors of both cruisers open and the officers spring out, coming toward them with their hands on their holsters. Another cruiser, lights on, chirps its siren as it pulls up behind them.

Trent shrieks, "Fuck!"

The nearest cop holds up a badge and calls out, "RCMP! Trent Reardon! On your knees! Hands on your head! You're under arrest for the murder of Hermine Schoenfeld."

WHEN CLINT FINALLY gets to his house later in the afternoon, Kiersten isn't home. He's not surprised, because she was at work. He swung by the Riverview on his way home and managed to get a kiss and a quick hug, but her co-workers were watching so the embrace was brief. He offered to pick her up after work but she said she already had a ride, so she'd see him at home. He decided to pick up groceries and surprise her with dinner ready when she got in.

He sets the grocery bags on the counter and is putting things away, leaving the salad fixings and hamburger for spaghetti sauce next to the stove, when the doorbell rings. He goes to the door and opens it on Kevin.

"Hey," Kevin says.

"You're finished with Trent already?" Clint asks.

"Yeah, well, they're not going to let him out until he appears before a judge in the morning."

"I guess that's how it usually works."

"Yeah. Er, you got a beer? I could use one."

Clint steps back and gestures with a wave, "Yeah, of course, come in. I was just getting ready to make dinner. Come grab a stool. Actually," he says as he glances at his Rolex, "I've got some time. I think I'll join you in that beer."

The two men head into the kitchen. Kevin takes a stool at the island while Clint gets two bottles of Heineken out of the fridge. He passes one to Kevin as he slides onto the stool next to him.

After opening his beer and taking a long swig, Clint says, "you didn't come here just to tell me this."

"Well, no. Fact is, I need to talk to you."

"What about?"

"That kid of yours. He worries me."

"Oh?"

Kevin draws a deep breath, clicks his tongue, and swivels his stool so he can look Clint in the eye. "He wants a meeting with Crown Counsel. He's talking about making a deal."

"What? What kind of a deal could he possibly make? What's he know that's worth enough to skate on a murder rap? Not boosting that hotel room…"

"No, not just that. Think about it. Kiersten claims she wasn't kidnapped but Trent knows she was. Or at least someone was. And where did he take her? To Bearon's." Kevin shakes his head slowly. "That might be explained away, but do you know what the job in Pillerton was?"

"Umm, no. I guess I didn't ask."

"Course you wouldn't ask. No one's allowed to ask questions. Everything's 'need to know' and I doubt Bearon would've thought you had a need to know."

"Trent said something about an old lady. I guess that's who they think he murdered. I should've asked him more about it but I was a little distracted."

"I know. It's about Kiersten, yeah?"

"Yeah. She's been acting peculiar."

"No doubt. You know why?"

Clint shakes his head.

"Because Bearon's been all over her the whole time you were away. If I didn't think it was impossible for him to have human emotions, I'd say he's smitten with her. Has she told you he's let her see him? I mean, *see* him? And that he's going to transfer her out of your house and into his?"

"What? No! He can't do that!"

"Yeah, I thought you didn't know. Bastard pulls this off when you aren't around. She didn't have a car. Gonna need one living out there, so he bought her one. She's quit her job. From now on her only job is to service him."

The fact Kevin called Bearon a bastard barely registering, Clint leaps to his feet and strides around the kitchen slamming cupboard doors and cursing. "Fuck! Goddamn *fuckin'* Bearon!"

"I know it's a kick in the nuts, Clint, but it's not the worst of it. Trent is a much bigger, more immediate problem. You don't think he has information to trade? Where did you pick him up from last night?"

"Well…"

"And that's not the first time he's been there. There were a lot more guests there the last time they stuck him down there, remember? He might not have seen them, but for sure he heard them. And then there's the hit he contracted for in Pillerton."

"A hit? Trent?"

"Yeah. He was hired to kill that woman who was snooping around, asking questions about Hank. He got her mother-in-law by mistake. That's the only part of it that was an accident."

"Trent was going to kill someone? Trent *did* kill someone? He said he didn't touch her."

"Well, there's a pile of forensics that says otherwise. And he's talking about the Saskatchewan operation. Knows Evan and Carl are involved. The bikers and their crusher. Who knows what else."

"What?" Clint slumps to a chair at the kitchen table next to the patio doors. "Trent?" The idea of his son being a stone cold killer is impossible to believe. "It can't be," he says. "He's as dumb as a post. You know him, he's like a ten year old. He's harmless. He couldn't kill anyone!"

Kevin swivels his stool around to face Clint. "Well, apparently he thought he could."

"But if he killed that... If that happened in Saskatchewan, why aren't they sending him back there?"

"They might eventually but they want to try him here first. It's not just for breaching bail conditions. They think they can tie him to a double murder last year on Vancouver Island."

"*What?* My god!"

They sit quiet while several minutes tick by. Then Kevin says, "I know it's a lot to wrap your head around. I'd give you time to process it, but time is a luxury we don't have. You have to talk to him, tonight. Before he can get with someone from Crown Counsel's office. Make sure he knows that you hired me to take care of him and if he takes Bearon or the Pillerton guys down, we all go down. Or at least get it across to him that you'll go down. Make him think you've got some deep dark secret and they could put you away for the rest of your life."

"Well..."

"I know. So, all he has to do to save you is plead guilty, just to the Saskatchewan charge. They haven't got enough to lay charges on the double murder yet. Maybe they never will. He'll be okay on that as long as he keeps his mouth shut. I've already told him I'm going to get the charge on the Saskatchewan thing reduced to involuntary manslaughter. He'll get ten years. What the hell, tell him five years. He won't even be thirty when he gets out and we'll set him up with a nice house, hot car or a new Bronco better than the one he keeps whining about, if that's what he wants. He just needs to keep his mouth shut."

"That might not be so easy for him to do."

"I know, he's yappy. Can you make him understand that if he yaps to other guys in jail, he won't be safe in there, either. Lots of nasty things can happen."

Clint nods and takes a few deep breaths. "You want me to see him tonight?"

"Yes." Kevin gets to his feet. "I think I can get him out on bail until his sentencing hearing, too. It would help if I could tell the judge he would be staying with you."

"I guess so. Sure."

"You'll have to be with me in court so the judge can confirm it with you."

"How long before the sentencing hearing?"

"Don't know. The old woman's family has a right to present victim impact statements so they'll likely give them time to arrange to be here."

"Okay."

"Come with me," Kevin says. "I'll get you in to see him now." He drinks the last of his beer, slams the empty bottle down on the island, and heads for the door just ahead of Clint.

CLINT IS SLOUCHED on the sofa having just drained his sixth beer when Kiersten comes in. He doesn't get up, just demands, "when were you going to tell me?"

"I—"

"Never mind," Clint says, "don't bother putting your purse down. You want to live with that asshole? Why not start tonight?"

"But Clint! It's not that I want to!"

"Don't give me that!" He gets up off the couch and wobbles slightly as he takes a few steps toward her. "All that moanin' and groanin' while you were fuckin' him—he enjoyed those fake orgasms so much he decided he'd like a steady diet, and you went right along with it, didn't you!"

"Clinton, baby, you told me to make it convincing! You know he takes what he wants! You said it would be a few times. I never thought I was going to have to live with him!"

"Oh no? Tell me you don't like his big dick! And the new car!"

"I—er—"

"Don't you lie! Don't you *dare* lie to me!" He strides toward her, grabs her by the shoulders and pushes her back against the wall.

"Clint, stop it! You're hurting me!"

"Oh yeah?"

"I—"

"Tell you what," he snarls, "let's see if you can moan and groan as convincingly when *I'm* fuckin' you!" He pulls her away from the wall and frog-marches her into the bedroom where he shoves her down on the bed. He pushes her uniform skirt up, hooks his fingers into her panties and pulls them roughly off. She attempts to sit up but he pushes her down again, unzipping and pushing his pants down to his knees at the same time. As he climbs on top of her, forcing himself inside her, he rips her blouse open and squeezes her breast. "Come on, bitch, let's hear some of those moans now!" he cries as he pounds away.

With a shock, he realizes she's crying and he is overcome with the enormity of what he's doing. She's right. It's not her fault. Bearon gets what he wants.

He rolls off and pulls her into his arms. "I'm sorry, baby. I'm sorry!" He holds her and strokes her hair while she cries.

"I love you, Kiersten. I just lost control. You know I love you! I can't stand the idea of him taking you away."

Her only answer is a sob.

He cups her chin and turns her face up so she makes eye contact. It's fleeting, though. She looks off to the side. "You know I love you, don't you?"

She won't meet his gaze but after a moment, gives a short nod.

"He doesn't love you! I love you more than anyone else ever could. It just made me crazy, him taking you away from me! I'm sorry, so sorry, for doing this. Forgive me? Please! Can you?"

"I guess so," she whispers.

He's stroking her neck when he realizes she's wearing a necklace. It's a chain. A heavy one. With a large gold pendant on it. He holds it in his palm to examine it.

"What's this?" he asks. "Something else Bearon gave you?"

She stiffens but doesn't answer.

"Yeah, of course it is." It's a gold coin in a rope setting. Who knows if the coin is worth anything, but the heavy chain would easily run a thousand. She wouldn't have the money to buy it.

"I don't even like it," Kiersten whispers. "It's too heavy. He insisted."

"I'm sorry, baby. Of course you have to play along." He doubts it's all playing, or that she gets no enjoyment from sex with Bearon. But it's stupid for him to take it out on Kiersten when she's much more useful as an ally than as an ex-girlfriend. One who wasn't even supposed to be a girlfriend. Lesson learned.

He's lying when he says he loves her. What really picks him is Bearon swooping in and taking her. If he'd asked for her, Clint would have given her to him without a second thought. Not that he'll tell anyone that.

"I have to move to his place. And I'm going to be working at the Lodge from now on."

"The Lodge? Doing what?"

"There's different things going on. Members are starting to book in. The software's the same as at Riverview so I already know how it works. They won't have to train anyone."

"So...I won't be able to see you at all? We won't be able to see each other at all?"

"I don't know."

"Well, you know my schedule is flexible. He wouldn't have given you a car if he wanted to keep you isolated up there."

"I guess not. But I'm not sure if I'm, er, if I can, you know, see other guys. Like see you, I mean. Like what would he do if I, er..."

Clint sits up and smooths Kiersten's skirt. When he fusses with her blouse, he realizes it's torn. "Sorry about this," he says, "looks like I ruined your blouse. Good thing you won't need it much longer. Tell you what. Get changed and we'll go out for something to eat. What do you think? Moxie's maybe? A nice dinner and then home to bed. Tonight, let's forget everything else except loving each other. We'll deal with tomorrow, tomorrow."

He realizes he has to be especially loving if he wants to keep Kiersten on his side. And he does. Having her living with Bearon might make her more useful than if she was just fucking him once in a while.

TWENTY-EIGHT

PLAN B

IT'S SIX A.M. and since the clocks have been set back to Pacific Standard instead of Daylight Savings Time, it's dark. Bearon is already in his office. His hip is on fire this morning. This time it's not because of a particularly athletic romp with Kiersten last night, though. She barely moved. Odd how that changed since she moved in. Maybe she needs a reminder of what can happen to Clint if she doesn't up her game. Or maybe he should move her along.

Kiersten won't be up for another hour, but the pain woke him early. He's taken a couple of pills and needs a soak in the hot tub. But it'll have to wait until he makes a phone call.

Since the lawyer called to confirm the Klein woman is claiming the five million and her butch lawyer friend did something to extend the time limit, he lives every day in a silent rage. He's not arrogant enough to think no one will ever discover the phoney invoices or the transfers into his own bank account that he has no way of justifying.

Not that he worries about the brainless idiots here, but Briggs and the other Big Guys in Pillerton are starting to act funny. He can't quite put his finger on it, but the sooner he gets everything paid back, the better. Then it was just a loan, he'll add interest, he is the owner after all and doesn't need their blessing to move money around in his own business does he? Of course he does, at least until he has more autonomy, but better to beg forgiveness than ask for permission, as they say. He's been planning on the last of his inheritance to cover it.

Even without the inheritance, he'll earn enough to repay it all, just not soon enough. And why should he live like a pauper when the lump sum that's rightfully his will solve everything?

That fuckin' Klein woman! She's all that stands between him and the solution to his financial problems. She still has to prove she's Hank Hazen's daughter and Robertson doesn't think she can, but Bearon is not going to wait and see.

Goddamn Reardons! First that fuck-up in Pillerton, and then Clint going against his orders and taking his moron son to the hospital! If he'd left him in the Basement, he wouldn't have been arrested. Clint and Kevin insist he'll take the fall, do the time and won't sing. Bearon is not going to wait and see on that one, either.

He thought about having Trent taken out before he has a chance to run his mouth, and then he learned that the Klein woman, well her husband anyway, is going to give a victim impact statement at the sentencing hearing. Will he come without her? Unlikely. He's going ahead on the assumption they'll come together. An unexpected gift and about time something went his way. But it means Trent has to be alive, at least until Klein gets to Dark River, so he can initiate Plan B.

All he needs is a way to get her to the Lodge. Dick-licker Briggs won't have any trouble making that happen. And if there are three others that go with her? Collateral damage. It's too bad about Rick, but unless he can separate them, there's nothing he can do about that.

With a time difference of two hours, it's not too early to call Saskatchewan.

"Hello, Bearon," Evan says.

"I've got you on speaker, Evan. You don't know for sure it's me," Bearon says. "This is a landline. Anyone could be using it."

"Yeah, right. Who would that anyone be?"

For a second, he thinks about telling him about his new living arrangements, but decides against it and says, "point taken."

"What's up?"

"Someone I'm interested in is going to be in Prince George for Reardon's sentencing hearing in a couple weeks."

"They are, eh? So. Why do I care?"

"You know we had to stand down on that job, short term anyway, so it wouldn't bring any more heat? Nix the job permanently. I'll deal with the problem at this end."

"Sure. So again, why do I care? What's it got to do with me?"

"They'll be connecting with fucking Danielsons. I want you to give Danielson a call, find out if that's the plan, and offer them four tickets to the dinner at the Lodge for the weekend of Reardon's hearing."

"What? Seriously? I'm gonna phone Danielson outta the blue, ask if his friends are coming and give him eight hundred dollars worth of tickets? Who says they'll even take them?"

"Don't be a fuckin' ass. No one passes up a gift like that. Make up something. Order more lumber for the Lodge. Work it into the conversation that way. Offer them two tickets for starters. When they say they have company that week-end, play the generous big shot you love to be and give them two more. For fuck's sake, Briggs, do I have to do all your thinking for you?"

"Maybe you doing the thinking isn't all that good an idea, at least on this subject, Bearon. You want all four of them at the Lodge? Do you plan on taking all of them out?"

"Leave the details to me."

"For fuck's sake, Bearon, think about it! When it comes to this woman, you're obsessed. It's irrational. Can't you see that? Just leave her alone."

Bearon's nostrils flare as hot rage begins to surge through him. "I have my reasons," he hisses through clenched teeth.

"Well, you can't grab her or whatever you're planning, without anyone knowing and I hope the hell you're not stupid enough to think you can. Which goes double if you think you can take both of them. What are you thinking, that when they show up for dinner, you can just hustle them into the Basement?"

"You really think I don't have a better plan than that?"

"Naww, of course not. You're smarter than that. I know it. It's just that when it comes to this one thing, this woman... I know a little bit about her, you know, from before."

"As if I don't! I was there, remember? They wanted her taken out."

"Sure, because they needed her out of the house. Even then, they were divided on eliminating her because she's a civilian. Now you're making the decision unilaterally and won't explain why? As far as I can see, there's nothing in it for anyone. I wasn't happy about it before and now I really don't like it. I have no idea why she went up there looking for Hank, but she gave up and came home. Why have you got such a hard-on about her? Are you really willing to put everything you've got at risk?"

"There's no risk."

"Whenever anyone is taken out, there's a risk. And I think you're so irrational when it comes to her—"

"When're you gonna quit selling me short?" Bearon snaps. "You know how treacherous the road from the Lodge to the highway is. Wouldn't it be a tragedy if someone lost their brakes in one of the steep parts?" After this outburst, Bearon takes a deep breath and sits back. He realizes he had lost his cool and raised his voice. *Damn it! Why does he always piss me off? Now I said more than I should have.*

But if Evan has more objections, he keeps them to himself. All Bearon hears is his breathing. Then Evan says, "I see you've got it handled. I'll call Denver."

"Great. Keep me posted." He clicks the off button on the handset and drops it. Groaning, he puts his hands on his desk and leans on his arms as he struggles to his feet.

He hobbles to the door of his office and is surprised to see Kiersten standing in the hall with a steaming mug of coffee. She looks as startled to see him as he is to see her.

"You're up early," he says, frowning as he studies her face.

"I, uhh, not as early as you," she says.

"How long have you been standing here?"

"I wasn't, er, I just, er, I wasn't just standing here. I was in the kitchen making coffee. And, um, when I didn't hear your voice anymore I thought it was okay to bring you this." She holds the mug out to him and makes eye contact briefly before looking away.

Was she eavesdropping? If she was in the kitchen when he was on the phone, she was too far away to make out what was being said, wasn't she? Then why is she nervous?

When he realizes she always stutters and quakes when face to face with him, he relaxes. Such a timid little mouse. Even coming up on his old six foot four body-builder body naked except for the oversized towel draped across his shoulders would have made her shrink away. So what he looks like now...

He takes her free hand and puts it on his penis; when it instantly begins to swell under her touch, he says, "thank you, darlin', that's sweet of you. But I'll drink it in the tub. Join me?"

TWENTY-NINE

ODD LITTLE DUCK

ASTRID IS AT her desk going over the contract for a new lease. A big multi-national owns the property so naturally, the lease is an inch thick. Four hundred pages of convoluted legalese. Some in-house lawyer's wet dream.

Denver is out with their arborist now, getting a sense of the amount of merchantable timber it contains. He's given the document a read-through and has highlighted a couple of clauses he wants to talk to her about when he gets back in the office.

She's been looking at it for so long now she barely sees it. She'll tell Denver they need to have their own lawyer look at it. In any case, a coffee break is in order. She's about to get up and go to the break room when Mary Ann sticks her head in the door.

"Someone to see you, Astrid," she says.

"Oh? Who?"

"Says her name's Kiersten."

"Kiersten? Sure!" Astrid gets up and comes around the desk, out the door and down the hall into the main office.

"Kiersten! Hi! Nice to see you! What brings you here?"

"I, um, can we talk?"

"Sure! Let's get a coffee."

"I can't stay that long."

"Oh? What is it?"

"Er, see...um, can we talk somewhere private?"

"Sounds ominous. Come to my office."

Kiersten follows Astrid back into her office. Once inside, she closes the door.

Astrid goes around the desk and sits in her chair. "Have a seat," she says, beckoning to a chair across from her.

"Thanks." Kiersten perches awkwardly on the edge of the chair.

"What's up?" Astrid asks.

"I had to talk to you. I'm on my way to get groceries but I have to get right back. I can't take more than a minute... good thing I have to drive by here anyway so I, er...it won't make me late."

"You had to drive by here?"

Kiersten ignores Astrid's puzzled look and says, "you and your friends are booked in at the Lodge for dinner on Friday, right?"

"Yeah. How'd you know that?"

"I'm working there now."

"What? Really? We need to get together and catch up. Why haven't you called me?"

"Well, um, just busy, you know. At the Lodge. Just no time."

"Really? It's that busy?"

"Yeah. With the members starting to come in. And then the dinner coming up, lots to do, organizing everything and all."

"Well, I'm looking forward to it. I've been bragging about it to Kathy. Hey, Kathy's coming. I bet she'd like to see you, too. She's only going to be here for a few days, though. Maybe we can get together."

"Maybe. I'll see if I can get some time off."

"Great."

"Why is Kathy here, though? Surely she didn't come all this way just for dinner? Or did she just want to visit you?"

"No. Her mother-in-law was murdered and they caught the guy here. Well, in Prince George. They're going to give a victim impact statement at his sentencing hearing."

"Murdered! Oh my god!" The colour drains from Kiersten's face.

"I know. It's hard to believe. They caught the guy, of course."

"Oh! Doesn't make it better, but it's something."

"Yeah. I don't think Kathy's going to say anything at the hearing, she's just coming with Rick. It's his mother, after all. But she's still looking for her blood relatives and it seems like the owner of the Lodge might be a sibling or a cousin maybe. She hasn't been able to get a name, and of course you know how hard it is to get into that place. Denver doesn't think she'd get past the gate if she just showed up and asked to speak to the manager. So she's hoping to get a chance to talk to him at the dinner."

"I... If he's there. He isn't always there. She shouldn't get her hopes up. He's very, um, a really private sort of person."

"I'll tell her." Astrid says. "I sure hope it's as good as last time. Same menu?"

"No. Um. I don't know. I wasn't there last time. Astrid, what I came to tell you is, when you go to the Lodge for dinner, have someone take you there and then pick you up when you're done."

"Oh, you're worried about drinking and driving? Like maybe there'll be a roadblock?"

"No, it's not that. Don't just have a designated driver. Have someone drive you there and then come and get you. Don't leave your vehicle there. And don't tell anyone that's what you're going to do."

"But that seems…"

"Please! Trust me on this. It's really important! Say you will!"

Astrid shrugs. Kiersten's face is pinched with concern. "Okay," Astrid agrees. "We'll get someone to drive, like you say."

"Don't tell anyone! Not anyone! And don't tell anyone I was here!"

"Okay! I won't."

Kiersten blows out a huge breath. "Great! That's a relief! I have to go. I'll see you then." She gets up and hurries out the office door.

As Astrid watches her departing back, she mutters, "what is that all about?"

As Kiersten goes out, Denver is coming in. He holds the door open for her and steps aside, then greets everyone as he comes through the office. When he gets to Astrid's office, he asks, "who was that?"

"Kiersten. Oh, you never met her, did you?"

"That was Kiersten? What did she want?"

"It was strange," Astrid says as she gets to her feet. "Come on, I was just going to get a coffee and I know you can always use one."

In the break room, they fill their mugs and sit across from each other at the table. "Have you had a chance to go over that lease contract yet?" Denver wants to know.

"Yes, but I've read through it so many times this morning I don't even see it anymore. We need Drew to look at it. I was just going to call him and then take a break when Kiersten breezed in. Well, breezed in and out."

"You didn't invite her for coffee?"

"She said she didn't have time. Then she warned me not to drive to the dinner on Friday. Or rather, to get someone to take us and then pick us up after."

"That would save one of us having to drink ginger ale while everyone else gets shitfaced."

"She said not a designated driver. Someone else entirely. She was really adamant about it. I promised her we would. I thought maybe Wilson could drive us. He might enjoy having Dora Mae around for the evening and she could stay with the kids when he's driving us. Or I guess, a cab?"

"A cab ride would cost more than the meal. Why would we do that? We'd be better off getting on that shuttle bus Danny Hardy got organized." Denver unzips his jacket and takes a swig of his coffee. "You might not have met him. Owen Hardy's son?"

"I've seen his name on the payroll but I haven't met him," Astrid says. "We could do that, couldn't we! We wouldn't have to drive all the way into town to get on it if he'd make a stop at our place. I bet he wouldn't mind. It's not out of his way."

"You know, that's probably a helluva good idea anyway. Can you get me his phone number?"

"Get Mary Ann to text it to you."

"Okay." Denver sips his coffee, then says, "that Kiersten. I don't know what to make of her. First she says she thinks there's something to the rumours about the new Lodge being just like the old Lodge. Now we shouldn't drive up there?"

"But maybe she's right. Both times she seemed scared. Not just scared, terrified. She begged me not to tell anyone. I really don't know what to make of it."

"Ay-yuh, me neither."

"She could be right, though. What if she's involved somehow, like against her will?"

"Then she'd ask for help, wouldn't she?"

"Maybe not, though. Maybe they're holding something over her."

"Like maybe they've kidnapped her kid?"

"No, it couldn't be that. When I asked her if she had kids, she said she got a cat when she moved in with her boyfriend."

"Then maybe they've kidnapped her cat."

"Not funny, Denver!"

"Sorry."

"Or—you've heard of Stockholm Syndrome?"

"Or maybe she's just a total wing nut."

"You said you believed her before."

"Yeah, I guess I did. Now that she's come up with this other nonsense... Something else to get you all worked up again..."

"It might not be nonsense!" Astrid's forehead creases in a frown and her lower lip quivers.

Just then, John comes in and goes to the coffee machine.

Denver reaches across the table and takes Astrid's hand. "Sorry, babe," he says in an almost whisper, "I don't mean to make small of your, er, *concerns*. We'll pay attention to her warning just to be on the safe side. But you have to admit, she is sure an odd little duck."

As John joins them at the table, Denver says, "that new lease looks promising. Lots of good Doug fir, and quite a bit of Western Red."

"We should meet with the Chilcotin elders to arrange access for them to harvest cedar bark, roots, whatever, then," John says.

"I'll get you to set that up once we get the lease signed," Denver says. He gives Astrid's hand a final rub before finishing his coffee and taking his cup to the sink.

THIRTY

NEW SOCIETY

KEVIN PULLS INTO the lot at Cherry Creek Bar and Grille just before three p.m. and spots Clint's Porsche. It's hard to miss, being unusual even in bigger cities, and then there's the fact he always parks away from the other cars and diagonally across two spaces. Good thing the Cherry isn't busy at this time of day or there would be complaints.

He goes to the pub entrance, pulls the door open, and once inside, scans the room. For a second he thinks Clint must not be here, even though it's unlikely someone else has a car the same as his. When he realizes the man at the corner table in the raised section at the back is waving at him, he heads his way.

"Hey," he says as he slides into the booth across from the bigger man. "Almost didn't recognize you. Where's your glasses?"

"Lasix."

"Short hair and a beard? How come?"

"Just decided to update my look. More 2020, less 1990. You know. Blend in better."

"Oh? I suppose."

"You know what they say, a change is as good as a rest. Check out my new watch." He holds out his wrist to show him. "Good-bye Rolex, hello Apple Watch."

The server comes up and asks Kevin, "what can I get you?"

"Umm, what's on tap?"

She rattles off five possibilities. When Kevin has made his choice, Clint lifts his glass in her direction and says, "another one of these for me."

"You got it, hon," she says, and scurries off.

"She's cute," Clint says as he watches her stop at another table and bend across it to wipe a spill. "Too bad that skirt's not an inch shorter."

"Yeah. I guess you're officially single now."

Clint scowls at him, swirls the last of the beer in his glass, then drinks it.

"About Kiersten. I was wondering what you think about Bearon moving her up to live with him."

"What do you think I think?" Clint snarls, eyes narrowing.

"I think you're pissed off about it."

"Wouldn't you be?"

"Sure."

"So why do you ask?"

The server comes back and sets their fresh pints in front of them. Clint puts a twenty on her tray and says, "I don't need change."

"Thanks!" she says with a wide smile, and leaves again.

"I just wanted to—well, it's a little awkward. I wanted to be sure. Because you're not the only one pissed at Bearon."

"Well, that's just ducky. So I'm not the only one pissed at him. What's this? The first ever meeting of the Pissed at Bearon Society? I'd go for a beer with you, Kevin. No need to skulk around about it."

"Yeah, well, there *is* a need to skulk. No one else can know about it."

Clint frowns and sits up straighter.

"That's right, buddy. Besides you and me, the Pillerton people aren't happy with him, either."

"What? Why?"

"They think Bearon's gone off the rails. I doubt Evan told me what the real problem with him is, but it sounds like this hit he put out on that woman who was looking for Hank is the last straw. Bad enough if it went without a hitch, but you know about the, er, collateral damage. And Trent's lucky the bikers didn't kill him."

"What? Just because he buggered off without paying them for an old piece of shit truck?"

"Not just that. He knows too much about their operation. You know how they deal with rats. Of course the Big Guys are worried about him yapping, too. Could solve that getting rid of Trent—no, no no! I didn't say that was going to happen!—but that's not enough for them. They tapped me to do something about Bearon."

"You? Why you?"

"I don't know. Nearest I can figure is that it's a kind of test. Initiation, maybe, since they discontinued that finger amputation thing."

"Thank fuckin' Christ for that!"

"Why do you care? Thinkin' you could move up?"

Clint shrugs. There's a lull in the conversation; Kevin slouches, one arm over the back of his chair, and scans the room while he waits for Clint to say more. Finally, Clint asks, "what are you going to do?"

"About Bearon? I haven't figured that out yet. About Trent? Well, I'm at a loss. You have to know he won't be safe inside."

"I know."

"He might make friends, though. He did last time."

"He might."

Clint scratches his head, smooths his hair and takes a drink of his beer. Then he looks Kevin in the eye and says, "you're takin' a chance tellin' me this."

"Yeah. But from the look on your face when I told you about Bearon and Kiersten—well, I thought you might be, how should I put it? Agreeable to making something happen."

Clint looks around the room to make sure there's no one close enough to overhear, before hissing, "you sayin' what I think you're sayin'?"

"What if I am?"

"Suppose he was gone. He owns the Lodge. Don't we need that? New owner might not go along with our, er, *business*."

"He's got no will and he's got no relatives. The Lodge will go to the government and with that lease we got registered on it, we'd have one foot in the door already. Pillerton can pick it up for a song. They *love* the business model, thinking about expanding their own business along the same lines. They already have tunnels they can put holding cells in."

"What's in it for me? I mean, besides getting even for him horning in on Kiersten? Just so you know, I don't care what happens to hoes, but I wasn't done with that one. He should've asked."

"I agree. What he did was underhanded. But as you point out, she's just a ho. You can settle that score, and get a pay bump at the same time. Pillerton agrees you don't get paid enough for all you do. For me, it means a promotion to Exalted Leader, so you can see why *I'm* glad they quit taking fingers!" he snorts. "It'll mean a bigger share of the pot. Once I'm in the Triumvirate, I'll make sure you get a better deal. I'd get you set up for Purification. Once you're Purified, you're in on Communions, too. You'll *love* the Mingling."

"You move up to Exalted Leader?"

"Yup. Third in command. No more second-rate room on the backside."

"Oh yeah? That sounds nice, *for you*. Doesn't sound like much for me, though. Once you're Exalted Leader, there's no way I can hold you to your promise of a better deal."

"That's true. You have to trust me."

"Trust a lawyer?"

"Don't go there."

"Kidding," Clint says, eyes narrowing. "Everyone knows lawyers are trustworthy. You wouldn't be in with these guys otherwise."

"Pfftt! You think you're being funny, but it's true. If they didn't trust me..." Kevin exhales with a scowl. "Anyway. You know I can't give you anything in writing. We can't even talk about this except face to face. If you're in, I'll set up a meet with Hayward and Preach. Totally on the Q.T., of course."

"Of course." Clint's jaw is clenched and his brow furrowed as he drinks but says nothing. Finally he sets the drink down, looks Kevin in the eye and says, "I'm in. So, me and you, partners? Didn't see that coming." He picks up his glass again and with his left hand, moves the coaster around in small circles. "You know Preach and Hayward better than I do. You think either of them's got the smarts to run the operation? Bearon does most of it. Bearon and Evan. Those other two are just dead weight. I think the only reason they're in is because they were left over from the old crew. What good are they?"

"Preach does the sermonizing."

"Not very fuckin' well."

"That's true. So what are you thinking?"

"I was just thinkin'. Why settle for third in command?"

THIRTY-ONE

PLANS FOR DINNER

BEARON'S ONLY PROBLEM now is to find out what Danielson drives. Since their yard is surrounded by trees, there's no way to see any of their vehicles and if he skulks around waiting for one of them drive away, it'll be noticeable. The Range Rover doesn't exactly blend in, not in this part of the world where everyone drives a pick-up, and the red Volvo's no better.

He's thinking of buying a beater. Private sale. It's going to be complicated, though. He could get Bob or one of the other guys to take care of it once he finds a suitable vehicle. He's settled on that idea and is at the computer looking at ads on Used Dark River when it comes to him there's a much easier way.

"Fuckin' shit," he mutters, and gives his forehead a couple of thumps with the heel of his good hand. *What's wrong with me?* he wonders. *My brain used to work better than this!* He doesn't need another car because he doesn't have to ID the vehicle himself. He has to sub-contract part of the job anyway; why not have them ID the vehicle?

Taking two days to come to this realization is troubling. His body failing is bad enough, and now his brain is letting him down, too?

Before, he was the guy who did everything. If he got under a car now, he'd be all week getting back out and it's doubtful he'd be able to see well enough to do what needs doing when he was under there anyway. He has to pay not only for the sabotage, but to have the vehicle ID'd in the first place.

Maybe he should put the idea on a back burner and think about it some more, in case Evan's right. But there might not be another opportunity like this one, and time is running out. Once this Kathy woman is out of the way, he needs Trent to disappear before the hearing, because he'll be taken straight from the courthouse to lock-up. The window of opportunity to have him dealt with is shrinking, too.

He leans back in his chair and rocks for a few minutes with his eyes closed, enjoying a mental slide show of his years when he was the go-to guy for the big bosses: first for Nick in Pillerton, then Hank in Dark River. The good times when his body was whole and the only pain he had was sore muscles after a workout or hangover headaches.

He wasn't running the show like he is now. His house was supplied by his employer and he never had more than a thousand dollars in his bank account, but he had a Harley, a five liter Mustang, and a beautiful dog. Someone else called the shots but they listened when he had ideas. His best buddy, Arnie, was President of the local HA and he was VP.

He was respected, even though he wasn't part of the Triumvirate, and he sure as hell didn't need the Communion or the Mingling or extortion to get laid. All he had to do was sit near the stage and he'd have the dancers all over him. He knew the upstairs rooms of every titty bar in town.

He knows it's a miracle he survived and he's lucky to be alive. But when the pain won't go away and it hurts to even move, it seems more like *bad* luck.

I don't have time to feel sorry for myself or to second guess myself either, he thinks. He gives himself a mental kick in the ass, picks up the phone, and dials.

RICK AND KATHY come up the stairs from the basement into the kitchen and take stools at the island where Wilson has set out a tray with crackers and antipasto. He's busy slicing cheese and garlic sausage to add to the spread.

"A snack to hold us over until dinner. Home made and vegan! Wilson and I made a huge batch," Astrid says, and points to the antipasto. "A beer, Rick? I don't think I have to ask Kathy what she'd like."

"Sounds great," Rick responds, and Kathy agrees.

Astrid hands Rick a beer and gets a glass of white wine from the box in the fridge, setting it in front of Kathy as she asks, "everything okay downstairs? Need more towels or anything?"

"Are you kidding? This place is better than a five-star hotel, Astrid," Kathy gushes. "I love it here! I can't wait until you guys come with our horses, so we can return the favour."

"That'll be soon," Astrid says. "We've got the clean-up and maintenance crew scheduled. Hopefully we'll have a new barn manager soon. Can't go and leave all the barn chores to Wilson."

"You could, if it come to that," Wilson says, "although I might git one of the boys from the mill to help with the grunt work."

"Sure," Astrid says, "if you can find one that doesn't mind shovelling horse shit."

"Or try to smoke it," Wilson scowls.

"Thanks for this," Rick says as he opens his beer. "That was quite a deal, your barn manager getting arrested. Wonder how long he'd been dealin' outta your barn, anyway."

"Probably from day one," Wilson says. "I think the little rat bastard was foolin' around with the girls, too. Course we'll never know fer sure 'bout that. Long's they's consenting adults, can't do nuthin' 'bout it anyhow."

"Bad reputation for Heather's House, though," Kathy says. "Just lucky you twigged to the drugs. Is he in jail? Or going to jail?"

"Dunno," Astrid replies. "Cops wanted us to keep him on. Said it would help with their ongoing investigation. We just couldn't."

"So, they're looking further up the food chain," Rick says. He takes a long pull on his beer, and reaches for a slice of garlic sausage. "Jake must've had other customers besides the girls in the house."

"He did," Astrid says. "There was a lot of traffic in and out. We were unaware. When we talked to staff about it, they said, 'oh yeah, we wondered how he had so many friends coming to visit and why they never stayed long'. Really stupefying they didn't mention it long ago. Besides the drive-ins, so many of the girls at Heather's are into drugs. What a great cover, working out of a women's shelter. Jake should've paid us to let him live there. Live and learn, I guess," Astrid chuckles as she pours herself a glass of wine, then slides onto the stool next to Kathy. "Any updates on the inheritance?"

"Mister Big Balls Robertson hasn't gotten back to me. I really didn't expect he would. Penny's been looking into the ownership of the Lodge, not getting far on that front either. It's owned by a numbered holding company, which is owned by something else. I can't follow it all. So convoluted! It would be so much simpler if she could find a name and a phone number, but no luck so far. Like we talked about, I'm really hoping to meet the owners tonight, since the Lodge is closed to the public most of the time. I might not get past the front gate if I just showed up there."

Denver comes in the back door in time to hear Kathy's last remark. He says, "No, you might not. In fact, you probably wouldn't."

"I thought they might let me in if I said I just wanted to talk to him because he might be a relative. Who could object to that?"

"No normal person. Worth a try, I guess. But it would be better if Kiersten introduced you," Astrid opines. "She said she would."

"But if he's not there tonight?"

"Then we can try tomorrow."

"Doubt the owner would be there Sunday."

"Haven't you heard?" Denver asks. "The owner is the last one who gets time off."

"That's true for our insurance agency, right, Runty?" Rick contributes.

"Well, if he's not there, maybe we could stay an extra day or two," Kathy says. "Godzilla's already freaking because she has to work Monday. Might as well give her something worthwhile to bitch about." She takes a cracker, scoops antipasto onto it and pops it into her mouth. "Yummy," she says, and washes it down with wine. Then she asks, "how are your girls? Where are they, anyway?"

"They're down in the playroom now," Denver says as he gets a beer and joins the others on stools around the island. "I'm thinkin' we're gonna have to build an unclimbable fence with a locking gate around the yard. When I went out to check on them just now, Lisey had juice boxes and granola bars in her lunch kit. She was leading Kylie out to the pasture when I caught up with them. Told me Heather was taking them down to the river for a picnic."

"Gawddamighty!" Wilson exclaims, "them little stinkers! They was in the sandbox last I saw them. I wondered why Lisey was up in the pantry. Didn't think nuthin' much of it though."

"You wouldn't," Astrid says. She looks at Rick and Kathy and explains, "Elise is the Keeper of the Food. I swear, she keeps a running inventory of everything. But going down to the river! They know they're not allowed to go there! My god, Denver!"

Denver reaches an arm around his wife and gives her a squeeze. "I wasn't kiddin' about the fence." He looks at their friends and explains, "Heather is Lisey's invisible friend."

"Oh, I remember you telling us she had one."

"And did we tell you Heather was the little Hazen girl who drowned down there? We named the shelter in her honour."

The colour drains from Kathy's face. "Yes," she says quietly.

"Dangerous time of year to be goin' to the river, usually," Denver says. "It's still low this year though, since the fall rains haven't showed up yet. Although it looks like there's rain further up the mountain, so the river could rise quick. Storm could be comin' our way. Wind's already pickin' up."

"We take them to the river when it's hot. There's a nice little swimming hole. But they're not allowed to go to the river without an adult and Lisey knows it! The Hazen kids weren't supposed to go to alone, either," Astrid tells them.

"Bridey was baking a birthday cake for her little girl and shooed her out of the house with Junior and the neighbour boy, Johnny Fletcher, so it would be a surprise. Bridey showed me where it happened. Oh my god, Denver! It was about this time of year! Heather's fifth birthday was the day she drowned. What is going on with Lisey?" Astrid bites her lower lip and draws a quick, deep breath.

"I'm sure it's nothing to worry about, babe," Denver says.

"But we'll get started on that fence anyway," Wilson says. "If we git that puppy we been talkin' about, it'll keep it in too."

"Lookin' for a puppy?" Rick asks.

"Yeah. Company for Tippy. The girls are at an age to enjoy a puppy, too."

The conversation turns to merits of various dog breeds, and then what is appropriate dress for dinner.

"When you told me how elegant and ritzy the place was, I brought a dress," Kathy says. "Rick brought a sports jacket."

"We'll all get gussied up, then," Astrid says; she pushes the thought of her daughters going to the river alone to the back of her mind. Still, she hopes for a good, unclimbable fence sooner rather than later.

THE FIFTEEN-PASSENGER van Danny Hardy rented for the occasion pulls into the Danielsons' yard as arranged. Everyone else got on at the Tempo Gas Bar on the outskirts of Dark River. They all introduce themselves as they take the last four seats, and enjoy lively chatter on the trip up the mountain. Once they turn off the highway the road is narrow with a steep incline. Dizzying drop-offs are a mere meter from the roadbed in many spots.

"I wouldn't want to be driving this road in snow," Rick observes, to a chorus of agreement from the other passengers.

"Or anytime," Kathy says. "I hope it doesn't start raining."

"It gets a little hairy sometimes," Danny tells them, "but I've driven worse roads up on some of our leases. Don't worry. I got this!"

They were the last passengers to get on so they're the first off when they get to the parking lot at the Lodge. As they get out of the van, a truck arrives and backs into a parking space nearby.

"Hey," Denver says, "that truck's the same model as mine."

"What are the chances? They're so rare," Astrid says.

"Yeah, I know. They're everywhere. That one is maybe a year newer, though. Wonder if he's had problems with rim leaks on those chrome wheels. Oh, that's Brent," Denver says when he recognizes the driver. "That's not his truck unless he just got it. Come on, Rick, I'll introduce you." The two men head across the lot.

"Oh great! A chance to talk trucks." Kathy says.

"This could take half an hour. We might as well go in and get our table," Astrid turns to Kathy and asks, "You don't want to stand around out in the cold to talk about trucks with them, do you?"

"Lord, no! I get enough of that back home. I'd like to go to the ladies room before we get seated, anyway," Kathy says. "That was quite a ride! It's not much of a road."

"Yeah. But like Danny said, he's driven these roads lots since he drives the crummy so he's used to the van, too."

"Crummy?"

"That's the van that takes the fallers up into the bush. It's not really *crummy*, we've replaced the crappy ones since we took over but it doesn't matter how shiny and new they are, they still call them crummies."

"Well, he's a good choice to drive this one, then. But it'll be dark when we go back down. I'm not looking forward to that!"

"Maybe it's better if we can't see out." The wind is billowing her skirt so she has to hold it down. "It's chilly! I'm not used to bare legs. Let's get in out of the wind."

Inside, they spot Kiersten between two large floral arrangements, marking names off the seating plan. With all the other people ahead of them, she doesn't notice them, so when she turns away and leads a couple in, they go down the hall to the ladies room.

"The manager, or owner, that's his office there," Astrid says, indicating the door at the end of the hall just before she pushes into the ladies room.

"Oh, good. I'll go see if I can talk to him."

"If you wait until after dinner, Kiersten can introduce you."

When they get back to the lobby area, they find Rick and Denver chatting with Kiersten.

"Hi, Kiersten! Wow, look at you!" Kathy says. "You look like a movie star!"

"Thank you." Kiersten leans forward and says in an almost-whisper, "I picked this dress out but they paid for it. And the hairdo. They wanted me to look high class."

"Well, it worked!" Kathy tells her. "Not too high class to join us peons later, I hope?"

"Maybe. I don't know. I, er, can't stay very long."

"Well, we have to go when the van leaves anyway."

"We'll see, then," Kiersten says. There are others waiting to be seated so she says, "I'll show you to your table now."

Once at their table, Kathy watches Kiersten scurry away, her long skirt swishing as she goes, then leans toward Astrid and asks, "did she say why she left the Riverview to work here? This is only once every couple of months or something, isn't it?"

"Yeah, but the members are booking in now, too, and she looks after checking them in," Astrid replies.

"Well, it is quite a step up from the Riverview," Kathy observes. "Riverview's nice enough but this place is something else! All the antiques, and giant flower arrangements everywhere! Just the flowers must've cost thousands. But I sure wouldn't want to commute on that road!"

"Me neither," Astrid agrees, and looks around. "I think there's more people here than last time, don't you, Den? There's Gary from the bank. I think I recognize a few others, too."

Denver nods and says, "I guess word gets around. If I was an investor looking at this as a business model, I never would've believed it would work, hey Rick? All these folks are paying two hundred bucks a head."

Rick lets out a low whistle. "Two hundred bucks! We owe you quite a chunk of change, then."

"Naw, like I said, we're all here as guests of the Lodge. Wouldn't've thought they'd be so grateful."

"Guess we didn't charge them enough for the logs," Astrid says. "I don't see Annie. Wonder if we're in her section again."

BEARON WATCHES THE monitors as vehicles arrive in the parking lot. When the shuttle bus pulls up and blocks the camera, he hisses, "Fuck!"

He tries some of the other camera views. There's a truck like the one he's looking for. Although he can see people on the far side of it, with no near cameras, he can't make out who they are.

He switches back to the main view and when the van finally pulls away, he gets a clear view of Kathy and Astrid, on their way into the building. Danielson and Schoenfeld are at the truck, talking to three other men. Probably truck talk. He experiences a jolt of sorrow, remembering how he did that in a previous life, too.

Then he sits up and takes a better look. Is that Brent and Wally? Panic washes over him when he sees Clint. He isn't yakking with the others, though. He's on his way in. Good thing Kathy didn't see him!

He pulls out his cellphone and sends Clint a text, warning him to come straight into the office. He's made a decision about Kiersten and he'll talk to him about that while he's at it.

He didn't know the two Illustrious Leaders were coming, either, and without their wives? Are they planning on staying over? Are they going to want to go downstairs? They should have given him a head's up. Another example of their puffed-up opinions of their own importance.

As for Clint, this might work out well. He was surprisingly pissed over the Kiersten thing. It'll give Bearon a chance to smooth his feathers. Give him a room with Kiersten in it for the night. They can have dinner sent up, and the Grotto to themselves once everyone else has cleared out.

Goddamn those three, showing up without letting him know! Why? And why stop to talk to *those* people? They know his feelings on them very well. He's the Imperial Leader and yet, Hayward stops to chit chat with Danielson anyway. Is it possible Hayward knows something? Is he warning him? Did Briggs yap? Would Briggs do that? No. Hayward doesn't know anything, and he and Danielson are friendly. Nothing to be suspicious about.

He sends another text.

There's a tap on the door. "Who is it?" he calls out.

"Me. Clint."

Bearon pushes the unlock button mounted on the side of his desk; the lock buzzes, and Clint pushes the door open. He comes in and lets the door close and lock behind him.

Bearon motions to a chair and gets a couple of glasses and the bottle of Crown Royal off the credenza. As he pours, he asks, "You know the Klein woman's here?"

"No."

"Well, you would have, if you three assholes had bothered to tell me you were coming."

"It was a last minute thing."

"Oh, yeah? Whose bright idea was it?"

"Er...I dunno. I was at the Fisherman's. Me and Brent just got talking. Figured we'd have a boys night out. What's the big deal?"

"Are you kidding? Don't you think Kathy might recognize you from the little chat you had behind Dot's that day you were supposed to grab her?" Bearon frowns and slams his glass down harder than he meant to.

"Back then I wore glasses and had shoulder length hair and no beard, remember? My own mother wouldn't recognize me now. Besides, how was I supposed to know she'd be here? Long fuckin' way to go for dinner."

"Well, she's here, thanks to your idiot son."

"What's it got to do with him?"

"They're going to deliver a victim's impact statement at his sentencing hearing on Monday."

"Oh yeah."

"Make fuckin' sure she doesn't see you. Get your ass up to my suite and fuckin' stay there. Kiersten can keep you company. Order a meal sent up. Don't go down to the Grotto until everyone's gone." He tosses the key card across the desk.

"How will I get home? I'm riding with those guys."

"They're not staying?"

"No. They both got stuff goin' on early tomorrow. Preach has an early service and Hayward has to take his grandson to a bike race in Prince George or something. I could barely talk them into coming."

"You need them for company?"

"Who else have I got? My girlfriend moved in with you, remember? Not by choice neither."

"Your *girlfriend*? *Your* girlfriend?"

"You know what I mean."

Bearon draws a deep breath and bites back a rebuke. Clint has been forgetting his place more and more often these past few months. If he didn't need him, he'd deal with it, but he has to keep him close. Clint is not someone who can easily be replaced. Right now, he has to throw him a bone.

As for the other two, he's mollified. At least they didn't expect their rooms to be made up and to have company, or maybe go to the Basement. Theoretically, they don't have to check in with him just to come for a meal. But they should have told him. He'll remind them the next time he sees them.

He says, "okay, then. Text them you're staying. I'll be back tomorrow for breakfast and I'll see you and Kiersten then. She can take you back to your place. She should take her things with her while she's at it. I'll send someone to collect the Volvo from your place next week sometime."

CLINT HEAVES A SIGH of relief as he leaves the office and heads up the back stairs, whistling quietly as he takes them two at a time. This is working out better than expected. Now he doesn't have to make up an excuse for staying in Kevin's room at the Lodge instead of going back to town with the other two. There won't be any awkward questions either from Bearon or the cops about why. And on top of that, he gets Kiersten back.

That part's puzzling. Why now? He would rather have taken her back instead of Bearon voluntarily returning her. Maybe he tosses her into the Basement. That would give Bearon the message: thanks for nothing, I didn't want her anyway. But not until tomorrow or maybe sometime next week. Or maybe not at all. She could be a good cruising partner.

Once in Bearon's suite, he texts Hayward and Preacher, then calls Kevin. "You can tell our guy it's a go," he says. "I'm stayin' over like we planned. Start the ball rolling on Phase Two...yeah, he's comin' here to pick me up tomorrow...no, I don't know what time. I'll text you when he gets here...have them take their positions." He ends the call.

Getting rid of Bearon will be easy. With Wally and Blake gone, no one will miss him. And Pillerton wanted him gone, so no questions from that quarter. As long as there's no staff, he can be taken out right here. No need to worry about an electric fence. This week-end, after tonight there are no customers, and no staff.

A window of opportunity like this won't come again until the next public dinner. All he has to do is think of a reason to make sure Bearon comes inside when he picks them up, instead of waiting in the car.

Maybe a problem with—? What? One of the girls in the Basement? Or maybe he'll accuse Kiersten of something so Bearon has to come in to discuss what to do with her. That would throw his big gift back in his face at the same time! Perfect!

At the bar cabinet, he pours a tall rye and ginger ale, then goes to the recliner and sinks in. He picks the remotes off the side table, turns on the propane fireplace and the TV, and scrolls through the guide, settling on a rerun of NCIS. His drink is nearly finished when there's a tap on the door. He opens it on Kiersten.

"Hey, baby," he says, pulling her into the room and taking her in his arms.

"Oh, Clint," she cries, melting into his embrace. Their kisses are passionate, fierce, then tender. At last she says, "you look so different!"

"Yeah. You like it?"

"I do! You look so, er, so modern!"

"Re-invented myself," he says. "How have you been? How's things in the Bear Cave?"

"I hate it! It's like I'm in jail."

"Well, that's about to change."

"What? How?"

He kisses her temple and smooths her hair, tucking a lock behind her ear. "I got the boss to give us his suite for the night. We'll have dinner here, same as what they're serving downstairs. Nice quiet two-hundred-bucks-a-plate dinner. Then later, a swim? Or just a hot tub. Nice, eh?"

"Oh." Her shoulders slump; she breathes deep and bites her lip. "But my things. I have nothing with me. I don't have a swim suit."

"Neither do I. There's extra toothbrushes. And once the caterers leave, we've got the whole place to ourselves. We sure as hell don't need swimsuits!"

"I guess not," she says.

He expected a more enthusiastic reaction, then realizes she was hoping for more of a change than just one night away from the cabin. He'll tell her she's moving in the morning. For now, it's time she learned not to hope for anything.

He kisses her again then starts opening the tiny buttons in the lacy top of her dress and says, "you look so beautiful in your pretty dress. Wouldn't think covering up right to your chin could be so sexy! But you're even more beautiful naked. Come on, baby, let's get this off. Make your man happy."

She pulls away from him and says, "There's a zipper in the back. But I can't right now. I have to do a few things..."

"Oh? What?"

"Just some computer stuff. And maybe I could have a drink with my friends?"

"Friends? I'm your most important friend."

"Just for a few minutes?"

"No," he says sharply. She has friends? Better if she has no friends, outside of the church, anyway. Time to remind her who's boss. "Come straight back here as soon as you're done your computer stuff."

"But—"

"No buts, baby. You never know who's out there, watching."

"Oh."

"Okay?"

"Okay."

ASTRID SEES KIERSTEN coming through the dining area, and remarks, "Kiersten looks like she's on a mission."

She stops next to Astrid. "Hi guys," she says, "I'm booked off now but I can't stay. Maybe we could get together later in the week?"

"Unless the court thing changes, we're driving to Prince George Tuesday to get a flight home from there," Kathy tells her. "Could it be later Monday afternoon? Maybe dinner?"

"Maybe," Kiersten agrees, "I'll see if I can work something out."

"Before you go, could you introduce me to the manager?"

"He left already. Sorry." Then she leans in close and says quietly, "tomorrow morning? I'll meet you here tomorrow morning. He always comes in in the morning. Just don't tell anyone."

"Awesome! Any particular time?"

"Um, would ten be too early? I'll text you when he gets here. Let me know your ETA so I can open the gate for you."

"Okay!" Kathy agrees. Kiersten turns and hurries away.

Astrid says, "she hasn't returned any of my calls for weeks. Now she's going to be here and we should meet her here?"

"Don't spend too much time wondering about Kiersten," Denver recommends, "and again with the don't tell anyone? She's an odd little duck."

THIRTY-TWO

OFF ROADING

BEARON KNEW HE wouldn't be able to sleep, so he didn't bother going to bed. He spent an hour in the hot tub and now he's sitting in his office next to the police scanner, drinking Courvoisier. The constant garbled, staticky messages on the scanner combined with the cognac has almost lulled him to sleep when at last he hears what he's waiting for.

He looks up a number, picks up the phone and dials it.

"Yeah?" the man answers.

"Sounds like it's done," Bearon says. "If you come to the Lodge later this morning I'll have your money."

"What?"

"The rest of your money."

"Whaddaya mean? Money for what? We didn't do nuthin'."

"I know. Nuthin' for nuthin'."

"No, really. We went all the fuckin' way up there on your say so but no truck. Thanks a lot."

"Whaddaya mean, no truck? I saw it, parked on the far side up near the garage."

"Yeah, we saw that one. Wrong year. Wrong plate number too. Tried callin' you but no answer on this line and not on your cell, neither. So we just buggered off."

Bearon is stunned into silence.

"Okay?" the man on the other end of the line asks. Then he chuckles and says, "but we ain't returning no money if that's what yer thinkin'. Call it what you owe us for our time and gas. And if you wanna pay us for finishin' the job, I guess we wouldn't say no."

"I'll be in touch," Bearon says. "Meantime, stay outta sight, would ya? I hear any more reports of you guys startin' trouble at the Fisherman's..."

"We ain't been at the Fisherman's."

"Well, someone was. Owner says it was bikers. Got into it with the guys from camp."

"I'm tellin' ya, it wasn't us."

"Fine. Wasn't Raptors who did the truck. Wasn't Raptors in the bar fight. I get it. I'll be in touch." He clicks the off button, drops the handset on the desk and collapses deep into the chair. His brain feels muddled, the effects of a combination of cognac and Oxy.

If the truck that went off the road and burst into flames was Danielson's, what caused it? And if it wasn't Danielson's, then whose was it?

It had to be Danielson's. It was the right make and colour, the only one in the parking lot, and he was standing there... It had to be his.

Definitely no point in going to bed now. He takes his bottle and glass and goes out onto the back deck. It has cooled off since the storm took hold and the wind, gusty and strong at times, has an edge to it. The feel of winter coming on. He stays in the screened-in area, puts his glass and bottle down on the table, and drops into a chair.

The trees sway as the wind whistles through them. There's lightning off in the distance, and then loud, booming thunder. The rain that let up earlier seems to be coming on again. Good. With everything so dry, a good, steady rain is desperately needed.

He goes inside to get a quilt and when he comes out again, wraps it around himself and settles back in the chair. The forest is always calming and soothing, even during storms. *Especially* during storms. If it wasn't raining, he'd be out on the uncovered part of the deck, but when it storms, he loves being here, with the rain thrumming down on the tin roof and the storm-scented wind whistling through the screens. There's something mesmerizing about thunder and lightning.

He pushes on the chair back to recline slightly, watches the lightning over the treetops, and breathes deep of the rain-cleansed, ozone-scented night air as he ponders what could have happened. The wrong truck? Just a coincidence? Maybe. It was dark. Windy. Raining. It could have been just an accident.

When his phone rings, he's surprised to realize he'd been sleeping and it's early dawn. The handset stops ringing by the time he unwinds from the quilt and pulls it out of the pocket of his robe, but it soon starts up again. He clicks the on button and says, "Yeah?"

"It's me," Kevin responds. "You hear about the crash on Lodge Road last night?"

"No," Bearon lies. "What happened?"

"A truck went off. Sounds like it was just past the second hairpin turn."

"Gawddamighty! Anyone hurt?"

"Yeah. Whoever was in the truck couldn't survive. It caught fire right away and started a forest fire, too. They're fighting the fire now. Thank god for the rain! It is raining up there, isn't it?"

"Yeah. It's raining hard. Oh my god!" Bearon exclaims. "Do they know whose truck it is, then?"

"Well, they aren't saying, and it's not safe to go to the wreck yet. But I'm wondering. Could it be Brent's? Or Wally's?"

"Brent and Wally?" Bearon takes several deep breaths before asking, "What makes you think it could be them?"

"Both their wives have called me to ask if I've seen them. They've heard about the crash, too, so they're worried. No preacher this morning and I guess Hayward had something going on with his grandson and hasn't showed. I said I hadn't seen them but I didn't think they were planning on going to the Lodge last night."

"I didn't expect them either," Bearon says. After a quiet moment, he adds, "I know they were there, though. Clint rode up with them."

"Jesus! Could he have been in the truck, too?"

"No. I gave him my suite for the night."

Kevin utters a low whistle. "Holy shit! Lucky for him." Both men are quiet for a few moments. Then Kevin asks, "what're we going to do if it's Brent and Wally, though? Two of our top guys gone? Hayward is one thing, but no preacher?"

"You ever thought of being a lay preacher?"

"Umm…"

"Never mind. When we know for sure, I'll call Pillerton and let them know," Bearon says. "Business as usual until we have confirmation. We'll meet when I have instructions from the Big Guys."

"Yeah."

"Keep me posted," Bearon says, and clicks the off button.

Yes, very lucky for Clint. He's been puzzling how to get rid of Hayward and Preacher for a while and now this falls into his lap? And Clint, his right hand man and the only one of the bunch he can't do without, was supposed to be in the truck with them, and wasn't? How did that work out so well?

Could it be it wasn't an accident? Could Clint be involved somehow? He thinks back over his conversation with him. There was nothing to suggest he wasn't going to go back home with the other two; in fact, he said he couldn't stay because he was riding back with them. It was Bearon's idea for him to stay. Is it just coincidence Hayward's truck did what was planned for Danielson's?

"I've always been lucky," he reminds himself. The way he is, the mutilation of his once beautiful body, is unfair, but he knows who's to blame and will make the bastard pay if it takes the rest of his life. Right now, he just has to get rid of that woman. And next, Trent.

KIERSTEN IS NOT in bed when Clint wakes up. It's unusual, because she likes to sleep in as much as he does. Last night he set an early mental alarm because he was hoping to wake her with a poke before telling her she would be coming home with him, and now she's not here?

She must be in the bathroom and will come back to bed. But there's no sound of activity anywhere in the suite.

He gets up and goes to the bathroom. When he's relieved himself, he dons the robe hanging on the hook, and as he washes his hands, notices the pendant in a heap on the vanity. He picks it up and examines it for a moment before slipping it over his head, then admires how it looks nestled against the smoothly-waxed skin of his chest. *Why would Bearon give this to a ho? Too good for her. Well, she just gave it to me.*

He goes to the door to look out in the hall. The trolley, left outside the door after last night's dinner, is gone. Since there is no staff on today, Kiersten must have taken it down to the kitchen and could be making breakfast now. Stupid! She should have just brought him a coffee. She knows he always has at least two cups of coffee before he can eat anything.

He goes to the kitchenette, makes a cup of coffee, and goes out on the deck with it. The wind is strong and scented with smoke. It's chilly, but the storm has let up. The clouds are clearing and the pre-dawn sun is glowing through the treetops, turning the bottom edge of the storm clouds deep pink. Sunrises like that are unusual for this side of the mountain range, and he's reminded of the saying, "red clouds at morning, sailors take warning". There's likely more bad weather on the way. It is fall, after all, so it's normal.

It's too cold to sit on the deck. He comes back in, finds the remote for the fireplace and sees the ambient room temperature is just eighteen. He turns the temperature setting up to twenty. The flames in the firebox come on with a whoosh. He gets his phone to see if there's a message from Kevin. There is. Just two words: two down.

"Yes!" he exclaims, pumping his fist. Two down! He responds with a thumbs up emoji, then takes the armchair next to the fireplace and scrolls through Facebook and his email. There are some likely prospects responding to his ad. He sends off the usual questionnaire with the *must be eighteen or over* warning, knowing they'll all tick the "yes" box.

By the time he's finished his coffee and Kiersten still hasn't returned, he decides to go down and hurry things along. Maybe she's setting up a breakfast table in the main dining room. If so, he'll tell her to scrap that idea. He'd rather sit by the fireplace in Bearon's suite.

Remembering to take the key card so they won't be locked out, he leaves the room and takes the elevator down. No smells of bacon frying when the doors open. No pots and pans noise coming from the kitchen, either. The trolley with the dirty dishes from their dinner is in the kitchen, but Kiersten isn't. He checks the rest of the main floor including the bathrooms, billiard room, then the great room.

Last night's tables and chairs are gone and the usual furniture—leather couches, loveseats, chairs, wood and glass tables arranged in conversation groupings—are back in place. He feels a moment of panic. Has she run off? But that doesn't make sense. Her dress was still draped across a chair upstairs; she's not going to head out down the road in a bathrobe, even if she wanted to leave him. And she is so under his thumb she wouldn't dare.

Maybe she's in the hot tub. It's an irritating thought. She should have waited for him to go with her. He glowers, and hurries down the service hall toward the Grotto, when he passes the door to Bearon's office and notices a sliver of light under the door. The room is windowless, so Bearon must be here, early as it is. He taps on the door. "Bearon? It's me," he calls out. No answer. Then he remembers he has Bearon's key card. Either Bearon has two, or someone else is here. Who else has a key card with access to the office? It must be Bearon. Why no response to his knock? Maybe it's just that the lights were left on. Clint uses the card in his pocket to unlock the door, and pushes it open.

Kiersten, in a bathrobe, is facing him, eyes wide as she backs up a step and bites her lower lip. Behind her is the bank of monitors. They're all dark except for one, which is just going dark now. Somehow, she turned them off when he knocked.

"How did you get in here?" he demands.

"I, um, work here. You know." She shows him a key card marked 'OFFICE'. "I have this."

"Yeah? What are you doing?"

"I, umm...I needed the liquor order. Um, to update it. From, er, what got used up last night."

Clint surveys the scene for a moment, then says quietly, "you don't have to work today, baby. Let's go back to bed."

"I, uh, was going to make breakfast. Isn't Bearon coming soon? I didn't want to wake you. Aren't you hungry?"

"Sure," Clint says. As she comes around the desk, he pulls her into his arms and whispers, "hungry for you. But breakfast does sound good. You go get it ready then come up and get dressed." He gives her a peck on the forehead before releasing her.

"Okay!" She smiles and scurries out the door and down the hall.

Clint watches her go, giving her a smile and a little wave when she turns and looks at him before going into the kitchen.

Things are coming together nicely.

THIRTY-THREE

SPA TREATMENT

"QUITE A STORM we had last night," Denver says as he reaches for the platter of pancakes and shovels another two onto his plate. "Pass the syrup, please, Wilson."

"Don't think it's done stormin' yet," Wilson opines as he hands Denver the bottle. "Raindrops're stickin' to the windows."

"Well, we need the rain, but it would be nice if it wasn't such a downpour."

"Yeah, but better than nothing," Astrid says. "Elise, are you sure you can eat another one?"

"I SURE! I WANT BACON!" Lisey has put another pancake on her plate and stands up on her chair to reach across the table to the bacon.

Astrid takes the plate before the girl has a chance to grab a piece. "You sit down and ask for it nicely," she chides.

Lisey scowls, but kneels down and says, "BACON PLEASE."

Astrid holds the plate out to her and pulls it back again when she's taken one piece.

"I WANT MORE!"

"You can have more when you finish what's on your plate," Astrid tells her.

"KYLIE WANTS MORE!"

"You want another pancake?" Astrid asks the little girl next to her.

"KYLIE WANTS BACON!" Lisey explains.

"Bacon, Kylie?" Astrid asks. When Kylie nods her head, Astrid tells her, "say yes please, Kylie."

"Yes please," Kylie responds in an almost-whisper and Astrid gives her another piece of bacon. She looks at Kathy and says, "see what you're missing?"

"We have three nephews and a niece, all under the age of eleven. I know pretty well what parents have on their plate," Kathy says with a grin. "Any time I think I need a kid fix, I take Jeanie's. She's pretty happy to have them gone even if it's only for a couple of hours."

"And a couple of hours is usually all we can take," Rick contributes.

"Did you always want kids, Astrid?" Kathy asks.

"Yup, ever since I was little. So it was wonderful that Denver wanted them, too."

"And me," Wilson interjects.

"And Wilson, the surrogate grandfather, of course!" Astrid chuckles. "Although I think Wilson sometimes wonders why he thought it was going to be so great, now that they're so busy."

"Wouldn't want kids that wasn't," Wilson says. "Something wrong with little uns that ain't busy."

"Some are a little too busy," Astrid says, giving her eldest a look that leaves no doubt which kid she's thinking of. Lisey looks up at her mother and then at Kathy with an angelic smile. Kathy gives the little girl a wink, and then does a double take. For the first time, she notices that Lisey's large, luminous eyes are brown.

Astrid's text alert chimes and she pulls her phone out of her pocket. "Hey, it's Kiersten. She stayed at the Lodge overnight. The boss is expected soon so we should come ahead."

"Great!" Kathy exclaims. "As long as the rain holds off, we can go up to the Lodge right after we clear away breakfast."

"Wait until we're done chores and we'll go with you," Denver says.

"But it might start raining again, and I think we should go before it does," Astrid says. "You know how bad that road was last night. You heard on the news, someone went off it on their way down. And there's no telling how long Kiersten's boss will be there. I'm sure Kathy and I can go without you guys."

"First you're all in a dither, tryin' to get me to agree the new Lodge is just like the old Lodge, and now you think I'm gonna let you go up there alone?" Denver asks. "Rain or no rain, not a chance!" He raps the table with his knuckles as if to punctuate his statement.

"I'm okay doing the barn," Wilson says. "You guys go ahead."

"You sure?"

"I'm sure. We'll git'er done without you anyhoo. I got two helpers."

"I HELP YOU, GRAMPA!" Lisey exclaims.

"Dunno how much help they'll be," Denver warns. "You know how quick they can get away on you."

"If Lisey don't stay in the barn, I'll hog tie 'er and lock 'er in a stall."

"I STAY IN BARN!" Lisey promises, nodding solemnly.

THEY ARRIVE AT THE GATES to the Lodge just as the rain starts again, huge drops that almost sound like hail on the roof of the truck.

"Damn, you see those flames down in the ravine? That fire can be up here in a heartbeat if the wind changes. I hope you get in to see him double quick so we can head out again right away," Denver says. "Don't fancy driving down that road tryin' to outrun a wildfire anytime, double goddamn not if the road's a river."

Denver pilots the truck into the parking lot where a gunmetal grey Range Rover is parked at the entrance.

"I've been wondering who owns the Range Rover," he says as he pulls up beside it and shifts into park. "Belongs to the Lodge? Briggs was the project manager for this place and had it when we saw him with your Pillerton friends at the airport."

"I wouldn't say they were friends," Kathy says as she opens her door. "I don't think this will take long. Wish me luck!" She slides out of her seat and closes the door behind her.

"I'm coming too," Astrid says. She gets out of the truck and follows Kathy up the steps and in the door.

It's eerily quiet inside and the building seems deserted. "They would've locked the doors if there was no one here, wouldn't they? Should we go and knock on the office door?" Kathy asks.

"There's a bell on the podium. Maybe try that first."

Kathy taps the bell a couple of times and then steps back beside Astrid to wait.

In a moment, a forty-something man in jeans and an untucked, half-buttoned shirt comes out of the manager's office and along the hall toward them, smiling as he approaches. "Good morning," he says. "You must be the gals who won the complimentary spa treatment!"

"Spa treatment? No," Astrid replies.

"Weren't you called?"

"I didn't get a call. Did you, Kathy?" Astrid takes in Kathy's silence and is puzzled by her shocked expression. When Kathy doesn't answer, Astrid continues, "I, er, um, no, we're looking for Kiersten."

He frowns as if not sure what to say. Then he says, "Sure! She's in the office. Follow me."

Astrid starts to follow, but Kathy says, "On second thought, I guess we, er, don't have time after all. Sorry to have bothered you." She turns toward the door.

"It's no bother." The man hurries to Kathy's side. "If you don't have time for your free treatments this morning, I'll get Kiersten to book another time for you. It'll just take a minute."

"No thanks," Kathy tells him, and turns toward the door.

The man seizes Kathy's arm and pulls her around to face him. "We have a great masseur. You'll like him."

Kathy jerks her arm to try and get it out of his grasp, but his fingers tighten and he doesn't release her. "Let go!" she cries out.

"Get your hands off her!" Astrid demands.

"Just being friendly," he says. But he instead of releasing Kathy, he pulls her close and propels her toward Astrid. "Come with me, girls," he coaxes, and reaches for Astrid's arm.

Astrid takes a quick step backward, bumping up against the antique buffet and causing the floral arrangements to wobble. Without releasing Kathy's arm, the man makes a grab for Astrid. His hand closes on her jacket but she breaks loose and turns away.

"I said, come with me!" The man shoves Kathy hard against the buffet, pinning her there as he grabs the fleeing Astrid by the collar and pulls her back to pin her next to Kathy. He releases his hold on her jacket and grabs her arm, but in that split second, Astrid grabs the closest flower arrangement, spins, lifts it over her head and smashes it down. The man jerks back so instead of hitting him squarely, the heavy ceramic vase smashes into his ear. Flowers and water cascade over him as broken pieces of the vase clatter to the floor. He staggers and flails his arms to keep his balance, releasing his hold on Kathy.

Kathy and Astrid dart to the door, pushing it open and racing out across the concrete apron and down the stairs to the truck.

"What the..." Denver says.

They slam their doors and Astrid yells, "Denver, go! Hurry!"

Denver takes in Kathy's expression; he backs the truck away from the steps, drops the shifter into drive and accelerates hard. "Where's Kiersten?"

"Not there. Please, let's get out of here!"

"What happened?" Rick asks, turning to look at Kathy.

"Astrid hit him over the head with one of those big bouquets. To make him let g-g-go of me!" She chokes back a sob.

"What? Hit who?"

"He was...he had a hold of her!" Astrid says.

"He had a hold of Kathy?" Denver asks.

"I need to have a chat with him!" Rick declares.

"No! We have to get away from here!" Astrid cries.

"He w-w-wouldn't let go of me," Kathy sobs.

"But he had a hold of you? A man had a hold of you? You look like you saw a ghost, Runty!"

"Not a ghost. A sn-sn-snake," Kathy moans. "A snake wearing my pendant."

"Oh my god!" Rick reaches over the seat and takes Kathy's hand.

Kathy draws a few deep breaths and collects herself enough to try and explain. "He looks different but I think he's the guy who wanted to take me to see his friend, Hank, the one he claimed lived where the carved bear is. We know that was a lie. Why do you suppose he wanted me to go with him so badly that time at Dot's? And now today...arghhh!" She gulps.

"You're safe, Kathy," Denver says. "You girls are both safe."

"What if he follows us?"

"He's a coward, Runty," Rick says. "Guys like that—big and tough when they're dealing with girls but he won't take us on."

"I'm going to call the cops," Denver says, "but not until we get the hell away from here! If the new Lodge is like the old Lodge, they got plenty of fire power. We have more than the rain to worry about. Seatbelts on, girls. It may be a wild ride down the mountain."

At that moment, there's an intense flash of light and almost simultaneously, a percussive roar of thunder. The rain begins pelting down with intensity as the wind picks up and the sky darkens.

"That one was too close," Denver mutters, and speeds through the gate. Rain and more lightning follows them down the road. Denver slows to little more than a crawl when they reach the switch-back section. The road is a river and mud flows wash down off the bank. Every pothole is a muddy pond. Then they round a corner and meet motorcyclists coming up three abreast.

"What the fuck are they doin' up here besides gettin' wet?" Rick asks.

"Maybe that's who they left the gates open for," Denver suggests. "They'll be glad to get there."

"I don't like the looks of those guys," Astrid says, as the cyclists split to pass them on either side.

"Me neither, babe. I'm glad we left when we did. I think I'll hold off on stoppin' to call the cops until we're back at the highway."

"I'll do it," Astrid says, and pulls out her phone.

"AND I'M SURE she was looking at the monitors," Clint tells Bearon, "all of them, including the Basement. Is there a key on the computer you can hit to make them all go dark? I figure that's what she did when I knocked."

"I think you're right," Bearon agrees.

"So, you took her phone and locked her in my suite? Why didn't you just put her in the Basement, since she's so interested in seeing it?"

"I figured there must be some reason people can be locked in as well as out. I wanted to discuss it with you first. Maybe you'd change your mind and take her back to your place. Maybe bring her into the team. She'd be a great help if we could turn her. What little girl worries about getting into a car with a nice, clean-cut married couple?"

"Hmmm." Bearon boots up the computer and turns to Clint as he waits for the monitors to come back on. He frowns and says, "I see you have some new jewelry to go with your new haircut."

"Yeah, uh, this." He lifts the pendant. "Kiersten gave it to me."

"You mean you took it from her," Bearon says, reaching his good hand out, palm up. "It wasn't hers to give. I'll take it now—"

He's interrupted by the chiming of the front desk bell.

"What the hell? Someone's here?" Bearon turns his attention back to the bank of monitors and growls, "goddamn fuckin' Kiersten, turning these off! A damn nuisance not having the monitors up!"

"Did you leave the gate open?"

"Damn! I'm sure I closed it. Still. If I left the gate open, they could get this far, but I came into my office the back way. How'd they get inside? Isn't the front door locked?"

Clint shrugs.

Bearon studies the monitors, now all online. "There's a truck," he observes, "but it's parked too close under the camera to see if there's anyone in it." He switches to the view of the front lobby area, and gives a low whistle. "Goddamn! Look who just showed up."

Clint takes a closer look and sees a small woman with a white streak in her short dark hair, and a tall blonde. "That's her? The short one?"

"That's her."

"What the fuck are they doing here?"

"Go and see. Think up some reason to bring them back here."

"Both of them?"

"For fuck's sake, do you think you can just bring one? And do *what* with the other one?"

"What if she recognizes me?"

"You said she hasn't seen you since you grew your beard and cut your hair. But if she does, just fuckin' grab them. Can't you deal with a couple of girls? *Go!*"

Clint jumps up and leaves the office.

Bearon sits back and watches the monitor. When he sees Astrid start to follow Clint, then Kathy say something and turn for the door, he curses. "Fuck! She made him!"

When a scuffle ensues, he thinks for a moment he should go to help, even though his hip is on fire and at best he can only shuffle along. He starts to rise but before he's on his feet, it's over. Astrid brings three hundred dollars worth of flowers down on Clint's head, and the two women run out the door.

He hits the close gate command key. The monitor shows the truck backing away from the steps, and he realizes there are two men in the front seat. The goddamn husbands!

The gate is within range of his rifle. Can he get his rifle and pick them off when they stop there? Do they have guns with them? Would they have time to arm themselves and return fire? More likely unless he took out goddamn Danielson with his first shot, which is not a certainty, as soon as he realized they were under fire, he'd crash the truck through the gate.

If they make a complaint about Clint's clumsy attempt at detaining them, that can be explained away, but shooting at them? It would certainly bring the heat down on the Lodge. He hits the key to stop the gate closer. The monitor shows the gate hadn't moved yet anyway.

Clint raps on the door and Bearon presses the button to unlock it.

"Sorry, Bearon. Couldn't make them stay. Something spooked them. And the bitch clobbered me." He touches the side of his head where the vase hit him, and when he pulls his hand away, there's blood on it. He's been cut. Blood trickles down onto his shirt.

"Yeah, I saw. It's just as well. If you hauled them in here, the husbands would've been looking for them anyhow. Damn Kiersten for taking the cameras offline! If I'd seen them coming, I would've known their husbands were with them and we could've stopped them before they got in the door. Is the fuckin' door locked now?"

"I'll check," Clint offers.

"You're gettin' awful goddamn sloppy, Clint. First you let Kiersten get into my office, then you don't notice the front gates are open, then you leave the door unlocked? To top it all off, you let two girls get the better of you. And you think you deserve a raise?"

"How is the gate my fault? You're the one who left it open."

Bearon scowls at Clint's tone, and might call him on it, but Clint has already left the office to check the front door. He turns to the monitor and watches him cross the lobby. But instead of throwing the deadbolt, Clint opens the door and goes out, letting the door slam behind him.

Bearon checks the front parking area monitor and sees Clint climb into the driver's seat of the Range Rover and buckle his seatbelt. He mutters, "What the fuck does he think he's doing?"

As he's backing the Range Rover away from the steps, Clint looks up at the camera and smiles, then lifts his hand in the middle finger salute before, turning toward the gate and flooring it.

"What the fuck? How'd he start it?" He opens the pencil drawer and sees the duplicate key fob is missing. "You just signed your death warrant, Reardon!" He hits the close gate command, then watches in dismay as the gate stays wide open. He hits the button again and again, with the same result.

The Range Rover is approaching the open gate when three motorcycles come up the road and stop. The Range Rover stops too, and one of the bikers rolls up to the driver's window, obviously conversing with Clint. In less than a minute, all continue on their way.

"What are they doing here?" he mutters. They admitted they hadn't done the job so they can't be looking for more money. Then as they come closer, he realizes he doesn't recognize them or their motorcycles. They aren't Raptors.

His guts clench and in that split second, he knows Hayward's truck going off the road wasn't an accident. And that now they're coming for him.

He rushes out of his office and heads to the front door, locks it, then scurries back. His office door is locked. *Why the fuck did I let this door close?* In a panic, he fumbles with the key card. The bikers are pounding on the front door before he's finally able to push the door in. As he turns to close it, he sees the window next to the door—a costly, custom-made stained glass work of art depicting a bear—shatter. A gloved hand reaches in to turn the lock.

Will the office door stop them? Not likely. It won't stop bullets. Should he go down into the Basement? Would Clint have told them about the hidden door? It doesn't matter. He doesn't have time to reach either the elevator or the stairwell to the basement without being seen and there's no way he can outrun anyone. *Goddamn this useless fuckin' body!* His only chance is to get to the secure enclosure of his cabin.

He takes precious seconds to push the credenza in front of the door so it can't be kicked in, then hurries out the back way, clenching his teeth against the fire in his hip, his lame leg dragging. He climbs into the Kubota and turns the key. It coughs a couple of times before the engine catches. He backs around and heads for the gate behind the garage, hoping they don't know about it, and that they haven't left someone outside to watch. As he passes the open area between the Lodge and the garage, he sees the three motorcycles parked in front, and no one on watch. So far so good.

He gets to the gate and pulls the cluster of keys out of his pocket. Cursing the rain and his mutilated hand that makes everything difficult, he manages to get the padlock on the chain undone and push the gate open. When he's driven the Kubota through, he shuts the gate again. The padlock has fallen off into a patch of Oregon grape. Should he take the time to look for it and lock it again? Probably wouldn't stop them anyway. Will they ride their bikes on a rough trail like this, even if they do find the gate? Would he have ridden his bike through here? Maybe.

He definitely doesn't have time to grub around in the bushes looking for the padlock. If they have cutters, the chain won't stop them anyway. He can only hope that if they know where he lives, they'll go back to the highway and come in that way. There's a chance they didn't see him go into his office and if they didn't, where would they start looking? It'll take time before they realize he's not in the Lodge.

He gets back in the UTV and drives off at speed, pounding over roots and rocks, fire knifing through his hip with every bounce. He's soon deep enough into the forest if there was someone at the gate they couldn't see him, and the rain is obliterating his tracks. He breathes a sigh of relief.

His situation is still desperate, but even if they saw him go into the office, break the door down, find the back door, and figure out he's not in the Lodge, it'll take them at least an hour to get to his house by the main roads. He can be home behind the electrified fence long before they arrive.

He has time. He slows the Kubota to a more comfortable speed. Once he's home, he'll set up his sniper rifle and have a surprise waiting for them!

The cab of the Kubota keeps him dry, but the wind is picking up. Branches are flying around, crashing down on the roof. He begins to worry there may be big branches coming down. The ones loggers call 'widow makers'. Branches that have broken off and are hanging up in the trees, just waiting for a wind strong enough to dislodge them. He grits his teeth and ups his speed again. He loves the forest and tells himself it will take care of him.

As he has that thought, a huge Douglas fir crashes down across the trail just meters in front of him. He slams on the brakes. Another smaller fir, partially uprooted by the falling giant, topples beside it. Yes, the forest took care of him. The tree didn't land on him. But it has stopped him.

There's a chainsaw in the Kubota, but it would take hours to cut through the big tree, and then he wouldn't be able to move the cut blocks out of the way. He scans the trail on either side. He has scouted the area and knows there is no way for the UTV to get through the forest except by this trail. The only way around the deadfall is on foot. He turns the Kubota off and gets out, pulling the rifle off the gun rack, and begins the hike around the fallen trees.

The tops of the trees are whipping around in the high winds, but it's surprisingly calm at ground level. He struggles through the dense underbrush, skirting rocky outcroppings until he's back on the trail, continuing homeward as briskly as he can. He checks his watch and calculates he still has plenty of time, as long as no more trees topple.

He's tiring fast. He stops for a second to catch his breath, notices the scent of smoke in the wind, and wonders how close the fire is.

He hears a *snap!* up above and a swishing sound. He flings his arm up just in time to ward off a falling branch, dropping the rifle as he does so.

"Arrghh!" he screams. Not the whole tree, but a decent-sized branch, maybe fifteen centimeters in diameter and three meters long. It would have killed him if it wasn't a glancing blow and if he hadn't shielded his head with his arm. As it is, it's excruciatingly painful to move his arm. It's likely broken. He clenches his teeth and lets it hang, picking up the rifle one handed. "No more of that! No more of that!" he groans as he lurches along.

At least the rain is letting up. Too late to make a difference, though. He's already wet and cold, and the path is slick enough to make the tough going even tougher. He slips and falls, screaming in agony as he reflexively throws out both arms, wrenching his bad leg under him. The pain from his injured arm is almost enough to make him pass out.

He pulls his leg out from under him and sits for a moment, cradling his injured arm, rocking and moaning, and is shocked to realize he's crying. "Get up, you stupid bastard," he commands himself; he works his way onto his knees, picks up the rifle and using it like a cane, gets back on his feet. He pushes on.

Finally the compound comes in sight. As painfully slow as his progress has been, a check of his watch shows he still has time to get inside before anyone could get here from the Lodge, even if they left right after he did.

Once in the cleared area next to the chain link fence, the going is easier. Still, it takes a supreme effort of will to get to the gate. His right arm is hanging uselessly. He drops the rifle and uses his left hand to flip the cover on the touch pad up and punch in the enter code.

Nothing happens.

He must have put in a wrong number. He curses, knowing he occasionally hits the six instead of the nine. Now he has to enter the correct number three times.

He straightens and looks anxiously up the driveway. Is that sound approaching motorcycles? Already? He takes several deep breaths. There is no one approaching and the sound he thought he heard was a trick of the storm and his imagination.

Commanding himself to remain calm, he carefully enters the correct code. He moans with relief when the gate begins to roll open. He hits the enter button when it's just wide enough for him to pass through, sending it back to the closed position. They won't be able to get in. Unless...has Clint given them the enter code? Even if he hasn't, he's a sitting duck out here in the open.

He can barely move his bad leg now, but with the rifle as a crutch, he manages to lurch across the yard and up the steps to the door. He drops the rifle and enters the lock code without mistake. He leaves the rifle, knowing it's useless with dirt plugging its barrel and he has no time to clean it. He'll get another one from the rack over the couch. But first, Oxycontin.

He pushes the door in and closes it behind him, then touches the button on the panel next to the door that disables the keypad for the gate. He blows out a long breath. Now he's safe.

It's oddly cold in the house and there's a hint of smoke much like the wind outside. He must have left a window open. That's not a priority just now. Safe in his forest womb, he'll take some oxy and get his rifle set up before he rests.

He nearly collapses onto the arm of the couch, but desperately needs Oxycontin. He must get the pain under control before he takes a look at his arm. At a minimum, he'll have to splint it. If it's serious. If bones have punctured the skin, he may have to go to a hospital. That prospect, with all its attendant problems, he pushes to the back of his mind.

He pulls himself up and shuffles to the kitchen, holding up in the doorway. The kitchen is filled with branches. There's an odd, pungent smell. In an instant he realizes what happened: one of the giant firs fell, crushing the house. There's no question the fence would be crushed, too. It won't keep anything out now. How had he not seen the tree on the house when he was outside? It must be big enough to hang over the peak of the roof.

There's a snuffling sound and Silverface pushes through the curtain of fir branches. A jolt of panic courses through Bearon. Where can he go to get away? If he barricades himself in a room, can the bear break through?

The bear lifts his head and turns his white-patched face to look Bearon in the eye.

"Aaarghhh!" he roars.

THIRTY-FOUR

BEAR MAN GONE

THE RCMP CRUISER rolls to a stop at the gate. The driver leans out and punches the intercom. After a couple of tries with no response, he says, "I think we should check and make sure everyone's out. Someone might be hurt, the size of those trees on the house— must be some serious damage."

"What about the electric fence?"

"Not likely it's still active, not with those trees down on it." He points at another clump of trees over the fence, then touches the gate and jerks his hand away. "Nope. Shorted out. I'm not happy about having to climb it, though. Maybe I can disengage the opener."

While the first constable is trying to get at the device that drives the opener by reaching through the barbwire, the second constable gets out, goes to the trunk and pulls out the piece of trunk liner that conceals the spare tire. "If you're sure we have to do this, when you give up on that opener, we can put this over the wire," he explains.

"Yeah, we have to. What if it's a woman with kids? We have to."

When the cruiser is moved up tight against the gate so they can use its bumper as a step, and with the heavy carpeting protecting them from the wire, the two manage to climb over.

"Jesus fuckin' Christ," one says as he grunts and gasps at the exertion, "I didn't sign up for this! Why'd this place have to be on *our* fuckin' list?"

The front door is locked and no one answers their knock. The first constable presses his face up to the window. "Something bad went on in there," he says, and steps back. "I think there's blood spray on the far wall there."

The other constable looks in. "I think you're right."

"Maybe we can get in the back."

They hurry around to the back of the house and see that a huge tree has demolished the deck. Branches and the massive trunk conceal most of the back wall of the house. The wall-to-wall, ceiling to floor windows are smashed.

The first constable carefully sticks his head through the broken window and calls out: "anyone home? Hello? RCMP! Anyone home? More blood, Dave. Look!" He points to dark red sprays on the wall. "Someone's hurt, all right."

He picks up a deck chair, breaks out the glass shards still stuck in the frame, and goes in. The second constable comes through behind him; they pick their way through glass and branches. The refrigerator and cupboard doors are standing open and there's food everywhere.

The first constable gets through to the back hallway, stops, and exclaims, "fuck!"

"What?"

"Don't think we have to worry about this guy, Dave."

Dave comes to stand beside his partner. "Holy shit!"

The partially-eaten body of a man in combat fatigues is lying in a massive spill of blood and entrails.

"Won't be easy to I.D. him," Dave says, looking down on the man's head. Most of the face has been eaten. His legs have been gnawed and his torso is torn open from the neck to the groin, spilling intestines onto the floor. "I think it ate his liver," he says quietly.

They stand, shocked, trying not to gag at the stench of the butchery. In a moment, Dave says, "Well, if there's an upside, he won't be very heavy to carry. Let's make sure there's no one else in the house, take a bunch of photos, then get a blanket and bundle him up. We need to get the fuck outta here. Whatever did this will be coming back for more. If the fire doesn't get here first."

"I'll call it in," his partner offers. "Tell 'em we're coming in and someone else needs to get out to the rest of the places on our evac list."

DENVER, ASTRID, RICK, Kathy and Wilson sit idly around the dinner table, picking at the remains of the salad and roast. "Well, Rick did his bit and I think his statement was perfect, but I doubt it'll matter much," Kathy says. "The judge didn't seem to be paying much attention. I think his mind's already made up."

"He wasn't even there so we couldn't get a look at the sick fucker," Rick tells them. "We got put off all day and finally they announce that his lawyer had an emergency. Don't you love how they can jerk everyone around? I think they only let me go ahead with my statement because I had to travel to get here."

"Will you have to come back?" Astrid asks. "Like for the sentencing?"

"I don't think I'll bother. I doubt I'm gonna think it's fair. You know, justice served. They'll go easy on him because he pled guilty."

"When is the sentencing, do you know?" Denver asks.

"Nope, they haven't said. Could be a month or even longer."

"Really? Why so long? How can it take a month? It's not like this is some frickin' rare crime, sadly," Astrid says.

"I think they just want a psych evaluation so they can come up with the idea he's not criminally responsible."

"I think they would've done that before now," Denver opines.

"Yeah. He's said all along it was an accident, like he only meant to grab her but she fell. Wasn't his fault she hit her head! What a fuckin' joke!" Rick draws a quick breath and shakes his head.

"On a brighter note," Astrid says, "anyone want coffee? I have decaf."

"I'm sticking with wine," Kathy says. She takes the wine bottle and at a nod from Astrid, shares it between Astrid's glass and her own.

"I'm with you," Astrid agrees. "Wine that comes in a bottle is a rare treat. Not gonna let it go bad!"

"Never any chance of that around here," Denver says. "You want that last Yorkshire, Rick?"

"I sure do! I gotta tell you, Astrid," Rick says as he spears the Yorkshire and smothers it in gravy, "these are great!"

"My, er, Bridey's recipe. They turn out perfect every time."

"I'll have to get the recipe," Kathy says. "I've tried lots of times and it's hit and miss. Rick doesn't care, though. His family's German. Yorkshires are more of an English thing."

"Yup. Bridey's mother was an English war bride. You know, as awful as she turned out to be, she was good to me. Well, except for that one time. And I don't know if she even knew what was going on by then. She went to Nechako Manor shortly after, and hasn't been out since."

"Speaking of Bridey," Kathy says, "do you ever go to visit her?"

"No. Why?"

"It's just that, well, you've said you liked her. I was wondering if she might agree to an exhumation order, just to get some DNA, if you asked her? If Hank Senior wasn't cremated?"

"I don't think we have to go that far," Astrid says.

Kathy wonders at the look that passes between Astrid and Denver. It's brief, and Astrid quickly turns back to Kathy and says, "we have all their things, boxed up, in the basement at Heather's House. I think they should be able to get DNA off something in there. After, well, after everything, I couldn't face it myself. I had packers come in and just throw everything into boxes. Didn't toss out anything. Not even the toothbrushes."

"That's right," Wilson says. "Canada Livestock Records uses twelve mane hairs for DNA testing horses. Doubt they need that many, think they just wanna be sure they got one or two pulled out by the root instead of broke off. You'd think there'd be hairs on something, at least."

"Would she, Bridey I mean, have to give permission for that?" Kathy asks.

"I don't know. Why don't you call Penny and ask? Meantime, I don't think we should wait until we find out. Since you're leaving tomorrow, we should go and see what we can find tonight. If it turns out it's illegal, we don't have to tell anyone."

"You think you'll be okay with that, babe?" Denver asks.

"Of course she will! I'll be with her," Kathy assures him. "And it's nothing compared to fighting off kidnappers! Remember, she's the girl who nearly knocked that bastard on his ass!"

"How about you wait until after the news?" Denver suggests. "I'm gonna go with you. Just to help, because there's a lot of stuff to go through. But I'd like to find out what's happenin' with that fire first. It was headin' for one of our leases last I heard."

"They said on the noon news it was ninety percent under control thanks to the rain," Wilson tells them. He checks his watch and gets to his feet. "Think it mostly stayed on the other side of the mountain. Couple of houses burned. One up on Bear Mountain Haul Road. News'll be comin' on now." He heads into the living room and turns the TV on.

"Oh yeah?" Denver exclaims. "Bear Mountain Haul Road? Only one house I know of up there!" He calls after Wilson, "Did they say if anyone was inside? Wonder if Bear Man made it out."

"Denver!" Astrid says sharply.

Denver grins and says, "I know. He's too deaf to hear my question."

"No I ain't!" Wilson calls back. "They ain't said nuthin' 'bout no one kilt in the fire but someone got kilt by a bear, likely fleein' the fire. And look here now! Somethin' went down at the Lodge."

Denver gets up and heads for the living room, with Rick right behind.

"Bring your wine," Astrid tells Kathy, and the two women join the men, watching the reporter with the yellow "do not cross" plastic tape across the Bear Mountain Lodge gates behind her. She's describing the rescue of seven girls and women from cells deep inside the sprawling log building in the distance.

"One man believed to be from Dark River is in custody," the reporter says, "and that's all we're being told at the moment. They promise an update at a press conference tomorrow morning. Back to you, Sophie."

"You were right, babe," Denver admits, and blows out a long breath. "I think we now know why that guy was tryin' to grab you."

There's stunned silence, then Denver says, "but when I called it in, Jacques said he didn't think the pendant was enough to get a search warrant for the Lodge, no proof the guy wearing it lived there, after all. You were going to give him your statements about the assault today, if Kathy hadn't been in the courthouse in Prince George all day. If nothing else, he was going to go up and ask some questions in hopes he'd see the guy wearing the pendant. He couldn't just stumble across this when he went to do that. There must be more to this."

The story of the bear mauling comes on next. The news anchor says the victim hasn't been identified, pending notification of next of kin.

"I wonder if it could be that bear we ran afoul of," Astrid muses.

"Maybe he got that crazy guy," Kathy suggests. "It would be a fitting end for him. Unpleasant, but fitting."

Lisey comes into the living room from the back hall and stands in front of the TV, staring at the news anchor.

"Lisey, we can't see through you," Astrid says.

"IT'S BEAR MAN," Lisey declares. She nods her head vigorously, spins and trots back out to the hall.

"Denver," Astrid says quietly, "what do you think she means?"

"I think it means that kid has a big imagination along with her big ears."

Astrid sighs. "Well, it's kinda creepy, but if she thinks he's gone and she doesn't have to build a fort around her bed to be able to sleep, I'm glad."

The news hour over, everyone gets up to go either to Heather's House or the barn for night chores. Astrid and Kathy clear the table and load the dishwasher. As Astrid passes the kitchen window, she looks out to see an RCMP cruiser pull up to the garage. Sergeant Villeneuve gets out from behind the wheel. and a woman gets out the driver's side.

"Den! It's Sergeant Villeneuve!" Astrid calls out. "And there's someone with him. In a long skirt? Oh, it's Kiersten!"

They both come up to the door, arriving there just as Astrid opens it.

Astrid says, "Kiersten! And Sergeant Villeneuve, hello."

"I hope it's not too late to drop in on you," Sergeant Villeneuve says. "We had to go by here anyhow."

"No, come on in! What's going on?"

"I let her tell you."

"Well, come in, don't mind the mess, we haven't cleared up from supper yet. Have you guys eaten? There's left overs."

"Not for me, tanks, but maybe Kiersten?"

"I, er...no thank you."

Everyone comes into the kitchen and hellos go all around. Sergeant Villeneuve and the other men take seats at the table, while the women slide onto stools at the island.

"I know you're a red wine drinker. Kiersten. I don't have red," Astrid says, "but you look like you might not mind a glass of white."

"That would be fine," Kiersten nods.

Kathy gets a glass and fills it from the box in the fridge. She passes it to Kiersten and climbs onto the stool next to her. "We went up to the Lodge to look for you yesterday, Kiersten, like you suggested, but when we got there, instead of you meeting us, a man came out and he was wearing my pendant and I... and then he grabbed my arm and... well anyway, we figured you weren't there even though you said you were and we didn't know why you would do that!"

"I was there. My phone was taken away."

Sergeant Villeneuve says, "she was one who was rescued. You see about the human trafficking on duh news, maybe?"

"Yeah. Just now," Astrid replies.

"But you didn't find the girls when you went to ask about Kathy's pendant, did you Jacques?" Denver asks.

"No. Dere's an informant. And before I forget, you will get your necklace back, Katy."

"Oh my god, Kiersten! They were selling people! But for a handy bouquet of flowers, we might've been with you," Kathy tells her.

"Flowers?"

"A story for another time," Astrid says. "But how did you end up there?"

"My boyfriend, Clint..." Kiersten lets out a sob and can't continue.

"Your boyfriend's name is Clint?" Kathy gasps. "That's the guy who accosted me that morning at Dot's!"

"It's okay, Kiersten," Astrid says as she hands her a box of Kleenex. "You're safe, and you're with friends who know what you've been through. You don't have to talk about it now."

"Duh reason I bring 'er 'ere," Sergeant Villeneuve tells everyone, "for a few days she need a place to stay. She 'ave only what she's wearing, so till she get 'er banking and so on, I wondered about 'edder's 'ouse."

"No, no, she doesn't have to go to Heather's. She can stay here," Astrid says. "But what happened to your, er, banking?"

"Everything's gone," Kiersten says quietly after blowing her nose. "All my i.d., credit cards, bank cards. Clothes. Everything burned up."

"At Clint's? Clint's house burned?" Astrid asks.

"No. He... he's the one who..." she begins crying softly and pulls another Kleenex out of the box.

"Mr. Reardon, look like 'e is involved. 'E is in jail till 'e post bail," Sergeant Villeneuve explains. "Dere's no one so far who post it for 'im."

"Not even his boss?"

"He's dead," Kiersten says. "The bear got him."

"Oh, my god!" Kathy exclaims. "That's who the unidentified victim is! But you know who he is, don't you, Kiersten? The Vampire?"

"I only know him as Bearon."

"Look like dis Bearon, 'e don't exist," Sergeant Villeneuve says.

"He has tattoos, though," Kiersten contributes. "A really beautiful one of a bear on his shoulder. And some that look like jailhouse tats."

"If he was in jail, his fingerprints would be on record," Denver says.

"Dey would be. 'Ave you seen a body predator 'ave been at it?"

"Oh."

"We might get some partials. Might be able to I.D. 'im trew 'is tattoos, too. Dere's one on 'is arm wit a woman's name."

"Yeah. I asked him who she was," Kiersten says. "He said she was nobody. But you don't tattoo a nobody's name on your arm."

"You saw him sometime when it wasn't dark?" Astrid asks.

"I, er, I was living with him."

"Oh, Kiersten! I thought you didn't like him! You broke up with Clint to go and live with him?"

"Not by choice," Kiersten murmurs. She makes eye contact with Astrid, then drops her head and studies the countertop.

"Oh."

Quiet settles over the group as the implications sink in. Finally, Kathy asks, "so the Vampire's, Bearon's, house burned?"

"Yeah, in duh forest fire out on Bear Mountain Haul Road," Sergeant Villeneuve explains. "Dat's why she lose everyting."

"Oh! Bear Mountain Haul Road! I bet it's the guy Astrid and I, er, *met* if you call that run-in we had, meeting him," Kathy says. "He scared the shit outta us."

"Me too. And pretty much everyone else," Kiersten says. "But he's...he *was* the boss. He owned the Lodge. That's why I went to work there."

Kathy draws a deep breath and thinks about what it was like for Kiersten, having to live with that awful man. Having no choice.

"So," Astrid says, breaking into Kathy's thoughts, "do you remember the woman's name? In his tattoo?"

"Yes. Jeanie," Kiersten responds.

"Oh my god!" Kathy exclaims. "I think I know who he is!"

THIRTY-FOUR

ONE YEAR LATER

A VERY PREGNANT Sarah comes waddling up the steps onto the deck and taps on the patio door.

"Come in," Kathy calls as she comes through the kitchen and gives the young woman a wave.

Sarah slides the door open and comes in.

"Everything okay?" Kathy asks.

"Yeah, sure, I just came to raid your herb patch."

"You know you can come and cut whatever you want, whenever you want. You don't have to ask," Kathy tells her. "But since you're here, how about some iced tea? I have a pitcher in the fridge."

"That would be perfect."

"Go sit on the deck. I'll bring you some. You don't mind if I drink a glass of wine in front of you, do you?"

"No, that's fine. I was never much of a wine drinker."

"At your age, I wasn't either," Kathy says. "I guess it takes time to develop a taste for it. Don't worry. You'll get there!"

They share a chuckle, and then Sarah turns and goes back outside. She's in a chair at the table under the pergola when Kathy comes out with the tray.

Before Kathy has a chance to sit, Sarah blurts out, "I'm going to miss you so much!"

"I know. I'll miss you, too. Think of it this way: you've got an awesome place to go for a holiday any time you want, and you can stay for as long as you want."

"That'll be nice. Not the same, though."

"Maybe better, Sarah! You'll have Jeanie and her kids right here. She'll be more help to you with the baby than I would be, with all her experience. And with Skype and Facetime, your Dad and I are just a call away. And of course, we're staying until after your little boy is born."

"I know," Sarah sniffs. After a moment, she says, "Jeanie's looking forward to moving into the big house. I don't know if I could live there, like permanently. I keep thinking about Mutti, you know, being murdered there. It creeps me out."

"Ghosts?"

"No, not really. It's just, the thought haunts me."

"Really? I'm sorry, I didn't know. You've been bothered about that all these months?"

"I try not to think about it. Jeanie says it doesn't bother her but I think it could be part of the reason she's going to have the kitchen renovated before she moves in."

"You could be right."

"Anyway, I'll be glad to move into this nice new house. And no rent? We just have to look after the farm? It's a real good start for us. I can't thank you enough."

"You're welcome. And you have thanked me enough."

They sit in companionable silence for a few moments, then Sarah asks, "but you really don't mind moving again? Being uprooted again?"

"You know, I moved so much I guess I'm kind of used to it." Kathy absent-mindedly strokes her mutilated ear. "Bad memories for me here, you know. I guess I never really put down roots. If not for your Dad, I don't think I would have stayed in Pillerton in the first place." She takes another sip of wine, and continues, "when I think that all those years growing up, when I wanted so badly to have a brother or sister like all the other kids, I had a brother right here and never knew it. A full brother, the sibling I went searching for, was right here all those years. He was such a cute little kid, too. Adored Jeanie. Those two were almost joined at the hip."

"Wonder what happened to turn him into such a monster."

"Who knows? Abused by his adoptive father. Bullied at school. He ran away when he was maybe in grade nine and got in with those bikers. Going to jail didn't do him any good, either. Then getting involved with the Children of Noah, first here and then in Dark River..."

"The family business, I guess?"

Yes, Kathy thinks, *my family both on my mother's and father's side. Maybe I would have been better off thinking that although my mother was insane and a murderer, at least I had a good father.*

The door alert chimes and there's the sound of footsteps coming through the house. Ryan appears in the doorway.

"Hey, here you are." He comes and gives Sarah a kiss.

"Grab a beer and join us," Kathy tells him. "Rick should be home before long."

"I saw his truck at Al's. He might be late."

"I guess he's getting his Big Al fix before we leave. He's really going to miss that place," Kathy says; she frowns, then sighs.

"Good thing they don't have rooms upstairs like in the old days, or he might never come home," Ryan opines.

Sarah gives Ryan a sharp look; he shrugs, then turns and goes back into the kitchen.

"Tsk!" Sarah takes her bottom lip in her teeth, then turns to Kathy and says, "don't worry about Dad. Why don't you come to our place for dinner? I'm getting pretty good at making vegan spaghetti sauce. Even Ryan likes it. And if Dad comes home in time, he can join us."

"Thank you, that sounds great! Can I bring something? Salad?"

"No, I've got a salad ready, just waiting to be tossed. Maybe you could fix the garlic toast while I do that."

"Sure thing."

Ryan comes back to the table with his beer, slides into a chair next to Sarah, and takes her hand. As Kathy takes in the look they exchange, she can't help envying them. High school sweethearts, so in love, starting a family. They talk about getting married, but it's some time off in the future. Right now, they're fully committed, without ink on paper as they say.

Kathy and Rick do have ink on paper. Does it make a difference? Are they more committed because of it? More and more she's coming to believe their commitment is fragile, a gossamer fabric, easily torn. Ink on paper hasn't made it strong.

Would Rick have even considered moving to the Lodge if it wasn't for the wealth she inherited because Max had no will and no other living relatives? She's moved so often she can't quite understand why it's such a big deal for him, no matter how many times she tells herself it's because he's firmly rooted here, as established as the Lombardy Poplar surrounding the yard, whereas she is cottonwood fluff, going where the wind blows ever since she was seventeen.

Maybe a change of scenery, especially being away from that pub that consumes so much of his time, will be a good thing. He's a good manager. He can really get his teeth into the new business. They will work together to weed out the members whose main interest is the so-called Gentlemen's Club, and build a new clientele. Maybe no members at all, just a destination resort.

Will the challenge be enough to keep him there? Will their marriage be enough of an anchor?

When she wakes up at three a.m. and can't get back to sleep because of her stampeding fears, she sometimes wonders if she even wants to keep him there. *I do. Of course I do. He's the love of my life. It'll be better when there's no more Big Al's.*

She looks across the table at the two faces watching her with puzzled expressions, musters a smile and says, "okay, then! I'll bring my wine."

AUTHOR'S NOTES

I hope you enjoyed *The Bear Mountain Secret,* Book Three of what was supposed to be the Secrets Trilogy. Unlike my other books, it didn't begin as a short story. Instead, the characters from *The Pillerton Secret* and *The Dark River Secret* kept talking to me. I thought *The Bear Mountain Secret* would put an end to that, but I think you'll have realized from the last few pages, Kathy, Rick, Astrid and Denver aren't done with me yet. Remember, Lisey has brown eyes. There's a rough draft of the opening scene in the fourth book in the series, tentatively titled "Astrid's Secret", on the next page.

If you have a few minutes to write a review on Amazon or Goodreads or any platform you are familiar with, it would be a great help. It takes only a few minutes and doesn't have to be lengthy, just a few words will do. Here are links to Amazon:

https://www.amazon.com/dp/B07PRDDVY9
https://www.amazon.ca/dp/B07PRDDVY9

It is much appreciated. Thank you.

Gayle Siebert, May 2019

ASTRID'S SECRET

One

Felix Helin, an Elder of the Tsilhquot'in Nation, sits across the table from Kathy, stirring a third teaspoon of sugar into his coffee. His driver is perched on a stool at the bar at the other end of the room, silent, watching.

Felix puts the spoon down, encloses the mug in both hands, and says, "Many dogs have gone missing."

"Oh, no! A cougar, do you think?" Kathy asks, and wonders, *did he really come up here to tell me about missing dogs?*

"Could be a cougar," he agrees. He lifts the mug and slurps noisily. He's a handsome man despite his large nose and the sculpturing of his face over his many years. Snowy-white hair cascades around his shoulders, held in place with a traditional beaded headband. It's not an official delegation of one, but it's definitely more than an informal visit. His black eyes are intense as he continues: "a cougar or a bear. If it's one of them, we usually find a kill site. We have not. People say the Spirit Bear is taking them."

"Spirit bear?"

"This is the reason I came to see you. So you'd know why many of our people avoid this place and don't want to work here even though the jobs are good. One of our elders is Sensitive. She had a Dream."

"I think I know who you mean. Joan, right? Joan had a dream of a spirit bear?"

"Yes."

"She did a smudge of the building when I first came here. She didn't say anything about a spirit bear then."

"The Spirits don't always come to her."

Of course not, Kathy thinks. Felix is more than just a prominent Elder of the Tsilhquot'in; he's so well-regarded it would be more accurate to say he's revered. She likes and respects him, so although she doesn't believe in ghosts or spirits, she doesn't voice her opinion. Anyway, if his people believe, it doesn't matter whether Kathy thinks it's nonsense or not. "But she had a dream? Since she was here?"

"It was last night. In her Dream, there was a Gathering of Spirits. They were angry. There was much blood," Felix slurps his coffee and for a moment seems to have lost the train of his thoughts. Then he says, "did you know a man who lived just over the ridge was mauled to death before you came here?"

Kathy draws in a deep breath. Yes, she not only knows it, but she knew *him.* He was a full brother, but she didn't know that until he was dead, and she, as his only living relative, inherited this place along with the five million from her biological father's estate. What a windfall! But tainted, because it proved her father was a serial killer. She feels the rush of emotions that courses through her whenever she remembers. "Yeah," she says.

"Silverface is a Spirit Bear now. He killed him. He has only one eye and a patch of white on his face. Spirits of the Bear People are powerful. Usually helpful. But he's angry. He hunts humans because they maimed him, and because he has found a liking for the taste of human flesh." Chief Helin's eyes narrow as he nods as if to punctuate this last statement, then lifts his mug and takes a long draft of his sweet white coffee.

Kathy shudders, remembering her meeting with Silverface when he was still very much alive. She pushes the memory to the back of her mind and rushes on, "so the spirit bear, Silverface, he eats humans?"

Felix gives her a look that tells her he knows she's skeptical. "Yes. As he did before he entered the Spirit World. When they trespass into his territory."

"And the dogs?"

"The Spirit Bear takes the dogs."

"Silverface."

"Not Silverface. Before you came, the old Lodge. The one that exploded. Those people killed him. He is a Kermode. The Kermodes are sacred to all my people. They are called Spirit Bears even before they die. Your people had one stuffed and used him as a decoration. We asked them to give him to us so we could keep him with us, to be respected. They refused. His spirit destroyed the lodge and began walking among us then."

"But they weren't *my* people," Kathy objects. Then she realizes they were, in fact, her people, if only by blood. "I guess they were, Felix, but I never knew them, you know…"

"I didn't come here to accuse you. I came to warn you."

"Oh, I see." Kathy takes a deep breath and tucks her hair behind her ear. "So there are two Spirit Bears."

"You have nothing to fear. You were tested and are marked as a Warrior," he nods at her ear. "Others will yet be tested."

Kathy had forgotten her mutilated ear. She pulls her hair forward to cover it. How does he know about her so-called test? She tells herself he didn't know. He noticed her missing earlobe and partially-amputated index finger, and took a guess. Neither mutilation was necessarily something that was deliberately done to her. Either could just as easily have been an accident, or she could have been born that way. Felix is intelligent enough to know that no matter what the cause, it could still be considered a test, so there was no risk of him being wrong. Still, a feeling of unease squeezes her insides. Others will be tested?

"But these bears, the spirit bears," she says, steering the conversation safely away from her 'warrior' status, "they can go anywhere, right? They aren't just here, right?"

"This place," he sweeps his hand in a half circle to take in the entire room, but meaning the whole property, "there was a sweat lodge here before The Ancestors were moved onto the reserve. There is a pictograph rock…"

"Yes! I know it. It's about halfway up the trail to Lookout Point."

"Only a few of my people have been seen it. Larson is one of them." Felix indicates the younger man, his driver, who waits respectfully on a stool at the bar. "He made a Quest to see it before the fence was put up to keep us out."

She considers telling him the fence wasn't to keep anyone out, but rather, to keep everyone in, but she doesn't want to open that discussion. Instead she tells him, "we're going to have to move it, you know. We're putting in a landing strip so people can fly in, small planes only of course. We thought we'd make that rock a feature of the patio out front here. Then everyone can see it. Your son," she indicates his driver with a nod, "all your people can come and see it whenever they want."

"My sons have all passed. Larson is the son of my granddaughter. He is one of the few still alive who has seen the Rock. It has been there since the time of the First People. It is a Gathering Place. The Bear People and my people have been linked together since Creation. The Ancestors gather there still. The Spirit Bears are anchored there. It is a mistake to move it. It is work there that has angered the Spirit Bears. They are taking dogs as a warning. If we don't heed the warning, they will not stop with dogs. I have come on behalf of my people to request that you leave it where it is."

***